SOFIA'S TUNE

Cindy Thomson

Sofia's Tune

Sofia's Tune is a work of fiction. Where real people, events, establishments, organizations, or locales appear; they are used fictitiously. All other elements of the novel are drawn from the author's imagination.

Con amore a mia famiglia,
Tom, Dan, Jeff, Kyle, Kelsey, and Aryn.

Family:
Like branches on a tree,
We all grow in different directions,
Yet our roots remain as one.

~Author Unknown

Acknowledgments

THE BIGGEST SUPPORTERS TO ME while I was working on *Sofia's Tune* were the fans of the first two books in the series. You told me you wanted the next book, and that is what truly kept me in my chair writing. My special team of promotors deserve a high five. Thank you so very much!

Holly Lorincz of Lorincz Literary Services did a fine job of editing for me. Holly had some terrific ideas for improving the story.

Thank you to the Twinless Twins support group for answering my queries and putting me in touch with someone whose personal story helped inspire Sofia's.

I owe a debt of gratitude to the Italian immigrants who came through Ellis Island and left their stories behind for future generations. I made good use of the Ellis Island website (www.ellisisland.org) and the National Archives (www.archives.gov) along with books such as *Imported Americans: The Story of the Experiences of a Disguised American and His Wife Studying the Immigration Question* by Broughton Brandenberg, which inspired, among other things, the scene of Antonio at Giovanni's.

Thank you to Ken Grossi, College Archivist at Oberlin College for answering questions and sending me a copy of "The First 100 Years of the Conservatory."

Rosanne Dingli, fellow author and member of the Historical Novel Society, was a huge blessing to me by reviewing the Italian words and phrases and suggesting changes. If I have made any mistakes, they are all mine.

Big hugs to Kim Draper who waited patiently to work on *Sofia's Tune*, supported me with Facebook messages, and who is without question a very talented designer. She was also helpful by reading an early copy of the manuscript.

Serious prayer partners at Etna UMC, and Sandy Beck, Cris Carnahan, and all those on social media, were critical to the process. Thanks for being so patient and faithful. Thanks also to Kendra Morgan and Cindy K. Thomson for their special support.

Kelsey Thomson was my photographer and Kaitlan Livingston my model. Thank you, girls, for being willing to tromp around old houses with me. You really did a wonderful job.

Thank you to Dean and Jodi at the Orchard House Bed and Breakfast for allowing us to do a photo shoot.

For his gentle shoves, moral support, brainstorming help, I thank my husband Tom for loving me through this process. It's not easy to live with an author sometimes. Thanks also to my kids Dan, Jeff, and Kyle, and to the girls Kelsey and Aryn, for your loving support as always. Our fun gatherings gave me much needed down time.

I'm grateful God has allowed me to keep publishing novels. His blessings every day continue to amaze me.

Thank YOU for reading! You are truly the reason I do it. Please visit me: www.cindyswriting.com

1

SEPTEMBER, 1903

THROUGHOUT HER TWENTY-ONE YEARS, Sofia Falcone had always been her mother's favored child, humored and made over more than her sister and three brothers. That is, until September rolled around. Every September.

The first autumn chill from the north brought about a palpable change that Sofia had learned to anticipate. The inaugural twinge of gold in the trees, the reddening of apples, the shorter days—all harbingers of her mother's impending personality change. Sofia's body responded like an old person's, with aching bones, as if a storm were gathering. Her hands grew cold and would not warm again until the new year arrived. She dreaded this season of sadness that made no sense. Autumn blues, Papà called it, and Mamma had it worse than anyone Sofia knew.

As Sofia and her mother tidied up the kitchen before beginning supper, Mamma grabbed the dish Sofia had put in the rinse water and plunked it back into the soapy dish pail. "Not clean enough," she scolded. "You cannot make up for what you lack, Sofia, no matter how hard you try. Some children are not completely what God intended them to be."

Sofia turned away, her heart pounding. Mamma's melancholy sometimes made her say hurtful things. She heard Papà's voice behind her.

"Angelina, please. Poor Sofia."

Her mother slammed a fist against the sink. "You know!" She pointed a dripping finger at him.

Tears burned Sofia's eyes. Mamma's demons had returned despite Sofia's prayers that God would banish them. They would have to endure the next couple of months until Mamma returned to herself. For most of Sofia's life, Papà and his cousins had made numerous trips to America, returning to their village with the money they had earned before winter settled on Manhattan. Immigration had not been Papà's intent. He hadn't initially planned to bring Sofia and the rest of the family over, but then he got the idea that living in a new country might help improve Mamma's autumn melancholy. Sofia had been in favor of trying anything new. Something had to be done. But after six months of living in New York City it hadn't helped after all.

Mamma let out a tense breath. "Never mind. Your father says, 'Poor Sofia.'" She shook her head. "Fetch the soup pot from the closet, Sofia. If you can open your eyes long enough to find it." Such sharp reprimands were a sure sign that the moodiness had descended. Mamma wasn't usually so curt.

Sofia paused to catch a look from her youngest brother Joey. At seventeen he was old enough to contribute to the household but he seldom worked. She never knew when he might show up at home. He grinned and shrugged his shoulders. They both knew Mamma's sad season was here but it didn't bother him as much.

She hurried to the back of the small flat where her parents slept, glad for the momentary escape. Back in Italy the soup pot had hung from the rafters in the kitchen, but here there was no room. The pasta pot was handy always, but the pot for stew was somewhere in this crowded storage space because they hadn't needed it all summer.

Sofia brushed strands of hair from her eyes. Mamma should not speak to her as if she were a baby. She was the eldest child. At her age, Sofia should be married and have her own home, and not be forced to endure Mamma's insults. One day Sofia would be free of this, but for now she had to cope with the annual autumn upheaval.

Thankfully, most of the time, Mamma wanted Sofia near. Sofia was the one Mamma taught her special recipes to, the one she trusted with the marketing money. They giggled together like sisters while escaping the summer heat out on the front stoop. At Christmastime they sang the songs Mamma's mother had taught her when she was a young girl. After Sunday meals, when the preparation exhausted them, together they made up stories about *la strega*, a creature from village folklore who came to sweep the house clean after everyone went to bed. Most of the year, Sofia and her mother were very close, and that's what made this melancholy now so unbearable.

When they'd first arrived in America, Sofia found work at a shoe factory to help the family meet the dear price of rent. Mamma had shed tears over it and said she hated to let Sofia go. She missed her during the day. And yet, when the blue months began, Sofia seemed to be the one person Mamma did not want around. The daughter she said was not what God fully intended her to be.

Sofia bit her lip and glanced out the tenement window toward the iron fire escape. They were a proud Italian family. *L'ordine della famiglia*, the rules of the family, meant they kept to themselves, dismissing the wider world, which had become more apparent now that they were in New York City, a place more heavily inhabited than anyone living in her native village would have imagined. Sofia met outsiders on the trolley and at work. But when you do not travel about, socialize, or even shop outside your neighborhood—as Mamma and many others did not—it was not so difficult to keep to your own.

Not even Sister Stefania, her aunt who lived in the abbey next to the Church of the Most Precious Blood, was exempt from the rules of *la famiglia*. First she was Mamma's sister. Second she was a bride of Christ. Everyone had his or her role. Most times Sofia found this comforting, like a cocoon of woolen blankets on a snowy day. She needed people around her. To Sofia, being alone was the worst punishment she could imagine.

She turned back to her task and soon found what she sought. But before she could grasp the pot, a box covered in flowered paper wedged behind it caught her eye. Mamma's sister had sent up some items from the abbey because there was no room for it there, due to the recent arrival of a group of

4

novices. Sofia's mother had reluctantly accepted these things, stuffing them into the already overflowing space. Sofia longed to know what belongings a nun could possibly wish to hold on to. She pulled out the box.

Glancing toward the door, she heard her parents arguing. She ran her fingers over the tattered paper covering. If Sister Stefania were here, she'd allow a look. She might be a peculiar woman but was not fussy in the least. However, if Mamma knew what Sofia was doing, she'd fume, saying Sofia was impetuous, unfocused, not capable of following directions.

Sofia shook her head, reminding herself that Mamma said those things now. The true Mamma would return to them in a few months.

She paused, gripping the box in her lap. It would only take a moment to see what was inside. She untied the brown string holding the top on and peeked in. The box contained a few embroidered handkerchiefs, a yellowed photo of a stern looking couple, likely Sofia's grandparents, and some folded letters. From underneath them, she pulled out something round, flat, and hard. She'd heard about these Victor records. The girls at the factory talked about them. If you have the machine to put them on, music comes out.

Sofia rubbed her hand over the image of the dog listening to the machine. "*La Mandolinata, Sousa's Band*," this one said. She didn't need to understand English to comprehend the meaning of the phrase, "His Master's Voice." Supposedly the sound was so good the dog was fooled into thinking he was hearing his owner's voice. Sofia wouldn't know, though. She'd never heard one of these played. Her aunt the nun was certainly full of surprises.

Sofia was about to replace the lid when a small photograph slid from under the pile. She gasped as she examined it. An infant in a long white lace dress lay in a tiny coffin. She turned the image over. Two dates were written in faded ink: 25/ *settembre* /1882. This was Sofia's birthday, September 25, 1882. Was it her in the picture then? Yet, this photo also had a second date recorded on the back . . . how odd. From the way the dates were written, they seemed to be recording the child's birthday and the day of death. If this was so, the child died on October 19, 1884, shortly after her second birthday.

She dug deeper in the box, flipping through official looking papers written in Italian, when something caught her eye in the handwritten texts: *Serena Falcone*. The same dates from the photograph were written on this page, but Sofia struggled to understand the rest. She leaned against the closet door and tried to comprehend the writing. She had not had reason to learn to read until they arrived in America, and now her schooling—at night, after her work at the factory—was in English. She squinted her eyes, hoping to send a message to her brain to concentrate harder.

The paper might be some kind of official document, like a birth certificate. But with those two dates? No, this was a record of the infant's death. Why would Sister Stefania have such a thing? Had she been hiding it? The *bambina* bore Sofia's family's name. And Sofia's birthday.

Had Sofia been born with a twin?

Her heart pounded. She did not want to believe her parents would have hidden this from her, but what other explanation could there be?

She rubbed a shaky hand over her face.

"Sofia! What are you doing, *figlia mia*? We shall never eat if you don't move quicker!"

Sofia slapped the lid back on the box and returned it to the corner. Gathering up the soup pot, she slipped the photograph into her apron pocket. Someone needed to explain this.

Later, after supper, when Papà was about to take his pipe to his favorite spot by the coal stove, Sofia brought out the photograph. Sofia's twin brothers, Frankie and Fredo, were away at work, and her sister Gabriella had likely slipped downstairs to sit on the stoop and trade stories with the neighbors. This moment might be her best chance to speak to her parents.

Sofia said nothing when she held out the photograph.

Mamma's face turned white. She snatched the photograph and handed it to Papà. He frowned. "I told you we should have told her, Angelina."

"You told me? This is my fault? You blame me, Giuseppe." Sofia's mother dismissed him with the wave of a dishcloth. She pinched at her eyes. "Serena. *Povera bambina!*"

Joey sat silently by the stove, not defending her as Sofia thought he should, even though he looked as shocked as she felt. Of course, he hadn't known this either. And it was done to her, not him. After a few moments he rose and slipped out the door.

Like many other Falcone conversations, this discussion rose in volume for the whole building to hear. Joey would not escape it unless he left the neighborhood. Never mind this had been a secret for nineteen years. Passion overruled privacy in these rooms. *La famiglia* must shout out when emotions turned hot.

"Who was she, Mamma? You must tell me."

"I must? May God wash your tongue!" Mamma reached out to slap her but instead kept her hand aloft as though some invisible force held it back.

Sofia turned away.

"Tell her, Angelina." Papà's face flushed scarlet.

"You do it." Mamma left the stove, pushed past them, and slammed the door to the bedroom behind her.

Papà lifted his gaze to the ceiling. "Always up to me, it is. All right then. Sit down, *mi figlia.*" Papà offered his seat.

Instead, Sofia dropped to the floor next to the chair. She longed for him to pat her head as if she were a child again, to speak softly, to understand how confusing all this was for her.

He sat and crossed his arms. Sadness choked his voice but he seemed to attempt to hold it back.

Sofia tried unsuccessfully to catch his eye. "Papà, I had a twin sister, *sì?*"

"You did. Your mother and I thought it best not to talk about this, Sofia." He drew in a long breath. "*La famiglia*, we do not discuss such unpleasantness. I thought your Mamma, she should tell you when she saw fit."

"It was wrong of you not to tell me!"

"It was best." He lowered his voice. "I am your papà and I tell you it was best. For you. For Mamma."

So this was the source of Mamma's demons. Sofia would never agree that keeping this from her was right. "What happened?"

Papà tapped his fingers together as he spoke. "Sweet Serena." He sighed the way someone does when recalling a pleasant memory. "The two of you together...*belle.*"

Sofia waited, looking away in case there were tears. He was an emotional man, but when his passion led to tears, he always tried to hide them. And right now she had no sympathy, no patience for his distress when she was the one who had been lied to.

He sighed. "Serena was just…she was not the lucky one. There was an accident."

Sofia's stomach clenched. *Not the lucky one.* Apparently, Sofia had been the fortunate one, the daughter who had lived. However painful, she needed to know what happened. "Please, Papà, tell me everything. I am a grown woman. I should know."

"*Sì.* I told your mother…ah, no matter. I tell you the truth, and then you forget about it, *sì?*"

"*Sì*, Papà." But she would not. How could she? This was why she had always felt less than whole, always needing someone near. She'd once shared her life with another. Her twin was gone, leaving an empty spot in Sofia's heart that was now explained. Suddenly all her peculiarities lined up before her like the English verbs she'd learned to conjugate. There was a reason for what had before seemed like irrational behavior. Her imaginary playmate growing up had not been truly fictional.

Images came to her mind like a rapid projection of glass lantern slides. Sofia had once held a hand, warm and heavy. She and Serena had toddled up the cobblestone streets of Benevento side by side. They had whispered their twin language at night in a shared crib, Serena lying on Sofia's right side. They had fed each other soft cheese. Laughed only because the other did. Pulled on each other's hair. In the hot afternoons when thunderstorms passed, they had plunged their bare feet into the same rain puddles. Their giggles had melded together in such a way that later Sofia's laughter had felt soft and hollow.

The shadowy memory of someone Sofia's own size had been real not imaginary in the least. Later, when Sofia had held out her arm and called to that shadow, when she had insisted that presence had been tangible, Sofia's loss had been passed off as mere wishful imagining.

Memories, not fantasy.

Papà's eyes moistened when he looked at her. "You missed the sister you never knew about, *sì*?"

She nodded.

"I suppose so." He drew in a deep breath, probably preparing to tell her the worst of it. "The extra plate you set at the table."

"*Sì*, Papà."

"Somehow you knew."

"And you told me I made things up."

He flipped his hands in the air. "A mere child. We thought you could not remember."

"But I did."

She thought about the times she had insisted her invisible friend listen to Papà read the Bible along with her. Her habit of bunching up blankets next to her when she went to bed had actually been an attempt to feel the presence of the twin who had once lain in that spot. It all made sense now. Her parents had known the reason while she had not. Sofia had simply been acting out the part of her that was missing. And her parents had chosen to dismiss it, pretend there was no reasoning behind her behavior. Perhaps they had so desperately wanted to act as if Serena had never lived, and they found that too difficult with Sofia around. Did she look like her dead sister? Was there some expression in her eyes or curve of her facial features that kept the memory of Serena alive?

She rubbed a hand over her face as realization dawned. All this time she had not realized her presence had been the impetus for Mamma's sadness. She had to know the whole story now. "Please go on. Won't you tell me, Papà?"

He tipped his dark head in her direction. "Accidents are no one's fault. They happen and we cannot stop them." He spoke in an even, no-nonsense tone, the one he employed when he was determined not to show what his heart was feeling. Sofia knew better. This was a difficult story to tell. If her own heart wasn't aching so much she might feel sorry for him. He rubbed his hands over his knees. "The two of you were playing inside our house in Benevento. You heard the shepherds coming." He made that wistful sound again. "Serena always loved the goats because we had none of our own. She thought they were furry playmates. She adored the clanking of their bells, their bleating...like a newborn baby, you understand. It was as though she had been directed toward those goats that day, Sofia, although I do not blame God for it. An accident is all it was."

"Papà, what Mamma said. This tragedy...was I responsible?"

He huffed. "I say to forget this. It will be better if you do. Your mamma? I am not so sure she does not blame God. And when you blame God curses follow. I tell her that."

"Please, Papà." Sofia brought her folded hands to her chin. "Tell me how it happened."

He nodded and pulled at the scarf tied at his neck. "The shepherds, they drive their goats to the market, *sì*? Right past our house and down *per la via*. Serena, she fell beneath a cart's wheels. We could not save her. There." He smacked a hand on the knee of his dungarees. "You wanted the truth. There you have it."

"Oh, Papà." She fought tears, biting her lip. The fingers of her right hand grew strangely cold as though moments earlier she'd held a hand that was now absent.

The bedroom door opened.

Sofia wiped her eyes. "Oh, Mamma. How awful. I am sorry this happened."

Mamma glared at them. "Sorry? You see, Giuseppe? Is this what you wanted?" Mamma's eyes held a look Sofia had never seen before, something she could not comprehend. Madness? Pain? Mamma seemed as though the top of her head might erupt like Mount Vesuvius. She sputtered her lips and marched past them to the stove and began stirring the soup Sofia's brothers would eat when they returned from the night shift.

Papà squeezed Sofia's shoulder too tightly. "And now you forget this, Sofia. Can you not see how it upsets your mamma?"

"But...she was *my*...where is she buried, Papà?"

He stood suddenly and waved one hand beside his head. "We will talk no more of this."

Sofia went to her mother. "I meant no harm, Mamma. I only wanted to know."

Mamma spun around, her expression melting from anger to sadness. "I never wanted you to worry about this, Sofia. It would have been better if you had never known. Now..." She sighed. "No peace. No peace for you or for me." She brushed Sofia to the side and returned to her bedroom.

2

ANTONIO BAGGIO CLIMBED the four sets of stairs to his one-room apartment. When he reached the landing he heard barking and scratching. "Hold on, Lu. I'm coming." He stuck a skeleton key into the lock on his door and when he opened it, Luigi lunged at the sack of apples. "Down, fella. These aren't for you." Antonio set his load on the square table next to the tiny window and gave the dog a rub behind the ears. Before Antonio's father died, Antonio hadn't cared much about having a pet. About six months ago Papà brought home a puppy he'd found shivering in the cold and now Luigi was full-grown, a welcome companion in the small space that seemed vastly empty now without Papà.

A sound behind him made him freeze. Luigi growled. Antonio swore under his breath. How could he have been so foolish as to leave his front door ajar with all the beggars about? He turned around slowly, holding firmly to Luigi's collar.

"You spend too much money feeding that mutt."

Antonio's uncle, Nicco, stood leaning on the doorpost. Antonio let out the breath he'd been holding. "Not completely sozzled today, I see." Nicco lived here and there, as he described it, but he would never accept Antonio's invitation to live with him. They were family, but Nicco insisted he would not stay. Perhaps because he knew Antonio would not tolerate his drunkenness.

"The night's early yet." The man let out a gruff laugh.

Antonio released his dog who ran over to sniff the cuffs of Nicco's trousers. The man kicked playfully at Luigi, causing the dog to flee yelping. Lu regained his stance and growled at Nicco from his post in front of the coal stove. A mutt with unreasonable bravado for his size, Luigi feared no one, not even a lump of a man like Nicco.

Nicco grinned at the dog. "Anyone ever tell you he looks something like that dog on the Victor records? You know, the one with that foolish pose, as though he's listening to that music machine."

"The phonograph. Yeah, some people have said that. I don't see it. Come looking for a meal, Uncle?" Antonio reached behind the man and closed the door.

"Can't a fella come see his boy for no reason?"

"Not some fellas." Antonio filled a pan at the kitchen sink and placed it on the stove.

"Don't be that way, Tony."

Antonio blew out a breath and turned around. "Oh, you know I don't mind having you come by, Uncle. You can stay as long as you like, but please stop calling me Tony."

Nicco sat on Antonio's bed, the only seat in the room save for the piano bench and a rickety kitchen chair that probably would not hold his weight. Antonio had told his uncle not to take the piano bench, so he knew better. The mahogany seat was Antonio's private space, the place where he practiced his gift, and he didn't want it relegated to mere lounging. Shortly after Papà's death Antonio had given away his father's bed to a family downstairs, not wanting it to serve as a reminder of his father's absence. Now the apartment seemed sparse.

Funny how grief has no practical constraints. It lurks to spring on you without warning, especially when death comes without explanation or reason as it had for his father. All they knew was Ernesto Baggio had been shot outside Cooper Union, a long way from their neighborhood. They didn't know by whom or for what reason or even why Antonio's father had been there in the first place. An unfortunate bystander, the police had said. Recently, when Nicco stopped by the theater while Antonio was working, to bring Luigi some water, he'd said some men had come asking for him. Antonio still did not know why.

Nicco scratched at his unshaven chin. "Might as well Americanize that name, no? Maybe then those men would leave you alone."

"No one has reason to bother me, Uncle." He said this with a bit a doubt. There *were* unanswered questions.

The man held his arms in surrender. "I don't know why your father was at Cooper Union when he was killed. Him, an immigrant, up there with all those educated types. He was a smart one, your father, but not of that ilk. Ernesto always helped a man who was down on his luck. But, up there, no one needed him. No one even knew who he was. It makes no sense. And I don't know why those men, when they saw your name at the theater and said they thought you were Ernesto's boy, were looking for you. I know nothing at all about this business!"

"What am I supposed to do, Uncle? I have to go to work. I can't be running down rabbit trails, and I certainly don't want your friends, or whoever they were, causing trouble for me at work." This had to be another one of Nicco's wild imaginings, the stories he came up with when he'd been drinking.

"I never said they were friends. I do not know them. I only want you to be cautious."

"Hard to be careful when you don't know what you're looking out for. I cannot have them jeopardizing my job. Someone has to work."

Antonio could see his words wounded his uncle, but it was the truth. Antonio's father's savings—what he'd stuffed under his mattress, warning Antonio not to trust the Italian bank— had run out. Only recently had Antonio found employment. When his father was alive, he hadn't wanted Antonio to work, encouraging instead his son's interest in music, urging him to practice rather than to labor as a bricklayer or painter, as most of Antonio's school friends were now doing. The only job his father had approved of for him had been the occasional substituting for the church organist. "You will go to college, my son. Learn all the great subjects and grow in wisdom. I could never achieve this dream for myself, but my son? He will be someone great using the talent God gave him."

Now that his father was gone, Antonio could not ignore his father's request, even though without his father's financial support it would be much harder to achieve.

Antonio had no choice but to accept that his father's death had been a terrible accident. If only his uncle would leave things be instead of stirring up trouble where it surely did not exist.

Nicco helped himself to an apple from the sack. "Stay away from those people, son."

"What people? We don't know who they are. I suppose I could talk to the New York police again." When he'd first sought answers the police reminded him folks had been fired up since the president's assassination. Mobs still gathered and rallied most everywhere. There had been an anarchy meeting going on at the Union when Papà was killed. He probably did not realize what he was walking into. At least that was what the police report had claimed.

Nicco shook his head. "Don't bother with the police. A poor immigrant is of less concern to them than an alley cat stranded on a fire escape. The Benevento people, over in the Bend? They were the ones asking for you. Stay away."

"So these men, the ones you know nothing about, they were from Benevento?"

Nicco brought a fist to his mouth and coughed. "They talk like it. I can tell from their accent."

Luigi growled.

"What would they want with me, Uncle? Offer condolences?"

Nicco sighed. "I don't know. A whole crowd of them from that village live over on Mulberry. Those men, they must live there. If you get theater work over that way, decline, just to be safe."

"There aren't any Vaudeville shows in that neighborhood."

"Good." He shrugged, his rumpled jacket making crumpling noises. "An old man from Northern Italy, they don't like. So I always avoid those thugs. If they think you are Tony, an American, they will leave you alone." He muttered under his breath. "Italians? They will not pray together in church, won't give you a match or tell you the time of day, but they will work wherever and beside whomever. Who can understand it?"

Nicco, Antonio's late father's brother, used to work like Papà had, for a *padrone*, an Italian boss, who had come to their village in Italy and promised them paid labor in America. For a time they had traveled back and forth, working in America for a season in order to feed their families in Italy, until one day Antonio's father decided he and Antonio would immigrate. Nicco came too. In later years, Papà worked for the street department.

"If your mamma was here, Antonio…" Nicco shed tears even though Antonio's mother had died almost two decades ago, giving birth to Antonio's sister who lived but one hour. "She would take care of you." Now he was weeping, wiping his eyes on his sleeve. Maybe he had been drinking more than usual, or else his constant binges had made him more emotional than he should be.

"I know, Uncle. It's all right. I am fine."

"Back then, the *padrone* get us work. We did all right. But now…"

Antonio had heard the story many times. America held the promise for a better education and a good life. Nicco worked with Antonio's father for a time, and had decided to stay in New York too. Life was hard at first, but they survived. Antonio went to school, learned English well. When Nicco started hitting the bottle and preferred not to share the apartment with them so he could come and go without scrutiny, Antonio's father supported them all with his paycheck.

"After all this time, Uncle, perhaps it would be best to move on with our lives and accept it was an accident."

The man shuffled his feet as though the floorboards were eavesdropping neighbors. "You just be careful, boy. Got work at the theater tonight?"

Antonio stirred oatmeal into the steaming pot. "A new vaudeville engagement. And Sunday I will be standing in for the organist again at mass."

Nicco slapped his knee. "St. Anthony's, God bless 'em."

The church helped support the Italian aid society where Nicco often found assistance. It seemed when it came to the aid society, the Italian immigrants from all regions could tolerate each other's presence. Tolerate, but without any real fraternizing. Mass was celebrated separately. The Northern Italians went to the magnificent St. Anthony's on Sullivan to say their prayers, worship, and observe confession. The impressive structure was built by a previous generation of Italian immigrants. But when large numbers of immigrants started arriving from Southern Italy, those people were regulated to the lower levels for their services. Eventually the Franciscans began helping to complete a church over in the Mulberry Bend area for the Southern Italians. He shook his head thinking about it. At St. Anthony's he'd heard people saying that the Mulberry church wasn't finished still, only the basement. Well, at least those folks had their own basement now for services and didn't have to endure a shunning from their northern countrymen. Antonio could walk from one church to the other in about half an hour. Why folks couldn't get along, he didn't know.

Nicco chatted on and on about what he had seen that day on the streets.

When the oatmeal was ready, Antonio handed Nicco a mugful and a spoon. "Finish up quickly. I have to practice." He tossed Nicco another apple and the man stuck it in his pocket. At least he'd have something in his stomach should he drop in on the saloon again. Antonio wanted to be kind to his father's brother, but he often battled a desire to send him away because of the man's propensity for liquor. A man should work for his food and not beg for his drink.

They ate in silence until Nicco was ready to leave.

"You watch yourself out there, Antonio. On my mother's grave, I tell you I do not know what those men wanted. But I would bet my last dime they are up to no good."

"Don't worry about me, Uncle." Antonio would be careful when he went back to work, bringing Luigi with him whenever he could. Most theaters didn't mind having the dog around, so long as Luigi waited outside the door. Luigi was well trained and faithful, a watchdog if not a weapon. Lu would stay as long as he was told and do his part. Uncle made a good point. Those men, whoever they were, might come back, and even if they didn't, it was time Antonio got some answers. With a man like Nicco, habitually bending his arm down at the nearest saloon, this might be the most help Antonio would get in trying to solve the mystery.

Antonio handed his uncle a blanket.

"Are you sure you have enough?" Nicco wouldn't look at him. Shame was not something any man wanted his kin to see in his eyes.

"I have enough, but you won't stay?"

"No."

He showed his uncle to the door.

"You'll be careful?"

Antonio nodded despite the dread creeping up his throat.

3

A WEIGHT PRESSED against Sofia's chest and she struggled to catch her breath. Now that the shouting had stopped, her mother's rejection, and the revelation that she'd had a twin that died, nearly knocked the breath from her lungs. The walls and ceiling seemed to creep in. She scrambled out of the house to the sidewalk as a coal truck rumbled by, sprinkling bits of black dust onto her grief. She should have realized when she found that photograph there would be an argument, a denial that hiding what had happened was wrong. But what she hadn't anticipated was how revealing the truth would make her mother so distraught. It had not been right for them to keep it from her, no matter how painful it was for Mamma. Winter could not come soon enough this year.

"I did not know." She looked up to find Joey standing at the curb. "No one told me."

She bit her lip. Who confesses a lie to their youngest child? Certainly not her parents.

He raised his brows and tilted his chin upward. "This was a bad thing."

His affirmation boosted her spirit.

"So long ago, Sofia." He wagged his head as he strode to her. Placing a hand on her shoulder, he leaned down to look into her eyes. "Thinking on it will only tear you apart, like Mamma. Try to forget."

She fought tears. "They should have told me."

"*Sì*, they should have, but it's all done now. That's what Papà told you, didn't he? I am sure he said to forget it."

"He did."

Joey nodded as though the matter was settled. He shoved his hands into the pockets of his dungarees and moved on down the sidewalk, softly humming a tune from their days in the old village. Stunned, she watched him go. What was wrong with everyone? Forget? How?

She dropped to the top step of the window well, where some newsboys huddled. Annoyed by her presence, they hurried out to trail behind the truck and collect whatever it dropped. Were any of them twins? Sofia had twin brothers, and, back in Italy, twin cousins. A spark of jealousy rose in her like a fever. It was not right for twins to be separated in death, especially before they had shared everything that needed to be shared. Her parents just did not understand. They had not trusted her with this knowledge. More than that, they had allowed everyone to think she was a bit loony for imagining she'd had a companion. She had not been delusional, and she certainly wasn't now. *La Famiglia's* code of silence. How she detested it.

Sofia wiped her eyes as a crowd of schoolgirls bustled by. Turning away from their stares, she thought about how she had been unable to meet her mother's expectations, the daughter who was "less than God intended." And Papà? He thought Sofia was too delicate to face life's harsh realities. She'd known they believed this all of her life, but now it made sense. Sofia was a painful reminder to them, especially when the anniversary of Serena's death came around.

A thought struck her like a blast of frigid air. What had Sofia done? She had to know. What if the reason they didn't want to talk about it was because it had been Sofia's fault? She glanced down at her cold hands. She had to know the truth. Papà probably had not been there when it happened. He would have been working in the lemon groves. Mamma would just have to tell her and Sofia would have to wait. Wait until the melancholy left.

The crisp air swept the aroma of sweat, soot, and musty rain down the street. She glanced around. Gabriella and Joey must have gone to play cards or sing at the Mazzones' or the Russos' home. If not there, then on one of the other stoops of any one of the families that had immigrated from their village. This had happened before Sofia's siblings were born. They could not understand.

Sofia covered her face with her apron. Someone tapped her on the shoulder. Thinking her sister had returned home, she shook her head.

"What's the trouble, lass? Sofia, isn't it? Can I help?"

Surprised, Sofia dropped her apron to find a red-haired woman she vaguely knew, someone she had seen at night school, staring down at her. "I am sorry. I thought you were…I thought my sister had come home, *signora*." Sofia glanced at the young woman's round belly. She'd noticed it when she'd first seen her, thinking to herself how different America was, where women did not shut themselves away during pregnancy. However, thinking about it, she realized she really hadn't seen any other pregnant girls out on the streets. Perhaps it was just this woman going about in public in this state.

The girl joined her on the step. "Mrs. Annie Adams. Do you remember me? I was at your night school, discussing the possibility of offering extra services for the girls there. I'm from Hawkins House."

Sofia barely recalled the conversation. "I am fine. I am...surprised to see you in this neighborhood"

"I was making some visits, as is my habit. Someone helped me when I first arrived and 'tis my extreme privilege to be able to help others now."

"You are kind. The sun is so low now, though. You should get along."

"Are you sure you're fine?"

"Please do not worry." Sofia was puzzled by this stranger's concern.

"All right, so." She reached into her pocket purse and pulled something out. She handed a small card to Sofia. "We have just opened a memorial library. Borrowing some books written in English might be good practice for you. If you've a mind."

Sofia stood, cradling the card as if it were a valuable thing. "*Bene. Grazie, Signora* Adams." Even though she could not accept, she was grateful for the offer.

"Annie, please. I hope to see you there. Sofia, correct?"

"*Sì.* Sofia Falcone."

Sofia watched the young woman march away, a market basket swinging from her arm. Incredible that when your world is crumbling around you, hoards of people walk down the street and pass you by without seeing your anguish. What was it about this Annie that made her notice Sofia's pain, when no one else had?

When Sofia went back in, she did not see Mamma.

"Off to her bed, Sofia." Papà paced the small sitting room. "I have never seen her so bad."

"She will be better, Papà."

"I do not think so. Her heart is broken."

Sofia closed her eyes a moment. "No. Like always, it will last a while and then she will get better. By Christmas, or just after, as always."

"No, no. Have you ever known her to leave her soup pot?"

Sofia turned toward the stove. Orange liquid dripped down the side of the pot while the flame underneath licked up spilled soup with a rhythmic sizzle. No, Mamma had never done that before. Her cooking was her joy, evidence of her delight in nurturing *la famiglia.*

"She is not herself, Papà. She will get better." Sofia hurried to clean up the mess.

The rest of the evening Mamma did not come out. Frankie and Fredo, Sofia's twin brothers, returned from their night jobs and Sofia served them slightly scorched soup. Then she washed and scrubbed and set the kitchen in order. No sign of Mamma.

Antonio stared at the playbill he'd been handed and tried to focus on his task. Tony Pastor's Fourteenth Street Theatre. He glanced to the page after the advertisements. For the week of September 21, 1903. Antonio had been a mid week fill-in, but a job was a job. He ran his thumb past the acts that had already performed to the end of the show where he came in. A trained monkey act and then he was on.Once he saw the creature and his trainer bounce off the stage through the curtains, he took his place at the piano. He had to improvise, something he despised, but he had a fairly detailed typed script in front of him, so at least he knew where the skit was headed. The act seemed to be going well until the performer veered away from the plan.

Perspiration gathered at Antonio's collar as he strained his neck to see around the piano. His tempo lagged behind the act.

When the piece was finished, the actor with a heavily powdered face stormed up to Antonio, threw down the scarf in his hands, and began shouting at the theater manager who had come to greet him. "This man is a disgrace. Sack him and get someone who knows what the devil he's doing! I will not be made a fool of, Mac!"

Not again. Antonio had been the victim of too many talentless performers in the last few weeks. Antonio had not been the one to change the skit. This actor had forgotten his lines or something. Apparently mediocrity was preferred in most theaters.

"Let's go, Otis. It's all over now." The theater manager, a man known simply as Mac, urged the irate actor back to his makeup table. When the manager returned, Antonio was already packing up his music. "Look, Tony, vaudeville ain't good enough for a classical musician like ye."

If the man hadn't called him Tony, Antonio might have been flattered. He liked the manager, a friendly fella of Scottish descent with wide blue eyes. "You are probably right, Mac, but I have to make a living."

"Don't we all." Mac wiped his forehead with a handkerchief, then returned the rag to his vest pocket and checked his timepiece. "I'll toss in an extra quarten for this next act. Not a bad deal for a couple of minutes of work."

"I'm finished. It's the end."

"Oh, no, it's not. You know we got to run the program again. Say, I've got another piano player coming in about thirty minutes. Some acts don't require accompaniment. Others do. If you stay just until he gets here, I'll pay you for the extra time, fair and square. I'm in a spot with the opening act, though. I need the piano. Help a *min* out?"

Antonio lifted his gaze to the rafters. He had read the playbill. "Dolly?"

"That's right. 'A Bird in a Gilded Cage.' You've played it before. No surprises there."

Antonio dropped back to the stool. "Fine."

Mac slapped his shoulder, sending him forward with the force. "Take fifteen minutes and then we'll be all set, aye? I'll tell Marcus."

"Just don't call me Tony."

"Sure. Righto." The man scrambled off into the shadows.

Dolly was a female impersonator, although most folks didn't realize it. His real name was Marcus, apparently. B.F. Keith, the owner of many theaters including Union Square, where they showed those new moving pictures called the Lumière Cinématographe, set the pace for vaudeville. He made a big deal out of offering theater suitable for women and families in his establishments. Tony Pastor, the owner of the Fourteenth Street Theatre was no different, for the most part. Wholesome entertainment was the fashion now in Manhattan, it seemed. Therefore, no one mentioned Dolly's masquerade. The farce was just another instance of what Antonio had to put up with in order to save money to fulfill his father's dream for him. One day he would be that classical musician Mac thought he should be. For now, this wasn't too bad. Antonio could do worse for his supper, he supposed. He'd been told that in the old days patrons were not prohibited from throwing vegetables at the acts. If he had to perform on stages like this, at least the Fourteenth didn't allow disgruntled mobs.

He stared down at the keys under his fingertips. This song, meant to make genteel ladies weep over a woman who had not married for love, launched the show nearly every night. While Antonio waited out the intermission, he brought his dog a cracker.

"Good, loyal mutt you got there." A stagehand offered Antonio a cup of coffee.

"Thanks. He is."

"He'll wait right here until you're done?"

"He will."

The man's face bloomed with a toothy grin. "Don't that beat all."

Antonio whispered instructions to Luigi although he didn't have to. The dog was more reliable than the humans Antonio knew. After a quick visit to the men's room, it was finally time to take his place at the piano again. He would play for this ridiculous act simply because he needed to eat. Antonio held on to the hope that one day he would rise above this, play in concert halls for wealthy patrons who had discerning tastes. If he continued to save as much of his earnings as possible to fund a trip west for an audition at Oberlin College, it could happen. A dream, perhaps unreachable, but one he was determined to pursue.

He stared down at his fingers hovering over the black and white keys like a bird of prey. Only one thing could throw a snake into the plan: the mystery of his father's death. Many times he had gone to sleep hoping to wake up from a bad dream.

He rubbed his hands together and flexed his joints. Right now he had a job to do. He had to put other thoughts aside and get through this.

As soon as Dolly hurried off the stage, to undeserved applause Antonio thought, a quartet scrambled up. One of them handed some music to Antonio. " 'Strike Up the Band?' Absolutely not." He stood, ready to leave, but Mac's firm hand pushed him back down. He dangled three dollar bills in front of Antonio.

"But this is a complicated piece," he complained.

"Can't you do it?"

"Yes, but probably not the way—"

"Just keep it up tempo. It will be fine."

Mac hurried away and the four men stood in the electric spotlight, waiting. Antonio inhaled deeply and then played an F to allow them to find their notes.

"Brum, brum, brum," they sang. "Jaaack...is the king of the dark blue sea...Jaaack...is as brave as the brave can be..."

Antonio began to speed up the pace and the singers followed. Then, when they got to the chorus, Antonio lunged into the song, hitting the keys with a syncopated rhythm he didn't know he had in him.

When the song ended he could hear the audience cheering and whistling. The quartet took several bows as Antonio packed up his things. The regular pianist had arrived. Even he applauded the performance. The four singers marched past them, out of breath.

"Bravo," Mac cried, handing Antonio his pay.

He'd earned it, all right. Antonio glanced toward the door and thought about his dog. "No one came looking for me tonight, Mac?"

"No one but your pooch."

"Thanks. You'd tell me, though, right? I mean if someone was here asking for me."

"I would. I owe ye that."

Antonio studied the manager's expression. He seemed sincere. He thanked him and hurried out. Later, as Antonio and Luigi hurried home with scraps he'd gathered for Luigi from behind a restaurant on Grand, Antonio paused, glancing in the direction of Mulberry. Nicco had warned him not to go there, but if the men from that neighborhood knew more about Antonio's father's death, why shouldn't he ask around?

He closed his eyes as an unwelcome memory rushed back. His father's body lying on the coroner's gurney was as gruesome a sight as he ever hoped to see. A bullet had traveled through Ernesto Baggio's head, an image that could not now be erased from Antonio's mind. *I'll find out, Papà. You had a reason to go to the Union that night, something you didn't tell me, but whatever it is, you did not deserve what happened to you.*

Perhaps the only way to erase the horror in his head and remember Papà as he'd truly been, a hardworking, generous man, would be to find answers. It was up to him. Papà would have wanted Antonio to find justice…and peace.

Antonio reached down and rubbed Luigi's head before urging him on toward home. "We have a tough task ahead, Lu. At least I'll have you with me to help charm folks."

4

THE NEXT MORNING Sofia handed Papà a cup of coffee. "How is Mamma?"

"Bad, so bad."

"Should I bring her a tray? I could boil an egg quickly."

"I do not think so."

"Did you talk to her? Did you tell her nothing has changed?" At least for Mamma. "This happened so long ago. What has made this worse?"

"I do not know, Sofia. You better forget night school this time and fetch our doctor when you leave the factory."

"Can't Gabriella?"

He glared at her. "She has the children to look after. Do not argue, Sofia."

Gabriella tended the neighbor's children while their mother worked. "I don't see why she can't just ask *Signora* Russo to watch—"

Papà made grunting sounds, waving his hands about.

Sofia swallowed a sour taste in her mouth. She knew she should obey. She had no choice, truly, but her respect for her parents was waning because they had treated her as a simpleton when all along they knew she missed her twin. She took a deep breath. Mamma needed her now despite it all. Sofia did not think their doctor—the healer from their village who lived in their building—could help. Perhaps she would also call on the priest.

The mantel clock gonged. Sofia was late. She'd lost sleep thinking about the accident, wondering how exactly it had happened, if Serena had suffered. And she'd prayed to remember it, but she had not.

Sofia paused on the stoop outside and turned to see her mother peering from the upstairs window, round-faced, white-streaked black hair pulled back in a bun, scowling. At least she'd gotten out of bed. Sofia raised her hand to wave. "I'll bring home the roasted peanuts you like, Mamma!" Mamma's face drew back from the lace curtain.

She bumped into Joey as she turned in the direction of the trolley. "Off to work?" he asked, tipping his cap away from his forehead.

"Of course. You?"

He frowned. "I do my best, Sofia."

She patted his arm. "Keep it up. We must all do our best. *Addio!*"

When Sofia stepped off the elevator, her boss, Mr. Richmond met her. "You're late, young lady."

"Sorry, Mr. Richmond. It will not happen again."

He bent his thick brows to a point. "If it does, Miss Falcone, you will be dismissed."

Sofia made her way to her sewing machine. She'd been fortunate to have this job. Much was expected of her by *la famiglia*. No one earned a lot of money. Living in America cost more than living in Italy, although there was work available, so everyone could contribute. Everyone but Mamma needed to earn money. Thankfully they had Mamma to cook, mend, and clean their tiny American *casa*, just a couple of rented rooms in an overly populated tenement building. Papà had sacrificed the bulk of his savings to bring them to New York in hopes that Mamma would forget her sorrow.

Mr. Richmond was too stern, too focused on productivity and efficiency, as he liked to say. But Sofia needed her position at the shoe factory, so she must be more careful. Now more than ever she needed employment, both for the money and for an escape.

As she examined the leather she was about to stitch, Sofia decided that on her way home, once she'd inquired after the healer and the priest, she would stop to speak to Sister Stefania. Her aunt would remember what happened. *Please, God, let the answers bring healing.*

All day long it seemed her supervisor stared at her. Several times she had to take deep breaths and remind herself that he had no reason to dismiss her. She was a hard worker. Still, her hands trembled as she worked.

Sofia rushed outside when the work whistle blew. She set off to find the doctor first, since that's what Papà had instructed her to do. Not the kind of person Americans called a doctor, though. The Falcones would trust their own before others. She would stop by the Russo apartment and beg *Signora* Russo to come see Mamma. Carla Russo had been a healer back in Benevento, and at times she continued the practice against her husband's wishes, who thought an American city was no place for the old ways. He never refused the healer's pay, though. Sofia quickened her steps, dodging dawdling walkers and boys with hoops. Perhaps *Signor* Russo had not returned home from work yet. If Sofia was quick enough, she might avoid the unpleasant man.

She shooed two cats away from the indoor stairs leading to the Russo residence and trotted up three flights. Reaching the Russos's door, she paused to pray the master of the home would not be there because he might not let his wife come. She rapped twice before the door creaked open.

"*Signora* Russo, are you all right?"

The door opened wider. "Oh, Sofia. What are you doing here?" The woman's face was partially shielded by a scarf, but Sofia could see purple marks at her left temple. She bit her lip and sucked back the disparaging words she wished she could voice about the man who beat his wife. No one talked about it. No one confronted him. It was just not done, but Sofia wished things could be different. "Mamma, *signora*. She needs your help."

"I can't help anyone today."

Sofia whispered. "*Signor* Russo is at home, then?"

"He is not, but I cannot help."

"Oh, please. It is the autumn melancholy and she is very bad this time. Much worse."

The woman's ample bosom rose as she took in a deep breath. "Tell her to drink the elixir. All a woman needs most times is a drop of grappa and soda water."

"Brandy? No, no, *signora*. This is different—"

"She will be fine." The door started to close.

Sofia grabbed the edge to stop the woman from shutting her out. "No, wait. You do not understand."

"It is you who does not understand, girl. I cannot come. Do not ask it of me."

"But, can I help you? Are you all right? Has something happened?" She asked even though the woman would never tell. At least *Signora* Russo would know someone had noticed what was happening to her.

"Go along, now." When Sofia pulled her hand back the woman shut the door.

Sofia closed her eyes a moment, praying the woman's husband might stay away forever. The sound of the cats fighting below jolted her. She scrambled down and hurried toward the church.

The Most Precious Blood Church was still under construction. Only the part below ground was finished and construction workers had scaffolds across the entrance. "Go next door," someone from high above called to her. "You can't come in here." They rambled on about how no one should come to church on a Thursday. Had they never heard of confession?

Sofia grabbed on to the iron fencing as she hurried to the lower level. First she would find Father Lucci and urge him to come see Mamma. Then she would seek out Sister Stefania at the convent house next door. She let herself in quietly, knowing people were lighting candles and visiting the confessional after their workday. She sat a moment in a pew, relishing the calmness she always felt when she entered. Ever since Sofia was young Mamma had told her the church was God's house, and Sofia had always felt a spiritual presence there. And now, entering her church, Sofia had managed to momentarily put aside the emptiness, what she now understood to be the absence of her twin. She gazed up at the altar, at the crucifix, candlesticks, vessels, and of course the reliquary of Saint Gennarro. When the upper church was completed, it would be more like the churches of Italy—white walls, fresco painting, life-sized statues of Jesus and Mary. The tradition and history of the church was precious to her, and even though she loved it for the way it connected her to her ancestors, she often pondered if the new church would still possess the specialness she experienced here in the temporary sacred space. Was that even possible? For a sacred space to lose its holiness once a grand chapel is built to replace it? In this lower church, Sofia felt as though she could almost touch heaven. Here in God's house.

The sound of someone leaving the confessional made her look up. She recognized Luisa Russo, the teenage daughter of the healer. She hurried over to the girl. "Is Father Lucci in the confessional, Luisa?"

"He is." The girl blinked. She had been crying.

"What is it?"

One of the old women lighting candles hushed them. Sofia ushered the girl toward the door.

"If Papà never comes back, it will be too soon. I hate him." She sighed and stomped her foot. "Now I have to go back to confession."

"God will forgive you."

The girl raised her black brows.

"Come now. You know He will. Go check on your mother, though. I think she needs you."

Luisa nodded and tugged her nutmeg-colored scarf over her head before she opened the door to leave.

Sofia turned back to the confessional. She would have to go in to talk to Father Lucci. The other priest might be available but she did not like him as well.

She peeled back the red curtain and ducked inside. She knelt, and when the door slid open she stared at the profile of the priest dappled by the wooden screen. She did not speak.

"Go on, child."

She asked for forgiveness because she was in the confessional for a different purpose. Then she stated her reason for coming.

"Sofia, you know what I am doing here." He blew out a frustrated breath. "Go on, now. I will come as soon as I get a replacement."

Satisfied he would, she asked for forgiveness for feeling angry her parents had kept a secret from her. He gave her a penance and told her to repeat the Act of Contrition, which she did as rapidly as possible. After he absolved her, she rushed out.

Darting up one set of stairs, Sofia swung past the iron fence to the door of the convent house. Sister Stefania happened to be on greeting duty.

"Sofia, *bella ragazza!*" She hugged Sofia tight and then drew back. Pinching Sofia's cheeks, her aunt clucked her tongue. "You are as red as a pepper. What is wrong, girl?"

"Mamma."

"Oh, *sì*. It is that time of year. Come in, I will pour you coffee."

Sofia followed her to the small kitchen the nuns used.

"The sisters are at prayers, but I am to offer hospitality to whomever comes by. And today it is you. You make me so happy."

Sofia had had few conversations with the woman, and never before alone. Sister Stefania was different than Mamma. Her heart was light where Mamma's was heavy. She smiled while Mamma seemed to prefer to frown, even when she and Sofia had enjoyed happier days. "I…I want to tell you something."

"What has happened? Frankie and Fredo? An accident on the job?" She lifted both hands beside her head. "They take too many risks, your brothers."

"No, it is not the boys. It is Mamma. And me. I…" She wasn't sure how to confess that she'd been snooping in her aunt's belongings. "Well, the truth is, I took a peek into that box you brought by. The one you had no room to keep here."

The sister busied herself pouring cream into a small pot. "Ah, *sì*. You probably wondered about that music recording. Annabelle gave it to me."

"Who?" Sofia took a steaming cup from Stefania.

"The gardener's wife. That's right. We have a small patch of roses and lavender, and the Father hires a gardener. The

44

poor man needed a job, that's why. I suppose that's all right now, isn't it?"

Sofia bit her lip. She loved her aunt, but talking with her was usually difficult because she could be *capriccioso*, flighty, as the Americans say. "Sister Stefania, about the box, the one covered in floral paper?"

"Ah, *sì*. The gardener's wife. She has one of those music machines. I will show you if you come by on Friday." She smacked her lips. "That is tomorrow, now isn't it? That is when I have my leisure time."

"I…uh, I have to work. Sister, there was something else in that box. Something that upset Mamma. And me as well."

Sofia's aunt didn't seem to hear. She must be thinking about the record still. Stefania began singing a tune Sofia didn't recognize. Certainly not a Latin hymn. "Sister?"

She seemed to float back from the clouds. "Hmm?"

"The box. There were other things in there."

Stefania shrugged.

Someone knocked at the door. Stefania sprang from her chair and rushed out to answer it.

This was why Sofia had rarely conversed with the woman. Her mother's sister was distracted by anything that moved in her peripheral vision. Flies, honking horns, bicycles, scurrying children. Just about anything could get Stefania to switch directions and lose track of what she was supposed to be doing. Perhaps this was why the sisters had given Sofia's aunt this duty. She was always noticing people. She would be the perfect choice to greet people and even pull lost souls in off the street.

As she waited for her aunt to attend to the new visitor, Sofia shifted uncomfortably on the spindly kitchen chair. The convent was too quiet. She did not like being alone in the kitchen. She picked up her coffee cup and moved to the doorway that led to the entry. She watched as Stefania put something into the hand of the man who had knocked, a beggar she supposed, and then blessed him as he hurried away. She turned and smiled at Sofia.

"Your mother needs you, child. No matter how harsh she might be at times, she needs you beside her. I help her when I can, but you are the one she needs most."

"Sister Stefania, I know. I know about my twin."

The woman just smiled sweetly, as though Sofia had commented on the weather. "Go along now. But come back soon."

"We should talk about it."

"Talk, talk. People talk when they should pray. That's what."

Sofia gave up. She thanked her aunt and handed the cup back. Father Lucci was probably on his way to see Mamma anyway, and Sofia needed to be there.

5

Antonio ate his midday meal when most people had their evening supper. That was the life of someone who worked in vaudeville. But it wouldn't be his lot forever. He didn't want the label of vaudevillian performer. He was a serious musician, or he hoped to be.

He stretched his fingers before he put the last bit of his cold bean sandwich in his mouth. Time to practice. He brushed the crumbs from his plate and returned it to the shelf above his sink. Then he scrubbed his utensils, giving Luigi a glance. "Good dog. You stayed on your bed while I ate. Whatever did I do to deserve such a faithful companion?"

Phonograph music wafted in through his lone window from somewhere below. Luigi turned toward the sound. "Do you hear that, boy? Someone's playing one of those records with your picture on it." It amused Antonio to think about the children he'd encountered outside the theater who were calling Lu "Nipper," the name of the dog on the label. "You may not look just like that dog, but you certainly are as loyal. Your demeanor has made you famous, boy."

Luigi lay down and put his paws over his ears.

"What's the matter? You don't like people thinking you're that other dog? Well, I don't blame you. People think I'm nothing but a low paid vaudeville piano player, and that's not who I am either. Not all together."

To prove his point he sat down at his piano and began playing Brahms. Fifty years ago Steinway & Sons was founded in this very building, or at least that's what the landlord had told Papà when they moved in, which explained the presence of the old piano. It had been left behind and somewhat neglected. Papà had bought it from the building's owner, paying installments for several years. Antonio and his father worked together on Papà's day off to clean it up, repair some keys, and tune it. Even the bench was unique, a prototype that was supposed to have been height adjustable with the turn of a key, now long lost.

Steinway pianos were made uptown now, but something besides this instrument had been left behind. Antonio could sense it in the walls of the Varick Street loft. Hope, creativity—he wasn't sure what to call it, but it seemed to envelop him every time he walked through the door. What others might see as dilapidated, drafty, and dowdy, he knew as a comforting shelter where inspiration bloomed like a hopeful spring weed through cracked pavement.

After he'd practiced long enough to begin to feel aching in his fingers and legs, he rose, shaved, and dressed in his best suit, a brown tweed his father had called his performance attire.

Most folks would be home from work by now and hopefully willing to talk. "For you, Papà. I go to Mulberry Bend for you."

Shoving his hands into his pockets he considered the fact that he had no weapon. He pondered whether it would be prudent to carry a gun or a knife when he went knocking on doors in a part of town where he might not be welcome. He wasn't sure, but it might be wise to arm oneself in such a situation. But it didn't matter. Antonio had nothing to take along. He didn't even know how to wield a weapon if he had one. For all his luck, some criminal would take it from him and use it against him. However, he did have one avenue of defense.

"Come here, boy." Antonio clipped a leash to Luigi's collar. "I know, you don't like that. Don't usually need it, do you boy?" He patted the dog to reassure him. "I trust you all right, but not everyone has a heart as good as yours." A clap of thunder outside convinced Antonio to collect his Mackintosh. He did not wish to ruin his best suit in the rain, and the overcoat was better protection than an umbrella. Plopping his homburg atop his head, he led Luigi out the door. Better to rely on something he knew how to handle: Lu.

Antonio climbed the steps to the el stop, confident Luigi would be admitted.

"Say there, Tony," the ticket taker greeted him. Everyone seemed to be so fond of nicknames these days. Antonio thought they were more suited to pets. "You've brought your theater dog with you. Nipper, right?"

Luigi growled. Chuckling, Antonio handed over the fare. "Call him whatever you like."

When they took a seat, Luigi didn't take his eyes off Antonio.

"Oh, come on, boy. What does it matter so long as you get to ride? Look there." Antonio glanced out the window. "The rain's letting up. Isn't that fine?"

A girl with long brown braids asked to pet Luigi and the attention helped to soothe both Antonio and his dog. The ride would be short. Antonio inhaled deeply and sat up straighter, telling himself there could not have been anything sinister in his father's death. Just a misunderstanding, as the police had said. The people in the Bend would just help clear things up for Antonio and satisfy Nicco, that's all. Then he could breathe easier, say goodbye to his father in peace, and move on toward getting trained at the best music school he knew of, Oberlin College in Ohio. Telling himself all this did nothing to stop the chill running up his neck.

When he got off the el, a church bell announced the hour. He paused, wondering if God recognized church bells as our call to prayer, or if God even heard our prayers. Antonio hoped so because he needed some courage. Pulling the collar of his Mackintosh up toward his chin, he knew where he'd head first. The church might be the best place to start. After asking three people, who each gave him an odd look and a dismissive shake of their heads, a small girl finally told him to head to Mulberry Street between Canal and Hester. "Mind yourself. You can't get in the front. Go next door."

It was only after he arrived that he understood her instructions. Men labored on various levels of a scaffold, sending clouds of dust down to the street. The lower level was nondescript. He was contemplating where to turn when a door suddenly flung open. He tied Luigi's leash to a basement railing more for his own comfort than to dissuade Lu from straying. "Sorry, boy. No dogs in church."

The dog whimpered a bit, but he'd wait. He always did. Antonio hurried over just before a nun closed the door. "*Mi scusi!* Wait a moment!"

The woman turned, smiled, and waved to him. Ah, he was right to come here. When one is a newcomer the church is often first to welcome him.

"*Buongiorno*, young man. I am Sister Stefania. Please come in."

Luigi began to bark.

"Quiet, Lu. I will be right back." He turned to the woman. "He is very faithful. He will wait for me."

She put both hands to her cheeks. "Ah, bring him in, too. But be quick about it before Mother Superior sees him."

Antonio dashed over, untied Luigi, and picked him up in a rush. He would not miss this opportunity to get information.

Once they were settled in a small kitchen, and drinking coffee with cream, Antonio introduced himself and explained his mission. "I have reason to think, Sister Stefania, that someone in this neighborhood may have information on…" How should he bring up something so vile to this gentle woman? "That is…you see, my father died."

A momentary look of surprise passed over her face, and then she frowned. "I am so sorry, *Signor* Baggio. Did he get last rites? Pray God he did." She rose to fetch more *pizzelle* to set in front of him, even though he hadn't eaten anything thus far. He recognized the regional Italian biscuit from street vendors' carts he'd seen, and this simple treat—something he'd never had on his own kitchen table—helped to remind him he was now in the middle of a culture different than that he'd grown up in. He took one and thanked her.

"Would you like me to light a candle for your father? I would be happy to. I do not mind that you are northern Italian."

He cringed, barely avoiding choking on the *pizzelle*. Perhaps he should not have given his last name. He better get right to the reason for his visit, since she realized he was from a different neighborhood. "Thank you. That is very kind of you. My father died under suspicious circumstances, Sister. You see, I believe someone from Benevento might know what happened."

She gasped and plunked down hard on her chair. "My home, Benevento? Why do you think so?"

"I do not say the people from there are bad people. Not at all. It is just that some men with the Benevento dialect have been asking for me, knowing that I am my father's son."

"So why didn't you ask them what happened, young man?"

"I did not have the opportunity to meet those men." This was a very difficult story to unfold, and a difficult fidgety woman to hear it. "I was working when they inquired. I'm afraid I missed them."

"Ah, so I see. You have come looking for them."

Finally. "I have, Sister."

She reached for his arm. "As I was just telling Sofia—"

"Who?"

"My niece, Sofia. You would like her. Very nice girl. *Bella figliòla!*"

"I am sure she is very...pretty, Sister. Certainly. But I have come to find out—"

She held up both arms. "Like I tell her, there is no use living in the past. In Italy, we understood the past is behind us and the future is not for us to know. We labor for the day. That is all." She snatched away his cup.

He gobbled down the rest of the biscuit and then rose, holding his hat to his chest. "*Grazie*, Sister. You are most hospitable."

Her wrinkled face brightened, as though he could not have offered a better compliment. She stretched out her arm and he bent to receive her blessing. Then he clicked his tongue and Luigi jumped up and followed him outside.

Dismayed that he'd not learned anything save for the fact that the southern Italian penchant for shutting out others still held true, Antonio shoved both hands inside his pockets, allowing Luigi's leash to trail along the uneven sidewalk back toward the train. This had been a bonehead idea. If the church would tell him nothing, what hope was there anyone else here would talk?

He sighed and stared down an alley at a string of white laundry flapping between two windows. He'd tried. That should fulfill his duty to his father. He clicked his tongue again, knowing Lu would follow. Antonio had trouble convincing himself his obligation had been fulfilled. The mystery would not unchain him so long as the possibility still existed that someone was trailing him.

The sound of children laughing made him turn to look for Luigi. The little brown and white dog was surrounded by giggling girls. A boy from a balcony above shouted down at them. "The Victor dog! Sure looks like him."

"No he doesn't," another said.

"Sure does, because he cocks his head, listening, just like that dog."

Antonio squeezed his way through the scarfed heads. Many of the children were without shoes and had been playing in puddles. Lu was enjoying their coos and pats on the nose. Antonio had to indulge them.

One of the girls glanced up at him. "*Signore*, he looks like the dog on that label, *sì*?"

"I suppose he does. You've said hello, Luigi. Come along, now."

"He is your dog?"

There was no doubt when the pup answered Antonio's command. The girls skipped down the sidewalk behind him, enjoying their discovery. "Come back tomorrow," they shouted as Antonio climbed the steps to the el.

Perhaps he should. Maybe it would not be raining and miserable out and the children could introduce him to their families as their friend. He leaned down and picked up his dog. "Good boy, Lu. You did your part."

When he was several blocks away he stuck his hand in his pocket and discovered a slip of paper that he had not put there. Thinking one of the children who had crowded around him had given him a secret gift, a sketching perhaps, he drew it out. The words scrawled there appeared to have come from a practiced hand, not a child's at all. He was able to make out the Italian words.

Come back. Mulberry Street holds the secrets you seek.

He spun around, but of course too late. No one seemed to be following him. Someone did not think of him as an outsider. This mysterious ally was enough to merit a return trip.

Before he went home he stopped by the Fourteenth to see if Mac was there. Antonio had no work for tonight, but it would not hurt to inquire. The man had been generous with him.

"Tony, there you are! I was hoping you'd come by."

Antonio sighed. It was hopeless trying to get Mac to address him by his proper name. "Got some work for me, then?"

"Ah, no. My regular is back. But wait here a minute. I have to go check on the seamstress. Dolly isn't happy with her hems. Don't go anywhere, lad. I have news." He closed the door when he left.

As Antonio waited in the dark office, moisture ran down the collar of his Mackintosh and landed on his shoes. He did not have the energy to wipe it off. The tension he'd worked up going over to the Bend had pilfered the pluck he normally tried to exhibit while at the theater. It would not do to have Mac and others think he was anything other than confident. No one here knew about the grief Antonio had endured. It had been all he could manage to muster up enough courage to tell the nun, and that had exhausted him.

He glanced around the small office. The room was nearly concealed in a hallway painted black, and with the door shut it felt like a dungeon. Such a dim workspace for a man like Mac, whose happy-come-what-may attitude beamed like a lighthouse beacon most days. Mac seemed to like Antonio. Hopefully he'd find at least a partial job for him tonight. While Antonio did have work this Sunday, the church did not pay as much as the theater. If only he could get a steady position.

He drew in a breath to calm himself and noted the smells of oil face paints and paper-mâché props, which nearly turned his stomach. He longed to be wearing tails and a white tie while sitting behind a gleaming piano in a concert hall. He pictured a place decked out with red velvet seats. Gold gilded chandeliers dripping from the ceiling like cake frosting. The longer he stayed in vaudeville, the less likely he would find himself in such a place. He needed to save as much as possible to move on to what he was truly called to do.

Mac's voice boomed from the hall. "Tony, you say? He's not our regular. I don't know where he's working now."

Antonio jumped up and gripped the doorknob. The door was stuck. He jiggled it while Luigi looked at him, tilting his head left and right. "Come on," he muttered. The door would not budge. Mac was loud, but Antonio couldn't tell what was happening. Putting his ear against the door, he could make out other, lower voices, but not what they were saying.

A few moments later the knob rattled. "Who's been mucking aboot with this door? Tony?"

"I can't get it open either."

"Stand back!"

Antonio pulled Luigi toward the shelves on the far wall just as Mac burst in.

"I tell ya, I'm gonna sack the superintendent. Are you all right?"

"We're fine, but who was that out there?"

"I don't know, son, but something tells me you don't want to meet them."

"You told them I wasn't here."

"You can thank me for that."

Luigi sniffed at the scent they'd left under an exit door.

"Did they say anything else? Did they say what they wanted?"

"Yeah. 'We'll find him, old man. Tell him the next time you see him that his Papà had our money and now his son must pay.'"

Antonio held up his palms. "Listen, Mac, I don't know what they were talking about. My father owed no one. They probably have the wrong man. Did they hurt you?"

"I am not hurt, but I think it's best you go along home, Tony. For your own sake, and for ours."

"I...uh, I will. Of course. Tell me, were they Italian?"

"They were. Glad they didn't see you. If you'd come charging out here, well, who knows what they would have done to you. Panned you in, I expect."

"They seemed...violent?"

"Might be just talk. You know how those type of thugs can be. I mean no offense."

"It's all right."

"Why take chances, Tony?"

"I'll be going."

"Wait. Before you go, sit down for a moment, you and your dog."

Mac and Antonio each took a wooden folding chair. Antonio ordered Luigi to sit outside the office, just in case, and they left the door open. Antonio leaned back on his chair, nearly bumping his head on a shelf of scripts and prompt cards on the wall behind him.

Mac's brows shot up as though a thought sparked in his mind. "Say, my news for you is even better now, in light of those fellas coming here."

"News?"

Mac dabbed at his perspiring forehead with a handkerchief. "That's right. You did a pure dead brilliant job improvising last night, Tony. You surely did." He poured himself a drink from a flask he'd stored in his desk drawer before offering it to Antonio.

"No thanks. I don't drink." And he never would, after seeing what the stuff had done to his uncle. "But thanks for the compliment, Mac. What news are you talking about? I should get home to practice and leave you to your work." And maybe he could get a glimpse of those men on the street.

"And you will. I won't keep you long. Practice, you say? Still waiting for Oberlin to come calling, then?"

He shrugged. "What if I am?"

"Keep the heid, Tony." The man liked to use Scottish colloquialisms. This one meant he was to stay calm.

"I've been a bit jittery, Mac. People asking after me and all."

He took a swallow from his flask. "I don't blame you. I'm just saying…you're a smart musician, lad. One of the best in vaudeville, whether you want to be or not."

"I don't mean to be ungrateful. You've been very kind to me. Please, Mac. Have your say and send me on my way."

Instead, the man took another long pull on his flask. When he finally put it away, he smiled. "That's better. Now the news. Good news, if you'll have it."

"I could use some. Spill it."

"Well, I was not the only one who noticed your talent. Those boys, the quartet?"

"I appreciate that." Antonio stood and whistled for his dog. "Tell them I'm pleased they liked it, won't you?"

"Sit down, lad. There's more."

Antonio waited but did not sit.

"Those boys told the manager at the Roman Athenaeum. Apparently they've lost their piano player. Terrible case of consumption, it seems. They want you over there. Half past six." Mac glanced at his pocket watch. "I'd recommend you skedaddle."

Stunned, Antonio struggled not to stutter. "Thank you. Thank you, Mac. Listen, I'm sorry about those fellas—"

"Don't mention it."

6

SOFIA MET FATHER LUCCI two doors down from the building where the Falcones rented rooms. As they walked together, the Father spoke toward the ground. "Your papà, he mentioned this to me a few months ago. He warned me your mother might need…well, some extra care."

"*Sì*, she gets the melancholy every year, but this time is worse than Papà anticipated, Father."

"Oh, why is that? Is there more I should know?"

"So much more, Father."

They paused at the stoop. A woman approached them, a parishioner Sofia recognized but didn't know. A recent immigrant from a village near Naples. "Father, *mio bambino*. He is ill. You must come pray for him. Just over here." She inclined her head toward a building on the opposite side of the street.

He took a step in that direction and then paused. "Sofia, a baby. You understand. I will be along when I'm finished over there."

"But, Father, I must tell you—"

"And you will. Soon." He reached for her hand and then kissed her cheek before moving away with the woman.

Sofia turned toward the steps blackened from the coal dust that rained on the streets in Mulberry Bend. Pinching her scarf tight against the lump forming in her throat, she made her way to Mamma, without the healer and without the priest.

She let herself in with her key. "Mamma, I am home. I am not going to night school." She chided herself for forgetting the roasted peanuts. She would get them tomorrow.

An odd light glowed from underneath the bedroom door. "Mamma?" Sofia slowly opened the door. The scent of smoke hit her. Shoving the door open wide, she could see a candle on the floor. It had ignited a newspaper, but fortunately the flame had not spread toward the bed where Mamma lay.

"What's going on here, Mamma?" Sofia stomped out the small fire in a panic. She threw open the window on the street side.

Mamma coughed and then thrashed about, throwing a blanket off the end of the bed.

"Have you been in bed all day, Mamma?"

The woman looked at her then, her eyes shadowed and her hair unpinned. "*I miei poveri bambini!* What could I have done? *Oddio*, what?"

Sofia urged her mother to lie back on a pillow. "It was an accident, Mamma. There was nothing you could have done. God knows that."

Mamma moaned but at least she wasn't wailing.

"I will bring you a damp cloth to wash up, Mamma. We will be having company, and Papà should be home from work soon."

Sofia's hands shook as she turned on the faucet in the bathroom outside their rooms. Mamma was worse. Much worse. She rambled as though in the middle of a dream. She should not be left alone.

Sofia had just gotten Mamma freshened up when someone knocked on the door. "Father Lucci, Mamma. Would you like to answer the door while I make coffee?"

Mamma just stared toward the open window. Sofia rushed over, shut it, and fastened the iron security bar before leaving the room, worried that the woman might hurl herself out of it while Sofia was busy letting the priest in. She could no longer predict what her mother might do and that thought landed in her chest like an iron anchor. Sofia quietly closed the bedroom door before greeting Father Lucci.

"Father, might I have a word before I get Mamma? She is…resting."

"How may I help, child?"

Sofia set a china plate on the end table beside him. She retrieved a slice of yesterday's bread from the tin she'd brought into the sitting room and placed it on the plate. "I am sorry I have nothing better, Father."

He smiled. "That looks wonderful to me. And you said you have coffee?"

"*Sì*. It will be ready in a moment. May I tell you something?"

"Indeed you may."

"My mamma, she's always had blue moods, come September."

"As your father told me. Even back in Italy, he said."

"Did he tell you why?"

"No, but I understand women her age have episodes of melancholy. Not all that unusual, Sofia."

"But do other women have them like anniversaries? At a certain time of the year?"

"I admit that is a bit unorthodox. What did you want to tell me?"

"I just discovered I had a twin who died. We were very young. I don't remember. She died in September."

"Oh, I see. That is most unfortunate."

Sofia sat on Papà's chair and put her elbows to her knees, leaning closer to whisper. "They did not tell me this, Father. I found out on my own, and, ever since I questioned them about it, Mamma has been in a terrible state."

He arched his brows. "I am very sorry, Sofia. I know many families, well…they do not like to discuss sorrows. I'm sure they meant no harm in not telling you."

Sofia rubbed her fingers around her neck. "That may be. Father, I am afraid I might have been the reason for this tragedy. I might have done something to cause my sister's death and that is why they didn't tell me. I was so young. Try as I might, I cannot remember."

He folded his hands in his lap. "You want forgiveness for this thing?"

She had not thought of that. Just of Mamma, and what this had done to her. "I don't know. I mean, I don't know the truth. I think if Mamma would tell me, if it would all come out in the daylight, she would get better. The truth is best, don't you think?"

He sighed and leaned back on the lumpy sofa. "Life is not as simple as that, I'm afraid. There are usually reasons, good ones, why families keep secrets. I cannot presume to know, but if your parents felt it was best not to discuss this I will not disagree."

She did not know what to say in response. The priest was supposed to help, and she could not understand how this dismissal would do any good. She went to the kitchen to grind the coffee.

Papà walked through the door just as Sofia finished boiling the coffee grounds. She hoped he would not scold her. They normally drank coffee only on Sundays. The rest of the week they had weak tea. She couldn't serve that to Father Lucci. She needed the priest to stay long enough to help Mamma. The coffee was the lure.

"Ah, Father Lucci. Thank you for coming." Papà gave Sofia a stern look. He did not want the priest to know *he* had not asked him to visit.

The men shook hands as Sofia returned to the kitchen. She poured the coffee into Mamma's best serving set, reserved for special guests. When she returned, Father Lucci's expression was grim. What had Papà said to him?

"Bring your mother in, Sofia." Papà took the tray from her.

This could be the moment she'd find out what happened. If she had been the reason Serena died, she was unsure how she would cope with that knowledge, but the truth must come out. One cannot go around troubles. The only thing to do was to go through them and come out on the other side. Her right hand grew icy as she reached for the bedroom's doorknob.

Angelina Falcone, normally a well-groomed woman, sat on the edge of her bed, her hair spun around her head as though whipped by wind. She wrung her hands in her lap.

"Papà is home, Mamma. He and Father Lucci would like you to come into the parlor now. I made coffee."

Mamma set her feet on the floor and without giving Sofia a glance, she shuffled out of the room.

Sofia stood in the cold bedroom a moment and listened to the ticking coming from the old clock Mamma said once hung in the *casetta* where she'd grown up. The coldness in her fingers had risen all the way up her arm. If someone were at Sofia's side right now, she might be braver. An overwhelming sense of neediness, like a driving hunger, gnawed at her insides. Not wishing to be alone with the ticking clock another moment, she hurried out into the sitting room.

Papà was helping Mamma to the sofa.

"How long has she been this way?" Father Lucci asked.

Sofia sat beside her mother, but Mamma didn't acknowledge her.

"This is the second day." Papà turned to Sofia. "How was she when you arrived home?"

Sofia bit her lip. She didn't know if she should say, but it was true that Mamma should not be left alone. "She was in bed, Papà." That was the truth, although Sofia couldn't yet admit Mamma rambled like a woman who had lost her mind, or that the room was about to go up in flames. The madness was temporary. Surely.

Papà stood and began to pace. "She doesn't eat. She barely answers me. We cannot hire a nurse, Father. We cannot afford it."

Father Lucci set his coffee cup down on a side table. "She needs to be looked after, Giuseppe."

Papà faced the priest. "Is there someone from the church who can sit with her during the day?"

The priest shook his head and turned to Mamma. "*Signora* Falcone is not merely debilitated. This is not a matter of a parishioner bringing her some soup or doing her laundry for a time. Those things the church can help with, but this? Your wife, she is not responsive. Her mind has taken her somewhere the rest of us cannot go."

"But prayer, Father. She can be healed."

"In God's time, Giuseppe. You must understand she needs medical help."

Papà drew in a deep breath. Then he knelt before Mamma. "You know I would do anything in my power for you, Angelina." He put his head in her lap and sighed deeply, like a mourner. "What happened took away not only my daughter, but the woman I love. The baby cannot come back to me, but you, my love, can."

Heartbroken, Sofia laid a hand on his shoulder. "Papà."

Papà lifted his head not to look at her, but at Mamma. "You must wake from this, Angelina." He clapped his hands twice as though that was all it would take. "I cannot hire a nurse."

The priest cleared his throat. "A doctor. They are making great strides with nervous disorders."

Papà did not look at him when he spoke. "Who is?"

"The doctors over at Manhattan State Hospital. Those who study the mysteries of the mind."

Papà stood and ran his fingers through his thick hair. "Doctors cost money. A lot of money." He flicked a finger into the air. "All the way out there? Long Island? Father Lucci, that is for the rich man, not me."

Sofia could stand by no longer. This was not the time for Papà to be stingy. "Having Mamma back to her senses, Papà. Think of that. You cannot worry about money at a time like this."

He ignored her. "Father, there must be someone else. Something else to help."

The priest stood and made the sign of the cross over Mamma's head, speaking a prayer. God knew what was happening. Sofia knew God always knew.

Father Lucci turned to Papà. "God blesses his children with gifts and talents. With special skills to help others. These doctors, the good that comes from their work, are a gift from God. But a worker is worthy of his wage, Giuseppe. You would not want your employer to hold back what you have earned."

Papà walked the Father to the door. "I do not deny these men earn their pay. I just do not have it to give, Father."

Sofia hoped her mother was not aware of Papà's unwillingness to help her. Mamma needed something to snap her out of this fog. She joined the men at the door. "Father Lucci, may I speak?"

He turned his warm, honey eyes on her. At last someone who would listen. "Can we not help Mamma by making her remember the accident?"

"Sofia!" Papà grabbed her arm. "You do not know what you are saying."

"I know, Papà. At least I understand what you've allowed me to know. There is more, si? It might help her to remem—"

The priest raised his hand, as he often has to do when the Italian people get too passionate in their conversations. "I have seen the dark side of depression. Prayer and medical help is what she needs. Not one without the other, but both."

Frustrated, Sofia turned and stomped off to the kitchen. It was rude, but what were they if not rude for not listening to her?

Later, after Gabriella returned from her job watching the neighbor's children, the four of them sat at the square table in the kitchen. Joey, as usual, was off somewhere else. He should be there to help.

Mamma chewed on a bread crust, the first thing they'd gotten her to eat since Sofia found the hidden photograph.

Gabriella chattered on about her day, barely aware of the crisis the family was facing. "*Signora* Martina, from downstairs? She says some wayward boys broke her window last week and the landlord will not fix it. She says she will not pay her rent until he does. You will see. She will be evicted, and I think the boys who broke it are her own." Sofia's sister was turning into a gossip. Finally Gabriella focused on Mamma. "Did our brothers look in on her before they went to their jobs?"

Sofia moved a fork around on her plate of pasta. "They said they did, but they are not much help. I could quit my job and look after her, Papà."

Sofia's father wiped his chin with a napkin. "I do not think that is wise, Sofia. You being here upsets her. You would be more harm than help. And we need your salary." Tension showed in the wrinkles around his eyes. "You say our doctor, the healer, she will not come?"

"No. Things are not well in her home, Papà." His words about her being harmful to Mamma wounded her already hurting heart, and she pondered whether they could be true, whether she was the cause of this.

Papà threw his napkin down on his empty plate. "Mamma will just have to sleep all day if that's what she wants to do."

It was time to tell him. "Papà, when I got home a candle in your bedroom was burning on the floor."

"What?"

"It had just touched a newspaper. It had not spread to anything yet, thanks be to God. I put it out. It must have happened just before I came in."

"And your Mamma? What did she do?"

"She didn't seem to notice, Papà."

He stood and gripped the back of his chair so tightly his knuckles turned white. "Her state has become a danger. To herself and to everyone in this building."

Gabriella's eyes grew round, as Sofia knew hers must be. Mamma began to rock back and forth, sending her wooden chair squeaking against the floorboards. Then she suddenly looked up at Papà. "Sofia. I saved her. I was right, Giuseppe?"

He went to her and tenderly put an arm around her shoulders. "*Sì*, my love. *Sì. Zitta*, now. Speak no more of it." He glanced up at his daughters, his eyes bugged out as though deep in thought. "Gabriella, from now on after you feed the children breakfast, you will come back and allow Sofia to go to work. Then when the boys wake, you will take the children home and

Frankie and Fredo will look after Mamma until it is time for them to leave for work. You will come back then and stay with Mamma between the time they are gone and until Sofia returns. No night school, Sofia. You understand? I cannot say when I will have extra work and not be able to come home, so no night school."

Sofia remembered Mr. Richmond's words. "I cannot be late for work, Papà, or I will lose my job."

He pointed at Gabriella. "You hear that?"

She nodded. "*Sì*, Papà."

He went back to his seat to finish the coffee Sofia had reheated from the priest's earlier visit. "I will ask in the neighborhood. I think the government provides some kind of nursing. I will find out."

Sofia's heart sank as she studied her mother's face. Mamma's mind was taking her prisoner. Someone had to find a way to pull her back.

The next morning brought shouting from the family that sent Mamma crying. Gabriella had been delayed cleaning up after a sick child. Finally, Papà convinced *Signora* Russo to come so that he and Sofia could go to work. Sofia ran all the way from the el station to the factory and up the metal stairs to the fifth floor. Sucking in air, sweat pouring down the back of her shirtwaist, she punched her card in the clock machine just in time.

Mr. Richmond waited for her at her station. "I saw you running."

"I am sorry, Mr. Richmond. But I did arrive on time."

He snapped his pocket watch shut. "Indeed you did."

When he left, Sofia took in a deep breath before sitting down at her sewing machine. Claudia, the girl working beside her, leaned over. "What was that about, Sofia?"

"He is threatening to dismiss me if I am late."

Maria, the worker directly opposite the table from Sofia, joined in. "I would not be late then. What is more important than your work?"

Sofia, sighed, knowing she needed more time than she had to fully explain. "My mamma is ill. Until Papà can decide where to send her, we all have to keep watch over her."

"Consumption? Typhoid?" Claudia asked while pulling thread through the needle on her machine.

"No. It's more…uh, nervous, I suppose you could say."

"Dear me," Maria piped in. "I do hope they don't send her to Ward's Island. It's a horrible place, I hear."

Sofia began to line up the soles she was to stitch. "I am sure it won't be anything like that."

"Must you go straight home after work today?" Maria asked, pushing her dark braid behind her as she worked.

Home was not appealing right now, and, besides, Papà thought she should not be around Mamma. "Perhaps not immediately. *Signora* Russo is with her. Papà will pay her."

"*Bene*. We should go to Hawkins House."

"Where?"

"You know, the library the Irish girl told us about, when we were in night school. I'd like to get a book. It won't take long."

She had thought they might want to shop the neighborhood vendors or gather outside their building and discuss the American styles in the *Sears & Roebuck* catalog or chat while they shined their shoes—the things they usually did. Leaving the neighborhood was not typical for them. Mamma never liked Sofia to venture too far. Although…Mamma wouldn't know this time. Her conscience seemed to tap her on the shoulder. Sofia ought to get straight home and check on her. "Oh, I better not. Mamma might need me." She hoped.

"Tomorrow then?"

"Perhaps."

Sofia arrived home to find a crowd of people standing in the front room. "Papà? Why are you home? What has happened?"

Even Joey was there. He gave her a sad look.

Father Lucci quietly called her to the side. "*Signora* Russo is quite concerned. Your mother has been wailing all day, mourning the loss of a child who died decades ago, as if it just happened."

Sofia glanced to Gabriella, who had her charges sitting on the floor around her feet. The youngest cried and pulled on her skirt. Sofia pointed at her sister. "Take them home and feed them, Gabriella. I am here now."

Her sister's shoulders drooped, obviously relieved. "Come Rico, Vanessa, Simone. Back to your kitchen now." They shuffled out, leaving space that seemed to help Papà breathe better.

Sofia wove around her father, the priest, and the healer until she reached the bedroom door. She knocked softly. "Mamma? I am here now."

Mamma lifted her head from her pillow. "Serena?"

Sofia entered and sat on the end of the bed. "No, Mamma. It is me, Sofia. You remember. Serena was my twin and she died long ago."

Mamma turned toward her with liquid eyes. "I remember. Twins."

"That's right, Mamma. Serena is not here anymore. But I am. I am your daughter, the one you like to cook with. Perhaps we should make some *zuppa di fagioli*. A nice soothing soup. You would like that, *sì*?"

"Sofia?" Mamma's face drew tight and red. "No! It is you. I cannot bear it." A guttural cry sent a crowd scurrying into the room. Mamma shoved Sofia with an open palm sending her tumbling off the edge of the bed.

Horrified, Sofia scrambled to her feet. Papà grabbed her arm. "Leave, Sofia. Wait in the other room."

Sofia went to the kitchen, wiped her face with a towel, and began grinding more coffee beans. Joey sat at the table. "It is bad."

"I know, but we will make it better. Somehow."

He left to join the men in the sitting room.

After she set some water to boiling, she reached for the flour tin. She would make cakes for the guests. She didn't know what else to do. A few moments later *Signora* Russo joined her. "I am so sorry I cannot help your Mamma, Sofia."

"You have done enough, *signora*. Let me get you some coffee."

Carla Russo bit her lip and squeezed her hands together. "I must get back home before *Signor* Russo comes looking for me."

Sofia reached out to her and kissed her cheek. "You let me know if there is anything I can do for you."

"*Grazie.*"

Sofia walked her to the door.

The woman's pitiful look as she glanced toward the bedroom door made Sofia feel even worse. "I do not know why, but when you are around she gets worse. She was sad today, *sì*, and I was alarmed, but this...the way she responded to you...I had not seen that before. I have never known Angelina Falcone to be...violent."

"She is not herself, but she did not hurt me. I am grateful you came. Will you be back? I hate to ask it, but my boss will get rid of me if I am late to work."

She nodded. "Your papà has paid me for the week. *Signor* Russo appreciates that so long as I work as a nurse." She lowered her gaze. "And not a healer."

As soon as Sofia shut the door, she noted Father Lucci and Papà in the sitting room. Joey stood looking out the window.

"I must be going now." The Father smiled tight-lipped. He turned to Papà. "I think it's best. At least for a while. Perhaps later, Giuseppe, when Angelina is stronger, she will confront her sorrow."

Sofia raised her right hand to speak, aware of the chill creeping into her knuckles. "Won't you stay for coffee, Father? It is nearly ready now."

He dipped his chin. "Thank you, Sofia. You are very kind. I have to return to my duties. There are confessions to be heard."

Papà saw him out. When he'd closed the door, he turned slowly to look at her.

She could not wait for him to explain what they had discussed. "What did he mean, Papà? What is best? You are not sending Mamma away, are you? I know you paid *Signora* Russo to come—"

He held up his hand. "You talk too much, Sofia. Bring me some coffee. Since you've already used most of what we have, and what I pay *Signora* Russo will mean we cannot buy more, I might as well drink it now."

As she stood stirring canned milk into a cup of the dark brew, a feeling of dread came over her. She worried Mamma might never get well. The priest had probably suggested Papà tell Sofia what she had done so long ago that had resulted in her twin's death—unlocking forgotten memories. The truth was probably painful for Papà. As Father Lucci said, folks do not like to talk about sorrows. Papà would need the strong brew to work up the courage to tell her.

When she brought Papà his cup, he set it aside. "The Father thinks it best if you don't live here, Sofia."

"No," Joey said. "Sofia belongs here with her family."

Papà held up his palm to silence his youngest son.

Her knees refused to hold her up. She dropped to the sofa. "What do you mean? You are putting me out?"

Her father rubbed his gnarled fingers over his face. "Of course not. You are my daughter. But, Sofia, you must see how you upset Mamma."

"It is not her fault," Joey said, pounding his fists together. "She should not be made to pay."

Papà did not look at him. "This is not your concern, Joseph."

"*Mia famiglia* is my concern, Papà."

"Silence!" Her father's stern rebuke ended her brother's protest. Joey stomped out the door.

"But why, Papà? Won't you tell me what I've done? I'll go to confession right now." Tears choked her voice.

He wagged his head and stared at the crucifix on the wall. "None of us know why this has happened, Sofia. It is best if Mamma puts this out of her mind as soon as possible. I will find you a boarding house." He grunted. "It will cost money. The healer costs me money. *Uffa*, what will we do?" He gazed at the ceiling, obviously more upset over that than the state of her mother's mind and the living arrangements for his daughter. "But if we are to keep Mamma here, it is the best way. You will see." He grabbed the newspaper from the table by his chair.

It was decided then.

Sofia glanced at the date on the back of the page Papà held in front of his face. Her birthday. No one had even mentioned it.

7

ANTONIO ROSE EARLY on Sunday, for once not minding that he hadn't had work the night before. The Roman Athenaeum had hired him on the spot to play for a performance lasting all next week, maybe even longer, if it went well. It seemed his crazy improvisation the other night had appealed not only to the singers he'd played for, but also to the manager of The Roman who had been at The Fourteenth as a paying customer. Why the man would spend his money on that vaudeville show Antonio didn't know, but he was grateful he had.

He had put off returning to The Bend. Today he was headed for the magnificent organ at St. Anthony's. His father had always loved hearing him play there, but there hadn't been much opportunity in the past. There was the regular organist and then an alternate who got the job because he had played the organ in cathedrals in Europe. But that man was getting older now and most often preferred to sleep through mass, which would not do at all when he was at the keyboard.

Antonio had been allowed to practice on the church organ during the week ever since he was a boy, not long after they had immigrated. Apparently the organist had noticed potential in him the first time he'd asked to give it a try. And with years of practice, he'd learned to use his feet on the pedals. The organ became his first love despite his access to the piano. He'd only taken up the piano because he had one. But it was nothing compared to the sound of a magnificent pipe organ. Even after all this time, he still had to keep to the simplest pieces, but when the regular organist was unavailable, the congregants and the priest seemed satisfied with his playing. He was in a jubilant mood because with a somewhat steady job, now he'd be able to save for Oberlin College where his talents would be challenged and improved.

He'd spent yesterday considering the men who'd said his father owed them something, making notes the way a police detective would do—facts that were known, speculation, details on what he remembered about his father's poor mutilated body—only to decide he'd wasted his time. There was probably no answer to the mystery of his father's death, and now he had no time to investigate anyway. Or maybe he didn't want to think about it, and the new job was his excuse. That was probably the truth. He would be better off letting matters lie. He spoke a quiet prayer in his mind, one he hoped God would attend to. *If I am to stay out of this business, God, let the matter drop from my mind.*

When he entered the church he immediately climbed to the organ platform and took in the morning light from the rosette shaped stained glass window. As he silently slid his fingers over the keys, he remembered the remarks people sometimes made about his playing. *A gift. God's music flowing through him. Pleasing to our Savior and the Blessed Mary. What he was designed to do. An ability few others had.*

Antonio shut his eyes. He did not want to become prideful. Besides, he was not the greatest musician. Far from it. If he were, he would not be cooling his heels during the week in the nickel theaters. But maybe the Roman Athenaeum would put an end to that.

The custodians at St. Anthony's took extreme care cleaning the place on Saturdays. He breathed in the scents of lemon oil, freshly cut flowers, and women's perfume. The smells always worked to bring clarity to Antonio's mind, the aroma of worship. Just sitting at the organ settled Antonio into the proper predilection for entering God's presence. In that respect, he did seem to be doing what God intended him to do. This would honor his father best, rather than uncovering old wounds.

Antonio played that morning with pleasure and delight. It ended all too soon. He gathered his music and prepared to leave, telling himself he should take Luigi to the park. A man approached him as he entered the gallery.

"Young man, was that you playing the organ?" The man was older, about the age of his father, with gray sideburns, and a husky build. He leaned on an elaborate walking stick.

"Yes, sir. I hope it was acceptable."

"Indeed it was. I'm visiting here from a small church over on Rayburn Street. Protestant, but I hope you will not hold that against me."

"Not at all." The man's appearance did differ from that of most of the parishioners. Definitely not Italian. Irish or English perhaps. American in speech certainly. He had welcoming blue eyes and a kind smile. Antonio took a deep breath and focused on the visitor. "I am happy you are here." Clearly, God was directing Antonio to set his thoughts on other things.

"Might you be going my way?" The gentleman pointed to the door.

"Uh, yes. Thank you."

Before Antonio could move toward the door, the man stuck out his hand. "I am Ronald Clarke."

"Pleased to meet you, Mr. Clarke. I am Antonio Baggio."

As they stepped outside into the sunny late morning air, Antonio matched his stride to the man's, which was surprisingly spritely. "What brought you to St. Anthony's, if I may ask?"

The man chuckled. "You may ask, but I may not have an adequate answer."

"You say you were visiting?"

"Yes. You see, I am a member of an aid society, a small one, which until recently has focused on helping young Irish women who come to America without relatives to help them."

"A valuable outreach, I would imagine."

"It seems to have been. We have vowed to follow God's leading in this endeavor."

"Admirable." They paused at a street corner to allow a horse-drawn wagon to pass. A new automobile followed, barely able to match the pace of the horse.

"Would you look there?" Ronald Clarke exclaimed. "More of those on the streets all the time, and what for? They don't travel any faster along these pedestrian clogged avenues than traditional modes of transportation."

"I suppose not."

"About this endeavor I mentioned. That seems to be why I visited your lovely cathedral this morning."

"Oh?" They continued on, dodging folks who were gaping at the automobile. Antonio had had few chances to speak to people outside his neighborhood other than those he encountered at the theater. Some Irish Catholics attended mass at St. Anthony's from time to time, but never a Protestant American like Mr. Clarke. Antonio was intrigued.

"Excuse me, Mr. Baggio, but I sometimes ponder whether or not I'm hearing God correctly." He chuckled again, his bright eyes almost disappearing behind wrinkled cheeks.

"I imagine we all struggle with that discernment, sir."

"I suppose so. But I'm fairly certain God intended me to meet you at St. Anthony's today, although I cannot say why."

Antonio found the man's pleasant demeanor charming. "Me? Well, I am flattered and I am glad we met. I hope you come back."

"Well, my congregants would not permit me too many Sundays away, I'm afraid."

"Your what?"

"Didn't I mention it? I pastor the flock at First Church."

"Uh, no." Antonio had not imagined a man of the cloth would not, on a Sunday, be wearing the cloth. "Well, that's…I mean, how wonderful…for them to have you."

"You are very kind to say so." The reverend urged him forward once the way was clear. "Say, I'm headed over to Hawkins House for supper. Won't you join me?"

"Oh, I don't think so. It wouldn't be right to impose. But, what, if I may ask, is this Hawkins House?"

"I mentioned the outreach to immigrants?" He tapped the brim of his hat with his walking stick. "Yes, of course I did. Hawkins House is part of that, a boarding house for girls, along with a night school and a lot of books."

"Excellent."

"Oh, it is. We would like to open ourselves to the possibility that God will direct other ethnic groups to us. After all, the city is quite diverse. In the past, we've had a German girl living there, and right now there are a couple of girls from Eastern Europe residing at Hawkins House, so we are not just Irish."

Antonio agreed that the city was indeed a diverse place. He had seen all sorts of people at the theaters and on the train, although he had not conversed much beyond comments about the weather. His trip to Mulberry Street had not provided much interaction either. Perhaps he should mingle with those not like himself. "They won't mind an extra person at the table?"

Reverend Clarke huffed as though Antonio had made a joke. "They will welcome you warmly. Do you like to read? As I said, we have quite the library over there."

"I would enjoy seeing it." They were headed south, not the direction Antonio would normally go. He might as well tag along, now that he was this far away from home. The elderly man hailed a cab and they set off toward Battery Park and the harbor.

8

AFTER SUNDAY MASS, Papà ushered Sofia out of the earshot of the rest of the family. "I do not want you to help with the meal."

She'd spent her hours after work yesterday preparing poultry with rice and saffron and baking a cake thickened with beaten eggs. Papà had scolded her for spending so much in the market, but Sofia had hoped the food would cheer Mamma. "What do you mean, Papà? I always do the cooking. I have everything ready to prepare, special things for Mamma. If I do not do it, who?"

"Your sister. She will manage. Perhaps if you are not here, Mamma will revive her spirit somewhat."

Sofia glanced around at the people leaving the church. They huddled in family groups. It was the way things were done. "Where will I go?"

He handed her a piece of paper. "I told *Signora* Carboni you might visit her boardinghouse today. It is not far."

Sofia's mouth went dry. She tried to swallow the embarrassment this news caused. "You told her I might?"

"*Sì.* You do not have to go, Sofia. I will not insist. True, they are Sicilians, but I think they will accept you all right if you show up there." He narrowed his brows. "And you will treat them with respect. Stay out of arguments."

"Papà? Must I? I mean, if there is another place…"

He glanced down the walk where the rest of the family was moving away from them. "You choose, Sofia, but please give your mamma this day of rest." He pinched her cheek. "For Mamma. Here." He pressed a few coins into her hand. "Go to one of those shows. Just for a few hours. Later we will consider…later, Sofia. Go on, now. Make it a festive outing, like all the young people seem to want these days."

She nodded and turned away, tears stinging her eyes. Festive? She would not go to the Sicilian boardinghouse. She would not go to the theater. She would spend this on the trolley and find the place the red-haired woman visiting her night school had told her about. Down near the tip of the island where the immigrants first arrive off the Ellis Island ferry.

When she stepped off the Broadway car, she glanced down at the address written on the card in her hand. She was on the right street but not all of the buildings were numbered. Maybe this had been a poor plan. The girl hadn't told her to stop by on a Sunday. What if they were Protestant? She had heard some Irish are. Sofia didn't know what time their church services ended. Interrupting a Sunday feast would be rude. The thought sent a tingle through her spine. She had missed the usual Falcone Sunday meal for the first time in her life.

Glancing at the pedestrians scurrying this way and that, she reminded herself that there was more to life than family. The idea, however, did little to comfort her. She'd had no choice about it. She'd had no say in matters concerning her twin, and she should have. Serena had been hers. They did not understand. They had not been born a twin.

Taking a deep breath, she continued on, noting what addresses she could see. She was headed in the correct direction. She remembered the American system of enumerating residences from a few months earlier, when she'd found the factory and had her interview for employment.

Eventually she found Hawkins House, identified by a swinging sign on the front stoop. She rang the bell, wondering what to say when the door opened. She needed not worry, though. The red-haired woman herself answered the door. "Hello, welcome to Hawkins House."

Sofia doubted her English. "*Grazie.* You told me...at night school...uh, you say to come for books."

The woman's face lit with pleasure. "Aye, I did indeed. Come in, please. You are very welcome."

A dark-skinned woman appeared and offered to take Sofia's wrap. She was unsure what to do. Was she a servant? She was certainly not related to Annie Adams, the red-haired girl.

"This is Minnie, our housekeeper," the Irish woman said. "She would be happy to hang up your cloak, Sofia."

Sofia was glad for the clue and removed both her wrap and her headscarf.

"We are about to sit down to dinner. Won't you join us?"

"Uh, I come back."

Annie took Sofia's arm. "Nonsense. You are here and you will join us. 'Tis what we do at Hawkins House, welcome others. Do not feel that you are imposing. Here you are not."

She was so cheerful Sofia could not refuse. She was led into a beautiful dining room with wood panels part way up the walls, a thick carpet on the floor, and sparkling gas lamps hanging from the ceiling. Three men already there stood as she entered.

Annie paused at the head of the table. "May I present my husband, Mr. Stephen Adams."

The man took his wife's hand and gently kissed it, causing the fair-haired young woman to blush. He turned to Sofia. "Very nice to meet your acquaintance."

Annie turned to the older gentleman and his companion. "The Reverend Clarke of First Church, and a new visitor Mr. Antonio Baggio."

Sofia had never met such gracious people who would so warmly welcome an outsider. There was even an Italian at the table, at least by name. He did not look like those from her village—he was fair-haired, lighter-skinned, more northern European-looking—but she was pleased she was not the only visitor. A hefty woman entered from the hall carrying a tray loaded down by a soup tureen and a basket of bread. The housekeeper Minnie followed behind with a tray of drinking glasses and a pitcher.

"And this," Annie said, taking the tray with the meal, "is the proprietor, Mrs. Hawkins. Mrs. Hawkins, this is Sofia Falcone. I first met her down at the English school for Italian immigrants. I visited there to see if we might assist with books or instruction. I mentioned it to you."

Mr. Adams took the tray from his wife and placed it on the long table.

The older woman grinned and lifted her chin, nodding as though strangers in her dining room were expected. "Yes indeed. Another guest. How delightful. Of course you will eat with us, love."

"I...uh...I came for the library. *Signora*, I mean...Mrs. Adams invited me."

Annie nodded, rubbing her middle. Sofia guessed she had a month at most before the baby's arrival.

"Sit down, love." Mrs. Hawkins motioned to an empty seat. "We have prepared our famous peas porridge. I hope you're hungry."

"*Grazie, grazie.*" Sofia sat down and the men did as well, the handsome male visitor with the Italian name taking the seat next to her.

Annie's husband pressed his hands firmly in his lap as he spoke to her. "Miss Falcone, are you new here to New York?"

"*Sì. Mia famiglia*, that is..my family...we came from Italy six months ago."

The man nodded his head. "Where did you settle? Mulberry Bend, perhaps?"

Sofia was puzzled that he should know this. Her surprise must have been spelled on her face.

Annie leaned in front of him as if imparting a secret. "He is a postman, Sofia. He knows where the various immigrant groups have settled in the city. He understands addresses, as well. I don't know how he keeps track of them." When the Irish woman laughed Sofia realized Annie Adams was trying to make her feel at ease and she was grateful. "Don't you know, in

Ireland the houses have names, not numbers, at least in the countryside. I traveled around with my da and I can remember a few of them. There was *An Diadan*, which in the Irish means The Hill, and *Cois Dara*, which means Beside The Oak."

Her husband chuckled. "Can you imagine if Manhattan tenements had names? There are not enough words in the dictionary for that."

Sofia forced a smile. "*Sì*, all our neighbors came from our village. They call it Little Italy there on those streets."

Mrs. Hawkins spread her arms out over the table while the housekeeper stood ready nearby. "Shall we say grace?"

Sofia crossed herself and lowered her head. The reverend gave thanks for the food and the company and soon dishes were being passed around, not unlike what was happening at that very moment in Sofia's home but without the help of a housekeeper. She took a chunk of thick bread, two slices of red, ripe tomato—uncooked, but she didn't mind, and a bit of a chilled soupy mix Annie said was a classic American staple, applesauce. Mrs. Hawkins collected bowls to dish out whatever she had in the large soup tureen in front of her. When Sofia got her bowl back, she stared unbelievably at the green mixture it contained, wondering how people actually ate that.

"'Tis pea porridge. My favorite," Annie exclaimed, dipping her silver spoon into the thick soup.

Slowly Sofia did the same. The soup was warm and tasted of cream and mint. Unusual, but not bad. Not bad at all. "You are very kind. *Grazie*. Uh, thank you, Mrs. Hawkins."

"It is my pleasure, Sofia. Now, what types of books do you like to read?"

Her question seemed to make Mr. Adams sit up straighter. He raised his brows and looked in her direction as he chewed his bread. The others seemed interested, as well.

"I do not read well. It is difficult for me, but Mrs. Adams thought books in English might help."

The plump Mrs. Hawkins nodded. "We all would be happy to assist. Right after supper Annie can take you up to the library. Please stay for a bit after you've chosen a book, won't you? We enjoy helping, so allow us that, if you do not mind."

She had a way of making Sofia feel as though she was doing them a favor instead of imposing. The periods of quiet between moments of conversation were as odd to Sofia as the peas porridge, but still fresh and intriguing. She liked it here. Mamma, however, would be appalled to know she was sitting at a dining table with Protestants, eating their strange food, but this was America, and perhaps it was what Sofia needed to help keep at bay that persistent iciness.

Just as they finished eating, *Signor* Baggio turned to her. "Miss Falcone, may I say your English is quite good for only being in America a few months."

"Thank you. My father, he came…for many seasons to work. He taught us…his children, to speak the language, although I am still learning."

Mrs. Hawkins nodded. "You do speak well, love."

"*Grazie.*" She felt foolish for slipping into Italian after that compliment.

Signor Baggio scooted forward in his chair. "May I ask what village you come from? My father and I immigrated from Italy when I was a young boy."

As she had observed before, this man did not look Italian and he spoke like the Americans she'd met in the shoe factory. Even those in The Bend who had been born in this country did not speak like Americans because the sounds of their village still echoed through the neighborhood as though no one had ever left. Perhaps he had been born in the north of Italy, which she'd been told might as well be an entirely separate country. Sofia's mother, in her more lucid moments, had taught Sofia many things about Italian art and history. The Italian unification had been created only a decade or so before Sofia was born, so of course the two regions *were* different. Old men and women from the south still considered their birthplace in Italy separate from the northerners, at times with a twinge of bitterness because of the favor the government showed to the north, spending taxes improving Rome and points north, ignoring the poorer regions to the south. Her mother had insisted this had been the cause of the hard times. If *Signor* Baggio thought he was the same as her, he was mistaken, but she didn't want to make suppositions just as she was enjoying the company present. She'd test him to see how informed he was. "I am from Benevento. It is a market village."

"Benevento?" He nearly choked as he sipped water from his glass.

"You know it?"

"No, I'm sorry. I have spent most of my life right here in New York. But I have heard of your homeland. I believe the people from that village do live on Mulberry for the most part, like Mr. Adams said. Is that correct?" He did not give Sofia a chance to answer and seemed a bit nervous the way he rambled, a departure from how he'd presented himself earlier. "I was actually over that way myself a few days ago."

"Oh?" She dabbed at her chin with her napkin, hoping he'd get her subtle message that he had pea mash on his chin.

His fair cheeks flushed as he mimicked her and wiped his face.

They exchanged smiles. She liked him already. "There is not much to see in Little Italy, I fear, *Signor* Baggio. Here it is much more..." She squeezed her fingers in her lap, shaking her head. "I'm afraid my English...it is little."

"Now don't worry, child," the reverend said. "We are all learning from each other." He nodded to each in turn. "Isn't that so, friends?"

They all agreed.

Mrs. Hawkins wiggled a bit in her chair. "Well, isn't that superb that you two are familiar with the same neighborhood. Mr. Baggio, do you live near Mulberry, then?"

"Uh, no I do not. I live with my dog over on Varick."

The woman grinned. "Ah, near St. Anthony's?"

"Not too far. I play the organ there, or rather I do on occasion when they need me."

"And that is how we met," the reverend said. "He has wonderful God-given talent."

Sofia was charmed. A man who liked dogs, had musical talent, and was interested in her neighborhood for some reason. Mamma would not like that he was of northern descent, but Sofia did not care.

Her palms perspired. She was being presumptuous, having only just met him. She'd only just met them all and she was already trying to impose herself on their lives. She had a family, but this one, or what seemed like a family of unrelated people, held much appeal in light of her current circumstances.

Antonio Baggio's face was red from the compliment. "Thank you, Reverend Clarke. That is kind of you to say."

The older man reached for the bread tray and passed it to Annie who sent it on its way around the table. "So, tell me, Antonio. Were you in Little Italy to play over there? There is another Italian church there, smaller, I believe. I've forgotten the name."

Sofia glanced at Antonio. Had he been to her church?

"Church of the Most Precious Blood," Antonio answered.

Sofia nodded. "My parish church."

"Lovely," Mrs. Hawkins said, taking a slice of bread for herself and passing the platter on to Antonio.

He paused to take a piece as well and then handed it on to Sofia.

"No, sir. I have never had the pleasure of playing there. I did visit briefly. I don't know anyone in that neighborhood and wasn't sure where to begin my inquiry. The church always seemed like the best place to go when you're new to an area."

"I agree. What inquiry, may I ask?" The reverend dipped his bread into his soup.

Antonio sighed. "I'm afraid it's a very long story. My father had some business and...I...well." He drummed his fingers on his thighs. "I am pursuing that business in his stead. I stopped by and spoke to a nun there. It's a matter that will never be resolved, though."

"I am sorry to hear that." The reverend put a hand on Antonio's shoulder. "If I can be of assistance in any way, please do not hesitate to ask."

This time it was Sofia who nearly choked on her food. "A nun? Do you remember her name?"

"I believe it was Sister Stefania. Very kind woman."

Sofia lifted her gaze to the ceiling. "I hope she didn't…she can be a bit…long-winded?" She hadn't meant to make that a question, but it came out that way because she was uncertain if she'd used the right words.

"Oh, not at all. I enjoyed our visit. She even allowed me to bring my dog into the nuns' kitchen. You know her then?"

Sofia felt her shoulders droop. "I do. She is my mamma's sister."

"Well," Mrs. Hawkins clapped her hands. "It is a small world."

Sofia caught Antonio's glance. "If you need me to intervene, to ask something for you, I would be happy to. My aunt, she can be a little…distracted."

He grinned, putting her at ease at once and slipping his way into her heart. "That is very kind of you. I will keep that under advisement."

After dinner, Annie escorted Sofia upstairs to find some books. The library was reached by ascending two stories to the top floor. Under Sofia's feet, the wood was dark polished, the bookcases lining the walls the same. Such a beautiful room in the attic. Who would have imagined?

Annie sounded out of breath as she leaned against the wall. "Whew, this babe. I have nearly no breathing room left, and I am more than ready for him or her to come." Annie gently touched Sofia's arm. "'Tis a lovely place here, aye?"

"*Bella.*" Sofia drew a hand to her face.

"My husband and I, along with a group of charity workers—we call ourselves The Benevolents—built this lofty library to honor my father. He passed away before I left Ireland. Later, when you're not in a rush to get home, I'll tell you more about it."

Sofia had told her she needed to get back to check on her mother. She hoped her family realized how much they needed her after having the Sunday meal without her help. She was anxious to find out.

Annie Adams turned toward her, a bit unsteady. She put a hand out toward the wall to balance herself and grinned. "Oh, there we go."

"Are you all right?" Sofia asked.

"Sure and I will be. Just a moment." She took a series of short breaths. "There, now. The babe's calmed down. Not as much kicking going on these days because there isn't much room. Sometimes I think I will be birthing a football team rather than a wee child."

Sofia smiled at the woman's candor. She chatted with her as a sister might.

"Now, you remember I spoke briefly about my father at your school, the famous Luther Redmond?"

"*Sì.*" Sofia remembered something about that.

"Although that was not his given name that is how most people know him." The woman roamed down one aisle, speaking about the care they'd taken to make sure the proper books were housed there. She said something about the stories her father liked to read. Or did she say 'tell?' Sofia could barely follow what the Irish woman said, so distracted as she was by the books. If it hadn't been for the time Papà spent in America and the English words he had brought back to teach them, Sofia wouldn't understand her at all. As it was she had to listen carefully to the woman's quick, melodic speech.

But, oh, the books. There were so many volumes that one could get lost browsing through them, but Annie seemed to know where to find the ones she wanted. She pulled one from a shelf and handed it to Sofia. Sofia carefully opened the cover. The letters she knew, but the words they formed were a mystery. She'd learned some English words, but could understand nothing on the pages she examined. She blinked and traced over them with her finger.

The Irish girl smacked her lips. "*The Poetical Works Of Elizabeth Barrett Browning*. She writes lovely verses. Truly, 'tis not a good place to start to learn English, but she's one of my favorites and I couldn't help but show this to you. Her words seem to float as though riding on a summer breeze. Here. Let's sit a wee while, so." She motioned toward a pair of high backed brown leather chairs.

Sofia hesitated only a moment. She could postpone her return home a bit. The room, so richly decorated and stacked with more volumes than Sofia had ever seen in one place, felt like a cocoon of literary possibilities that she could not resist. Each book contained a mystery waiting to be unlocked. When they were seated, Annie took the book from her fingers.

"Indulge me, won't you?" She wrinkled her button nose as she stared at the page. "Hmm. Let me see. Ah, you will find this fascinating. This poet lived in Italy. She was English, of course, but moved to Italy with her husband Robert Browning, who was also a poet. You might like some of this." She cleared her throat and began to read.

You remember down at Florence our Cascine. Where the people on the feast-days walk and drive, and through the trees, long-drawn in many a green way...

Florence? That was not Sofia's Italy, and yet she could still envision the people on feast days strolling down the *strade*, singing in the sunshine like skylarks. That world seemed distant now that she was in America, cast away like her voyage ticket after she'd crossed through Ellis Island. Like something that no longer had relevance for her life. She knew it must seem so not only for her, but for the Northern Italians as well, and even for this young woman who had been born in Ireland. An immigrant might still possess the tongue of her native land but yet be as far removed from their countries as their ancestors buried beneath it. This fact, this common thread ran through so many lives, people crowded on streetcars together and marching in clusters to the factories. Sofia could no more ignore the others than she could Sister Stefania. They were there in her path. All are God's children bound together in a common struggle to belong. As lonely as she sometimes felt, how much worse would it be if she shut herself off from those outside her community? Or what had been her community? She needed to draw a new circle, one that encompassed everyone. Oh what this outing to Hawkins House had taught her in just one afternoon.

Sofia was aware that she'd not been listening when Annie stopped reading and looked up from the book. Sofia coughed softly. "You are right, *Signora* Adams...uh, I mean Annie."

The mother-to-be smiled approvingly at the mention of her given name.

"The words are...as you say, lovely."

"I'm so pleased you think so." She leaned over and grabbed a couple more books from a nearby shelf. "These are fine, as well." Annie seemed to treasure each bound copy as though they were rare jewels. "We'll give these a go and see what you like. You can borrow them all, of course, if you want."

"You are generous, Annie." The woman's bright eyes and thin pink lips glowed from the compliment.

Being in that snug library was a welcome reprieve from the shouting in the Falcone household. Sofia snuggled deep into the soft leather as Annie held another book aloft so they both could see it. Together they spoke out some words in *Riley Songs O'Cheer*, the poetry of an American named James Whitcomb Riley.

The Little-red-apple Tree!—
O The Little-red-apple Tree!
When I was the little-est bit of a boy
And you were a boy with me!

The reading was somewhat difficult, but Sofia managed a few words without help. Just being able to decipher some of it was a victory, at least Annie said so.

"Do not worry about the poem's meaning. You are just learning words, English ones. Eventually the pages will speak to you of deeper meaning."

Finally, Annie handed her the books she thought would help her the most. Not for pleasure reading, but for instruction, books she said American children used in school. "There is so much happening in Manhattan right now in the matter of education for immigrants, Sofia. I realize your night school utilizes hand gestures and pictures to teach English, and they do indeed have some success with that method. But I want girls like you to know there is much more to be learned by using books. These are called *McGuffey Readers*. 'Tis a simpler way to learn than the books I've shown you so far, but you're a smart one and you'll be ready for these others soon, so take them all." She handed the books she had collected to Sofia.

"I do not understand this 'happening' in education you speak of."

"Do not worry. You'll be hearing plenty in the coming months, and 'tis wonderful news for women and for immigrants."

"I am afraid in my neighborhood, we keep to ourselves."

"You work at the shoe factory, you say?"

"I do."

"Then you will be hearing about it. Everyone will be talking about Miss Julia Richman, even strangers on the trolley. She's an educator. I am so pleased the education of those arriving here is becoming a top priority. She is focused on the wee ones, and that is important, but I believe adults should have access to learning and to stories."

"I see. America is a wonderful land, Annie."

"Oh, 'tis indeed."

"I am grateful for your help. I will not be able to go back to night school for a while. My mamma, she is ill."

"Oh, I'm so sorry for your trouble, Sofia. Whatever you need, please ask."

"*Grazie*, we have a healer. I mean a doctor, and a priest, and my papà will get my mamma the help she needs." At least Sofia hoped so.

"Very good. In the meantime, come back here. We would love to help you learn to read the English, Sofia. And you are already speaking it quite well."

If only she knew how difficult it was.

"Like I said, 'tis an exciting time for women in the immigrant quarters. *The Times* is reporting that Miss Richman is to be named Manhattan's first-ever woman superintendent of a public school. She has already been working as the principal of the girls' department at Public School 77 over on the corner of First Avenue and 85th street."

New York's public schools seemed as far removed from the Benevento immigrants as the European continent, but this news seemed to please Annie Adams very much. The woman, of course, knew where these places were because she was married to a postman.

"I must be going now. *Grazie, Signora.*...Annie." She kept forgetting how Americans greeted each other.

"Just Annie."

Sofia nodded to show she understood, but addressing strangers by their Christian names was something she was still trying to get used to. They marched back down the stairs to the parlor where the men were.

Antonio Baggio took Sofia's wrap from the housekeeper and helped Sofia drape it over her shoulders. She'd never received such attention from a man before. The gesture warmed her. If only they could spend time together.

"May I walk you to the trolley?" he asked.

She agreed. Thankfully he would be going the other direction. It was enough that he'd met her aunt already. If he knew her mother was not in her right mind, he might flee from her on the day they'd just met.

9

AFTER SEEING THE BEAUTIFUL SOFIA Falcone to her trolley car, Antonio encountered the reverend on the street.

"I am on my way to my church. You will pass the corner going to Varick Street. Care to walk with me?"

"Certainly."

"You say you came over as a lad, Antonio?"

Reverend Clarke liked to ask questions. Antonio wondered if he'd already shared too much. When people learn your father had been shot, even by accident, they tend to back away from you as though your bad luck might follow them.

"Yes. I have very few memories of the land of my birth."

"And your father? You mentioned his business. What kind of business is he in?"

"He worked for the street department. I'm afraid he has passed away, six months now."

"Oh, I am so sorry to hear that. What kind of business was the street department doing over in The Bend?"

"Nothing unsavory, Reverend."

"Oh, of course not. It's just that he didn't live there, and as you probably know from your own visit, folks don't go into that neighborhood without a good reason. Much despair and poverty, but hopefully one day we will all accomplish the goal of eradicating it. I do hope you don't think I'm too nosey."

"Not at all. I think it's quite good that folks like you bring charity where it is badly needed." Antonio cleared his throat. "My father's death, it seems, was an accident. He was killed up at Cooper Union, though my uncle and I don't know why he was there. He seems to have been caught in a protest. He was an innocent bystander."

"Oh, my dear boy. I am so sorry. That must have been difficult for you and your family."

"Yes, sir."

"But Cooper Union? That is no where near The Bend."

"It is not. This is difficult to explain. The police say my father was in the wrong place at the worst time. However, my uncle believes someone from Benevento knows something. Someone from that village, who would probably live in The Bend, has been asking around. I went to the church, talked to the nun, but so far I've uncovered nothing."

"We all have to carry on despite life's sorrows, son."

"I thank you for your understanding."

"Please, let's stop in here a moment." He indicated a set of red doors and Antonio followed him. It was a church Antonio had never been in before.

"Are you sure we should be here?" He glanced around for a priest or holy man who would surely order them out for trespassing.

The reverend lowered his plump body onto an oak pew and sighed. "We are Christians, and this is God's house. Who is to complain?"

Certainly not Antonio. He admired cathedrals but he'd only been in Catholic ones thus far. This place was likely Protestant, judging from the lack of holy water. It was still elaborately adorned. Episcopal perhaps, or maybe Lutheran, but yes, God's house.

"Are you in danger as we speak? I mean, can you be sure your father's death was an accident? It occurs to me that blindly asking around might be harmful to your well being, son."

"No, I don't think I'm in danger. There were some men asking for me at a theater where I sometimes work. I didn't get an opportunity to talk with them, but they seemed to be under the false impression that my father owed them money. I assure you, he owed no one."

The reverend grunted. "I see. There could be more to this than you know. I unfortunately have little confidence in the police department. Some are upright and respectable, but many are not."

Antonio sighed and leaned against the hard pew. "I'm afraid I'm no good at detective work. I assure you I have no part in any gangs or anything of the sort and neither did my father."

"I have no reason to think otherwise. After all, the Lord directed me your way this very morning. I do think you need to be careful going blindly into that neighborhood."

"My uncle agrees with you."

"Good man."

"I am careful, but Reverend, someone knows what happened."

"God knows. Do not run ahead of him in this."

"My search was not fruitful anyway. No harm done." Antonio stood. He had an ally, but there no use in mentioning it without knowing who it was. "I thank you very much for your kindness and for including me at your meal with your friends, Reverend. I don't want to trouble you further."

"God's work is never a bother to me, son. I am in his employ." He pulled himself to his feet. "You come by and see me on Rayburn Street anytime, you hear?"

"Thank you."

"And you be careful out there, young man. Heed my caution. I deplore you. And stay out of Little Italy. If you do not live there, you don't want to be wandering about, even with your dog."

10

As she approached Mulberry after exiting the trolley, Sofia thought about what the reverend had said to her before she left Hawkins House. When no one else was around, he asked if she felt safe. She had tried to reassure him. "Things are difficult at home, and I find I must leave in order to give my mother time to rest. But I am not unsafe."

"Just the same, my dear, I give you my assurances that Hawkins House is at your disposal. Our girls stay here under no obligations."

"You do not charge rent?"

"That is correct. The girls who live here do some chores, but otherwise there is no charge."

"Rent...it is very...precious...uh, that is, expensive to find housing in New York. My papà says we must live together and support each other in this new country because we can trust no one else."

"Your papà is right to caution you, my dear, and that is precisely the reason I'm addressing you in this manner. There are many aid societies that exist to help young, inexperienced immigrants, just until folks get settled in, you understand. It is our charge from God to do so, and we are happy to. If you and your family are doing well, that is wonderful indeed. But I do believe—and I've learned over the years to listen to these urgings from the Holy Spirit as they occur—that I must make you aware there are those in this city willing and ready to help others in need. Please remember that, should you ever find yourself in troubling circumstances."

"You can afford to do this thing?" Papà would never accept help from someone like this reverend and the affable Mrs. Hawkins, but perhaps she could.

"This is not a difficulty for us in the least. We have benefactors at the ready. We are not at liberty to speak specifically about where the money comes from to support our girls, but you can trust me when I say it is gained from legitimate means, mostly inheritances."

"I see. Truly, I do need a place to stay, Reverend. Just until my mamma is better."

"Say no more. I will speak to Mrs. Hawkins about it in the morning. You come whenever you want."

"I will return after my shift at the shoe factory tomorrow. My papà will be pleased because he cannot afford any additional rent." So long as he didn't find out she would be staying outside Little Italy. Eventually she'd have to tell him, but by then she'd already be settled in and he would have to agree. "Are you sure this is all right with Mrs. Hawkins?"

"Indeed it is."

"Is there a church for Italians nearby?"

"Most certainly. St. Anthony's, where I met Mr. Baggio. I will see you are escorted. And we will be delighted to have you at Hawkins House."

This conversation had actually happened. God saw her need and provided. Papà would have to understand. Sofia wrapped her shawl tighter and skipped over a break in the sidewalk. She rehearsed in her mind how she would tell Papà. She would make it sound as though it was precisely what he'd hoped for.

When Antonio arrived home he found Nicco camped outside his apartment. The sounds of Luigi sniffing and whimpering drifted from inside. "Wake up, Nicco. Did the aid society kick you out?" Nicco stirred and then his eyes bolted open. "Huh?" He scrambled to his feet and struggled to shift the strap of his accordion over his shoulder. The instrument his father had brought over from Italy was smaller than most accordions, but still a burden to keep on one's person all day long.

"I don't know why you lug that thing around. If you insist on staying away from my apartment most of the time, so be it, but I could keep that for you here." Antonio unlocked the door and shooed his dog back inside. Nicco lumbered in behind him.

"Keep it, but not me, in your apartment, *figliòlo*. That is how it should be."

"I told you before, Uncle. You can stay here if you stop drinking. My father told you the same thing."

"My own brother, God rest his soul."

The man was soused. He would not remember this conversation in the morning.

"I have to keep the...instru...music...th...th...ing...with me. *Mi capisci*? It is the inheritance of *la famiglia* and your father trusted me with it."

Antonio wanted to laugh as his uncle spit out the ridiculous assertion but held back. It would not be right to ridicule a drunken man who could not help his foolishness. Not only was it amusing to think the family treasure was an accordion with malfunctioning keys, but Nicco trustworthy? Not quite. He assumed his father had urged Nicco to keep the old thing to give him some hope, some encouragement, by placing some responsibility on Nicco's shoulders. As you would do with a child. You give him something worthless, something you aren't afraid to lose, until he proves he can handle the trust you put in him. He shrugged as he knelt to stroke Luigi's neck. Antonio was losing hope that his uncle would ever pull himself out of the gutter.

"What? You do not believe me, Tony? Your father, he says, he said, 'Do not lose this. Take it to...'uh, that's right. I forgot. You are supposed to have it." He shoved it toward Antonio.

"And now I have it." He placed the case between the wall and his bed. "There, safe and sound. Would you like some supper?"

11

If SOFIA HAD THOUGHT her father would put up a fuss about her moving across Manhattan, she was wrong. Perhaps he would have, if times were less tumultuous, but Mamma was worse and the healer was required to stay with her all day. He had to pay her, so having Sofia move without paying additional rent helped ease his worry.

"You will visit me at work, Sofia, to tell me you are well, *capisci?*" He lifted both hands toward the ceiling in a gesture of anguish.

"*Sì*, Papà. I will. Maybe now you can afford the doctor."

He flipped his hand to dismiss her statement. "You cannot know. Everything in America...it costs so much."

"*Sì*, Papà. But...you just have to make sure Mamma is cared for. If I am not here to cook and check on her—"

"Such foolishness, Sofia. She cannot have you here. I have told you that. *Signora* Russo will do what needs to be done."

"But Papà, her husband."

"What about her husband?"

Sofia was sure the man beat his wife, but Papà wouldn't listen. He thought every man from Benevento was an upright *compagno* and he would never believe otherwise.

"I do not know if her husband will like her being away, is all."

"Sofia, you cannot know these things. My daughter believes she knows more than all the men on Mulberry Street. You should not think so much. Go to work, be a good girl for your papà, that is all."

It wasn't all. Not for her. "You have not told me why, Papà. Why does my being here bother Mamma when this happened so long ago?"

He flew into a rage even as his eyes glistened with tears. Waving both arms toward the ceiling, he shouted loud enough for the blessed Virgin Mary to hear from heaven. "You think I say nothing for no reason? You think I am not the Papà who tries to save my eldest daughter from misery?" He slammed his fist against the wall, leaving an impression. Seeming to be as startled by this as she was, he flung himself down on his chair, pulled the handkerchief from his neck and dabbed his eyes.

She sat, too, as they listened to Mamma's soft sobs coming from behind the bedroom door. Such passionate displays were not unusual in the Falcone home, but this time Sofia did not want to dismiss it. She wanted answers.

He drew in a long breath, causing Sofia to do the same and take in the scents of home: dried basil, hot peppers, freshly cut lemons. And then the smell of heartache: *Signora* Russo's concoction of olive oil and soap used to make the sign of the cross on a sick one's forehead to ward off *malocchio*—the evil eye. Sofia had seen the woman do it before, and not only her. Others back in Italy had their own rituals for expelling the curse. Sofia didn't believe in the evil eye. Because she might be the only one from her village who did not, she didn't mention it to anyone. She imagined that if Serena had lived, the two of them might talk about it. She wondered if someday she might discuss matters of the old country with Antonio Baggio. But for now, and with Mamma ill, she had no one to talk to. She rubbed the back of her neck and stared at Papà, who worked his lips as though contemplating what to say next.

Only God heals, although he often does so through the hands of others. Sofia believed Father Lucci could bring God's healing through his prayers. Perhaps the Reverend Clarke could, as well. She believed doctors at large hospitals could heal people at God's command. She wasn't so sure about Carla Russo, who was as worn down and battered a wife as Sofia had ever seen. If she had the power to heal, why didn't she use it on herself? A nursemaid. That was the best they could hope for from that poor woman.

"Papà?"

"Shush." He held up a hand. He was still thinking.

"I can leave now."

He turned to her, his eyes red from the strain of holding in his emotions. "Listen to me, *figlia mia*, my precious daughter, when I tell you I only do what is best. Your mamma and your papà, your brothers and your sister, we love you. That is why this is best. You understand."

It was not a question. She was expected to accept his authority without argument. She would only do that if he sought the best doctors for Mamma. "I will check on Mamma, discretely, so she doesn't know I am here, Papà. I will consult with *Signora* Russo. Will that be acceptable? May I do at least that if you must send me away?"

He dabbed perspiration from his forehead. "So long as you promise me, Sofia. Promise me you will keep your job and you will stay out of Mamma's sight until I say you may come back."

"I promise." The words grated in her throat like sand, but this was the best arrangement she could hope for.

On Monday she carried an extra bag to work, filled with personal items. It was small, made of unbleached linen and closed at the top with a drawstring, a typical traveling bag that anyone might recognize. She felt a twinge of embarrassment having the bag at her side. Inside she'd stashed a bone comb, her Sunday dress, an extra skirt and apron, and her Italian Bible given to her by Sister Stefania when she was born, or so Mamma had told her. Inside the Bible was a rosary made of wooden black beads strung together with small bits of chain and adorned with a wooden crucifix. Every good Italian girl had one, and although Sofia's father wanted her to be good, or at least his interpretation of such, she would do what the mind God gave her told her to. Keeping her prayers thus focused, she was sure she could help Mamma even if Papà would not.

"Are you going somewhere?" Claudia pointed to the bag Sofia had dropped next to her sewing machine.

"I...uh, I am moving out."

That caught Maria's attention, a Benevento girl like Sofia. "Away from home? Where. Sofia? Why?"

"My mamma is ill."

Claudia wrinkled her upturned nose. "Oh, I see. They don't want you to catch it."

Maria knew better. Everyone in their neighborhood either heard about Angelina Falcone's affliction from someone else or witnessed with their own two ears through the paper-thin walls. "Not that kind of ill, Claudia," Maria said, pointing to her temple. She turned back to Sofia.

"I do hope they don't send her off to Ward's Island," Maria said.

She'd mentioned that before. "What is Ward's Island?"

Claudia jiggled her chin as she threaded her machine. "Haven't you heard about Nellie Bly?"

Sofia shook her head and busied herself with her job, aware that Mr. Richmond must be watching them from some platform or another.

But Claudia was not finished. "Nellie Bly investigated the place. She works for a newspaper. She got herself sent there as a patient, under false pretenses of course, and almost didn't escape. Her boss had to come vouch for her, and even then they were reluctant to release her. I am sure they didn't want the whole city to know how cruelly they treat their patients." She whispered as she spewed information. "Ice baths, starving them, keeping them locked in rooms without any human companionship, and most of them as sane as you and me. Some of the women didn't speak English. That was the only thing wrong."

How could such a thing be true? "What do you mean? Aren't there doctors there?" Doctors have the blessing of healing, Sofia believed.

Claudia withdrew a swatch of leather from her stack. "Aye, doctors, all right, but you could better call them sadists. *Ten Days in a Madhouse*. It's a book. I've read it."

Maria sighed loudly. "Your reading tastes are so…pleasant, as the Americans say."

Maria's attempt at sarcasm did little to relieve Sofia's anxiety.

"That's Blackwell's Island you are talking about, and it closed several years ago." The man stationed behind Sofia, one of the few men working in the stitching room, looked over his shoulder. "The island Nellie Bly was at."

Sofia felt herself relax.

Claudia frowned at the man. "Ward's Island is home to the insane, as well. Everything's just moved, but it's all the same." She leaned over to Sofia and whispered. "He's probably been a patient."

Sofia didn't think that was funny. Neither was scaring someone whose mother had been in a melancholy state.

After work, Sofia prepared to go straight to Hawkins House, hoping and praying they could take her in that very day. She tied her bag to the waistband of her skirt, trying to give the impression that she had a simple but large handbag, rather than a traveling satchel. Looking like a newly arrived immigrant was humiliating. On the trolley a girl asked her where she was headed. She didn't usually talk to strangers, but her heart was full of hope so she loosened her tongue.

"Don't go there," the girl said, wrinkling her nose.

"Why not?"

"Listen, those boarding houses for new immigrants? They make you work every hour you are there, scrubbing floors, cleaning chimneys, sometimes worse."

"I will be happy to help out. These are very kind people."

"They want you to think that. Come with me instead. I know a wonderful place with featherbeds. You're Italian? They feed you pasta and fresh fish, not mushy American food."

"Oh, no. I cannot pay."

"Don't you worry about that. You can earn your keep, and without working that hard." She winked at her.

Sofia thought perhaps she had been too hasty in agreeing to go to Hawkins House. She stared out at the darkening street. There wasn't time to investigate boarding houses, as she should have. "I will try this one out. They are expecting me."

The girl urged her up when the trolley stopped. "Before you make up your mind, come see. Try this one first and then compare it to the other. No harm in visiting, just to be sure, you know? I promise it won't take long. You can spare half an hour, can't you?"

The girl was persuasive. She was well dressed in a satin suit and fashionable hat.

When they arrived at the boarding house Sofia was surprised to find not a tidy brick building with a hanging flowerpot near the door, but a wooden clapboard structure with a sagging front porch. Music and laughter spilled out onto the street like an oil spill she didn't care to walk in. "No, thank you, I must go."

Before she could get away, a burly man hurried out the door and took her arm. "A new one, Margie. Good work."

"No, there is some mistake!" Bile rose up in Sofia's throat as she tried to fight the brute off.

He managed to get her inside and close the door. The smell of whiskey and stale cigar smoke made her eyes water. Several people lounged on a filthy sofa. One of them, a tall woman dressed smartly like Margie, the girl who had lured Sofia there, approached. Her fine clothes were as out of place in that house as dungarees would be at Carnegie Hall. "Come now, honey, this ain't so bad. Hungry? I can get you a sandwich."

"No." She stomped her foot, sending a cloud of dust high enough to reach her nose. She resisted the urge to cough.

The brute grabbed her again, this time pushing his body against hers. She was helpless against his strength until she remembered what her brothers had once taught her. She managed to stomp on the man's toe. He wore thin shoes and hers were well made. When he winced, he loosened his grip on her just enough that she was able to thrust her knee between his legs, sending him howling in pain. The crowd laughed and this time no one tried to keep her from leaving.

She pressed a hand against her heaving chest as she ran down the street. By the grace of God she found the trolley stop and made her way to Hawkins House.

Minnie the housekeeper met her at the door. "Why, come in, darlin'. These folks don't never turn girls away, certainly not ones they've met before. Here now, let me take your bag. You go on in the parlor. I'll send Mrs. Hawkins in shortly. She's upstairs ironing."

Sofia smoothed her hair with her hand, hoping that she bore no evidence of her encounter in a bawdy boarding house.

Minnie kept blabbering. "Don't you know I told her I'd do that but she likes to keep busy, she says. Reckon' she'll like having another girl here. Let me see. Kirsten's moved on now. She was from Germany, you know. She and her brother saved up and bought some land out west. She met him out there. Kansas or Oklahoma or some such place. Now we've got two new girls just in from Ellis Island." She popped her fingers once over her mouth. "Can't keep my gob shut, that's what Mrs. Hawkins says. You will meet them soon enough, darlin'. Don't need my blathering on. You just sit down and I'll get you some tea. Or would you rather have coffee, you being Italian and all?"

Sofia felt light-headed and foolish for being so gullible. She focused on the housekeeper.

"Coffee, please."

Minnie winked. "I got this way of knowing what our girls prefer. Those new ones, they like drinking chocolate. Ever have it? Hot like tea. Well, no matter. I will be right back. Now you relax here, darlin'."

A few moments later Mrs. Hawkins entered. "Sofia, love. How delightful to see you back so soon."

Sofia stood and squeezed her hands together, willing the English words to come. "I was hoping...I don't mean to...I just would like...a room?" Her voice squeaked like a mouse.

"Minnie told me, love. And Ronald, I mean Reverend Clarke, he told me you might be stopping by. Of course we have a room for you. Let's talk a bit."

The woman was patient with Sofia, encouraging her to take her time when she spoke. Sofia managed to do much better with her English when she was at ease. She explained her situation, leaving out the part about her deceased twin. She did not want Mrs. Hawkins to think ill of her parents.

"I do hope your poor mother recovers soon. You wouldn't mind a few preliminary questions, my usual information gathering?"

What if Mrs. Hawkins did not allow her in? Sofia wasn't sure if the woman liked Italians. It was too late to go anywhere else. A trickle of sweat ran down her back.

"Don't look so dismayed, love. I only need to know your parents' names, their address, what chores you are best at."

Sofia nodded.

"You are welcome to stay as long as need be. You say you work at a factory, Sofia?"

"Oh, *sì*, yes. I stitch shoes. I even designed these." She stuck out a foot to show her elevated boot. "For women like me of short stature."

"Short? You are taller than the rest of the women around here."

"Ah, perhaps an inch or two, but I like being able to see over heads, to be the height of a man, so I can see what's in front of the crowd." Sofia explained that she'd won a contest at her work and was given the chance to design a new shoe and to try out a sample so the owner of the company could decide if they'd be manufactured. She hoped her efforts would impress.

"And do they like your shoe, Sofia?"

"I don't know. No one has said they'd be making them. But I like it."

They laughed over that and Sofia relaxed. Minnie returned. Sofia wasn't sure she'd be able to keep up with the housekeeper's speech because of the odd lilt, something Sofia had heard referred to as a southern drawl, very different from the night school teacher's accent, or even Mrs. Hawkins's, for that matter. This place would challenge her language interpretation skills, but she'd endure that with pleasure after the place she'd mistakenly visited earlier.

Thankfully, the housekeeper said little, pouring coffee for Sofia and tea for Mrs. Hawkins. Judging from the flowery smell of Mrs. Hawkins's cup, Sofia was pleased she had coffee instead. Minnie excused herself, leaving them to sample some apple tarts.

"I've two other new girls at present, love. They are Eastern European Jews. Aileen will be sharing your room, but she is only here on occasion. She works as a nanny for the Parker family and often stays over, in her charges' nursery. Annie, whom you've met, lives next door with her husband and they attend First Church with me. I'm so sorry there are no other Italian Catholics to go to church with you. It's peculiar indeed, but you are the first Italian girl who has inquired here."

"We keep to our neighborhoods, *signora*."

"I see. Well, don't you worry. You are most welcome here and I will see that you are escorted to mass on Sundays."

"*Grazie*."

The woman showed her upstairs to a spacious room with two beds. "Aileen is Annie's cousin, but, like I said, most nights you'll have the room to yourself. There is a washroom with a tub at the end of the hall. Minnie will show you how it works. The other room is occupied by sisters, Etti and Leena Maslov."

A heady feeling washed over Sofia. In only one day she'd been transported from the Italian corner of New York City to the part of town where people from all over the world congregated, and she had landed safely at Hawkins House. She would miss Mamma, but this was something she could never have imagined before Mamma took such a bad turn. An adventure, now that she knew what types of people to avoid and what streets to stay away from. Like visiting an entirely different country that was only a trolley ride away. Perhaps this was one of those times Father Lucci called a blessing in disguise. Not that God created Mamma's affliction so that Sofia would come here, no. But rather he had turned an unfortunate occurrence into a grand adventure for Sofia.

She sighed, looking around. She would not like sleeping alone in this big room, however. Perhaps she could leave the door open.

Sofia could not stand there daydreaming for long. "I must go, Mrs. Hawkins. My papà, he expects me to meet him at the gate of the building where he is working. He wants to know I am all right."

"Of course, love. Can you find your way? I could call for the message boy to lead you."

"I can find my way. *Grazie, Signora* Hawkins." She'd meant to use more English but she didn't have time to consider her words. She needed to be there to give Papà her new address and tell him not to worry. She couldn't possibly check in with him every day, not from this place way down on the tip of Manhattan.

Papà stared down at the paper where Sofia had written, "*Agnes Hawkins, Hawkins House.*" He couldn't read it, of course, so she told him what it said. "This place, a Christian woman runs it?"

"*Sì*, Papà."

He wagged his head. "Hawkins? Not from Benevento."

"No, Papà. I told you that. But you do not need to worry."

He rubbed a hand over the stubble on his chin. "A papà will worry. Do not tell me different until you have your own children."

"*Sì*, Papà." She could not read his expression. Relief? "The house is a good distance from here. But it is a nice one, clean, spacious, run by a good-hearted woman."

"Well, that is a proper thing, I suppose. My children are in America now." He huffed. "You are sure of this, Sofia?"

"Absolutely sure. Would you like to come by?"

He ran a hand through his hair, contemplating. "I have no time."

"Please, Papà, I will come by your work…once a week. That should be fine, *sì*?"

He put a hand to his forehead. "My daughter leaves my house, leaves her neighborhood, tells me not to worry, and now she decides for herself what will be fine? Is this what America brings?" His voice escalated as an argument seemed to bandy about in his mind. "Because if so, I will walk you back through Ellis Island right now and put you on a ship to Italy."

"Papà, no, please. You decide. I will tell you all about the boarding house, but you decide."

"*Sì*. I will."

"The church watches over the women at this house. They promised I will attend mass. In fact, they require it. I will have to go to St. Anthony's, because it is closer, but I will go. They will see to it." She was careful not to mention what church the others attended. But she hadn't been untruthful with him.

He nodded his head. "Just until your mamma is better."

"*Grazie*, Papà. I will walk home with you now to check on her."

"No, Sofia."

"I will stay out of sight. I promise." Her voice took on a pleading tone. She hated that.

"You come in the morning, if you must come. Before work, *sì?* Mamma will be asleep then and you can talk with the healer. And from time to time, you will come to our church for confession, to let Father Lucci know you are well. You will do this, Sofia."

She thought about how this would add to her long days, but after he agreed that she could spend part of her salary on trolley and train fares, she kissed him good-bye.

As she walked back to Hawkins House, the street lamps began to glow over the sullen sidewalks. Even surrounded by so many people on the streets, she felt alone, worse than normal. The nip in her side rose up her spine and seemed to settle in the back of her neck. Perhaps Mrs. Hawkins and Minnie would allow her a warm bath when she returned.

As she neared Hawkins House, she could see oil lamps glowing from the windowsills. Someone's shadow seemed to be lighting them. Minnie Draper, she assumed.

The housekeeper met her at the door. "Evenin', Miss Falcone. Your room's all ready. Would ya like a bit of supper? Got a mess o' beans on the stove."

Sofia didn't know what that was, and the confusion of hearing English spoken so differently made her head ache. "*Grazie*. I have…" She mumbled the Italian under her breath before forcing out the English. "I eat already, *Signora* Draper."

"Uh, just call me Minnie, honey. Now if you need anything a'tall, you just holler. Can you find your way up to your room, child? Would you like a bath this evenin'?"

"A bath? *Sì*, yes, *grazie.*"

As Sofia snuggled under a floral quilt, an extra pillow pressed firmly against the emptiness on her right side, she watched the moon shaded by lace curtains. She thought she'd see the other boarders, but Minne had told her they had gone to see a vaudeville show. Sofia's day started early, so she decided to retire. She was so relaxed from her bath that despite the quiet in the house she drifted off to sleep almost immediately.

The rest of the week Sofia scrambled around trying to figure out which trolley to take and when they would arrive. It took her several days to get the timing right, but she hadn't been late because she left Hawkins House while the moon was still out. She remembered the names of the streets where the repugnant houses were, and avoided those deftly. She'd only had one brief conversation with Carla Russo, but the healer assured her Mamma was no worse.

"Time, Sofia, this will take time," the healer had said. "I rub her shoulders with oil and sprinkle holy water on her bedcovers. I light a candle at church, too. Try not to worry. God will hear."

But she did worry. She was so far away from Mamma now.

On Sunday, Mrs. Hawkins walked her to St. Anthony's and said good-bye at the door so she could get along to First

Church on Rayburn Street in time for services. She explained that while the reverend was willing to come for her, he was too busy for his own good, and she had told him she would bring Sofia to church.

Sofia smiled at the folks moving around her as they entered for mass. Strangers. Not smiling, not returning her glances. Finally, she drew in a deep breath, straightened her shoulders, and marched in. God knew her, didn't he?

She was a little early, but she could pray while she waited. She knew God would not want her to be noticing the other parishioners—she was here for worship—but she couldn't help it. Their clothing seemed finer, their mannerisms more…American. Most were speaking a dialect she couldn't understand. She gathered the ends of her fraying scarf in the palm of her right hand as much to still her jitteriness as to hide her poverty. *You belong*, she kept telling herself. *Stop feeling as if you don't.*

Someone brushed past her just then. A man. He slipped behind a door and she heard his footsteps clatter up stairs. The organist, she presumed. He looked like *Signor* Baggio. He hadn't minded, when they'd met, that she was southern Italian. These others shouldn't either.

Putting on her best posture, feeling elevated in her specially made shoes, Sofia held her head high when she entered the church and found a seat. But no one seemed to notice her anyway. She wondered, after her horrible experience at that other boarding house, if it might be better to be ignored. She was safe if no one knew she was there. She was also woefully alone.

12

ANTONIO WAS NOT AS RESTED as he should have been that morning. Playing the organ was his joy, but he'd stayed up far too late, making sure Nicco had a bed at the aid society. His uncle had left Antonio's last night after getting something to eat, but much later a troubling feeling prodded Antonio to grab his coat and hat and go looking for him. It had taken several hours of waking up vagrants and asking after Nicco to finally find him passed out in an alley. Dragging a drunken man along the streets on a Saturday night when every dive and brothel was filled to capacity and spilling out onto the sidewalks was not an easy thing. Taking him back to his apartment seemed to be most prudent, but Uncle wouldn't have it. Even in his stupor he refused to allow Antonio to renege on his father's principles. "I'm a bad, bad influence," the man kept muttering. The truth was, keeping him in his apartment could cause Antonio to lose his lease. His landlords were strict teetotalers and made no mistake about it. Antonio didn't want to think about having to move. His apartment was less expensive than most others and he was still saving all he could to get to Oberlin. Regardless, he would have snuck Nicco in if his uncle had allowed him to. He was, after all, his father's brother.

The only place Antonio felt secure about leaving his uncle was the Italian mission several blocks east. It must have been two in the morning when he and Luigi got home. Antonio had rushed out this morning while his dog barely noticed, snoring away on the end of Antonio's bed.

After the mass, he waited until most of the folks had left and then descended the stairs from the organ loft. The priest met him in the vestibule. "Antonio, my son, how are you?"

"I am well, Father."

"Working?"

"I am indeed. I've been hired to play at the Roman Athenaeum and I'm hoping..." He cleared his throat. "Praying, I mean to say, that God will allow me to continue playing concert music."

"Well done." He placed a hand on Antonio's shoulder. "There are some Italians, Antonio, who.....engage in behavior that is not becoming the Church. Do you know this?"

"There are some like that in all walks of life, Father."

"We must discourage this, but we must also protect our parishioners from ill repute, bad influences, you understand. That is why I must address you like this."

The priest's condescending tone irritated Antonio. "Please don't be vague, Father. Which Italians? Southerners? Sicilians? Or more specifically, Father, The Black Hand?" There were many prejudices and perhaps not enough caution in the right places. "I know nothing of any ill repute, as you say, among the people I spend time with."

The priest shrugged and whispered under his breath. "I cannot bear these jabbering women's complaints one more moment." Placing a hand to his collar, he cleared his throat. "What I mean to say is, better not to be seen in the company of those southerners, just because of appearances."

"You mean the young woman I walked to the train the other night? *Signorina* Falcone?"

"Whomever it was." He lifted his gaze to the rafters. "For all that is holy, just be careful. That is all I want to say." He started to turn away and then stopped. "A young girl asked the name of the organist and then gave me this for you." He sighed and then placed a note in Antonio's hand. "I am not a messenger, Antonio."

"Oh, no, Father. I have no idea—"

"Once is fine. No more." The priest moved on toward the doors.

Antonio looked at the note. It was written in the same hand as before, in Italian. He narrowed his eyes and concentrated until a rough English translation came to him.

Your father was a caretaker. Now that he is gone, the men worry. Will you take up his cause?

It made no sense. What cause?

Antonio walked outside, stunned that he'd been spied on and reported on to the priest, and now he was receiving cryptic messages. He glanced around at the parishioners still assembled on the sidewalk, wondering who among them was judging him. Antonio had accepted an invitation to Sunday dinner at Hawkins House. Sofia had been the only Italian there, but who would have known that? No, she couldn't be the reason someone had complained. Most likely a gossip had seen him staggering down the gas lamp lit streets with Nicco last night and assumed something worse than the truth—that he'd been helping his very own relative. No matter that one of the parishioners would have been out late as well in order to report it. Whomever was bending the Father's ear was probably also filling the church's coffers. Money rules hearts, despite what we all tell ourselves. Perhaps the "cause" was nothing more than the church offering. Maybe it was no different in The Bend.

He balled his fists in the pockets of his overcoat as he walked down Broadway. He didn't want to give up playing the organ. Tears filled his eyes as he thought about how proud his father had been of his playing. He stopped and turned the opposite direction when he remembered he'd been invited again to dine at Hawkins House. In fact, Mrs. Hawkins had asked him to…oh, no!

Antonio spun on his heels and hurried back to the church. He found Sofia leaning on an iron post out front. She was gazing down Sullivan, presumably looking for him. What would the busybodies think of that? He didn't care.

"Miss Falcone, I am so sorry. I am not accustomed to escorting anyone. I'm afraid it slipped my mind."

She glanced over to him. A momentary smile was replaced with a serious look. "I did not know they sent you."

"Not who you were expecting. I am sorry."

"No, it is not that. I am happy…uh, I mean I am able to escort myself. I could have, since you are busy with your music, *signore*."

"Not at all. My fault entirely." He held out his hand.

She slipped her long fingers tentatively in the crook of his arm. "I only wish the mass did not let out after First Church. Everyone will be cooking without my help."

"Well, let's hurry along, shall we?" He quite enjoyed having a girl on his arm. He'd never courted before. He reminded himself not to forget his mission, even as the scent of lavender emanated from her hair and her jaunty walk on those...those boot-like shoes she wore put a spring into his own step.

Later, as they sat in the dining room at Hawkins House, Sofia gave him a look with those deep, dark eyes as though he were an invading yellow jacket ready to sting someone. "Are you all right, Miss Falcone?"

She nodded. "I was just thinking of something." She looked away. "I am sorry."

Mrs. Hawkins cleared her throat and said a blessing over their meal.

"I must hurry today," Sofia said, staring at her lap. "I have to speak to Papà."

"I understand, love. We all have things to attend to. But I do hope you'll enjoy your Sabbath meal without apprehension."

The red-haired woman who ran the library upstairs agreed. "Don't worry about us, Sofia. You go see your parents right after dinner. When you return I'll have a few more selections placed on your bedside table. Later, when you have time, we can talk about the books."

"Books? I am so sorry I haven't yet—"

Annie jiggled her chin. "That is perfectly fine, Sofia. There will be time later."

The room held an awkward air. Antonio shifted in his chair. The librarian woman's husband laughed nervously. "Nothing better than discussing books. Did you know, Mrs. Hawkins, that the latest children's book by that English author Beatrix Potter has arrived?" He turned to Antonio. "Because Annie's father was published by a British publisher, we often get books from overseas before they arrive at the bookshop."

The hostess clapped her chubby hands. "Splendid. I did so enjoy *The Tale of Peter Rabbit.* Some are saying Miss Potter's writings are inspired by your father's stories, Annie."

Annie Adams sighed, bringing a napkin to her lips. "Well, I don't know about that, Mrs. Hawkins, but it does seem so that animals are extremely popular with children."

Despite the friendly banter, Antonio could feel Sofia's stare bore into him. He could ignore her no longer. "I believe I will call on your aunt again, Miss Falcone. I do hope she doesn't mind. Perhaps you will allow me to see you to your family's apartment." Dash all those looks from the members of St. Anthony's, he would see whom he wished.

"She'll be at the church." She stared at him a moment and then looked away. There must be some kind of message she was trying to send him. This time he knew he did not have pea mash on his chin, but for the life of him he didn't know what she was hinting at.

Sofia looked down at her lap, her black lashes flickering on the brim of her cheekbones. "Tomorrow will be best to see her, I believe. But truly, *Signor* Baggio, I do not think Sister Stefania...that is...I cannot say if the Sister will answer your questions."

"Perhaps not. But she may be able to send me to someone who can. Tomorrow, then."

She nodded, and turned her long neck away from him. This girl was troubled but lovely. Under other circumstances…

He lifted his chin toward Mrs. Hawkins. "My apologies, Mrs. Hawkins, for imposing business on the day's conversation."

The hostess clicked her tongue. "We do not mind, but may I ask what business you are seeking to conduct there?"

"It is complicated, but the priest at St. Anthony's insists, if I am to stay employed there, that I wrap up some affairs as quickly as possible." That wasn't what he'd said, but Antonio reasoned that was what he meant. His father. His uncle. Benevento men. The entire mystery. The priest probably assumed some gangsters were involved in his father's death, but his father had no unsavory acquaintances. He would prove that, once he figured out who was looking for him.

"Well, I wish you Godspeed, love." She passed around a basket of soft buns.

"You are very kind."

After the meal and a short time of conversation over coffee in the parlor, Stephen and Sofia donned their overcoats at the same time and headed toward the trolley.

"I would be happy to take you to my aunt, but I have to get home. And like I said, it is Sunday."

"I understand. You are correct that tomorrow would be a better day for business. Truly, I wouldn't want to impose. Indulge my curiosity, though. You did not have your Sunday meal with your family?"

"Uh, no. I planned to arrive after they had eaten. It is…difficult to explain."

He held up a hand. "No need. I am happy I had the pleasure of enjoying the meal with you."

She smiled. "As am I. But…why? Why do you seek a nun in Little Italy? *Non capisce.* I do not understand…it is a bit unusual?"

He nodded to acknowledge her puzzlement. "I have to start somewhere. The church seemed as good as any place. I'm afraid my father left some unanswered questions and my uncle believes someone in the Benevento area of the city might have more information." He gripped the note inside his pocket, deciding not to reveal the written clues just yet.

"*Signore*, do you mind if we say farewell here?"

His heart sank. "I would be happy to escort you, but not stay of course."

"That is very kind, but no, please. I mean, I can find my way. I do not mind. And with *mia famiglia* it is better not to bring visitors just now."

"I see." He was certainly an outsider. "Tomorrow I will have my dog with me when I drop in at the abbey. Your aunt seemed to like him when I was there before. Perhaps after your work tomorrow, you might meet me over there. I'd be happy to walk you back to Hawkins House. That is, if I'm not being too forward."

She beamed and he was getting the idea that speaking in English was what was causing her to look distressed, not him. "I attend night school next door. At least, I am trying to. There is so much to do and the working day is so long. But tomorrow, I hope to go. Perhaps our paths will cross."

He could not contain his delight. "I would like that. Are you sure you would not prefer that I see you to your family home today?"

Her smile left. "I do not mind going alone from here. Good-bye, *Signor* Baggio."

He started to walk away and then retraced his steps. "I would consider it an honor if you would think of me as your friend and call me Antonio."

"*Sì*, Antonio."

His name rolled off her tongue pleasantly to his ear, the way it should sound when spoken aloud.

13

SOFIA REHEARSED over in her head what she should have said to Papà during their short exchange in the tenement's corridor. *I can take care of myself. I'm a grown woman. It's Mamma you should worry about.*

She finally managed to drift off to sleep. She dreamt she saw Mamma behind iron bars calling out to her over the river. She was locked in an island cell with no one to help her keep her sanity, and, try as she might, Sofia could not get to her. She spotted Papà out on the river in a rowboat. She shouted to him but soon realized he had been the one who left Mamma there. He was moving away from her. It felt as though the solid land Sofia stood on was drifting backward. Against her will, she was abandoning Mamma just like Papà, leaving in the rowboat.

Sofia jerked awake, sweating. The entire night became a sieve, poked through with moments of wakefulness.

The next thing she knew, Minnie was shouting at her.

"Wake up, sleepy head. Don't ya have a job to get off to this morning? Know what time it is?"

Sofia tossed her pillow aside and stared at the woman standing in the doorway of her room. "Time?" A panic rose in her belly. She glanced out the window. It was light outside. Much too light. "I am late." If she hadn't been alone in the room, she might have roused earlier. She sprung from the bed, visited the washroom, and then grabbed her dress from the wooden chair where she'd slung it the night before.

After she dressed and wound her hair into a bun, then covered up with her scarf, she left her shoelaces undone as she scurried down the stairs toward the front door. She had her buttonhook in her hand, planning to find the right moment to tie up her shoes while on her commute.

"Take this with you, love." Mrs. Hawkins shoved a brown paper package at her. "For lunch. It's all prepared. Now, God bless your day, Sofia."

She nodded, flashed a smile she hoped was appreciative enough, and then rushed out toward the trolley stop. She'd never overslept before. Never. Perhaps the company of her boisterous family had been for the best. She hadn't had the opportunity to become lazy.

"This is the second time, young lady!" Mr. Richmond glared at her as she punched the time clock.

"I am on time, Mr. Richmond."

He twisted the ends of his waxed mustache. "Perhaps, but this is the second time you've come perilously close to being tardy."

He made it sound as if she were traversing a canyon cliff.

"I caution you to remedy this before it causes you to lose your job."

He obviously wanted her out. No time had been lost, no productivity sacrificed. He watched her like a hawk, just waiting for a reason to dismiss her.

Sofia could barely breathe as she stowed the paper-wrapped lunch under her desk.

"Is your mother worse?" Claudia asked, already at work on her stack of shoes for the day.

"She is the same."

"But you've moved out, haven't you?" Maria chimed in, tilting her head to the side to look at Sofia around her machine. "Carla Russo's daughter, Luisa, told me."

"I have. Just until Mamma is recovered. Luisa should mind her own business, though."

Maria's face fell, as though Sofia's insult had been aimed at her.

Sofia waved her fingers toward her friend. "I am sorry. She is a lovely girl. Today I am just…not used to how things are, where things are…the location of the trolley stops. They moved one, and I slept too long." There were no adequate excuses. "Forgive me, Maria."

Maria gave her a tightlipped smile. But Claudia was not yet satisfied. "Your brother Joey is spending a lot of time at the Irish dances, Sofia. Does your mamma know? I only ask because Italian mothers…well, everyone knows how protective they are over their families. I wouldn't want him to cause discord. I thought you should know."

Sofia's exclamation about Luisa's nosiness was lost on Claudia, it seemed. Sofia nodded as though she agreed, although it was just as well known around the factory that Irish mothers were the same. Sofia's grasp of English might not be perfect but she recognized a gossip when she saw one and wished Mr. Richmond would move Claudia to another station. Joey, the youngest in the family, was not as compliant as he should be. But, of course, Mamma didn't know where Joey was spending his leisure and Papà didn't have time to correct him. Neither did Sofia if she had wanted to. Perhaps Joey had the right idea—get away, meet new people.

Claudia would not stay silent. "You went to Hawkins House without us, didn't you?"

How? Sofia rubbed her temples and felt her supervisor's stare. "I had to find a boarding house. They took me in."

"Is that so? At the dance, Joey told me he'd seen you walking from that direction with a gentlemen, Sofia. Quite young and handsome." She winked when Sofia looked up.

"Joey said handsome?"

Claudia laughed. "Of course not, but he was fairly certain it was a man named Antonio Baggio you were out walking with. Some of the folks have seen him and his dog over at the nickel theater. Plays the piano, I hear."

Antonio said he had a dog. How meddlesome Claudia was. And why would Joey be talking about her to strangers?

"Truly, Sofia, I don't mean to be a busybody. Your brother is quite polite. I've even danced with him. But this Antonio is not one of them, so your brother says."

"Oh for heaven's sake, Claudia!" Maria nearly came out of her chair. "She is not out walking. She is just getting settled in. Whose business is it if someone showed her the way to the trolley?"

"My brother should speak to me directly if he does not approve." Sofia hoped that would end the conversation, but to be sure, she pulled a square of leather from her bin and held it high enough to hide her face, pretending to examine it. The city was huge, crowds of people crammed the narrow streets. Joey would not have accidentally seen her, as though they were back in the small market town of Benevento. He was watching her. He knew Antonio for some reason. Papà had put him up to it, but Sofia would end it.

Sofia took a quick look at Claudia, who was reaching for her second sole. Sofia had not stitched her first yet.

Maria leaned over toward Sofia and whispered, a thread hanging out of her mouth. "She is nothing but a *ficcanaso,* a nosy parker."

At noon Sofia chose to eat alone at her desk, hoping to gain a reprieve from Claudia. She unwrapped the paper-covered lunch and found a cold beef sandwich, an apple, and a pickle that she gave away to the boy sweeping up. Such thoughtfulness from the boarding house's matron and her housekeeper. She'd not had time for breakfast. She rose to get a glass of water.

When she returned from the cafeteria, having stopped for a brief chat with Maria, she found her sewing machine missing, along with her lunch. Glancing in all directions, she finally spotted Mr. Richmond in a far corner. "Come here, Miss Falcone," he called.

She hurried over and saw her machine and her work—more leather pieces than she'd had before she left, she was sure—squeezed into the corner facing a brick wall. Her lunch had been haphazardly placed on her chair.

"I believe you'll be more productive here. No chance of chattering the day away."

"But it was not me…" She gave up, realizing she spoke to his back and he would not give her another look. Claudia should be in this dark corner, not her.

After a long afternoon Sofia's knuckles stiffened. As she leaned into her chair and bent back the tips of the fingers of her left hand with her right, she gazed at the stack of finished soles. Amazed at how high it was, she realized her banishment had actually made her more productive. Now Mr. Richmond would never move her back.

He approached her with his clipboard and pen ready. Frowning, he examined her work. He nodded to the floor boy who loaded up his cart. When the boy had gone he shook his head. "I'm docking your pay this week ten percent, Miss Falcone."

"But why? I've done better than I ever have."

He narrowed his falcon eyes. "And just imagine how much more you would have produced this morning had you not been fraternizing with the other workers." He turned on his heel and moved to the next station.

A few minutes later the dismissal bell rang and Sofia stomped off to wait in line to punch her time card. After they had collected their coats, Sofia met Maria out on the sidewalk and told her what had happened.

"His niece," Maria said. "He wants to replace you with her. I heard him on his telephone." She snickered. "Fool does not know he doesn't have to shout into that talking machine to be heard. My uncle has one. I know."

"He wants to give my job away?"

"Well, Claudia works so quickly. I'm catching up to her. You are the one who bursts in like *fattucchiera* on her broomstick, barely ready to work. I know your mamma has not been well, Sofia, but it is still the truth. He believes you are the most likely to give him just cause to dismiss you."

"I won't, I tell you." Sofia rushed toward the trolley and hopped on just in time. As she faced the open side of the car, she swung her prized shoes out into the air, and tried to ignore the worry threatening to make her cry. Papà would have to understand. One week with less pay shouldn't send them into a debtors' prison. Still, it made her mad and she pouted. She would not lose her job, not while she had an ounce of gumption left.

Hopping off, she saw her brother waiting for her. She was glad she'd spotted him. They needed to talk. "Don't you have a job, Joey? You always seem to be lurking about."

"I thought you'd be happy to see me."

She hurried ahead of him down the walk. "Happy that you're out in the open instead of hiding in a window well or watching me from behind someone's sandwich board." And she was pleased he hadn't noticed her wandering into that first boarding house like the greenhorn she did not want to appear to be.

"Don't be that way, Sofia. I'm just looking out for you. It's a dangerous city." He smirked. "And who told you I was behind a sandwich board?"

She spun to look at him. A few men following behind collided when Joey halted. They glared but wound their way around them and proceeded down the walk.

Sofia tugged Joey closer to her. "I am fine. I am in a safe place. Go look out for Mamma instead of following me."

He frowned, but did not reply.

"Joey, I do not yet know why, but I believe you are more interested in a man named Antonio Baggio than my safety."

"Hush, sister." He clutched her close as they continued to walk. "You do not understand. It is my job to, uh, watch some people."

"Oh for the love of Saint Peter, Joey. That is no kind of job. I don't know what business *Signor* Baggio has in our neighborhood, but I assure you he means no harm."

"I was surprised to see you with him."

"Is he a burglar? A murderer?"

"No. How did you meet?"

"He was having lunch at the boarding house. He was a guest, and presented himself as a very fine gentleman."

A man in a long duster coat and a brimmed hat sitting low over his eyes bumped Joey hard enough to cause him to scoot out to the street. While the avenues were always teeming with pedestrians, this seemed intentional. Her hot-as-a-pepper tempered brother oddly gave no response.

"Who was that?"

"Keep walking."

When they were one block from Hawkins House, Joey stopped and bought a newspaper from a boy and pretended to read it. "I told you there are dangers about, Sofia."

"That man accosted you, not me."

He folded the paper and slapped it across his knee. "You are right. I should not be here. You tell Papà I did my duty. It is not my wish to treat you as my younger sister when you are the eldest, Sofia. I came only to warn you."

She was running out of patience after the day she'd had. She glanced around at the brownstones, at a woman pushing a *carrozzina*—what Mrs. Hawkins called a pram—and cooing to her baby. She noted the baskets of sunny chrysanthemums placed near doorsteps. This was a quiet, gentle place, not a neighborhood where warnings need be made. They sat on a bench outside a pharmacy shop.

"I think you should tell me what you've been up to, Joey Falcone."

He turned his palms upward. "I told you. Just making sure you are well."

"Not just this time. You've been all over the city, even to the Irish dances, so I hear."

"Is that what you hear? I can go where I wish. People are speaking ill of me just because I'm Italian, Sofia. An Italian man in Manhattan must be in a gang. He must be threatening folks and beating whomever the *padrone* tells him to—that's what people think."

"Is that who bumped you? A *padrone*?"

He let out a sigh. "He was just reminding me that I have a job to do, and it does not involve chats with my sister. I wish it did."

"He should have introduced himself."

"Sofia, you know that is not how Benevento men are."

His little boy smile melted her heart. She pinched his cheek, glad that he did not know about her blunder at that first boarding house. He did not need to worry about her. "People know you in your own neighborhood, Joey. You should stay there."

He jiggled one foot as he spoke. "It is not fair. We are in America. The land we were told was paved in gold bricks."

She laughed. "Who told you that? Papà traveled here many times. He knows better, and so should you."

"But at Ellis Island. Do you not remember?" He stared at the sky. "Hope. We all felt it when we arrived. We thought our lives would be better. We only had to step off that ferry and our poverty would be in the past."

She nodded. "Oh, *sì*. The ship agent, the *padrone*, they were the ones...so many promises." She patted his shoulder. "But see? I have a job. I have a nice place to live. You will find steady work. God will guide you."

He drew in a deep breath that made his chest swell. "I thought Mamma would be better here."

She blinked as a knife-sharp pang hit her heart. "I thought so, too, my brother, but do not give up hope so quickly. America has fine doctors. Papà will see. Mamma will get the treatment she needs and then we'll rejoice that America truly is the land of golden promises come true."

He hugged her. "My sister, Sofia—always the cheer giver."

14

EARLY IN THE EVENING on Monday, Antonio dug out some sheet music and began practicing. Luigi, lying on the striped rug next to the piano, perked up his ears. By the time Antonio was satisfied he knew the tunes he'd likely be playing on his next vaudeville job, he rose stiffly from the bench and began searching in his cupboard for something to make into a meal.

"Rice today. What do you think, boy?"

Luigi sprung to his feet, stretched with front paws extended, and then wagged his tail.

"I purchased this from a Chinaman's cart. Let's give it a try."

Luigi barked in agreement.

Antonio thought about Sofia as he filled his pot with water from the faucet. He'd been going about this the wrong way. He hoped that while he was at the church in Little Italy, Sofia would stop by on her way to night school. Why not have Sofia make introductions for him? Those men, the ones asking for him, said they wanted something. So did Antonio. Answers. Proof that his papà was not wrapped up in anything nefarious. The trouble with the southern Italians was they didn't know how to get answers without bullying folks, and that's what had given the priest and others a bad impression.

While the people in Sofia's neighborhood distrusted outsiders, perhaps if they thought he was *her* friend...

He rubbed a thumb over the stubble on his chin. "What do you think, Lu? Is it bad to use an acquaintance in such a matter?"

Luigi flopped back down on the rug, probably disappointed the music had stopped and supper was not yet ready.

"Of course, I would not mind if Sofia Falcone became more than just an acquaintance." He told his dog things he wouldn't tell humans.

After they ate, Antonio checked his pocket watch. Seven o'clock. He should get along so he didn't miss her. School for immigrants who work during the day normally started at eight. He'd seen enough flyers on doors to know that. "Just enough time to check on Uncle Nicco, I suppose."

Luigi whined and scooted down to lay his head between his outstretched paws.

"I know you don't care for the man, but he's all I've got. Father would want me to make sure he's all right." He glanced to Nicco's accordion. "Come along." He whistled and opened his door. As always, Luigi followed at his heels.

"He's been asleep most of the time?" Antonio stood with the charity worker gazing down on the mountain of blankets covering Nicco.

"Except for meals. I expect he's only sleeping it off." The gruff man, who said he was a retired schoolmaster, was the only volunteer in the building at the moment.

"But I brought him in on Saturday. Should the doctor see him?"

"Our health and sanitation volunteer has already examined him, along with the other men. Purely an alcohol slumber, he assured me. Your uncle left our facility for a time yesterday. The saloons should not be open on Sunday, but you know how it is."

"Very well. I mean, if the volunteer thinks that's all it is."

The man sneered at Antonio's dog. "He should not be in here."

Antonio turned to leave. "Are you saying the place is not fit for a dog?"

The man flipped away the insult with his fingers and returned to his desk. This was the best place around for vagrants, but it was no Peacock Alley in the Waldorf-Astoria.

"Come on, Lu. We've a mission."

When they got off the trolley, Antonio and his dog were once again met by an admiring tribe of children. They circled them, sighing and clicking their tongues. Antonio moved through them and Luigi, despite enjoying the attention, followed. "It is getting late, children. You should get on home." He wished he knew more Italian. One thing he did figure out was that the children in Little Italy adored his dog. They kept shouting something he thought was an announcement, that the famous dog and his owner had returned. This couldn't hurt his reputation.

He knocked on the abbey door.

"*Sì, sì,* come in." The diminutive woman he had met the other day waved them inside. She whispered. "Mother Superior is away for a few days so your dog is welcome, *signore.*"

"Sister Stefania, we met before but I've just learned that you are the aunt of an acquaintance, Sofia Falcone."

She swept her hand toward the chairs in the kitchen. He sat and waited for her to pour coffee into china cups.

"Lovely girl. I think I told you so, *Signor* Baggio."

"You remembered my name." He sat up straighter.

"Ah, *sì.* And your friend here. What do the children call him? The Victor dog?"

"Yes, I think so. He looks a little like that advertisement for phonographic records. I think it's more the way he behaves than how he looks. Have you seen those records?"

She smiled broadly. "I have one myself."

"How nice. His true name is Luigi."

She patted his head. "Why would you give him an Italian name?"

He set his china cup down. "I am Italian."

She brought a hand to her forehead. "Baggio. Why do I forget this? Some would think you are an outsider, but your father *was* Italian."

"You are quite perceptive. I was born in Pavia, but my father brought us to America when I was only five years of age."

150

She nodded. "America. Sometimes I can even forget I am here, what with all the Benevento people here at the church."

"Yes, that is what I would like to talk to you about, Sister. I have heard my father acted in the role of helper of some sort, for the people here. Do you know anything about that?"

She smiled sweetly, like a child. "That is a good thing, *signore*."

"Then you know what I am talking about."

"We are brothers and sisters, made in the Lord's image. I am happy to know the kind of man he was."

"Uh, yes. Do you know what cause he might have taken up?"

"I suppose the cause of loving our fellow man."

Antonio muttered a silent prayer while the nun answered a knock at the door. Where was he to go from here? *Help me, Lord!*

The nun returned and handed him a folded piece of paper. "A message for you."

"Who is it from?"

She shrugged. "One of the church workers brought it down, but he doesn't know its source. Signed, perhaps?"

He unfolded it. At once he recognized the handwriting. The same person who had given him clues before. Feeling weary, he struggled to understand the words.

"I can help," the nun offered.

He handed it to her.

She smiled as she read, giving him the impression that she could know something about it. Was she the informer?

It says: "Your father once helped the people of this neighborhood." She paused and looked him in the eye. "Ah, as you said." She nodded vigorously and then continued. "We are a proud people. Others will not say they distrust outsiders, but I will say it for them. Please find out what your father did with our money." She wrinkled her brow as though this surprised her.

"I don't know what it means, Sister. Please tell me where these messages are coming from."

She frowned. "I do not know."

Sofia said good-bye to her brother and entered Hawkins House. "Hello, love." Mrs. Hawkins stood in the hall, chubby hands clasped in front of her waist. Her sharp facial features would make her appear foreboding if it weren't for her sing-songy voice.

Sofia focused on her English. "Good afternoon, Mrs. Hawkins."

"Come and sit down in the parlor. I know you have night school to ready for, but after a long day at work you should have some tea and relax a few minutes."

"You are very kind." What had she done? Her boss wanted to fire her, and now Mrs. Hawkins seemed disturbed.

As they settled in, Minnie entered with a tray. "Coffee for Miss Sofia, and tea for Mrs. Hawkins."

Sofia was not used to being served. It made her even more jittery. She'd heard about how the American slaves had suffered only a generation earlier and she didn't want to give this woman the impression she expected to be served. She jumped to her feet. "Let me help you."

"I don't mind a bit, Miss Sofia. Now you just sit down and rest. I will get you a sandwich since you won't be here for supper. Kick off those big shoes of yours if you want, honey. We don't stand on ceremony at Hawkins House, do we, Mrs. Hawkins?"

The hostess didn't immediately agree. Sofia was learning that various cultural groups had different mannerisms and expectations. It was a lot to keep up with when one had been living among such a small circle of people. And to top it off, something was bothering the woman and Sofia had no idea what.

Mrs. Hawkins sipped from her floral teacup. "If you would like to go upstairs and freshen up, even put on some slippers for a bit, I do not mind at all."

"Oh, I am…quite comfortable, but…*grazie*." She lowered herself back down on the plump sofa.

After stirring a bit of cream into her coffee, Sofia glanced up to see the woman staring. What had she forgotten? Did Mrs. Hawkins expect her to "freshen up?" It was the housekeeper who had mentioned taking off her shoes. Mrs. Hawkins had urged her to sit. She tried to relax her pounding heart.

"Love? Was that a family member walking you to the door? Or a beau, perhaps? I only ask because I want you to know you are welcome to have visitors here."

"Beau? Uh, a sweetheart you mean? No." She had answered too quickly because Mrs. Hawkins cocked her head in a way that suggested she did not believe Sofia. "My brother. You saw him outside." A nervous giggle escaped her lips. "He could not stay. But, *grazie*, thank you."

"Anytime, Sofia. Invite him to Sunday supper. Your papà, too."

Oh, no. Never. She could forgive this woman who could not possibly understand. Sunday suppers are sacred for Italians. You would never find any Italian, other than Sofia, at the table of an English woman on Sunday. She rubbed her chilly arms.

A few moments later, having consumed the ham sandwich Minnie brought her, she excused herself and quit the room to go upstairs and collect the books Annie had left for her. She would show them to her teacher at night school with the explanation that her boarding house let her borrow them, not what boarding house or who owned it or what guests visited there. For now she would tell no one, not until she could explain fully. She could not imagine why the men from her village were suspicious of Antonio, but Sofia had been naïve before so she would proceed cautiously.

Darkness had fallen by the time she exited the train and walked toward the building adjacent to the church. Lamps flickered in the windows, casting a welcoming amber glow at her feet. She was glad to be back. As challenging as the English language was to learn, she liked the night school because it was what remained for her of *la famiglia*, of her village. Mamma had rejected her, she'd felt the loss of her twin deeply, Joey no longer resembled the delightful younger brother she'd helped raise, and the mass she now attended made her feel like a leper everyone tried to avoid. But this classroom was her nest of security.

"Wait there, Sofia!" The door to the abbey kitchen flung open.

"Sister Stefania, I will be late for school."

"I am here with a young man, and he says you have met, Sofia. Come, come."

She had almost forgotten Antonio Baggio had said he was coming to speak to her aunt. She was sorry she did not have more time, but she had only now reminded herself to be cautious. "Say hello for me. I must go. Tell him I can speak to him after class, please." She would warn Antonio that the people in her village were wary of him and ask him why.

The woman marched up the steps from the kitchen and grabbed hold of her arm. Sofia had no choice but to follow.

Antonio rose from his chair at the table when he saw her. His curly hair and the gleam in his eye made him seem gentle and attractive, not someone who might be a threat. Surely Joey and his *padrone* trailed the wrong outsider.

"Nice to see you again, Miss Falcone."

"And you, *Signor* Baggio." She felt heat rising to her cheeks. Something about the man charmed her. Joey would like this young man, if he attempted to become acquainted. She nearly forgot her quest to get to school on time.

But she did need to go.

"Sit, sit," her aunt ordered.

"Just for a moment, Sister." Sofia dropped down on the chair directly across from Antonio, stacking the books in her lap. It was infuriating at times how Sister Stefania did not seem to care what others might be doing or how busy they might be. When the woman wanted to talk, she talked. Even *Signor* Baggio seemed held against his will.

"Do you know why *Signor* Baggio has come to the abbey?"

Sofia whispered. "Sister, I am sure that is his own business and he doesn't care to share it with everyone." But she wanted to know. Very much.

A whining sound came from under the table. She bent to look. "Oh, this is your dog?" She patted the white fur on his nose and he licked her hand.

"Miss Falcone, meet Luigi."

She laughed. He was a well-behaved, charming pet with brown eyes that focused on hers, melting her heart.

Antonio cleared his throat. "I have come to find out what the people in this neighborhood knew about my father."

"I understand you have questions, and I wish I could help you." She glanced to her aunt. "We cannot. I am sorry. The people here, they are not like those at Hawkins House, *signore*. You will not find what you seek." She stood. "I am happy to see you again, but I am afraid I must go."

"Not yet." Stefania gripped Sofia's arm a bit too hard. "I want you both to stay."

"I really must. It was delightful to meet your dog, signore."

Antonio's face softened as though by admiring his dog she was welcoming his attention. She broke from his gaze, reminding herself she had studies to catch up on, things she had missed during the process of her move. She bit her lip. There was something about this handsome man, something mysterious, that she knew nothing about. She should be mindful. Joey might not know why he was following Antonio, but there could be something she was not aware of. Pausing to take another look at the man, she hoped she was wrong.

Stefania relented and let her go. She shouted at Sofia's back. "All God's children. Doesn't matter who you are or what your circumstances may be. Even if the *padrone* steals from you, the Church will be here."

Sofia closed her eyes as she ascended the steps to the street. That woman could embarrass her without warning, and now in front of Antonio.

She inhaled the night air, which seemed to smell less of burning coal once the sun set. The smell of Italian suppers being prepared around the neighborhood wafted to her senses and her soul. Being away had been enlightening and exciting, but she did miss her people. Even Stefania, the enigmatic, quirky, but sensitive nun. She was surely the key, the one who would be most willing to share the details surrounding Sofia's sister's death. But Sofia would have to be alone with her to get the information she was somewhat afraid to hear but needed in order to reach Mamma.

15

"I DO NOT UNDERSTAND." Antonio thought the nun had a purpose in mentioning a *padrone*, but it made no sense. Even Lu whimpered from his spot under the table.

Sister Stefania rose to putter about the kitchen, putting away items, wiping off the counters. "When people do not understand, which is almost always how it is, they should pray. Ask God for wisdom."

"Yes, sister. Perhaps you will help me understand what you meant just now when you said something about a *padrone* stealing. Was that for your niece or for me?"

"Hmm." She shifted her shoulders. "Both."

"But I'm afraid I have no personal dealings with any *padrone*. Are you saying an Italian boss sent me these notes?"

"No, I do not think so. No dealings? I am happy for you. Usually, when there is trouble, it is because of labor, a lack of jobs and money. Who controls these things?"

"The *padrone*?"

She nodded and toasted with an empty coffee cup.

"Where can I meet such a person, in case he can shed light on the circumstances of my father's death?"

"*Banca Stabile*, of course."

"The Italian bank?"

"*Sì*."

"But it's closed until tomorrow."

"Of course."

A bell tolled and the woman scurried away for prayers. Antonio scratched his head. The woman was simple, kind. A nun wouldn't lie to him, surely. What had her warning to Sofia been about? Was *she* in some kind of danger? He wondered if perhaps that was why her father had sent her away, to protect her. All kinds of fanciful scenarios came to mind, but of one thing he was sure. He felt affection for the girl and an overwhelming sense that she needed his help. Certainly that's what the sister was suggesting.

He decided to take Luigi on a stroll around the neighborhood until Sofia's school ended. He would look out for the note writer in case he tried to drop another message his way. Two messages had come while he was in Little Italy. The other was delivered at St. Anthony's. And then there were the men who had come to the theater. Someone obviously knew where to find him.

A glance at his pocket watch told him Sofia would be no longer than three-quarters of an hour. Even though most of the students lived nearby, many had to rise early for their jobs and would be headed to their beds directly.

Luigi tugged slightly on his leash. He wasn't used to it. "It's okay, boy. Just for looks. Wouldn't want anyone mistaking you for a stray."

Luigi paused and looked back at him, his ears raised at alert.

"Sorry. No insult intended."

They rounded a corner, where music came from a basement window. Accordions, tambourines. Antonio was curious. He stopped a man who was about to enter the building. "What kind of music is that?"

The man frowned beneath his heavy black mustache. "*Musica?* No, no. *Ristorante.*" He slapped Antonio on the arm. "*Maccheroni!*" Then he descended the steps and went inside.

Antonio and his dog exchanged glances. "That rice didn't fill us up, did it?" He tied his dog's leash to the railing in front of the window. "Wait, Lu." He trotted down the steps and let himself in the door the way he'd seen the man do.

When he stepped inside most of the chatter ceased, although the musicians kept playing. Those who had glanced up at him turned back to their plates and their conversations, but in a hushed manner that made Antonio feel unwelcome. He even wondered for a moment if he'd mistakenly wandered into a private home but dismissed the thought because there were diners seated at several tables and no parlor. A young man approached him. "Do not mind us. We do not get many newcomers at Giovanni's. Would you like pasta *e fagioli?* Macaroni?" He waved a woman over as he directed Antonio to a table just a few steps away.

"Thank you, *grazie.*" Antonio nodded toward the woman. "Whatever you are serving will be fine." He turned back to the young man. "I am Antonio." He decided it best to leave off his last name.

"*Sì*, I know."

Antonio was confused. "We've met?"

"Uh, no. The children. They said you come with your dog."

"That's right."

"I am Joey."

Antonio pointed to the chair across from him.

"*Grazie*, no. I am washing dishes here tonight and as little work as I get, I cannot afford to lose it. Enjoy, *signore*." He left, weaving through the tables of male diners—Antonio noted no females save the one who had waited on him. The diners still spoke in hushed voices, and in Italian, which Antonio understood little of so they needn't have bothered. He gave them sideways glances, wondering if they knew his father, knew what mysterious thing he had done.

Moments later the woman placed a large platter in front of him. It smelled of rich tomato sauce and spices, much more appetizing than what Antonio had back in his apartment. He smiled up at her and spoke one of the few Italian words he knew. "*Delizioso!*"

One corner of the woman's mouth curled up. She reached behind her and snagged a basket of bread from another table. A few moments later, she returned with a narrow bottle of olive oil and placed it beside the bread. Then she turned to the men at the table who were now without their bread and nodded firmly. They waved their hands as though they hadn't wanted any anyway.

Antonio ate and watched the musicians who were assembled in one corner. They were quite talented in their cultural manner and he was thoroughly enjoying himself, and sure he had found a way to fit in, when he heard a clatter coming from outside. The aproned woman appeared again from the kitchen and scurried up to the window, flapping her apron to and fro. She turned to Antonio and said in broken English, "The children, they should be…night…in bed!"

He realized they were playing with his dog so he paid his check quickly and left, but not before putting a roll into his pocket for Lu.

As he was freeing his dog from the entanglement of children, he heard his name called. Sofia was waving to him as she approached from up the street. "Let's go see the lady, Lu." He headed toward her.

The leash slipped from his hand and Lu dashed away, as eager to see Sofia as he was. She ordered him to sit and then patted his nose. "He's such a good dog, Antonio."

"He is. Would you like us to walk you home?"

"Oh, I don't know about the dog on the trolley." She glanced down the street. "I must hurry, though. I am not certain when the last one runs."

He offered his arm. "You have time still, and the conductors always allow Luigi to ride. I know most of them working at this hour."

She slipped her small hand into the crook of his arm. "How is that you are riding the trolley at night?"

"I am a musician. Most theater is in the evenings, when working folks are out and about."

"Ah, that explains why you were in Giovanni's. To hear the music." She arched a dark brow.

"At first, yes, but the food was exceptional."

She laughed. "I can make better. Tell me, did my aunt help you with your business?"

"No, not really."

Sofia flung her free arm above her head and then back down. "She is...uh, flibbertigibbet? Is that what you Americans say?"

He chuckled. "Well, she may be a little distracted. She had to go off to prayers."

"It was not the prayers. She is always like that. I have been trying to talk to her myself and cannot talk...uh, converse very well with her. There are rumors in the neighborhood about you. Do you know what it is about?"

"I would like you to tell me."

"I do not know why the people are curious about you. That is why I asked. You do not know?"

"Before God I tell you I do not, but I came here hoping to find out."

"Just talk, then. Nothing to listen to," she suggested. "I am sure they are fond of your dog."

Whether it was the night air or being in the company of a woman he found charming, Antonio didn't know, but something compelled him to confide in her about his father's death and how the priest had insinuated that he prove his father had been an innocent bystander when he was killed. He even told her it was Uncle Nicco who had suggested men from Benevento might have the answers.

After they were seated on the trolley, he noted Sofia's eyes glimmering in the light of the gas lamps. He had upset her. He bit his lip and allowed silence to open up a space between them.

The trolley bumped along the shadowy avenue as the riders shifted in unison. *Not everyone has to deal with a family tragedy.* He hoped sharing his hadn't made her shy away from him. Sofia was the one Benevento native he knew best, however she had made it clear she could not help him.

Finally, she spoke. "I am so sorry to hear about your papà. That is a terrible thing to happen."

"Yes. Thank you."

"You must miss him very much."

"I do." No one had ever suggested that Antonio might feel pain over the incident, not even the priest. It was as though feeling anything would be unmanly and weak. He blinked back his own tears. "I have had to adjust to being alone." He felt Luigi nudge his ankle. "I have my dog, of course."

"And he is a good companion." She invited Lu onto her lap and nuzzled him under her chin.

"He likes you." And he had a way of lifting spirits, as he had just done for her.

The stop closest to Hawkins House was approaching. If he were going to ask, he needed to do so now. "Sofia, your aunt. She seemed to be warning you about something. Is there anything I can do, because I'm more than willing."

Sofia drew in a deep breath and then allowed Luigi to jump down where he sat at Antonio's feet. "Thank you. Very much thank you. But there is nothing."

"Are you in any kind of danger? I mean, she mentioned a *padrone*, perhaps a troublesome one."

"My aunt. She is a bit…" Sofia patted her forehead with the heel of her palm.

"I understand, but—"

"My troubles are many, but there is no danger. Thank you for being concerned."

"May I ask then, have you any idea who might be passing me notes about my father?" He explained the best he could.

"That is indeed odd. I have never heard your father's name before I met you. Perhaps someone is…how do you say it?"

"Playing a cruel joke on me?" Being unwelcome in Little Italy, it was possible. "Why would they come looking for me at the theater, though, if they only wanted to run me out? It seems they drew me to your streets." His throat tightened. Perhaps his father had also been lured.

She covered her head with her scarf. "I wish I knew the answers."

After they stepped off, Antonio gently took her arm. "You must call on me, Sofia, if you encounter something threatening. I am happy to help."

She nodded and paraded down the walk toward the boarding house with the swinging sign out front, marching on those outrageous shoes of hers. He didn't care if her troubles did not involve personal danger. They were causing her grief and he wanted to help her resolve whatever it was. A woman this beautiful should not be so weighed down with life that her smile stayed forever hidden. He didn't care anymore about the priest's meddling. He knew his father had been an upstanding, hardworking moral man. There were people in the world who really needed help, who needed joy in their lives. That was why Antonio took pleasure in playing his music for them. He should invite Sofia to the theater to hear him play. Perhaps then she would forget her troubles and smile again.

He looked again at the note the nun read to him. What money? If he went to the bank and asked, perhaps he could help both Sofia and himself.

16

After seeing Sofia home, Antonio headed up to the theater district. Union Square was busy, the streets bulging with vaudeville performers he had to push through. They were all looking for work and many could do his job. Thankfully the manager at the Roman Athenaeum liked him. Without this employment Antonio might have no extra funds for his savings. First he should give the society housing his uncle a hefty donation. He hadn't meant to insult them the last time he was there. Without them, Nicco might have been killed out on the streets.

As he neared the entrance of the theater, a man approached them, a manager who had not been there last week when Antonio was hired. He chuckled when he saw Luigi. "The Victor dog, don't you know. How extraordinary the way he listens to you."

"Yes, well, not really. Just resembles him." He stuck out his hand. "I'm the pianist tonight, Antonio Baggio." He'd been hired for the late, late shows.

The man flipped pages on a clipboard. "Have you been booked by the agency?"

Antonio knew booking agents were everywhere, he'd been approached by quite a few, but the theaters had been moving away from such arrangements, according to Mac and the manager at the Roman he had met last week. "No. Must I be?" Booking agencies required a fee and he didn't much like dividing his earnings.

The fellow laughed and handed a female dancer a fan as she scooted past them. "I understand Cox booked you. That's fine, then. Superb." He leaned in. "The other performers will despise you should they learn you've not paid a booking fee, so I should not discuss it if I were you."

"Very well."

"What about your dog?"

"Lu? He'll wait for me like he always does."

"How incredible. Nice pooch." The man made kissing sounds. Lu growled and the man jumped back.

Good dog. Keep on letting folks know you can hold your own.

Later, Antonio watched as the theater manager counted out bills and put them in his pay envelope. "It was a good night, son. A packed house."

Antonio had played a mixture of ragtime and classical. It was a compromise he didn't mind making. He'd enjoyed it. He'd relished the applause. God was blessing Antonio's plans at last.

"I…uh…I was wondering. Mr. Cox told me I would work all week. Should I come back the same time tomorrow?"

"No." He slapped the envelope into Antonio's hand.

He swallowed hard. "Earlier then? Should I come by and check?"

"I wouldn't if I were you." He started to turn away. Luigi growled. "Your dog seems a bit aggressive. Move along. Your work is done here."

Antonio put a hand on the man's arm. "You didn't like my playing?"

The man lifted Antonio's fingers from his navy suit sleeve. "Look, you're very good. Cox recognized your talent. However, there's a multitude out there like you." He smiled. "You're a good fella. Go down to Longacre Square. Mingle with the performers there. You'll learn about new opportunities as they come up."

"But…you see, the Roman Athenaeum is the kind of place where I want—"

"You want, huh? They all want to work here. Just a bit of advice. Take it or leave it." He bent down to pet Lu who immediately jumped up and stood behind Antonio. "Or, if you want steady work you could go over to 28th Street and work as a song plugger." The manager shrugged and then disappeared into the long, tenebrous hallway.

Antonio caught a whiff of cigar smoke that nearly choked him. He left the theater thinking about his options. Tin Pan Alley, they called it, the place where sheet music was produced. Antonio cringed to think of working as a plugger, someone who plunked away at a new tune the publisher was pushing to sell. There was no art in that job. No applause or lingering enjoyment by listeners. "Come on, Lu. I need work, so off to Longacre Square we go. We'll skip Tin Pan Alley for now." Papà wouldn't have liked Antonio roaming around the nocturnal city like this, but he wasn't here now and there was nothing else Antonio knew how to do to pay his rent. His father hadn't taken anyone's money. He couldn't have. There was never any extra. If it weren't for the mystery of his father being at Cooper Union, Antonio would have dismissed those crazy notes. However, since his father had been there, there was obviously something he kept secret. He glanced at his watch. Still several hours before the bank would open.

Luigi trailed after Antonio as he paced down sidewalks intermittently shadowed by shop awnings. The businesses themselves were locked up tight for the night, but there was plenty of light spilling onto the street from saloons and billiard halls. Men and women wearing stage powdered faces passed him by, accompanied by normally attired folks. Actors and musicians he assumed. This was the part of the city where they lived and lolled while waiting for work. The Beach, some liked to call it, as though waiting around was akin to a holiday. It wasn't. To be beached meant you were always out here and never inside a theater working.

He drew in a breath and the smells of ale and cigarettes accosted his senses. Pausing to listen to a singer practice an aria, Antonio thought about that moment of quiet before a curtain is lifted, the time when both audience and performers inhale in anticipation. The revelry out here was lacking that sacred moment, that specialness he craved. Why had God teased him by only seeming to answer his prayers?

He continued on. The agents also hung out in this area. Those leeches whose only employment consisted of taking money from starving artists for setting them up with theater managers.

He paused and leaned against a cast iron pillar framing a shop entrance.

"Is that the Victor dog, Nipper?" A man with a cane came trotting up to him from across the street.

"Looks a bit like him, people say." Antonio replied. "His name is Luigi."

The man pursed his lips as he stared at the dog. "I thought for a moment, sir, that the dog was looking for a new job." He laughed and stroked his white beard. "He is about the same size, although his ears are different. Probably his demeanor is what reminds people of that advertisement. Are you looking to get him into an act?"

Lu turned his whole body away from the man and stared at nothing on the wall.

"No, he's not a vaudeville act, sir. I'm not either."

"Pity. What are you, then?"

The diamond pin in the man's lapel told Antonio this was not an ordinary grubbing agent. He was a successful one. How much cut did he take in a deal? "I'm a musician."

The man groaned. "Accordion? Fiddle? Guitar? Listen, son, there's not much call for that in today's theater, not unless you've got an animal act to go with it." He tried to pet Lu, but the dog inched away from him.

"I am a pianist and an organist up at St. Anthony's."

"Well, good evening to you, young man." The agent marched off, waving to a group of men waiting outside a gentleman's league.

Antonio looked down at his dog, who whimpered. "He'll be off smoking cigars in a velvet room and forget about you. Don't worry. They'll be no vaudeville act for my dog."

That sent Lu's tail wagging.

Antonio and Luigi kept moving down the sidewalk. "We'll stop into an all-night cafe for coffee and a biscuit, what do you say?"

Antonio had never gone searching for employment before. So far his work had come from referrals and now he realized how much he preferred it that way. He paused to gaze up at an electric sign. Glass bulbs spelled out *New York* in letters that arched like a sun peeking over a horizon. Underneath it spelled *Burlesque Ballet and Varieties*. The architecture of the building resembled a fine theater, but those gaudy light bulb letters suggested otherwise.

The overwhelming thought that he was more out of place here than he'd been on Mulberry Street swam in his mind. Burlesque, from the Italian word *burla*, a parody, a joke. What had he lowered himself to?

He clicked his tongue and Lu jumped up. They approached the massive structure of Hammerstein's Victoria Theatre at the corner of 7th Avenue and 42nd Street. Variety theater was everywhere, and that was good for musicians and actors alike, but the times were changing, or so the newspapers kept saying. Moving pictures would take over someday. Maybe these pictures would swallow up variety shows and burlesque ballets, but not concerts and operas that had been around for centuries. Definitely not. We would always have Tchaikovsky, Mozart, Strauss, and Wagner. So long as there were European opera houses and music academies, there would be music performed in front of audiences. Oh, how he longed to study at Oberlin, where folks understood the beauty of a well-performed piece of music and also the value of a well-rounded education, like Papà had wanted for his only son. Song plugger? Not him.

The Fourteenth Street Theater was probably his best bet. He'd go back and talk to Mac. But first coffee for himself and a treat for his dog. He was near the construction site of the new Times Building. Despite the crowds still on the street, the walkways were dark and treacherous, so he had to pick his way carefully. He lifted Luigi and carried him beyond a pile of lumber and bricks until his feet hit sound pavement again. At the rate they were building in this city, there would be no more room for people.

It was not difficult finding an open cafe in this district of late night theaters and vaudeville, but finding one with an open stool was quite another matter. After placing his dog outside of two cafes and then coming right back out again when he found them too crowded, he finally ducked into a corner cafe called Healy's and sat on a stool where he could see out the window and keep an eye on Luigi.

He ordered coffee. Putting his elbows on the bar, he closed his eyes. Voices drifted to him from a nearby booth.

"Honestly, Viola, if you take a break from plays now you'll cost yourself a lot of earnings."

Plays? He wondered if he was overhearing a conversation with the famous actress Viola Allen. Women weren't normally admitted in saloons, and this place was more tavern than restaurant. She had to be someone famous to garner such an exception.

He turned just enough to get a glimpse. A man in a striped shirt and suspenders was talking to a woman. She outdid him in elegance, wearing one of those French evening gowns, the kind with flowing, frost-like skirts. The bodice dripped in lace, as did the sleeves.

Distracted by the grumbling in his stomach, he glanced up at the man tending the bar. He should get something more substantial than a biscuit. "Hard boiled egg, please." It was all he could afford.

The man barely moved.

He had to get something for his dog. "Two, that is. Thank you." Antonio hoped he had enough in his pocket to cover the bill. No wonder this place had open tables, what with the prices he saw written on a board above the bar.

"If you want a meal, we have a dining room in the back."

"Uh, no thank you. Just coffee and eggs, please. Do you mind if I have it in here? I can see my dog out there." The place was virtually empty.

"That will be fine, sir." He glanced quickly at the lady and then back at Antonio. "She will only be here a moment."

"Doesn't bother me," Antonio said.

The barman huffed. "It is not *your* sensibilities I'm concerned with. See that you mind yourself while a woman's in the room."

"Of course." After the man left behind a door, Antonio couldn't help but observe what was happening nearby. A man approached the booth where the fancy woman sat and she left with him. The other man waited just a moment and then rose to throw some money on the table. He must have felt Antonio staring because he turned to him. "Beautiful but temperamental."

"Are you an agent for performers, sir?"

The man took the stool next to him and chuckled. "Oh, no. Nothing of the sort. I'm an author, of short stories, but don't look so worried, son. She's more likely to show up in one of my tales than you are, or at least her attitude is. Sydney Porter's the name."

"Pleasure to meet you." He wasn't sure why, but at that moment he remembered Mrs. Adams's father, the short story writer she'd dedicated her library to. "Have you heard of a man named Marty Gallagher, who wrote under the name Luther Redmond?"

The man smiled and accepted a cup from the waiter although Antonio had not seen him order anything. "Who hasn't?"

Antonio told him about the charitable library and about Hawkins House.

"I'm all in favor of benefaction, my son. Now tell me your name. What brings you here tonight?"

"Antonio Baggio." He extended his hand. "I'm a struggling pianist, I'm afraid. Trying to get to Oberlin to continue my studies."

"Oberlin? That's in Ohio, right?"

"Yes, have you been there?"

The barman interrupted them to bring Antonio not only his coffee and eggs but toast and sausages, as well.

He held up a hand. "There has been a mistake."

The waiter smiled for the first time. "Anyone who is a friend of O. Henry is a friend of this establishment. No charge at all."

Antonio reached for his wallet. "But I must insist. I pay my own way."

The man seated next to Antonio held up his palm. "Please, it's my treat for allowing me to bend your ear."

"Thank you, Mr....Henry, is it?"

"Just Sydney is fine. Go ahead and eat."

Antonio dug in.

"Ohio, you say?"

Antonio nodded.

"Indeed, I've recently come from that state. The people there were...shall we say, most hospitable. Oberlin is a fine choice, if you like the Midwest. Nothing like New York, though, where you can meet people late at night at a cafe and have a conversation. Very Twain-like, that Ohio, isn't it?"

"I don't know. I only know about the college." Antonio felt so at ease with the man that before he knew it, he'd told him the story about his father. Tiredness, or perhaps anxiety, had been loosening his tongue lately.

"Nasty business what goes on in this city sometimes. My condolences and sympathies." He waved the barman away when he tried to bring him a scotch. Cupping his coffee between his hands, Sydney leaned over the bar.

"Let me tell you something, Antonio." He cleared his throat and straightened his neck the way an actor would before beginning his lines.

And then he talked till the sun went down
And the chickens went to roost;
And he seized the collar of the poor young man,
And never his hold he loosed.

Antonio wasn't sure if he might have just bared his soul to a drunken man.

"From a poem I wrote a few years back. You will have to tell me, young man, if I talk until the chickens roost. Sometimes I am unaware of the possibility that I might be becoming a bore."

"Not at all. Please, continue."

"Thank you." He twisted his hand in the air as though he were about to take a bow.

Antonio swallowed the last bit of egg and toast and tipped his head forward to hear over the banter of a group of men who had just entered.

"A writer, you see, has to be an excellent observer of human activity. He has his ear to the wind during every party and in every conversation on the train and in the street. This is not rude eavesdropping, you understand. It's much more important than that. If he does not do it, how else will he create characters that charm and intrigue and stimulate the modern reader?"

"I suppose you are correct." Antonio slipped the uneaten shelled egg into his pocket. He would need to make his apologies and get back to Luigi soon.

"I'm glad you agree. Then you will not think less of me when I tell you that due to my keen observation I may know just the man who could help you."

Antonio set his water glass back down on the rough oak surface of the bar. Here he was as removed from The Bend as one could be, and he meets someone who knows something. "What did you hear, Mr. Porter? Something about my father?"

The man chuckled. "Call me Sydney, son, or I might be tempted not to tell."

"Sydney." One of these monikers—Henry, Porter—was probably correct. The man obviously used a pen name. Like Annie Adams's father. Like Dolly at The Fourteenth. He tipped his chin to show he was listening.

"Now, Antonio, I am not in the habit of…well, ever since I returned from Ohio…uh, from Honduras for that matter, I do not put myself in situations where anyone will think I'm doing anything unscrupulous."

Antonio stiffened. What did he know? "Please, if you have knowledge about how or why my father was shot, tell it."

"I wish I could, but I know nothing about that."

"I thought you said—"

"I said I knew someone who could help you. Help you get into Oberlin, or concert halls. Shucks, as Twain would say, maybe both."

"Oh." Antonio swallowed hard, embarrassed that he'd guessed incorrectly. Of course the man, an artist of words, would be more interested in Antonio's musical aspirations than his personal troubles. "Who might that be, sir?"

"A benefactor." He pulled a scrap of paper and a pencil out of his pocket and grinned. "A writer must always be prepared. In fact, I've written several stories right over there in that booth."

Luigi barked. Through the window in the dim lamplight Antonio could see some street urchins teasing his dog with a stick, boys who should be in bed at this hour.

The author scribbled something on the paper. "I live in a section sometimes dubiously referred to as Genius Row. It's really mere red brick row houses on Washington Square South between Thompson Street and the 5th Avenue el, a place where musicians, artists, and writers dwell. One man in particular is in residence there for only a short time. This man, Paderewski, is a concert musician. You've heard of him?"

Antonio had. He was quite famous. "He is Polish. Just performed the American debut of his opera last year. I wish I had the funds to attend his concerts. Solo recitals. No one else sells tickets to a solo performance, but he does it to great success."

"He gives very few, as I understand. I have had the pleasure of meeting him through an acquaintance. Here is his New York address. As I said, he is in the city at the moment. You should go see him because an opportunity like this may come only once in a lifetime."

Antonio glanced out the window again. Luigi was holding his own. "I don't think the man would see me." Certainly not without someone to make introductions. "And I don't see why he should."

"I happen to know, my keen observations you understand, that he endorses aspiring young musicians. He supports them with cash. A charitable sort, like that library you were telling me of." He held out the paper.

Antonio stammered. "Uh, why, if I may ask, would you, a stranger an hour ago, want to help me?"

"Because someone assisted me once. Take it from a middle-aged man with more life experience than you, son. If you don't grasp the brass ring when it comes around, it could be forever out of reach and you'll be left with regrets. No one wants that." He lit a cigar. "And besides, strangers are just friends you haven't met yet. Wouldn't you agree?"

Antonio thanked him, took the paper, and hurried outside.

17

SOFIA COULD NOT CONTROL her yawns as she worked in the dim corner that had been assigned to her. It was not that she hadn't been tired on other days, but the darkness and lack of conversation with co-workers made the work especially wearisome. She glanced over her shoulder. Mr. Richmond was watching her much too closely. If she hadn't won the design contest that the management had promoted for seamstresses, he would have fired her already. She needed a plan, a way to make herself so valuable to the company he would never be allowed to dismiss her. But today was not a day for plans. Mamma and Serena, her long lost twin, consumed her thoughts, making concentrating on her work extremely challenging.

She focused on the leather sole in her machine. Work was essential. She had to keep her head about her. When the whistle blew Sofia rose from her chair and stretched her back. A boy collected her work while Mr. Richmond looked on. She smiled at him even though he glowered at her.

When she got to the cloakroom, she found Maria. "Last night I brought books I borrowed from Hawkins House to English school and my teacher said we could bring in any American or British reading material we would like to practice with, so long as it did not come from the Free Library on Mulberry."

Maria whispered. "What's wrong with that place? My younger sisters go to a sewing club there. They are teaching them so they can get jobs better than working here."

"The teacher believes the evangelicals over there are trying to convert us. In any case, I've been practicing my English with books I got from Hawkins House. You should come by, bring Luisa Russo."

Maria's dark eyes widened. "I should bring her. She spends too much time over there, listening to conversations."

"Oh, she is not happy at home."

"I suppose that is it."

They walked outside and toward the trolley. "Mr. Richmond is worried about a worker's strike even though there has not been one yet in this company," Maria said.

"Strike? You mean walk away from our jobs?"

"*Sì.*"

"I could never do that." As much as she didn't like the man, she would have to assure him she was faithful.

Sofia hurried toward Mulberry Street. She wanted to catch *Signora* Russo before her husband came home, maybe even talk to Luisa. Between them, they had to figure out how to convince

Papà to get Mamma the help modern American medicine could offer.

She shooed the tabby cat away from the interior stairs leading to the Falcone rooms. "I have not been away that long," she said to the cat in English, out of the strange notion that cats living in America listened to you better in the native tongue. Joey did it, too. Edging the cat to the side with the tip of her boot she mused about how cats, whether they knew what you wanted or not, made up their own minds about when to move. When she got to the door, a thumping sound came through the walls like someone knocking a chair against the baseboards. "*Signora* Russo?" Sofia put her hand on the doorknob just as it turned from the other side. She let go as Carla Russo opened it.

"Oh, Sofia, your Mamma...I just don't know—"

Sofia pushed the door wide. Mamma sat on the edge of a chair, thumping her head against the wall.

"Stop it, Mamma!" Sofia tried to urge her away but the woman kept doing it, each time with more force. A trickle of blood appeared at her temple.

Carla ran for a pillow and placed it between Mamma's head and the wall and after two more thumps Mamma stopped and hung her head toward her lap.

Sofia could not get her mother to meet her gaze. She looked up at the healer.

"She is despondent, Sofia. My herbs and tinctures cannot help with this."

A sour burn rose in Sofia's throat. "We will take her to the hospital. Papà will just have to accept it. I will work extra shifts."

Sofia and Carla worked together to bathe and dress Sofia's mother. They left her head uncovered because she complained of a headache and wailed whenever they brought a scarf near. "I have money for a cab," Sofia offered.

Carla sucked in a deep breath. "Good, because I cannot go with you."

"Oh, please. I need help."

Carla's deep shadowed eyes spoke of more worry. Her husband, most likely.

"All right. Go home. But please stop and tell Gabriella where I've gone. She and the children can wait here for Papà."

Carla helped her find a cab and guided them inside. "Go with God," Carla said, shutting the door of the carriage.

"Bellevue," Sofia told the driver. No matter what it cost, Mamma would have the best care.

But once there, to her surprise, they were directed to a waiting room filled with people who coughed, gagged, cried, and even bled in plain sight.

"There are not enough nurses for all these immigrants," a woman in a pressed white uniform told her when she complained.

"But my mother is not ill, not like that. She does not have…" Oh, how she despised it when her English failed her.

The woman looked at her over her wire spectacles. "Are you saying your mother suffers from, shall we say, an unstable mind?"

Sofia nodded.

"You do not belong here, my dear. I'll have an orderly give you directions."

She returned to the hard wooden chair next to Mamma. A serene looked passed over her mother's face as she watched some children playing with a top at their mother's feet. At least there had been no more wails or complaints about her head. Sofia's presence did not seem to bother her mother anymore. Papà had been wrong about that. He'd been wrong about a lot of things.

They waited quite a long time as people moved in and out of the room. Mamma seemed entranced by them and hardly acknowledged Sofia. Perhaps this was the only treatment she needed, to go out among other people, folks who had not come from Benevento.

Sofia tried to relax. The sun was getting low, casting waving fingers of light across the floor. Papà would be coming home soon and hearing from Gabriella that Sofia had defied him. Sitting there with nothing to do allowed Sofia's mind to wander. She thought about Pope Leo who had died last month. An account of his last days had been printed in the *New York Times* and Claudia had read it to her on lunch break. The article mentioned how his mind betrayed him in his last days. He'd seen someone in his room who wasn't there. He'd acted afraid. These were signs that he was on his deathbed. Mamma had seen things that weren't there. She'd been afraid. *Please, God. Do not take her. I need her.*

Maybe Papà wouldn't come, but if he did he might not know where the orderly had taken them. She returned to the nurse at the desk. "*Mi scusi.*"

The nurse frowned. Sofia had fallen into Italian by mistake. "I…uh, where will the orderly be taking us?"

The woman had a puzzled look.

"My mother." Sofia moved to the side so the woman could see Mamma waiting in a chair along the opposite wall.

"Oh, certainly." She rose and disappeared behind a door. When she returned a man, also dressed in white, followed her.

"Come along," he said. "We will begin the assessment for Ward's Island."

"Where?" Perhaps she had misunderstood.

"Ward's Island. You said your mother is mentally unstable, yes?"

"Uh, no." Sofia grabbed her mother's arm and urged her down the hall to the foyer where they descended the steps and left the building. They would have to walk home. Papà would shout the roof off their building, but Sofia could not worry about that right now. After what Claudia had said, and the way the nurse looked at her, she knew she could not take Mamma to such a place. But when they were away from the distraction of the children Mamma had been watching, she began to fade like dying embers. As Mamma's mood became more agitated, Sofia noted a change in herself. The lonely feeling of isolation crept up her arms to her neck. If only she had her twin with her. Someone. Gabriella was entirely self-absorbed, and her brothers were working so much they hardly even noticed their mother's decline.

"No!" Mamma wrenched away from her and ran down an alley.

As Sofia rushed after her, she realized that while her shoes gave her greater visibility and protection from muddy, muck-filled streets, they were no help when it came to hurrying after a disturbed woman bent on escaping her. "Wait! Help!" She shouted, quite naturally in Italian. But she was nowhere near Mulberry Street and no one bothered to help her.

It was getting dark and Mamma was leading her through a labyrinth of alleys. Shadows faded into garbage cans, boxes, and alley cats so that she couldn't tell what was what. She held to the corner of a brick wall. *Where was she?* She called out again.

Voices came from the windows and fire escapes. Nothing she could decipher. Someone grabbed her arm. Surprised, she cried out. A beggar held out his palm. She pushed past him, dark thoughts swirling with the fading light. She should never have left the hospital. The danger to Mamma on the streets was probably worse than what the doctors had planned. She shouldn't have let Claudia spook her with stories.

"Mamma? Please, where are you? Mamma!"

As she rounded the corner and crept into the depths of an alley behind a stable, she heard a scuffling and people yelling in English.

"Get out of here! 'Tis a mad woman if I ever saw one."

Mamma!

But it wasn't her. A woman in a long black cloak was handing something toward the people who cowered back as though she offered the plague on a platter.

"God's Word. It's free. Take it."

Sofia approached her and accepted the book she held out, hoping that in return she would help look for Mamma. "My mother, have you seen her? She is not well. She ran…" Sofia caught the woman's eye, hoping her pleading look would say what she was having trouble expressing.

"Oh, my dear. What is the trouble?" The older woman wrapped an arm around her, shielding them both as they turned away from the others. "Whatever it is, you will find the answers right here." She pointed to the small black volume.

"No!" Sofia smacked it against her palm in frustration. "Did you see my mamma?"

"No, dear. Is she lost?"

Sofia's chin trembled. The two of them hurried out of the alley toward the street. They approached a carriage. A policeman stepped out to meet them. Tall, imposing, but with a kind expression. The woman gestured toward him. "Sergeant McNulty, this woman is in distress."

Sofia glanced around, doubting the New York police would care to search for a lost immigrant woman.

"Tell him what your mother looks like, dear."

Sofia struggled to find words.

The kind lady inclined her head toward the tall man. "Go on. You can trust this man. He attends my church."

"My...mamma," she spurted out.

"Has your mother gotten lost out here?" Sergeant McNulty asked.

"She has. She is...ill. Please help me."

He held some kind of lantern and began peering down the dark alley, shouting the name Sofia had given him.

"That will scare her away!"

He turned toward her and nodded, lowering the volume of his voice.

Sofia ran down the street, searching in window wells and behind iron fences. "Don't be afraid, Mamma!" she shouted in Italian.

"Over here." A boy selling newspapers waved wildly with his free arm.

She rushed over to him and found Mamma huddled on the sidewalk weeping. Sofia spread her arms over her mother's head like an umbrella. "Thank you," she said to the boy. She got Mamma to her feet when the policeman approached.

"I will transport you home. The police wagon is right over here."

"Sofia," Mamma whispered as they sat in the darkness, the horses trotting along at a good clip.

"*Sì*, Mamma. I am here."

A low groan emanated from deep in Mamma's throat. "I cannot bear it."

"Mamma, you can. Remember what you taught me when I was a little girl. It can't be darker than midnight. You remember that old Italian proverb? You told me that so I'd know things would get better, not worse."

"Sofia?"

"*Sì*, Mamma?"

Sofia's mother gazed out at the street lamps. "It is always midnight."

Papà was in a rage when they arrived. The policeman stayed by the door, probably wondering if he needed to intervene.

"Sofia, she could have been harmed. Killed! Isn't that right, Mr. Policeman?"

The large uniformed man took one step forward before Papà stopped him in his tracks with his ranting. Mamma rubbed her hands over her face and then retreated into the bedroom. Gabriella sat on the sofa, eyes wide.

"This is no place for her. She has to be safe," Papà insisted, stomping his foot.

"*Signor* Falcone," Sergeant McNulty shouted above Papà's rising temper. "There is no harm done. I have seen both your daughter and your wife home. Please try to remain calm."

Papà narrowed his eyes and dipped his chin. "My daughter does not live here. Please take her to her boarding house."

Sofia tried to explain on the trip back to Hawkins House, but Sergeant McNulty was driving the horse and couldn't hear her. After he helped her from the wagon, she tried again. "My papà, he wants to send Mamma away. But I am sure she will be better now. I upset her. That is why I stay here."

He turned kind, warm eyes toward her. "You owe me no explanation, *signorina*. I know Mrs. Hawkins will take good care of you here."

They trotted up the steps toward the door together. "You are familiar with Mrs. Hawkins?" Sofia asked.

"Oh, yes. My wife Grace used to be one of the girls here."

The door opened before Sofia grasped the door handle. Minnie gave her a surprised look, her large chocolate eyes widening. "Oh, my gracious. I was just about to pay the neighbor a visit to borrow a cup of brown sugar for the Apple Betty. Thought I'd get a jump on tomorrow's baking. Well, no matter. Come in, you two. What brings ya around, Mr. McNulty?"

"Just escorting this young lady home, Minnie."

"Please come in and sit down." She shook a finger at the sergeant. "Don't you be running off, ya hear? We don't see enough of you and Grace around here. I'll just pop over to get the sugar and then come right back and put the tea kettle on."

"I would not miss it," he said.

Sofia was weary and would rather go to bed than socialize but she saw Mrs. Hawkins marching down the hall toward them and knew she would have none of it.

18

Antonio rose early on Tuesday because his thoughts would not let him rest. As much as the writer's suggestion intrigued him, he had other things to attend to. "Come on, Lu. We will accomplish something today. Off to *Banca Stabile*."

Antonio did not know much about the Italian bank, just that it catered to Italians, helping them send steamship tickets to family members or wire them money. He imagined, like most banks, they also lent money. This was where the *padroni* often loitered, waiting for unemployed men to show up. As they walked up Mulberry Street, Antonio patted his dog's head. "Let me know, pal, if there are any perfidious characters I should avoid."

Lu let out a whine, echoing Antonio's own apprehension. But the lovely Sofia needed his help. Her aunt had certainly insinuated as much.

They passed a business with an Italian sign: *Farmacia Italiana*. The Italians' pharmacy. He congratulated himself on knowing that bit of Italian. Perhaps his limited Italian would assist him on this venture. He was aware that in this neighborhood he was as out of place as a fly in soapsuds. His skin was lighter and his hair not as dark as the Southern Italians. He remembered what Nicco had said. Perhaps he should present himself as wholly American.

As they continued down the street, only stopping once so a girl could pet Luigi, he paused outside another storefront bearing Italian words. A man standing in the doorway bid him to enter. "For a respite." He indicated that Lu should come in too.

"Thank you." Antonio ducked through the doorway after checking his watch and determining that he had a few minutes to spare. He shook the man's hand.

"You are not Italian, are you, sir?"

"Yes. I mean, I was born Italian but have lived in New York since I was a boy. And...I am not from this neighborhood." Whatever he had considered before as an appropriate way to introduce himself around was now lost due to his nervous tongue. He'd always believed honesty was best anyway. "Name's Antonio Baggio."

"I am Lieutenant Delfino. Please come in."

The hall was filled with empty wooden chairs. Banners hung from the walls. One read, "All For Jesus." But it was the red sign, "Salvation Army," that told him where he was despite the Italian writing on the outside windows, which must say the same thing.

The man offered Antonio a cup of coffee. "If you are not from here, mind me asking what brings you to Mulberry Street?"

"It's a fair question." The coffee tasted good. He hadn't taken time to make any for himself before he left home. "I suppose no one would come down here for no reason. Uh, not that it's not nice. It certainly is. I mean no offense."

The man chuckled. "We cannot deny poverty, son. There is no way to cover it up here. We are happy people, hardworking and proud, but no one who lives in these tenements would say it's a wonderful place."

"I suppose not."

"But as to no one coming here without reason? Ah, that's not entirely true." The man spoke with an accent but his English was very good for an immigrant.

"Oh, I understand, sir. You are here to distribute charity. I did not mean any disrespect. I have attended your doughnut fundraisers and I always drop a coin in the bucket when I see one."

"None taken. But I am happy to hear you're aware of our efforts." He raised an eyebrow. Antonio had not yet answered his question.

"I have come to aid a friend." Yes, honesty. "And to have some questions answered for myself. I need to go over to the bank, but...I fear they won't talk to an outsider."

"Just be friendly. Wear a smile. Hold your head up as though it's the most reasonable thing for you to be walking through the door. So many Americans in this city harbor morbid contempt for the Italian. They dislike the vast numbers arriving daily. They turn their ignorance to fear and declare that the Italian is of low intelligence at best and a rapscallion at worst."

197

Antonio tapped a finger on the side of his cup. "I believe that is prejudice. A disillusioned evaluation of newcomers. My friend is a good example of how untrue such perceptions are."

The man nodded his head. "If you show that you will treat them well, they will respond. In time. Be persistent if you need cooperation from the bank in order to help your friend. We have had great success reaching out to the poor here, and God bless them, they arrive in such desperate circumstances."

Antonio lifted his coffee cup. "I appreciate the advice. Perhaps you can tell me, have you heard of the name Ernesto Baggio?"

"No, I can't say I have heard that surname around here."

Lu whimpered.

"Down," Antonio ordered and Lu immediately quieted.

"Fine dog you have there, *Signor* Baggio. Well trained."

"He is a good dog, but I cannot take credit for his training. His temperament seems to come naturally."

"A loyal companion. If you and your dog ever want to join us here and become soldiers for Christ, stop by for a meeting."

"You are very kind." Antonio rose to leave. "May I ask one more question?"

"Certainly."

"Do you know the Falcones from Benevento?"

"Gabriella Falcone? She brings some neighborhood children to the reading room a few doors down. Sometimes accompanied by her neighbor, a young lady named Luisa. I can't say that I know either family well, though."

"Thank you, Lieutenant." Antonio chided himself for asking that question. The man wouldn't be able to tell him if the Falcones were in peril from a *padrone*. Still, he stored away the information about this Gabriella and Luisa in case it could be helpful in some way.

As he marched down the sidewalks, he tried his best. But an organ grinder barely tipped his chin at Antonio's greeting, and a grocer pushing a straw broom across the step of his store did not even lift his head to return Antonio's, "*Buona sera!*" He focused his eyes straight ahead. Short of faking a southern Italian accent, there was nothing Antonio could do to fit in when he opened his mouth. *Be friendly. Smile. Hold your head up.* He concentrated on Lieutenant Delfino's advice. He glanced down at Luigi. Isn't that what his dog always did? It worked for him.

Leaving Lu outside, Antonio entered the bank and stood in line behind several men, all of them with thick, black hair. They spoke rapid Italian. Many wore ragged clothes they had brushed and straightened to look as much like businessmen as possible. Several had probably just arrived from Ellis Island.

When it was Antonio's turn to approach the teller's cage, he smiled broadly. "*Parla l'inglese?*"

"*Sì.*" The man's dark eyes bore into him, making Antonio's hands perspire.

"I am looking for the *padrone*, the one who works with Benevento men."

The man huffed. "What business do you have with this man?"

"I…uh, for a friend. I need to ask a few questions, is all. Might he be here?"

"No." He motioned for the next man in line.

"Wait. When will he be back? What is his name?"

The man just shook his head.

"Please, help me. You see, my father…something happened that I do not understand. But I'm told my father was known around here, for…helping. And now my friend has some trouble. Somehow there is a connection to the misfortunes we are having. Have pity on me, won't you? I know I don't belong here. You don't want me here. But I must be heard." Antonio's words surprised even him.

A man stepped out of the queue. "The Benevento *padrone*? The man who employs Benevento men, you say? You are looking for him?"

Antonio approached him, excited. "Yes. *Sì.* Can you help me?"

"Not here, *signore*. This is an honest bank. That man is no…he is…not here. That is all I know."

"But where?"

The whole line shrugged their shoulders. Giving up, Antonio returned to Lu and slid his back against the wall until he was seated on the pavement with his dog. Those men knew something. They all knew something. Only one person was willing to tell him things, but that was in parables and anonymously. Their lips were shut tighter than a clamshell.

It had begun to rain steadily. He watched rivulets flow from puddles down to the street gutters, his resolve slipping away with the rain.

The door to the bank opened and a man walked out at a quick clip. He made a motion with his hand that Antonio should follow. Leaping up and pulling on his dog's leash, Antonio trailed the man to a bakery and then ordered Lu to wait. When he went inside he waited patiently while the man purchased something. The man spun around and held out a pastry. "*Anisette.*"

"*Grazie.*" Antonio took it and followed the man to an aisle near the rear of the shop where bins of flour were stored. "Another bank you are looking for. West one block and then north three. A small place where *Signor* Parrella recruits men. That is who you look for, *sì?*"

"I don't know."

The man cocked his head the way Luigi sometimes did when he didn't understand a command.

"No one told me his name," Antonio explained. "Perhaps if I can just ask him if he knew my father. Then I would know if he was the correct *padrone.*"

"No!" The man grabbed his arm. "I do you a kindness, *sì?*"

"Indeed. *Grazie.*" Antonio began fishing in his pockets for something to give in appreciation.

"No, no. You do not understand." He let out a frustrated breath and glanced around before speaking again. He lowered his voice. "Find out first if he is the right one. Ask your friend. You are an outsider walking on shards of glass, my friend. Take care you are not cut." He spurt out the final word as his eyes flared. "I must go."

His dog had waited patiently. "Sorry it took so long, Lu. Here, maybe this will help." He handed his dog the Italian cookie.

The unsettling visit to Little Italy had at least turned up one bit of information: a name. Perhaps Sofia or her aunt would recognize it. When he found the other bank, however, it was closed. He would have to come back.

As he prepared to board the el, he glanced down to the street below. A young woman stared up at him. When he waved, she darted off out of sight.

19

ONCE AGAIN SOFIA had needed to race to work as though wolves were on her heels. Last evening's conversation, poetry recitation, and exhibition of Grace McNulty's photographs were proper evening pursuits in an English woman's boarding house, but Sofia had been exhausted and was worried about her mother, and would have preferred to be excused. She hadn't asked, however, because she did not want to appear unmannerly. To make matters worse, she'd missed another session of night school in the process.

Claudia whispered to her as they walked to their stations. "Mr. Richmond is afraid we will form a union and if we do, he won't be able to replace us. And he should be afraid unless working conditions improve. People deserve to be treated with respect." She lifted her brows menacingly. Americans, along with the Irish and other fair skinned people, seemed so expressionless to Sofia that they were hard to discern. Just the eyes. How odd. She preferred the passion of the Italians. That she understood. No mistaking an Italian's melancholy or pleasure.

When Sofia went to her dark corner the wheels of her imagination cranked up. People could join together to convince others to do what was right. She might find a team of people to support her belief that Mamma should get proper help. She wasn't sure about a union at the factory. If things were so bad here, why didn't people leave and get other jobs? Claudia could not have been serious. Nellie Bly had not come snooping. Still, she did not like knowing that Mr. Richmond could fire her on a whim. She supposed a union could be useful.

Sofia did not see Claudia later. Sofia had been forced to work through her lunch break because her reflecting had resulted in her falling behind. When she punched the clock and readied to go home, she turned to find Mr. Richmond blocking her way.

"Miss Falcone, I have heard the rumors, as I am sure you have."

"I…uh…I do not know what you mean."

"Unions. Protesting in hopes of gaining high wages and shorter hours, which could mean ruin for the company's profits, which in turn would cause people to lose their jobs. Those Progressives even want to take away my floor boys. They are twelve years old, not six. Well capable of the work I ask of them. I will not have rebellion on my floor, Miss Falcone."

"No, sir." She knew the boys were younger than twelve, but children working to help their families was not something she ever considered improper.

"You understand that I have been disappointed in your performance as late."

"I am sorry, Mr. Richmond, but I will make up, catch up." She was unsure how to explain.

"Yes, well, come to my office. I have a little proposition for you."

"I must check on my mother. And then night school."

"I promise this will only take a moment." He took a step toward her, forcing her to turn around and walk toward the open door to the room where he smoked and shuffled through papers most of the day.

He shut the door behind them, something he never did. The door had always been open. He leaned against the desk, letting one leg dangle over the corner, and folded his hands in front of his belly.

"What do you want to tell me?" She managed to blurt out. The secretiveness of the meeting made her nervous.

"I want you to be my ears on the floor. All you have to do is tell me what the girls are talking about." He laughed. "Not fashion or gossip, mind you, just whatever they say about unions or striking or any kind of disgruntled talk so long as it has to do with the factory."

How could he ask this of her? A woman of character was loyal to family and to friends. "I do not think—"

He slid his foot back to the floor and banged a fist on his desk. "You will do this, Miss Falcone, in order to stay employed here."

She jumped involuntarily. So he wasn't asking at all. Her hands began to tremble as nippy air whisked down from the paddle fan on the ceiling.

"Besides, in accordance with our arrangement, I will see to it that you once again regain your position in the middle of the floor. You will need to be there to listen, of course. I will make sure you get an extra fifteen minutes for lunch."

"I…uh, Mr. Richmond, this is a difficult thing for me—"

"Of course it is. I will increase your pay two dollars a week. But that is just between us, you understand."

"Taking money for this?" Her head began to ache.

"All right. Don't take the increase if you insist against it. But Miss Falcone, you understand the choice here is simple, don't you? You do the job I'm asking of you, or you collect your final pay and don't come back. Those have always been the terms." He stood too close to her and touched his index finger to her sleeve, stroking her arm.

Every muscle in her body tensed. She couldn't move, though. She must not lose her job.

"There could be more benefits, my dear." He withdrew his hand. "If you handle this well, I will find more pleasurable tasks for you. You would like that now, wouldn't you?"

She agreed. She wanted him to like her. She did despise that dark corner. "I understand. But Mr. Richmond? I do not think anyone is serious about unions."

He stood and opened the door. "See that it stays that way, Miss Falcone."

As she walked away she felt as though she'd done something terribly wrong, when in fact she had done nothing but listen to her boss. If she had understood him correctly, he wanted her to give him information. There would be nothing to tell, but by being agreeable she hoped to save her job. He had touched her, though, and she had not wiggled away. Thoughts of that house of ill repute she'd stumbled into and the man who had forcibly accosted her came rushing back like a bad dream.

Out of breath when she reached the Russo's apartment, she paused to regain her composure before entering the building. Joey found her there.

"Sister, I thought you had to stay away. Papà should not find you here."

"He doesn't want me *inside* the apartment. I want to talk to the healer. Is she back at her home now?"

"She is." He turned to walk away.

"Where are you going?"

"*Banca Stabile.* I need to see the *padrone.*"

"*Padrone?*" She remembered her aunt's rambling, a warning about a *padrone*, the man who finds work for Italian men for a price. She'd heard rumors that the cost was often equal to being enslaved. Not only do you pay a fee, but you pay for transportation to the job, buy food from the company store at inflated prices, and even pay to have your clothes washed. At the end of the day there was not much left, and some were even indebted to the *padrone* and the company they worked for. "You do not want to do that, Joey. Do not work for that man I saw with you the other day. Some of those bosses are not fair and take advantage."

He hugged her. "Some, but not all. I will be careful. You were right, Sofia. I should find steady work." He smiled and waved as he left her.

She shouted after him. "Maybe you should try the Free Library. *Signor* Arrighi sometimes helps men find work. You know, where the children go sometimes. Luisa is always over there. She likes it." It would be better for her brother to be converted to another religion than to be enslaved. She didn't know if he heard her but she had to hurry. She turned and rushed up the stairs.

20

AFTER ANTONIO AND HIS DOG returned home and finished breakfast, Antonio realized Lu was staring at him.

"I know. I should go look for Uncle."

As he completed shaving, he realized he had hardly considered the suggestion the author he'd met had made, although he had kept the name and address, just in case. A benefactor was a long shot, though. Antonio wasn't good at imposing himself. If the man had come to him it would be different.

He turned to his Bible before heading out the door and read in Psalm 10: "Thou art the helper of the fatherless." He shut the book. He wasn't sure what help he had. He didn't seem to have any, truly. He knew what his gift was, but for some reason God was not guiding the way. He thought a moment. He would do what he could not only for himself, but also for Sofia. And his uncle. Even if he received no help in his endeavors, he could still serve others.

He found Nicco eating scrambled eggs with five other men and two boys. He waited at the door while they finished.

"*Saluti, Signor* Baggio," the cook called to Uncle as he headed out the door with Antonio. "Stay out of trouble!"

Nicco lifted an arm, either to say farewell or mind your own business. Antonio opened the door to allow him to exit.

"Tony, my boy. What brings you to St. Anthony's mission? God bless 'em."

"Antonio," he whispered. "Call me Antonio."

They paused outside Antonio's building. "You better come inside. I think Papà had a coat you might want for winter."

The man didn't argue and followed Antonio up the stairs to his apartment. When Antonio opened the door, Luigi yelped at Nicco as usual.

"Crazy mutt." Nicco nudged Lu away with his shoe and then slouched on Antonio's bed, reaching for the accordion case and placing it onto his lap. "Your papà, he did not want you to know his business, Antonio. He did not want me to know, for that matter. So I only know a little bit, but what I know, I tell you."

"I would hope so, Nicco. I am not the neighborhood gossip. I'm his only son. Now, what is it?" He sat on the piano bench and Luigi leaned against his leg.

"I only know he visited a lawyer, the day he was shot."

"What lawyer? What's his name?"

"Now, son, do not go looking. It is not safe."

"You let me worry about that. What haven't you told me?"

Nicco's eyes filled with tears. "I do not know. If I did, I would tell you. Your papà, when he give me the accordion, he say, 'Keep this until Antonio comes home from organ practicing. Give it to him.' Then he mumbled something he thought I did not hear. Something about the Union and that high priced lawyer better be worth the dough."

"Cooper Union?"

"I suppose so, since that is where he died. I did not know what he meant at the time. I tell you the truth when I say I just remembered about the lawyer, Antonio. I forgot before." He rubbed his eyes. "I forget a lot."

"Anything else? Think hard."

"No."

Luigi sat and perked up his ears.

Antonio almost felt sorry for the man. Hard drink had a grip on him nothing on earth seemed to be able to break. "It's okay, Uncle, but if you remember something later, you must tell me." More clues. Nothing adding up.

When Nicco Baggio was sober and smiling he almost looked like a regular fellow. Hoping to encourage this state of being, Antonio invited him to go out with him. "I'll give you one of Papà's coats, a shirt, too, and you can use my razor in the washroom down the hall."

"Where are we going?" He seemed delighted. Perhaps there was hope for the man.

"Want to come to Longacre Square with me? I'm looking for work."

"Fine, fine." He scurried out to the hall washroom with a pan of warmed water.

It was early evening when Nicco and Antonio arrived at Healy's Cafe where Antonio had earlier met the writer. No sign of him now, however.

"Are you sure you can afford to feed us here, Antonio? You, out of work?"

"I am not entirely unemployed, Uncle." He would have to pay his bill this time but going to new places, like that Italian eatery he had been to in Sofia's neighborhood, could be unsettling. You never knew if you'd like the food. He preferred to return to restaurants he'd already visited.

"I remember you," the barman said, setting two glasses in front of them. "Nice to see repeat customers. What can I get you?"

Antonio noticed Nicco staring at the glass bottles filled with golden liquid lining the shelf behind the man. "Uh, mind if we take a booth?"

"Not at all. We do have a dining room in the rear, though, if you'd prefer it."

Antonio pointed to the booth where Mr. Porter had said he'd written stories. "We will sit over here."

The barman checked his pocket watch. "It's available until about nine o'clock. That's when he comes in."

"I understand." They sat and looked at the paper bill of fare a waiter brought them. There were only a few choices, but the prices would not send him to the poorhouse. Not this once. He had been paid well at the Roman Athenaeum. The entire menu was a la carte. Both of them were famished, having not had anything since breakfast and then spending hours searching for piano engagements. Antonio decided to order two pork chops, the vegetable d'jour, and bread.

"Mighty nice of you to bring me here," Nicco said, still eyeing the bar.

"We will not be drinking. Just coffee."

Nicco looked down at his hands. "Of course. Coffee's fine." He was perspiring.

"Here." Antonio handed him his handkerchief. "It is hard for you, isn't it?"

Nicco lifted his head with an expression that was a mixture of grimace and grin. "I am fine. Do not worry about me."

Antonio chose to redirect the conversation. "Looking for work took much longer than I expected."

"*Sì*. Well, my boy, you did find work." Nicco lifted himself from the seat to lean over and pat Antonio on the arm.

"I did." With Mac again. He prayed it would last awhile.

"I just hope those fellas don't come around when you're there. God himself only knows what they want." He chopped at the air with his hands. "Are you sure you have to go over there?"

"I will be fine, Uncle."

"When we first come over, many years ago, we worked in that neighborhood, me and your father. Of course, there were not so many Southern Italians then. It was not bad. I was younger. More vigorous."

"And then the drinking?"

Nicco gazed at the corner of the ceiling behind Antonio. You do not lock eyes with a man when you are feeling guilty.

"Uncle, if you just try to be more diligent. I mean, God will help you if you try to help yourself. Stay out of the saloons.

Give up begging and rag-picking for beer money. You know I will help you however I am able."

A lone tear rolled down Nicco's cheek. He ignored it. "I will tell you, although it is my shame. You are my only family. You should know, now that my brother is gone." He held a hand to his heart. "I could not keep working. I was not well. But I owed the *padrone* still. The reason times were very hard then, the reason your father never took a day off? He repaid my debt. It took a long time, but he did it. He paid it free and clear. There is a receipt at the bank. Those Benevento men know it, too. They had the same arrangement. We saw them at the bank those many years ago. I remember it because I went with your father, so that he could vouch that he was doing this in my stead and it was paid off. Afterward, we drank ale with those others. At an Irish pub, I think it was, McSorley's.

"Truly? Why there?"

"I don't recall now, but I tell you the truth, I have not been there since." He chuckled. "I remember your father was miffed with me, but it was only one pint. I confess, Antonio. Only one."

"I see. Well, my father was a good man to pay off your debt."

"He was, God bless 'em. And this is how I repay him now? I am a miserable gutter rat." He mumbled under his breath. "Hobo. Bum. Drunkard. What people say is true."

"No." Antonio reached for his uncle's arm, but the man pulled away. He thought about how he had enjoyed what people said about him—talented, gifted, blessed. Words float over people's heads sink into their minds and remain, good or bad.

Nicco wagged his head. "But…our companions that day were Benevento men. And those who asked after you at the theater? They are, too. Some things I forget, but this I remember." He sucked in a sob. "I would pay Ernesto back today if I could. But I can't." His eyes brightened. "But I can get sober, Antonio. For you, Antonio."

"I would like that very much."

The waiter brought their meals. Thick pork chops smothered in gravy, creamed peas, and generous slices of bread smeared with butter and garlic. They ate in celebration. It was a new start.

21

"She is gone, Sofia."

"Gone? Where?"

Carla Russo stepped out into the hall to talk to her. Apparently her husband was at home but Sofia didn't care. How could the healer leave her mother?

"Your father took her to Bellevue for an evaluation. I think it is for the best. She is so bad."

"No." Sofia grabbed the woman's arms, shaking her before she realized what she was doing. The fear in the woman's eyes made Sofia release her. She drew in a deep breath to calm herself. "*Signora*, please. I tried to take her there myself. They would not help. They just wanted to cart her off to a terrible place. You must tell me. When did they leave? I must go right over there."

"No, child. You know *tua famiglia* has no money. If you can't pay and you are that bad, they send you to an asylum. But we light a candle. Together. Let's go." She turned and looked at the closed door to her apartment and then led Sofia down the stairs.

Sofia was happy to not be alone as she struggled to find options. Hopefully, Carla Russo accompanying her would not come at a cost to the woman's safety.

As they made their way to the church, Sofia considered how she should pray. Prayer might bring clarity to her thoughts. There had to be something she could do. God would hear her, but would he answer? Her mother was gone. Gone. People rarely come back from places like Ward's Island. As desperately as she'd tried to hold on to her mother, she hadn't been able to.

When they knelt together at the altar, all Sofia could do, even while clutching her rosary, was to reel at God. *You've taken my twin. You have the half of me that I will never get back. Must you take Mamma, too?*

She sensed a presence at her side, opposite of where Carla Russo knelt beside her. Another parishioner had joined them. Sofia felt comforted when people were around her. A complete circle always felt the most secure. Prayers said around her made her feel as though God would be more disposed to answer.

A sense of peace, the feeling she usually had when she came to the chapel, radiated from her and even the fingertips of her usually cold right hand warmed. She ended her prayer and crossed herself. Not wanting to disturb the person next to her, she waited a moment to allow whomever it was to leave the altar before her.

Carla Russo touched her arm. "Are you ready? Shall we go?"

Sofia opened her eyes and nodded to her. She turned to her right. No one was there. She glanced behind her and saw no one leaving the railing.

Sofia and the healer parted ways outside the church. "Just remember," *Signora* Russo told her, "you cannot help what has happened. God will provide."

Sofia said she understood, but she didn't. There might have been something she could have done when her sister died, something to prevent her from running after the wagons. And now there might be something she could do. For Mamma.

Sofia rode the Third Avenue el to Bellevue, hoping either Mamma was still there or they could tell her where she was taken. When she at last was directed to the ward where Mamma was being seen, she spotted her father sitting in a metal chair in an area designated for waiting family members. She rushed to him. "Papà, what has happened to Mamma?"

He lifted his head, smiled briefly, and then resumed staring at the tiles on the floor. "There is not enough room for her here, Sofia. There is too much consumption, too many insane patients. They say they are building more hospitals, but how does that help us? Those with consumption stay. The others, like your mamma, must leave."

"Do not let them send her to Ward's Island, Papà. We will take care of her at home. The healer and me."

"No." He stood and straightened his coat. "What must be, must be. She will be sent to the state hospital ward. I have been waiting for the papers to be prepared."

"Papà, no. You do not know what it will be like there for her."

His face reddened, his posture stiffened. "You are the one who does not understand, Sofia. Your mamma, she is not as she was. We must accept this. The doctors will help her. In America, they have arrangements for people who cannot pay. We cannot care for her any longer at home."

Sofia's chest ached. Her head swam with worry. "Accept this? I will not. I can't, Papà. They will not help her!"

He put a hand on her back and they walked to the stairs. "Go home now. Our home. You do not need the boarding house anymore."

"I won't go there." She forced the words through clenched teeth. "I will not so long as Mamma is not there. Where is she now? I want to see her."

"They have taken her to a ferry to go to the asylum. It is on an island in the river. I am waiting for the clerk, but your mother is on her way there."

Sofia pulled on his arm. "Papà, no. Please don't send her there. Nellie Bly put it in the newspapers. It is a terrible place. Everyone says so."

He whispered into her hair the way he had done when she was a small girl and upset over losing a coin or having a friend move away from the village. "Your mamma is in a terrible state. So terrible. God will send an angel to watch over her, *mi figlia*. Go on, now."

As they left the saloon, Antonio and Nicco strolled down the street in good humor. Men do not need alcohol to enjoy themselves. He hoped he had proven this to his uncle. When Antonio noticed a directional sign across the street illuminated by a street lamp, he realized they were not too far from the address the writer had given him, near Washington Square. Thinking he might as well stroll by just to see if someone wealthy enough to be a possible benefactor might live there, he steered his uncle down 5th Avenue. As they approached some red brick houses, music floated on the air, piano music worthy of Carnegie Hall. "What's that?" Nicco looked around, not understanding what had halted Antonio in his steps.

"Beethoven's 'Moonlight Sonata.'"

A crowd began to form around them. Antonio closed his eyes to listen to the master.

"You can play like that," Nicco said, shoving him with his elbow.

"I do not think so, Uncle."

"Sure. I've heard you play that exact thing."

"But not like that. Do you not hear the beauty?"

Nicco grumbled and shuffled his feet.

"Will you stop that?" Antonio held on to his arm. "Close your eyes. Concentrate only on the music." Antonio did just that. The artistry he heard was breathtaking. The sound made him feel weightless. It stirred him. Then the music stopped suddenly before morphing into Chopin. This was a practice rather than a performance but the only clue had been the change of pieces. The playing was flawless, smooth, and mesmerizing.

"Move along," someone shouted from behind. A policeman came marching up to the crowd from the direction of Washington Park, blowing his whistle and shattering the magic, the dream, into shards of words and shouts. There should be a law against that.

Antonio glanced up at the windows. Most were shuttered so he was able to spot the musician easily. A man with a mad mop of red hair leaned out the window and shouted to the bystanders below. "Thank you for attending my practice. Do come again!" Then he disappeared back into the room.

Paderewski seemed amiable enough, but Antonio would not bother him simply because a writer who had had too much to drink had told him to.

As they walked home, Antonio encasing Nicco's arm in his, he felt his uncle tremble from withdrawal. Staying off the sauce would not be easy. He almost pitied him. "You are doing fine, Uncle."

The man's words slurred just a bit even though he'd had nothing to drink. "I...Tony, you hear the master...you hear that fellow's playing in your mind when you perform and all will work out fine."

If only that were possible.

As they neared the mission, Nicco broke free. "I will stay here."

"But, Nicco, you are fine with me. You do not need to. I can make up a bed for you."

Nicco shook his head and plodded up the cement steps, leaving Antonio alone on the sidewalk. Nicco turned before he opened the door to the mission. "Hurry along and take care of that mutt of yours."

22

SOFIA COULD BARELY CONCENTRATE on her work. Even though she was once again cocooned within the nest of sole makers in the center of the large workroom, her heart ached for her mamma. She counted the hours until her shift was finished, planning to head directly for Ward's Island. They would have to let Mamma leave with her. Where they would go, she didn't know. Sofia was not used to going against Papà's wishes, but this time she had no choice. He was not listening to Sofia or even trying to consider her opinion. So she would have to do the things she knew to be right. Sofia could not be sure Mamma would submit to leaving with her but she had to try.

Flinging a finished sole down on the top of her pile, she strengthened her resolve.

"Daydreaming again?"

Sofia turned to find Mr. Richmond hovering over her. "No, sir. I am working."

He leaned down and whispered into her hair. "In my office as soon as the whistle blows."

"But—"

He spun on his heels, ignoring her protest. How would she explain to him that there were matters of critical urgency that overruled his worries about a strike, something that was not going to happen in the first place?

She jabbed a needle into the end of her thumb. "*Ai!*"

"What is the trouble?" Maria called out from behind her machine.

"Nothing." Sofia squeezed her thumb inside her apron and prayed it would not bleed so much as to cause her to have to change. It was too late in the shift.

"You have hardly said a word," Claudia complained, wiggling a bit in her chair next to Sofia.

"I, uh. I have been focusing."

"I hear that you have become Mr. Richmond's favorite. That for some reason he has decided to prefer you." She examined Sofia's pile of soles. "Very nice work." She inclined her head toward Mr. Richmond's office. "Be warned, he doesn't care about his workers."

Impatient, Sofia resuming her sewing. "Do not worry, Claudia. Everyone knows your stitching is superior."

The girl grinned and turned the wheel on her machine. "I am happy you think so, but I am trying to help you. Don't be blinded by the promise of more pay."

"What are you talking about?" How on earth could word about their arrangement have gotten out already? "I did not accept more money from him."

"So, he offered, didn't he?" Claudia blew out a breath. "That humbug."

"Stop it," Maria cut in. "She is more worthy of respect than most."

"I didn't say she wasn't." The crimson-haired girl, smug as though she was privy to information—and of course she could not be—shrugged her shoulders and counted her own day's pile of soles. Sofia thought the girl's estimation of her own value as an employee was inflated. No one's job was completely secure. That was the nature of business. Sofia had come from a hardworking family that understood there were no guarantees in life.

Sofia darted into Mr. Richmond's office seconds after the dismissal bell rang. "Should I punch my card first?" she asked as he began to close the door.

"No. This won't take long. What did you find out?"

"Nothing, sir."

"Don't play games, Miss Falcone."

"I...uh, I am most serious. No one is talking about a strike."

"I don't believe you." His face turned tomato red.

"Truly. Please, I have to leave promptly. My mamma...she is not well. I have to go to her."

He stood with his back against the door. "It's that Claudia, isn't it?"

"Who?"

"Come now, Miss Falcone. The little redhead beside you. She is firing everyone up, isn't she?" He grunted and swore under his breath. "A hardheaded carrot top. If she wasn't such a good worker...well, don't think I am completely bamboozled."

"Completely what? I am sorry. I do not understand this word. And carrot? What do you mean?"

"Never mind."

She tried to push past him but he held on to her wrist.

"You should learn English, Miss Falcone, if you're going to stay in America."

"I...uh, I will. I do..." He held her too tightly for her to get away.

"I know what they say about me out there. But I am much nicer than I look."

She could smell licorice on his breath. She'd often seen him eating the candy but had never before been so close she could smell it. "I must leave, please."

He cupped her cheek with his palm. "I am quite the pleasant fellow once you get to know me."

"Yes, sir. May I go now?"

He flung the door open. "All right go. But know that I am watching. The girls need to make me happy if they are to stay employed."

Happy? He wanted something more than information. Sofia would keep sidestepping as long as she could.

She rushed out of his office, hurried to the clock, and got in line behind the last two girls to leave. Brushing away the strands of hair that had tumbled loose from her bun, she considered the feasibility of quitting. She could find another job. Papà wouldn't force her to stay, not if he knew what her boss was like. But she would never tell him. God only knew what he'd do if he knew how Mr. Richmond treated her. She didn't want her father sent to Sing-Sing while her mother wasted away on Ward's Island.

Before she left the sewing floor, she glanced back to her station. She was now nearly in the very center, a position of esteem. She turned toward the corner where Mr. Richmond had placed her earlier, a lonely location where her fingers had grown numb along with her mind. There had to be another choice besides staying safe or becoming an outcast.

She headed north on the el, wishing she had time to petition Father Lucci to join her. She didn't know how late hospitals allowed visitors so she wanted to go straight there. Anxiety built with each squealing rotation of the train's wheels on the metal track. She would much prefer a companion on this journey. If her twin had lived, she would have come. But, if Serena had not died, none of this would be necessary. *Oh, God. Did I cause this?*

Her urgency would not be satisfied on the el. The ride was exceedingly slow. At irregular intervals, and not at the scheduled stops, the train halted and the passengers had little choice, if they didn't care to walk, but to wait. The attendant had told her where to get off, as close to 116th Street as they would go, near the north end of Central Park. Dusk was not far off and she still had a long way to go. She gazed out the window the best she could. A fine film of dirt and soot cast the city in a dull light. She bit her lip and focused on the announced stops. Tears began to sting the corners of her eyes and when she willed them away her eyes overflowed all the more.

She had not been aware of the man next to her until he spoke. "Miss?" He held out a handkerchief and bobbed his head, indicating that she should accept it.

"*Grazie.*" She did not even bother to speak English.

"You may keep it." He stood at the next stop and exited.

Sniffing, she tried to summon an image in her mind, a map of where she was.

"St. Mark's. Tompkins Square," the conductor bellowed.

She leaned forward to get the attention of a woman seated in front of her. "What number street?"

The woman turned. She was dark complected, like Sofia. She would understand her difficulty with English. The woman pinched her lips together as though trying to remember. Finally, she shrugged her shoulders and blurted, "Ah. Eight. Maybe nine."

Sofia moaned and leaned back in her seat to rest her eyes. Much later she heard the conductor shout, "Central Park." She had nearly missed getting off. At some point she knew the train would end but how far that was and at what distance from her destination, she couldn't guess, so she was pleased she hadn't dozed for the entire trip.

She exited and rushed down the iron stairs behind others whom she assumed had only been visiting or shopping in the lower part of the city and were now on their way to their colossal dwellings. Here, everyone was dressed in fine clothing and spoke smooth English with no hesitations. She had never felt so foreign in America, not since stepping off the Ellis Island ferry in Battery Park.

After some searching, she finally found a street sign. "Sixty-fourth Street?" She hadn't missed her stop. She had gotten off too soon! She stepped in front of an elderly couple about to cross the street. "Central Park?" she asked, unable to keep her voice from warbling.

"Just a few blocks west," the man replied, curling his wife's fingers over his right arm.

"Please, wait. I am…looking for…" She swallowed hard. "One Hundred Sixteenth. Is that not close to Central Park?"

The man chuckled. "Indeed, but Central Park is vast, my dear." He exchanged looks with his wife. "Perhaps you would care to share a carriage with us. We are headed that direction."

Sofia nodded, fully aware that the change in her pocket needed to get her back to Hawkins House. She had to get to her mother, though. That came first.

She sat across from the couple, nervously jingling the coins in her pocket. She knew that sixty-four was less than one hundred sixteen, and with paper and pencil she might be able to calculate how far they had to go, but what a carriage ride cost, she didn't know.

The elderly woman cleared her throat. When Sofia looked up the woman asked her name.

"Sofia Falcone."

"Well, I am Amelia Whitfield and this is my friend, Mr. William Price."

"Please to meet you," Sofia said, the echoes of her night school teacher's instruction meeting her ears. So the couple was not married. They were acquaintances, like she and *Signor* Baggio. Another person who might have helped her had she taken the time to ask.

The woman, face pale with chalky powder, smiled like a kind Italian *nonna* might, calming Sofia's anxiety just a bit. "Might I ask where you are headed out here alone, Sofia?"

"The ferry to Ward's Island."

"Ward's Island?" The woman began waving an ornate paper fan about although the evening was cool.

"Are you perhaps an employee at the hospital there, my dear?" Mr. Price asked.

The woman sighed as though that would explain everything and she no longer had to worry that they had given a lift to a crazy immigrant girl.

"No. They have taken my mother there, but she is not mad."

"Oh, dear. I have heard of such things." Amelia Whitfield quickened her fanning. "I do hope you get her home soon, dear."

"*Grazie*. Uh, thank you, *Signora*...uh, Mrs..." Was she married? Sofia's stomach turned with the realization that her poor English inhibited her ability to be polite to these people who were quite sympathetic toward her.

"Just call me Miss Amelia. That's how all the young people refer to me."

The man interrupted. "I am afraid you won't be going over to Ward's Island this evening, Miss Falcone. The ferry doesn't run this time of day."

A tear ran down Sofia's face as frustration gripped her like a vice. "I see. I will take the train back. How much do I owe...for the carriage, *signore*?"

"Nothing at all, my dear. Are you sure you can find your way?"

"I can. You are so kind." Emotion choked her voice.

"There, there, child. I am sure your mother is fine," the woman said, waving as Sofia left them.

She walked to the 116th Street dock anyway, just to get a glimpse of the place where her mother was. The dock was deserted. She wandered around but she supposed the boats had been locked up somewhere beyond the rope blocking the way to the end of the dock. It wasn't like she could row over anyway or, then, having done so, convince the hospital staff she herself was sane enough to warrant a visit with one of their patients.

The buildings on the island in the river were not far, she could see them clearly. But in the absence of a ferry, the place they had taken her mother to seemed as distant as the moon. A smell of fish and murky water turned her stomach. It seemed America smelled rank on every street, making her miss the Italian countryside and hills. The streams and seashore back home held sunshine and warmth, despite the fact that when they lived there Mamma had still drifted into a seasonal melancholy. In Italy, however, she had always risen from it. Now, here, the hope that she'd get better was sinking with the sun.

Sofia made her way to the train. She was a penny short but a kindly man paid the rest of her fare. He offered her a small book, which she could not refuse after the kindness he'd shown her, and then he moved on to the back of the car and struck up a conversation with a Chinese woman.

In the fading light, she studied the English words in the book. The small numbers among the letters told her this was a Bible very much like the one on her nightstand that the stranger in the alley had given her when she was looking for her mother. She glanced out the window at the dim buildings rushing toward her as they traveled to the southern tip of Manhattan.

Was God out there? She felt the smooth binding of the Bible in her lap. Or was he here in the gift of a stranger at the moment she'd felt the most alone?

23

ANTONIO DID NOT WAIT until he fed Luigi to examine the piece of mail he'd picked up at his post office box. He did, however, check his pocket watch. An hour before show time at the theater. He ripped open the envelope from Oberlin College and thumbed through the pages of a general catalogue containing information on tuition and courses. He sat on his bed to study it and his dog jumped up beside him. "Hey, Lu. There is an elective course for organ now. It must be a sign." He flipped through the pages until he found the fees. He gulped, sweat forming at his collar. Five dollars a week for room and board. A year's tuition plus room and board was estimated to be approximately $500. Way beyond his means, and that was only if he completed an acceptable recital, proved that he was of good moral character, and met a few other requirements. He stuffed the book under his pillow. He would study it more carefully later.

There had been another piece of mail but not from the post office. He had stopped by St. Anthony's to check on the schedule. He wasn't needed this week, but the janitor handed him a note. It was from the same mysterious informer. This one he had dismissed because he was beginning to think these notes were meant to keep him off the trail. Yes, the person said he was needed on Mulberry Street, and yes, Antonio should find answers, but the note writer wanted something from him. Whatever money had been exchanged, for whatever service Papà had done for the Benevento men, there was none of it left now. This note warned Antonio away from visiting the *padrone*. Perhaps that was where he would uncover the deal that had been made and that would be the end of it. Or, perhaps the *padrone* knew why Ernesto Baggio had been shot, a conflict over something Antonio had no part in. He should go find out.

He sighed as he looked at the message again. There was no time now for a visit to Little Italy. He had to report for work

When he got to the theater, Mac waited in the hallway. "Finally, my lad."

"What do you mean? I'm not late." Even under the dim electric sconces, Antonio noticed something different about the man. "What's wrong with you, Mac? You look like someone's been handing out free gold dollar coins."

The theater manager spoke toward his open office door. "He is here now, gentlemen. Thank you for waiting."

Gentlemen? Not the thugs, apparently. Before he could ask, the writer referred to as O. Henry burst out of the room. He gave Antonio such a big smile that Antonio wondered if they were all inebriated.

"Come to see the show, Sydney, because I have to warn you, it's—"

The writer held a finger to his lips. "I've brought the master to meet you."

"What master?" Antonio looked at his watch. "I go on in ten minutes."

He glanced up to see a man with a shocking mass of red hair fill the doorway. Antonio looked back at the writer. "You don't mean…"

Mac cleared his throat. "Mr. Paderewski would like to speak with you, Tony."

Antonio nearly dropped his sheet music.

The master pianist waved his long fingers toward the room. "Come in, son, and sit down a moment. The manager can do without you for a bit, can't you, sir?"

"I'll say I can."

They stared at Mac a moment until he seemed to realize he was no longer needed. He scrambled down the hall toward the seamstress's room.

Sydney leaned against Mac's desk and motioned for Antonio to sit on one of the chairs while the famous musician took the other. "I hear he is quite talented, a young ragtime pianist," Sydney offered.

Paderewski crossed his thin legs at the knee and nodded toward Antonio. "What are your aspirations, son?"

"I…uh, I do not intend to keep playing vaudeville. It pays the bills, you understand."

"I do indeed. What would you like to do? If there were no boundaries, no obligations you are honor bound to fulfill, what would you be doing, Antonio Baggio?"

He gave no hesitation. "I would be playing the organ or the piano in concert halls for a multitude of people. I want my music to bring pleasure, not just passing entertainment. I want people to feel something when I play."

The musician laughed lightly. "Isn't that what we all want? Even you, Sydney?"

The writer returned the laugh. "I suppose so, although I want to make enough money with my stories to be able to enjoy the lifestyle to which I have become accustomed. Which reminds me, we are expected at the club for a drink."

"In due time, man." The master musician turned to Antonio. "Are you following these dreams of yours? Are you doing anything to see them come to fruition?"

The sounds of laughter and bawdy music drifted down the hall. "I am trying. I would like to audition to be admitted to Oberlin College in Ohio, sir."

"Oberlin, you say?"

Antonio nodded, feeling his throat grow dry.

"You do not wish to stay in New York?"

"It's not that. It's just that my father, he's passed away, wanted me to go to get a well-rounded education."

"I see. Your father was a wise man. I was in London earlier this year. Have you ever been?"

"No, sir."

"The world is a big place, son. New York is the largest city in this country. There are many opportunities here."

"Yes, I understand."

The older man turned to the writer. "The Academy of Music? Can't he go there?"

Sydney shook his head. "It's vaudeville now."

"The National Conservatory of Music?"

Sydney pinched the bridge of his nose as though thinking was painful. "I would imagine they'll be closing their doors the way things are there."

Paderewski drew in a breath. "Well, most unfortunate. With all the wealth in this country, who would have thought?"

"I am sure there are plenty of schools," the writer noted.

Antonio bit the inside of his lip.

Paderewski pointed a thin finger at Antonio. "This man is set on Oberlin, and it's a fine school, I dare say."

"If you like Ohio," Sydney added. "Personally, I do not."

Paderewski waggled his head. "This is not about you. I tell you what, young man. Let me hear you play tonight. If I am pleased by what I hear, I would like to help you out, introduce you to some concert musicians, see if you can learn something while you are here in New York. I want to see if I can convince you to stay, not because I do not like Oberlin, not at all. It is a long way off, however. Because you live here, you should see what opportunities are in this city first, in my opinion. Following them could lead you to places like London, Brussels, and Paris. But I'm getting ahead of things. I must see for myself how talented and dedicated you are. If you are willing."

He stood and Antonio jumped to his feet. "Thank you. It was a pleasure to meet you. Your invitation to speak with you has been a great honor." He had no idea how to perform for a man whose practicing had earlier brought Antonio close to tears of joy. It seemed wrong, that man being here in this place. Like a nightmare of sorts. And Antonio had to go to Oberlin even if someone of Paderewski's talent believed otherwise. Even if he judged Antonio as not having the ability for

Oberlin. Surely the will to do something could supersede shortcomings. He hurried to the stage, praying that Mac had had the piano tuned that morning.

Antonio's stomach clenched. Why Dolly now?

He arranged his music, shifted on the piano stool, and readied his fingers, telling himself that if folks liked his playing before, he need do nothing different now. He let his fingers hover over the keys while he whispered a prayer. *Just let me do what I know how to do, and do it to the best of my abilities.* He drew in a breath, wondering if his prayers were wasted. He was probably not offering them in an acceptable manner but he had little time.

He remembered scarcely worrying after that. His music brought him to a place of enjoyment, shutting out the world around him, even Dolly.

24

"WHERE HAVE YOU BEEN, LOVE?" Mrs. Hawkins fussed over Sofia, claiming she would catch a terrible cold if she didn't hurry to shed her rain-soaked clothing.

Sofia said as little as possible as she went to her room to change. She met Aileen, her roommate, in the hall.

"Well, don't you look like a drowned rat."

"Hello to you, too." The two of them had teased this way since Sofia arrived. They did not see each other much because of Aileen's job as a nanny, but somehow they shared a sense of humor that Sofia found a delightful momentary escape from her worries.

"Come on, I will help you out of those clothes. The sisters are in the bathroom, cutting each other's hair."

"Cutting? Why?"

"I don't know. They say it's what modern American girls do. I've no need to be a modern American girl." She rolled her eyes.

Before long Sofia was attired in one of Aileen's nightdresses. She seemed to have more than enough to share.

Aileen sighed as she drew a brush through Sofia's long tresses. "Never cut your hair again. 'Tis your crowning glory, Sofia. So shiny and black."

"I cut it when I started at the shoe factory, thinking it would be easier to manage, but I was wrong. I wish it were thicker, like my sister's."

"We all wish for hair different than we have, but yours is so shiny and dark. Very pretty, lass."

Sofia tried to smile but sadness hung over her like a heavy brocade curtain. "They have taken Mamma away. I tried to get to her, but the ferry had stopped for the night."

"Where?"

"Ward's Island."

"You poor girl. No wonder you look like you've been wading in the East River." She tapped Sofia's shoulder with the brush. "You haven't, have you?"

"No." She couldn't even laugh at the joke.

"As soon as she gets better, she will come back. Annie, my cousin, you know the library lady?"

"*Sì*, Annie Adams."

She tied Sofia's hair with a blue satin ribbon as she spoke. "She had to go away to a place much worse than that when we lived in Ireland. And look at her today. She survived, and she's more congenial now. I don't know, perhaps that place even helped her. She was angry about it, of course, but some people need a doctor's care away from home to get better. You'll see. Your mamma will be fine."

"Aileen!" A shriek sounding as though someone had been attacked came from the doorway. They both stood with a jolt and Aileen dropped the brush to the ground. Mrs. Hawkins marched in and picked it up. She pointed it at Sofia's diminutive roommate. "You are never to say such things in this house. That 'laundry' was no place for Annie, and you'd be well advised to remember that."

Sofia didn't know what this was about, but her own fears for her mother's safety escalated with each word her landlord spoke.

"Do not speak of things you haven't experienced, Aileen."

"I am sorry, Mrs. Hawkins. I only meant to assure Sofia. I didn't want her to worry."

"There are legitimate reasons to be concerned sometimes, young lady. You treat such matters too lightly." She sat on the edge of Sofia's bed to face her. "Excuse me, Sofia, but Aileen has broached a painful subject with me. Love, what has happened with your mother?"

"They took her to Ward's Island, and as soon as the sun comes up I am going there to get her back. Papà? He will not listen to reason. He says he cannot pay for doctors. I am going to stop giving my earnings to him so I can use it for Mamma's care." It was a bold idea, and one that rattled Sofia's mind so much she had to grasp onto the bed frame to steady herself. But she would not be swayed, *l'ordine della famiglia*—the order of the family—or not.

Mrs. Hawkins reached for Sofia's hand. "Oh, my. Your mother is worse, then?"

Sofia nodded.

"I will go with you."

"No, I can go myself."

"Of course you can, love, but at times like this our concern for our loved ones can cloud our reasoning. You need someone with you to clearly hear what the attendants have to say about your mother and to help you make proper arrangements."

"I am not assuming to bring her here, Mrs. Hawkins. I will convince Papà—"

"Now, now. We will sort all this out tomorrow. That is, if you will consent for me to assist you. I am perfectly willing."

"*Grazie.* I appreciate your help."

"Well, then. I will make you some lavender and licorice tea. That will help you rest." She rose and folded her thick arms in front of her bosom. "Tea calms the nerves and mind." It was as though she was trying to settle objections no one had made. Mrs. Hawkins paused at the door and turned back. "And I will telephone Mr. Richmond's residence and let him know you will not be able to report for work tomorrow."

Sofia gasped. "He will give my job to someone else."

"Oh, no, he won't. Don't you worry. I will convince him it's an emergency. I have plenty of experience dealing with my boarders' employers."

Aileen piped up. "Oh, that's a fact. Mrs. Hawkins certainly gave our Kirsten's boss an earful. That's the girl that was here before you. She was in some awful trouble. And Grace, she married the fine police sergeant, Owen McNulty. She was in some trouble too when she lived here and Mrs. Hawkins always came to her rescue, so I hear, it was become I came over."

"That will be enough, Aileen."

Aileen bit her lip. The woman she called The Hawk was forceful yet soft at the same time. On occasion she seemed to be trying too hard to be a matriarchal substitute for the girls. Sofia had a mother and didn't need another.

The Hawk lifted her eyes toward the ceiling medallion. "Watch your tongue, Aileen. Make sure everything you say is kind and helpful."

"Yes, ma'am."

"I will get the tea now. Minnie has the night off and she is staying with her cousin in Jersey. Let us proceed to the parlor, ladies."

Sofia sighed. No Minnie meant no coffee. She even preferred the Falcone's weak black tea to the stuff Mrs. Hawkins brewed, but she would be gracious and get it down with plenty of milk. Once downstairs, Sofia fluffed up the sofa pillow and positioned it next to her to wait.

Sometime in the night Aileen shook Sofia awake. "Don't you hear that, now?"

"What?" Sofia sat up as Aileen went toward the window.

"'Tis a gully washer as I've never seen before. We've had floods, but not rain this hard. 'Tis as if the water pipes in heaven burst."

Sofia rubbed her face and then listened. Rain was indeed coming down in sheets. "Go back to sleep, Aileen."

Aileen crawled back beneath her covers. "Makes me happy I work uptown. Down here, the water creeps over land so often that one of these days I'm sure Lady Liberty herself is going to come knocking on Hawkins House's door."

Sofia giggled, thinking about the statue. "She doesn't have a free hand, as I remember, so don't worry about her rapping on the door."

Some time later Sofia was awakened again, but by Mrs. Hawkins. "Get up girls, we've got to do some bailing."

"What?" Sofia tossed off her covers. The rain was pelting the window so hard she thought it might break.

The landlady held a lantern and wore her gardening boots. "Throw on your workaday dress. This will be a dirty chore. We've got at least half a foot of water downstairs already. The other girls are gathering the buckets and mops. Skedaddle, now."

Sofia and Aileen sprung to their wardrobe and chose linen skirts and cotton shirtwaists. They tied on their oldest boots and rushed downstairs. Leena and Etti were in the hall. There was not room for them all so Sofia and Aileen stood on the stairs. Water covered the sisters' ankles. The effort of scooping up the muddy flooding was futile because more rushed in under the door and through the jam. The reek of stagnant river water struck Sofia's senses like smelling salt. The beautiful parlor and the carefully polished staircase were being ruined. No matter how fast they bailed, they could not stop it.

"Grab what you can save," Mrs. Hawkins shouted. "Thank the Lord the library's on the third floor where the books will be safe."

Sofia picked up a chair, delivered it to the second floor landing and then returned. When dining chairs were secured, she and Mrs. Hawkins lugged the woman's favorite overstuffed chair up the steps. The Hawk had to rest in it a moment before scrambling back down to wade through the waters again and gather the quilts from her bed and Minnie's. Soon they had the lightest furniture, Mrs. Hawkins's sewing basket, a pile of magazines, and a book or two stored in the crowded upstairs hall.

"Everything else should weather all right, save the rugs. Those will have to be replaced if this doesn't cease soon."

"Are we safe here?" Aileen asked, looking at the door that led to the library.

"As safe as can be," Mrs. Hawkins sighed, holding a hand to her heaving chest. "Thank you all for your hard work."

Leena shivered as she held a lantern aloft. Her now short stringy yellow hair stuck to her face and her sister's looked no better. Her eyes were wide, her face pale. They did not seem to have lived through flooding before. Sofia had. Her home in Italy near the river flooded often. They were so accustomed to it that they hung their chairs on the wall. But, of course, the rivers in Italy were much cleaner and smelled more of spring water than fish. And this much flooding? She had never witnessed a rainstorm like it. There was one comforting fact about floods that she could share.

"The water will recede," she told the others. "In time it will slither back like a fox to its den. Water knows it does not belong on land or in houses and it will go back. We just wait."

Mrs. Hawkins pressed her fingers together. "You are right, Sofia. Let's take the most important things on up to the library, girls. Just be careful of the books. Don't drip on them."

Sofia grasped the back of a chair.

"No, not that, love. It's just furniture. We need it, yes, but it's replaceable. Bring whatever books you have, your Bibles, your rosary, Sofia." She turned to Etti. "You and your sister, get the tapestries your mother sent over with you." When they turned toward their tasks she shouted one more order. "And photographs. Get your photographs! Oh, dear. I've forgotten Harold." She rushed down the steps.

Sofia was about to offer to get the portrait of the woman's long dead husband for her when she saw Mrs. Hawkins slip on the bottom water-logged step and fall face up.

"No!" Aileen slipped past her.

The sisters dropped their crates and papers drifted into the air as they hurried to help.

Etti and Leena sat in the water while Sofia held the woman's head in her lap. "She's out cold," Sofia said. She tapped her palm on the woman's left cheek. "Check to see if she's injured."

Leena examined the woman's limbs. When she laid her ear to the woman's chest she waved an arm. "The missus, she does not breathe."

"Quick, roll her to the side." Sofia helped the girls push the plump woman so that any water blocking her air would run down her face. Mrs. Hawkins was pale, her chubby arms flopping like a rag doll.

"What do we do?" cried Etti.

"Thump her on the back," her sister ordered.

Dread encircled Sofia like a bad omen. She made the sign of the cross before putting an open fist between the woman's shoulders. She smacked the unresponsive woman firmly then held her opposite hand over Mrs. Hawkins's mouth to check for air.

Nothing.

The room seemed to freeze in time. *She can't die. Please forgive me for not wanting her to mother me.*

Sofia thumped again. And then a third time.

Etti began to cry. Aileen gasped.

Once again Sofia struck the woman, but this time with more force. Water spurted from the woman's mouth and nose. They urged her to sit up. After a couple of coughs, Mrs. Hawkins blinked her eyes. She was going to be all right.

"What happened?" Mrs. Hawkins brought a hand to the back of her head. "Oh, dear. I've fallen." She turned slowly toward Sofia. "Whatever you did, love, was the right thing. I am fine now."

"Are you sure?" Leena asked. "Should we get your friend, the doctor?"

"No, love. Not with the tempest brewing outside. I am fine." She rubbed her face. "Don't worry."

Etti continued to pat the woman's hand.

"Should we move up to the third floor now?" Aileen called from somewhere behind the others.

Mrs. Hawkins allowed Sofia and Leena to help her to her feet. She toddled a bit. "I suppose we better. I'm dandy. Just had the wind knocked out of me for a moment. Now try not to worry, lovies. As the Irish say, 'There's no flood that doesn't subside.'"

Sofia's hands shook. She had never before thought about how fleeting life could be.

"Let's start moving things up, girls. Mind the books, and don't get anything wet near them. Oh, yes, I was about to get Harold."

"I have him," Aileen shouted, holding up the framed image of the man in military uniform. She handed it to Sofia and whispered. "Time I started showing the old woman I really do care about more than myself." She moved toward the kitchen, hollering over her shoulder. "I will get a piece of meat from the icebox for your head, Mrs. Hawkins. Off with you. I will be up shortly."

Mrs. Hawkins held her hands to her cheeks. "Aileen! What kindness. All you girls make me so proud."

Once the five of them were settled in the library, Mrs. Hawkins in a leather chair, the sisters on a settee under a window, and Sofia and Aileen on a pile of quilts against a bookshelf, Sofia could not stop the tears.

"What's the matter, love?"

Sofia looked past the Shakespearian bust on the top of the bookcase toward the window where rain beat against the house driven by a howling wind. "I am happy you are all right, *Signora* Hawkins."

"I am fine. You kept a cool head in crisis, love."

"My mother. The asylum is on an island. What will happen to her?" Her voice trailed off in a sob that even she had not anticipated.

Mrs. Hawkins waved a hand in the air. "Aileen, fetch that map over there, would you?"

Aileen glanced around. "That?" She pointed toward a glass case against the wall.

"Indeed. The map of Manhattan. Bring it to me, please. And come over here, Sofia. I want to show you something."

Aileen went to the case, which looked something like a window mounted flat on long table legs. She lifted the top and drew out a flat sheet of paper. When Sofia looked at it on Mrs. Hawkins's lap, she noted three large letters at the top, an English word she knew: MAP. Mrs. Hawkins drew her index finger underneath the words that followed.

"As you can see, this says 'Map of New York City.' Now along the left side here is the Hudson River."

"The rest of it looks like wee window panes," Aileen added.

"Streets," Mrs. Hawkins said. "See this dark line here? That's the elevated train track. And over here, the East River. If you follow that north…" She pushed her finger upward. "There. Ward's Island."

Sofia stared. The island seemed even farther from the tip of Manhattan where they were than she had imagined.

"Look carefully, love. See the land so close on either side? Ward's Island is protected. They shouldn't see as much flooding as we'll have down here. That's my estimation. So, no reason to worry."

Sofia felt her shoulders droop. "In the morning I am going to her."

Mrs. Hawkins struggled to her feet. "Anyone hear from Annie and Stephen?"

Aileen shook her head. "I will check, if you'd like."

"No. The door up here to their residence will be locked and I think it's best we don't go downstairs in that mess right now. I will knock."

She wove her way through the book stacks. Sofia heard her rap firmly on the opposite wall. She had forgotten the lady librarian lived in the adjacent house.

"Haalooo?" Mrs. Hawkins shouted. "Are you quite right over there?" She knocked some more. She was a strong woman and even after the accident she'd had downstairs she had no trouble making herself heard. Not even the rain beating against the roof could drown her out.

A few moments later voices drifted from the eaves. Aileen hurried over. Sofia heard the librarian's voice, stronger now that the door had opened. "We are fine, Mrs. Hawkins, Aileen. Everything all right over here?"

"Indeed, love. We are planning to sleep in the library tonight. You don't mind?"

"Not at all. Do you have everything you need?"

After they assured her they did, Annie told them she and her husband were fine in their extra third floor bedroom.

"The baby has even settled his kicking for the evening so there is hope I can rest."

The door shut and The Hawk and Aileen returned to where Sofia and the sisters waited.

"I...uh, I meant to return the books she gave me," Sofia said, feeling guilty.

"She is not concerned about that, love." Mrs. Hawkins handed Sofia another pillow. "Try to get some rest, girls. Let's all make a bed for the night."

Some time later, Aileen shook Sofia. "'Tis morning, wake up."

"Morning?" Sofia rubbed her eyes and looked at the window. Little light streamed in and rain continued to coat the panes.

"Aye. The sisters have left for work. Mrs. Hawkins says to wake you. The downstairs is flooded but she is determined you and she will get over to Ward's Island."

"And you are dressed already?"

"I am off to work as well."

Sofia rose and gathered up the quilts. "I am sorry I slept so long. What time is it?"

"Only now seven. You will have to skip breakfast. Here, I snatched some apples from the scullery." She handed Sofia one. "The stove's not working. Leave everything up here. 'Tis storming still and we might be spending another night with the books."

Just when Sofia and Mrs. Hawkins were about to go out the front door, the back door slammed opened. Leena and Etti had returned. "Streets are flooded, missus," Leena said. "Trains not running. Wagons stuck. Cannot even walk on some of the streets."

Sofia glanced from them to Mrs. Hawkins. "I have to go."

"It does not sound wise, love. We won't get very far. They did not."

Sofia ignored her and hurried out into the street. Water the color of caffè latte flowed past like a stream. Surprisingly, there were people out and about, trying to get by. She dismissed the calls for her to come back. She slopped through, grabbing on to the side of a slow moving wagon as she walked. She would likely ruin her prize-winning shoes, but she could make another pair. She had to get to Mamma.

When she arrived at the el station she learned the sisters had been correct. Transportation in lower Manhattan was slow moving, if available at all. Rain pelted her so hard it stung.

Defeated, she waded back toward Hawkins House. Her heart sank with each step.

Sofia's thoughts raced to Sister Stefania and The Most Precious Blood Church. They were in the basement. She turned and headed toward Mulberry. The Second Avenue el was fairing a bit better, so she was able to get back to her neighborhood.

25

THEY'D HAD A GOOD RAINSTORM last night, something Antonio didn't normally worry about, but it was still raining hard so he decided he should check on his uncle. He whistled for his dog and put on his Macintosh.

Outside the streets were flooded but still passable.

"Much worse at Battery Park," a passing newsboy told him.

"Stay out of the basement window wells," Antonio hollered after him.

Lu didn't like the rain and lashed out at it as though it were a rat he could frighten away.

"Sorry, pal. I should have left you at home. As soon as we find Uncle, I'll make coffee and get out that bone for you that I saved from last night's supper."

He hoisted his dog under his arm and dashed up the steps of the mission. He found an attendant mopping up near the washrooms.

The man spoke as he continued his work. "Terrible storm, aye?"

"I'll say. Everyone staying dry here?"

"Everyone that would come in. Stubborn, some of the bums."

Antonio cringed. He knew others thought of his uncle as a no-good vagrant. But he knew the real Nicco Baggio. The man who had once been a hard worker, who loved his family, and who could sing, when he was sober. He was still Nicco, under it all.

"I am here to collect Nicco Baggio." Antonio and Luigi started toward the men's quarters.

The attendant tapped a pencil on a clipboard. "He is not here."

"Did he leave?"

The man shrugged his shoulders. "I haven't seen him on my shift. Can't say when he was last here."

"So he did not spend the night in the shelter?"

The man wagged his head.

Antonio and Lu hurried outside. "Maybe he's inside the church."

He wasn't.

Lu ran on ahead and stopped outside a tavern Nicco frequented.

A ruddy, bearded bartender wiped a glass with a rag. "Haven't seen him in a week at least."

"Come on, Lu." The dog lagged behind as the rain pelted them. Antonio could imagine how much it must hurt a dog Luigi's size. He scooped him up and cradled him under his Macintosh. "I'm worried, Lu. We better keep looking."

Lu licked the raindrops off Antonio's hand as the shower slowed to a soft patter. "Thank God." Antonio pushed back his hood and sloshed through puddles, looking behind alley trash bins and inquiring of men standing in front of small fires.

"Ask Paulo," one of the men suggested. "You'll find him in the alley behind St. Anthony's rectory. The priests give him bread. He knows everything that happens in this neighborhood."

"Thank you." Antonio handed the man a quarter and Lu did his part by sticking out his nose for a rub on his head.

Antonio cautiously approached the tenements beside the church. He'd never ventured toward them before. Normally he entered and exited the church by Sullivan Street. He had told himself he had been minding his own business, which truly is something New Yorkers must do with the number of people one encountered in a single day. He had to ignore most of the corruption and unscrupulous behavior for his own safety. Maybe it had not been that way in Italy. Maybe Nicco had not been strong enough to avoid the vices, having grown up in a quiet village. But Antonio was raised on these streets and seeing only what he wished to see had helped him survive. Now he had no choice but to look the degeneracy in the eye, right here beside the church, where the poor lived. Many suffered from alcoholism like Nicco did. Antonio couldn't save them all, but he'd never even managed to acknowledge them with a nod or a smile. He knew he could do that now, though. In this neighborhood, he was not an outsider.

"Paulo?" he asked one man after another.

Luigi sniffed around, seeming to understand why they'd come there. But so far neither one of them had any luck finding Antonio's uncle.

"Why you look for Paulo?" a wizened man asked, pulling up his collar.

"I'm looking for a man named Nicco Baggio. I am told Paulo knows things."

"That's what they say, huh?" The man grinned, a wide gap exposed on his lower gum.

Obviously, this was Paulo. Who else would be so delighted to hear the compliment? "Nicco is my uncle. I'm worried about him."

"Your uncle, you say? Well, I am Paulo."

"Very nice to meet you."

"He is your uncle? Then you should know. They should have notified you, young man."

Antonio drew in a breath and snapped his fingers. Lu stood obediently at his side. "What's happened? I was working late uptown. No one notified me."

"Ah, well, the police. They have some kind of order from the commish. I listen. I hear things over at the police headquarters. In the old days you used to be able to sleep there, you know." He lifted one boney shoulder to his jaw. "Still a good place to get a hot cup of coffee."

"My uncle?"

Paulo closed his eyes a moment. "They rounded up men sleeping on the streets and took them to Ward's Island. Not me. I got away."

"Why? Nothing like this has happened before."

"Like I said, a new order or something." He held out a grimy hand.

Antonio reached deep in his pocket and drew out his money clip. He held out a one dollar banknote but drew it back when the man reached for it. "And how do I know you aren't mistaken? How do you know my uncle was taken away with the others?"

Luigi growled and Antonio did nothing to correct him.

"It was him."

"Again, why should I believe you?"

"Nicco? He is usually up at St. Anthony's? *Si?* He sings that song, uh...*There's a time in each year that we always hold dear, good old summertime...*" He coughed as he squeaked out the last note.

"Yeah, yeah. That's him. Thanks." He handed the man the money and directed Lu out of the alley. "Uncle's costing me my savings. He better straighten up this time. Let's head to the el."

When Antonio and Luigi exited the ferry onto the island, the rain began again. Antonio dared not take out his pocket watch and risk ruining it, but it was now afternoon and if he didn't take care of this quickly, he'd miss his evening engagement. He didn't expect Mr. Paderewski to return. Antonio was convinced there would be no sponsorship after the classical master heard the ragtime music. Therefore, he had to keep working to fund his education himself. If only his uncle would stop drinking.

He walked several blocks to pick up the Second Avenue el, dodging folks who scurried to get out of the rain. The streets were flooding now, dirty water rushing along the curbs as though it too wanted to escape the downpour. He sloshed on, holding Lu tighter inside his coat. The dog whimpered. "I know, I know. You'd rather be home curled in front of the coal stove. You don't even like Nicco. But we have to make the best of it."

Antonio swallowed hard as he realized he'd spoken the words he'd so often heard his father say. *I promise, Papà. I will get back to this padrone business and find justice.* If others like Sofia had also been harmed by this man, something had to be done. And just as he could no longer ignore the poor near his own church, he could not stand aside while someone else's loved one was shot down on the street.

Justice came so seldom to the hard working poor in Manhattan. Antonio tried to study the faces of those hurrying past, despite the driving rain. He'd always told himself his music was for them. For the people who came to hear him. Every time he realized his music uplifted someone's spirit, helped to bring the listener somehow closer to God, he worked harder. Surely bettering himself at Oberlin would achieve that. God would certainly agree and make a way.

A crowd gathered at the el platform. "Has the train stopped running?" he asked a man.

"Not yet, but everything else has. Better hurry on, young man, before they shut it down."

"But it's elevated. Far above the floods."

"Powered by electricity. The floodwaters will turn it off soon if the rain doesn't stop."

As if to punctuate the man's contention, a thunderclap struck overhead. Antonio hoisted his dog up to his shoulder, paid his fare, and squeezed onto a car stuffed with drenched passengers.

At the 92nd Street station, the lights flickered out and the train's wheels ground down slowly, sending a squeal of metal against metal that caused Luigi to wiggle free. He jumped to the floor at Antonio's feet and began to howl. No one could hear him, however, due to the loud groaning of the train's occupants. Antonio leaned down to hook the leash to his dog's collar. "Time to go, Lu. Easy now. Let's let the pushy folks go first."

They inched along behind others from the aisle of the car into the damp station and out onto the rain swept street. When they finally broke free Antonio was relieved to find that they were only a few blocks from the ferry to Ward's Island. When they arrived at the dock the ferry was still operating.

"A little water never hurt anyone," the ferryman proclaimed as he drew up a thick rope and waved the all-clear to the captain.

Once on the island, Antonio tried to ignore the water oozing through the seams of his leather shoes as he followed the directions he had been given toward the intoxication ward.

26

SOFIA SLOSHED HER WAY through the abbey's kitchen. Several inches of water covered the floor. No one seemed to be there. She opened the door that led to the nun's private rooms and jumped back with a shock. Standing in front of her was Stefania with a Victrola hoisted above her head.

"Are you going to hit me with that?"

"Oh, Sofia! What are you doing here?"

"I came to check on you. Have the others left?"

"*Sì.* Gone to the upstairs church. I will make you a hot drink." She didn't move, the music machine balanced on her shoulder.

"There is no electricity and too much water near the stove. Let's get you upstairs." Her aunt didn't budge. "Come along, Sister Stefania. The water will not recede tonight."

"I cannot."

"Why?"

She whispered. "The Victrola."

Sofia put an arm on her aunt in an effort to steer her toward the staircase. "I'm sure the priest will overlook it. No one wants to see it get ruined."

The sister stared straight ahead, pinching her lips.

"It belongs to the gardener's wife. Isn't that what you told me, Sister? I'll help you find her."

She nodded her head once and then shook it side to side.

"Uh...perhaps you did not have permission to borrow it?"

Stefania stared toward the flooding floorboards.

"And you do not want her to see you with it?"

"She let me borrow it once. Just not this time. I didn't think she'd mind, and I was going to ask her. If she saw me with it now, she would not understand."

"Give it to me." With some effort Sofia finally got the thing placed on top of the icebox, somewhere her aunt couldn't have reached. They were finally alone, but this wasn't the time. "Later, Sister, you will tell me about my lost twin. We will talk about it, *sì*? But later."

"She is not lost, Sofia. Jesus holds her in his arms."

After they went upstairs and Sofia was satisfied her aunt would be fine, she said good-bye.

"*Sì*, child. Go check on the family now. Just be careful."

"They are fine, Sister. They are on the third floor. Mamma—"

"*Sì*, go anyway and make sure my sister is well. She has had such terrible melancholy."

She didn't know. As much as Sofia disagreed with Papà, she still felt the order of the family in her heart and she would not disgrace Papà to Mamma's sister by telling her where

Mamma was. It had been a mistake and Sofia was about to remedy that anyway.

When she got back to the Second Avenue el she learned it was running sporadically. "Is it operating now?" she asked a woman in a waist length black scarf.

"*Sì*, now." She pushed past Sofia and scurried up to the platform.

Sofia paid her fare and settled in, desperate for the train to get her all the way to the ferry. The rain sounded like marbles beating against the car's windows. A child seated in front of her cried out as though in pain. The train lurched, the electric lights flickered, the child wailed. But they were in motion. Clutching the rosary she had snatched from her bedside table the night before, Sofia pleaded for God to keep the wheels moving.

Much later, at one of the station stops, a conductor marched down the aisle shouting instructions. "The weather has become unpredictable. You will have to leave the train. The mayor urges everyone to return to their homes or to find a place of safety."

Shouts of protest rose up. People wanted to know how they would get home if the train wasn't running. The conductor dodged the complaints by exiting through a side door and walking along the rail. Sofia rose and followed the displeased child and her mother out of the car.

"Where are we?" she heard someone ask.

"Close to 88th Street," another answered.

Sofia would have to walk several blocks, in the pouring rain, but she wasn't dissuaded. She would bring Mamma home that very night if she could manage it.

An hour later she arrived at the asylum drenched to the bone but accustomed to the dampness. A man with a mop frowned at her as she approached a receptionist.

"I'm looking for my mother, Angelina Falcone."

The woman looked up at her over a pair of oval spectacles. "She is a patient here?"

"*Sì*, yes, but there has been some mistake. I come…" As usual, she struggled with English when others intimidated her. "I have come to take her home."

"What was she brought in for?"

"I do not know what you call it, ma'am."

"What sickness?" She raised her voice as though Sofia was hard of hearing. "Lunacy? Drunkenness? A suspicion she might harm herself or others?"

"No. A mistake, I said. She is none of those."

The woman rubbed her temples. "She had to have been brought here for some reason, even if you do not agree with the doctors, miss. Now, what was it?"

Sofia pinched her coat collar closed, feeling a breeze from an unseen open window. "I believe it would be called lunacy." The words burned her throat.

"Very well. I will check for you." She returned her pen to an ink well and then clattered down the hall, her footsteps pounded with the pulse in Sofia's ears.

She turned to a wooden bench and sat down, soaked coat and all. The sound of voices near the door where she'd entered caused her to look that way.

"Not this building. The ward for men with vices is next door."

"Vices? What kind of place is this?"

She knew that voice. She rose and took a few steps toward the door. There with his little dog at his side stood Antonio Baggio. They locked gazes. "What are you doing here?"

"Sofia? Is something wrong? Is it your mother?"

"*Sì.* Why have you come?"

He hurried over to her despite the attendant's objections and the janitor's impatient sighs. "It seems they've brought my uncle here. I'm afraid he spends too much time in the local tavern."

"You have come to take him home, then?"

"Yes. And you've come to get your mother. I'm afraid a terrible storm is raging. I'm not sure if either of us will be able to get back."

She nodded. She would sleep in Mamma's bed with her in the asylum ward, then, and return in the morning.

He glanced behind at the door and then turned to her. "I have to go to another building. Will you be all right?"

"*Sì.*"

He seemed reluctant to leave. She bent to pet Luigi. "Such a fine dog. Sorry you got so wet, my friend."

Luigi leaned against Sofia and thumped his tail. She laughed. "He remembers me."

Antonio took a step back. "He does like you. I will check in before I leave. If you are still here, I'll be happy to escort you both to the train."

"You are very kind." She selfishly wished he would stay with her.

The sound of the receptionist grunting her disapproval told Sofia she'd better hurry over to the desk. "*Grazie, signore.*

Grazie." She rushed toward the woman. "*Sì?* I may take my mother home now?"

The woman glared. "You certainly may not. Your mother is in a delicate state and is scheduled for a procedure."

"A what? It was a mistake. I will take responsibility for her."

"That is not possible." The woman disturbed some papers on her desk as though she intended to return to her work and ignore Sofia.

"But I have come so far in the rain. I must see her."

Another irritated sigh. "I suppose there's no harm in you looking in on her."

As Sofia followed the woman down the hall, they passed doors with bars across the windows. Wails and cries shot through her heart like a bullet. There was no denying this was a horrible place. Claudia had been right about that. Perhaps Sofia could sneak her mother out. If only this weren't an island. Her fortitude plummeted. Of course that's why the place was built here—an isolated, lonely island with no easy escape back to the city.

They stopped in front of a door. The woman grappled with some keys on a ring. Sofia gazed around. A fire escape must surely lie beyond the door at the end of the hall. Light peered from a small window at the top, suggesting it led outside. A vicious-sounding dog's bark echoed through the hall. Sofia tensed.

"Hounds," the woman said. "For security." She shook her ring of keys. "Blasted mess of metal. The regular attendant is at lunch," she explained. "I don't know why I consented to bring you down. Should have made you wait." She got the door open and then stared at Sofia. "I suppose your emotional state made me feel sorry for you. Well, see that you don't dampen the linens on the bed. Ten minutes and then you must be on your way, miss." She tapped Sofia's arm before moving past her. "The doctors know how to handle the poor souls, child."

Mamma was lying on a cot facing the wall.

"Mamma?"

She jolted into a seated position.

"Mamma, don't be afraid. It is Sofia. I am here to take you home."

Angelina jiggled her head, her eyes wild-looking. If this confinement was intended to help, it was not working. There were no doctors. Just caretakers. No, not someone who takes care, just custodians. Mamma wasn't some stray dog that needed to be contained in a pen.

Sofia stepped carefully toward her, holding out her hands. She spoke softly in Italian. Mamma backed into the farthest corner of her cot. Sofia stopped and Mamma let out a breath. "It is all right, Mamma. I will just sit here with you." The cold metal chair sent shivers to Sofia's bones.

Ten minutes.

Sofia began to recite a rhyme her mother used to say when Sofia and her siblings were children. Mamma seemed to relax, so she repeated it over and over.

Bolli bolli pentolino,
fa la pappa al mio bambino;
la rimescola la mamma
mentre il bimbo fa la nanna;
fa la nanna gioia mia
o la pappa scappa via.

Boil, boil, little pot,
Cook the food for my baby.
Mother mixes it
While the baby sleeps.
Go to sleep, my joy,
Or your food will run away.

Mamma smiled. Then she laughed. "A silly little rhyme."

Sofia had not seen her mother coherent in some time. She did not know if it would last. "Mamma? What happened? Can you tell me what happened to my twin?"

Mamma's eyes glistened.

"Would you tell me?"

She nodded. Sofia dragged her chair closer. "It's okay, Mamma. No one will hurt you. It was a long time ago. You will tell me?"

"I chose you, Sofia."

"What do you mean?"

"That day." She sighed and glanced away, as though the memory lay beyond the locked door. "I was home alone with my twin girls." She pointed a finger at Sofia. "You were mischievous, always tearing about the house." She smiled.

Sofia patted her hand.

"One moment. In one moment. I say, 'Sofia, Serena, hold hands.' To keep you out of trouble."

Sofia could see the two of them in her mind, like a photograph. She thought she remembered holding her sister's hand in her own. She glanced down at her fingers. In her own right hand.

"You, you, Sofia…" She began to weep and keen for Serena.

"What happened? What did I do?" The knuckles in her hand cramped. She tried to rub out the pain.

Mamma shook her head.

"I did something, didn't I? I was naughty?"

Mamma's cries echoed against the cement walls.

"Oh, Mamma." Tears flowed down Sofia's cheeks. She wiped them away. "Would you like to go home now, Mamma?"

A voice boomed from the door. "She's not going anywhere, young lady. Who let you in here?"

Mamma turned her face back toward the wall.

Sofia stood. She would not be bullied. "This is my mother and I am here to take her home. Who are you?"

The man marched in. "Dr. Hansley. This woman's husband remitted her into our care. She is despondent, without proper mental facilities, but I believe with some electrical stimulation she has the potential for some improvement. But these things take time. She cannot go home now, if ever."

"What?" Sofia wanted to slap the man.

"You must face facts, miss. Your mother is clinically insane."

Sofia raised one hand. She would slap him. But the chill she could never keep at bay tingled from her fingers to her elbow so that the pain would not allow her to do anything but lower it again. "There has been a mistake, Doctor."

He laughed. "No mistake, I assure you, other than you coming out here on a day like this. I do hope you can make your way back to the city safely."

Antonio was allowed to collect his uncle after a bit of persuasion. The authorities had to be convinced that Nicco was not without relatives and a place to stay. "But I warn you," a man who called himself Master Davidson, because he was master of the house of indigents, said. "Keep your derelict relative off the streets."Nicco hung his head and hardly said a word as they returned to the building where Antonio had seen Sofia. Luigi ran ahead and scratched on the door. The janitor opened it a crack. "What the devil?"

"I've come to collect someone. She was visiting her mother," Antonio called to him.

The man nodded his head and held the door open as Antonio and Nicco tucked inside and escaped the wind-driven rain. "Worst I've ever seen it. Be glad we are not on the coast."

Antonio settled his uncle and his dog in a waiting area and hurried over to the receptionist he'd seen talking with Sofia earlier. Before he could inquire, a door slammed and Sofia came running down the hall, wailing.

"They won't let her go!" She wept into Antonio's shoulder.

"Doctor's orders," the woman at the desk said. "Now, you must be leaving. You're upsetting the patients."

Sofia sat down on the chair next to Nicco. "I am not going."

Antonio glanced to the woman who kept her gaze on her paperwork. Nicco frowned. Luigi trotted over to Sofia and lay down at her feet. Antonio touched Sofia's shoulder. "You can't stay here."

"Why not? If my mamma can lie all day on a cot in a locked cell, I certainly can wait here on this chair."

"But…what do you hope will happen?"

She covered her face with her hands. "I do not know. I should have let Mrs. Hawkins come with me."

Antonio shifted on his feet, his damp socks making him miserable. "Would you like to telephone Mrs. Hawkins?"

Sofia brightened. "*Sì.*" Her shoulders drooped. "She owns no telephone."

"Oh, I see. Well, I can't just leave you here."

"*Sì.* You can. I am fine."

The receptionist grunted. Antonio knew that if he left, the woman would throw Sofia out by the scruff of her collar. So he sat too. A few minutes passed by and then Sofia rose and went back to the desk.

"*Mi scusi.*"

"What?" The woman lifted her head, her brow wrinkled.

"I mean, excuse me. Tell me. The doctor will not perform any procedures before I return?"

The woman drew in a deep breath. "I would not know."

"Please. Can you…can you find out? Please?"

Antonio joined them. "She's come all this way. Surely you can grant this one small request before we leave?"

At the mention of them leaving, the woman managed a faint smile. As she walked away from her desk, she muttered, "I don't know why I'm doing this."

Sofia inhaled deeply. "I know why."

Antonio looked into her beautiful, weary-looking face. "You do?"

"*Sì.* I have been praying. God heard me. He may not always answer my prayers, but he hears me."

Antonio thought about that all the way home. The train wasn't running so he hired a wagon to take them back to Hawkins House. After he saw Sofia home, he and Nicco would walk back to his apartment. The doctor had agreed to postpone treatment. A miracle, Antonio thought. Sofia's prayers had been answered, at least in part. Her belief that God always heard her supplications intrigued him. Perhaps he had been going about finding his father's murderers the wrong way. Since no one felt like conversation anyway, and thankfully so, because the horse's clopping through the streets would have made that nearly impossible, he decided to whisper his own prayer. *Forgive my unbelief, Jesus. Tell me what to do next.*

27

SOFIA WOKE the next morning shivering. No matter how many quilts she covered up with she could not get warm.

"Good thing the factory's closed down for flooding," Aileen said, patting the foot of Sofia's bed. "You are too sick for work."

"I am not sick. I feel fine. All but my heart."

Aileen turned up the oil lamp. "Can I do something for you?"

"Thank you, no. I must go see my father today."

"How far?" She peered out the window to the street below. "The streets are still flooding. 'Tis an awful storm, so much rain."

"Mulberry Street. I am sure I can make my way there."

Aileen clucked her tongue. "Not a good idea when you are sick, lass."

Sofia threw off the covers and slid on a robe. "I am not sick. I just...you would not understand."

"I would be happy to try."

Sofia grabbed her hairbrush. "I get cold sometimes. It is...a matter of the heart not of the blood. I miss my twin."

Aileen sprung to her side and took the brush. "You have a twin? I didn't know. She lives with your father, I imagine. You Italians have such big, wonderful families. The Irish do too, mostly, but not me and Annie."

Sofia was not up to Aileen's blathering. She took back the brush. "I have to hurry."

Aileen was waiting when Sofia returned from the washroom. Normally Sofia enjoyed the company. She didn't like being alone in a room. Today there was too much to explain and she did not have the fervor to try.

Aileen seemed more than happy to fill the silence. "Annie and Stephen have a good start on a big Irish family. I'm looking forward to being an auntie."

"As you should."

"Are you going to tell Mrs. Hawkins you are going out again? She was as worried as a cat up a pole, Sofia. You gave her such a fright running off yesterday."

"*Sì*, I will talk to her."

Sofia found The Hawk in the kitchen placing the teakettle on the stove.

"Ah, there you are, love. You had me concerned you'd catch your death of a cold out there yesterday. Did you get to see your mother?"

"I did. She even talked to me."

"Oh, that's wonderful. The treatment is helping, then?" She retrieved two teacups from the cabinet Aileen called a dresser and then filled her teapot with the steaming water.

"They are not helping her, Mrs. Hawkins. I wanted to bring her home, but they wouldn't let me. Finally *Signor* Baggio insisted we come back."

"That young man Antonio? He went with you? It's good you weren't alone. I wanted to come, you know."

"I am sorry. I was so distraught. I went alone but happened to see *Signor* Baggio there."

"Truly? Whatever would a musician like him be doing at Ward's Island?"

"I am afraid it was required for him to…uh, he needed to escort his uncle home."

"His uncle was there, too? And he was able to bring him home but they would not release your mother?"

"His uncle was in the Inebriate Ward."

"What? That place closed decades ago. Are they taking men there again?" She pounded her fists together. "I will certainly consult with Dr. Thorp and The Benevolents. This wiping the streets clear of the poor people is ill advised. It aids no one and offers no solution."

Sofia had heard the woman talk about these people, Dr. Thorp and the committee with the odd title. They were a kind of family that didn't share bloodlines. She was beginning to understand that relationships could be formed even if you weren't born with them.

Mrs. Hawkins handed her some tea. Sofia poured as much milk in the cup as would fit.

"But he did retrieve his uncle, you say?"

"He did."

"So kind of him to see you home. I am sorry I did not realize he was the one who did so. I would have come outside to thank him."

The rain had slowed but it was still coming. Thankfully the water on the bottom floors at Hawkins House had been contained. It would take a few sunny days to dry things out completely.

"You should not have been out in the storm, Mrs. Hawkins. I am sure he understands."

"Well, now, let's ponder the situation with your mother. I am sure there is something to be done. That's what The Benevolents do, love. Give aid wherever God leads. We will get your mother the help she needs."

"No. I mean, *grazie, signora*...uh, Mrs. Hawkins, but my father will not allow it. It is a family matter."

"And we are family." She smiled and chose a gingersnap from the tea tray.

"I still do not think—"

"Do not worry a minute about it, Sofia."

Sofia began to cry, unloading the day's frustrations. "They are going to do a treatment. I mean...the doctor promised to wait, but I fear he won't. Why, Mrs. Hawkins? Why will God, who hears all prayers, not answer mine? I have been to mass. I have confessed my sins. I've said my rosary every morning and night and still my mamma does not return to me." She could not hold back the dam of emotions now that she'd allowed some of it to seep out. Her despair flowed unstopped like the gutter water outside.

Mrs. Hawkins rose from her chair and stood next to Sofia. The sisters returned from mopping the hall as Aileen entered the kitchen from the back stairs.

"What's the matter?" Aileen stroked the back of Sofia's neck.

Sofia heard the sisters' lyrical murmurs as they offered sympathy in their language. They were considerate but none of them could truly understand. They had family. None of them were twin-less twins as she was. Their mothers were not facing electric shock to their brains or, worse, an operation the doctor called a lobotomy. Sofia feared leaving her mother on that island only to return to find her catatonic and completely lost to her.

She waved away their clucking. "I don't understand." She covered her face with her hands. Why was God refusing to help Mamma?

The papers were calling the rains an epic storm of inconceivable proportion. Some even compared it to the infamous blizzard of '88. "If it were winter New York would have been blanketed in one hundred inches of snow last night," one declared. Well, Antonio was happy it was not yet winter. A blizzard shuts down theaters. A blizzard would mean several months, unproductive months, had passed and time was running out in order to get accepted into Oberlin. If he didn't get out of the city by the new term, he feared it would never happen. He would take October rains in stride knowing he had time to put his plans into motion. The prevailing thought of the musicians he knew was that whatever you were doing by age twenty-five would be your life's work until the day you died. Antonio did not want to be playing ragtime on his twenty-fifth birthday.

Nicco stirred on the makeshift bed near the stove. He'd adamantly refused Antonio's offer to take his bed. "I should be on my way, nephew. I washed up down the hall when you were asleep."

Antonio motioned for him to stay. "It's storming out. You're better off here."

"No." He rose and batted his hands at the wrinkles on his trousers. "I do not want those men to find me here. If they are watching, they will follow me away from you."

"What do you mean?" Antonio blocked the door. "No one has followed you. I went to talk to the *padrone*, but he wasn't there. I'll go back. I will get this straightened out, Nicco. You can't go out there. Look." The two of them turned toward the window where rain covered the outside panes like a clear, liquid curtain.

"Who do you think took me to that island, Tony? They knew you'd come after me. I am a worm on a hook, son. I suppose the only reason they didn't catch you there was because of the rain. Makes it hard to keep watch so long. Now, move away."

"Nonsense. You are talking foolishness, Uncle. I'll make some coffee. At least wait that long."

The man sighed and slumped onto Antonio's bed. "Only a moment. I must go." The accordion case made a sound against the wall when Nicco flopped down on the bed. He turned to look at it. "Is it safe there, son?"

"Of course." Antonio was beginning to wonder if years of drinking had deteriorated Nicco's brain.

Later, when Antonio handed Nicco a steaming cup, his uncle offered to explain himself.

"You do not believe me, but it's true. I was minding my own business. I was not even intoxicated. Yet." Tears formed at the corner of his eyes. "I was trying hard, Tony. For you, I try very hard. But I was weak. Some men approached me as I came out of the saloon. I had just bought a jar of whiskey. Business was slow, because of the rain, and the proprietor let me buy it with the coins folks gave me that day."

"It's okay, Uncle. You don't have to—"

"It is not, Tony. Hear me out."

"Go on."

"I should have realized something was wrong when they took a look at the wrapped bottle in my hands and told me they would buy me ale at the corner pub. I should have realized that did not make sense. But…" He tapped a finger to his head. "I do not think so well when I have been long without a drink. A sad fact." He toasted with his coffee cup. "You stay away from strong drink, nephew."

"I intend to."

"Well, the next thing I knew I was on the ferry to the island. They told me you would be coming for me but probably not for a few days. I thought they were taking me to St. Anthony's, but now as I think back I realize I had been on the train for some time. It just got all mixed up in my head. They brought me to that place, Ward's Island, and waited. There were no doctors. Not that I saw. They just put me on a cot and told me to sleep it off. You did not come that night."

"I thought you were at St. Anthony's."

"Of course you did. I did not see the men when I woke. They probably gave up. This time. But if they see me again, if they take me again, you must not come after me." His gaze flew to the accordion. "And you must not lose that."

Antonio scratched his head. "This doesn't make sense. At St. Anthony's they knew you had been taken to Ward's Island."

"Who knew? *Signor* Mudazo?"

"No, not the attendant. He just knew you had not come in. A man named Paulo in the alley."

Nicco set his cup down on the table. "Maybe he was a Benevento man?"

"Uncle, if they really wanted you to lead them to me, they would have camped out on the steps of the shelter. I am always coming there to get you. Or the theater, for that matter." He considered the notes. Someone was trying to lure him away, perhaps to a place where no one would know him. Nicco may have been right when he warned him to stay out of Little Italy.

"Maybe they don't know this?" He rubbed his thumb and forefinger together. "They incubate a plan after they just happen to learn you are there looking for me." He jumped to his feet. "I must go now!" He pointed to the accordion. "Get a safe for that thing. Lock it up."

"Uncle!"

Nicco scrambled out the door and jolted down the stairs. Antonio leapt after him. When he got outside he saw his uncle jump up on the foot rail of a sanitary wagon—the kind that collects garbage. Nicco put one hand on a shovel that was affixed to the side. With his free hand he pounded on the wagon. He was volunteering to work as the wagon clattered off down a side street. It was too late. Antonio had to let him go. Perhaps he would have been better off at Ward's Island where he would be safe, dry, and fed. One thing was certain.

He turned to go back inside when someone called to him.

"*Signor* Baggio, *sì?*" A thin young man leaned against a lamppost, rain dripping from the brim of his hat.

"Do I know you?"

"No, but I know you. That was your uncle you were chasing after, *sì?*"

Antonio studied the fellow's face as well as he could in the downpour. He thought he recognized him. "Won't you come into the hall out of the rain?"

They stepped inside when suddenly the man pushed Antonio to the wall. Pulling upward on Antonio's shirt collar, he blurted through his teeth. "Where is the money?"

"I haven't got any money." He tried to still his chattering teeth. "If you're hungry I can get you a meal. I have a tab at the place across the street." Because he didn't see a weapon, he told himself this was just a misguided youth.

"The money. I have been sent here to get it. You hid it somewhere after your father took a bullet to the head. Isn't that right?" The fellow spoke in a heavy, stunted Italian accent.

"What? Who are you?"

"One of the men who took your uncle up the river. My boss told me to tell you that if you don't hand it over by midnight, this time your uncle will not be floating on the ferry. He'll be floating face down in the East River." He let go and then gave Antonio a shove.

"I don't know what you're talking about." He returned the evil gaze. "What do you know about my father's death?" The fellow was young, unsteady. No reason to let him intimidate.

"I will be back. With others." The thug darted out the door.

"Fine!" Antonio shouted. "I will be at work!"

This kid knew nothing. He looked an awfully lot like the dishwasher at Giovanni's. What a shame he stooped to such ill-advised behavior. He heard Lu barking as he climbed back up toward his apartment. He would put on his MacIntosh and go ask questions over at St. Anthony's.

After donning his raincoat and gathering up his dog, who at least served as a watchdog should someone try to surprise him again, Antonio paused with his hand on the doorknob. Nicco might seem like a crazy old coot, but he'd been right about someone looking for him. He glanced back toward the bed. "What do you think, Lu? Since the thugs know I'm here, should I bring it along? For safekeeping?"

The dog gave an approving bark.

Antonio hurried to the bed, leaned over, and retrieved the accordion case. "Might be foolish, but it's the only thing my father hung on to. Might be made of money or something."

Nicco wasn't at St. Anthony's and neither was the regular attendant.

"Mario's got the night off," a man with a walrus mustache said.

"Do you know who the janitor was last night?"

"Davy." He nodded to a Chinaman who was picking up discarded newspapers and stuffing them into a barrel. "He's the only janitor I know of."

"His name's not Davy."

The man picked up his damp copy of the *Times*. "Is to me."

Antonio called out to the janitor. "You there."

The man looked up, surprised. "You here last night? You see another fellow pushing a mop around the lobby here?"

The mustached man chuckled. "That won't do you no good. Davy doesn't speak English."

The janitor shrugged and went back to his work.

Frustrated, Antonio put a hand on the newspaper to pull it down from the man's face. "Well, how do you talk to him?"

The man grimaced at the wet handprint Antonio made across the front page. "Good thing I already read that part. Blasted weather we're having."

Antonio clicked his tongue and Lu followed him to the door.

The attendant called out to him. "I just point and he does what I need. I'm telling you, there's no other janitor."

A spy then. Antonio had been gullible. He wanted to go back to the Italian bank and have a word with the *padrone* there, get him to fill in the holes in what Nicco had been saying, but what would that do other than get him a bloody nose? He would not fall for a trap, having surely escaped one at Ward's Island without knowing it.

His father had no money. Someone was after him for no reason, or for misguided reasons, and he was helpless to stop them without more information.

His father's mysterious death.

A handful of nonsensical clues from his often drunk uncle.

A few puzzling anonymous notes.

A worthless accordion that seemed to be the most important but most ridiculous clue.

A beautiful young woman who had her own mysterious connection to the Italian *padroni*.

A nun who was so distracted all the time that if she did know something Antonio would have a devil of a time getting it out of her.

"Come on, Lu. We're going to see the sister again in her nice warm kitchen." He patted Lu's damp head. At least he had a smart, obedient dog. Lu let out an approving yip and they went back out into the rain, the accordion case thumping against Antonio's thigh, making him feel like a fool on a fool's errand.

That nun knows more than she is saying.

28

MRS. HAWKINS HUNG UP HER APRON on a kitchen wall peg. "I will go next door right now and telephone. I'm so pleased that Annie and Stephen are close by. That nosey neighbor on the other side, whose telephone I used to borrow, was turning into a busybody. Even if she is an excellent baker, I prefer the company of those young people."

Aileen collected the teacups. "You should get your own telephone, Mrs. Hawkins. They really are quite handy contraptions."

"So your cousin Annie likes to remind me, love. But, she has one so why go to the trouble?"

After she left, Sofia helped Aileen wash up from tea. "My priest says there are doctors on Long Island that are very good with…uh, that can help people like Mamma. Perhaps Mrs. Hawkins or her doctor know of them."

Aileen flipped a ticking-striped towel over her shoulder and headed to the dish cabinet. "It always amazes me how many people The Hawk knows. She's quite a wonder. Sofia, do you mean to say your mother is suffering from what people in America call poor mental hygiene?"

"I suppose so. Such odd phrases Americans have for things."

Aileen chuckled. "Indeed they do."

"Whatever you call it, Mamma's condition was caused by something that happened long ago. Usually, for most of the year, she is fine."

"Some kind of trauma, so."

"*Sì*. We have to help her get over it and then she will be well. We will be *una famiglia* again."

"The people in Ireland? A great many have poor mental hygiene. We liked to call it Irish crazies. And some, like my da, handle it by finding the bottom of a whiskey glass. I hope the new doctors can do something. I truly do."

"*Grazie*. Thank you."

It was approaching the dinner hour. Antonio had little time to see the Sister. He needed to be at the music hall over on 23rd Street by eight. He didn't want to be late for the new job Mac found for him if he could help it. Mac had given Antonio some music and that was what he'd been practicing before his worries about Nicco drove him to make the journey uptown.He hummed the notes to himself, hoping he had learned the piece well enough. He'd be playing for something called ragtime opera. It sounded ludicrous, but he actually enjoyed the music composed by a man of color from St. Louis. The song titled *Swipsey* was quite pleasant.

His mind wandered between keeping his job and protecting Nicco and himself from some Italian gang thugs. At times it all seemed too much. This was what it meant to be a man, he supposed. He needed to get this settled on his own terms and not because of the kid who visited his apartment or because of some handwritten messages. If he missed his set and lost pay, well...he hoped it wouldn't come to that. Antonio was determined, however, not to be sent to slaughter like his father had been. He would do what he had to do.

The rain settled into a steady rhythm, no longer sending a pelting assault against Antonio's back. The Most Precious Blood Church's outside walls were gray with dampness, but the structure had been built well. He imagined it would long stand proud and invincible. He adjusted the accordion strap over his shoulder and knocked on the kitchen door.

"*Avanti!*" The woman he'd met before, Sofia's aunt, hauled him through the doorway. "And the little dog, too. No beast should be out in this rain." She apologized for the muddy floors and water stained cabinets. "We were flooded. We only now make things nice again."

"I do not mean to intrude." Workmen pulled off ruined boards and hammered on wainscoting and cabinet doors. The place was anything but the quiet kitchen he'd hoped for.

"No intrude, *signore*. There is always welcome in our Father's house."

He pulled off his coat. "I should help." He grabbed a mop and ordered Luigi to wait by the table.

After an hour of sponging up floodwater and picking up scraps of leftover wood wainscoting, he was finally able to tell the sister why he'd come. Lu sat licking a soup bone by the door as the sister poured two small cups of deeply dark coffee. Espresso. A treat.

"Sister, I would like to know about this *padrone*, the one you say has caused trouble for families."

"For yours?"

"Why, yes, mine it seems, but also for yours, as you told me earlier."

"You go to the bank?"

"No. Well, yes, but he was not there. I was going to go back, however, I felt compelled not to. Not until I know more."

A worker returned, bounding down the stairs toward the kitchen, muttering in Italian. Antonio thought he'd said he was returning for a forgotten tool but his Italian was less than proficient.

"*Avanti*, Joseph," the sister called out. "Come meet my friend."

She whispered over her coffee cup. "Sofia's brother. Always looking for work. I send him to the priest. Joseph does very good construction work."

Antonio turned toward the stairs as the man descended, at first only his feet and legs visible. When his lean form passed below the overhang, he and Antonio gazed at each other. It was the thug who had accosted him just hours earlier. "You move around neighborhoods very quickly, Joseph," Antonio said, breaking the stunned silence.

The sister reached for Antonio's arm. "You know each other?"

The man backed up the stairs and hurried off. Antonio ran after him, Luigi barking at his heels. Without his Macintosh, Antonio was soaked in minutes. The kid called Joseph slipped and fell in front of a line of waste barrels, allowing Antonio to catch up. He grabbed the rascal and hauled him upright. "What is this about? You better tell me right now. I am tired of the shenanigans. Decent people have more to do with their lives than go around threatening strangers. You're the dishwasher, aren't you?"

"Only a hired hand."

"Well, you better look for more respectable work, fella."

Someone pulled Antonio off the thug, and shoved a fist into his jaw. He went down to the pavement hard and a pain shot through his arm. Then another blow to his stomach. He looked up and in the gray light he thought he saw two, maybe three men. A strike to his ribs. Another to his thigh and then blackness.

He woke up back in the sister's kitchen, lying on a cot next to the coal stove wearing just his shirt and trousers. His wet suit coat had been hung over a chair next to him and his Macintosh dripped from a wooden hanger on the wall. He clicked his tongue. His jaw hurt.

"Where's my dog?"

Movement from the far corner made him try to look that way, but his head pounded and shards of pain rose up his leg from knee to hip.

He heard the sister's voice. "Joseph helped get you inside. I am very sorry for this trouble, *Signor* Baggio."

"Joseph needs another line of work. My dog, Sister?"

"I call for him, but he not come. Those foolish boys. Will they ever learn that a stranger to the neighborhood is good and welcome? Not to be feared." She moved into his line of vision, shouting in Italian so rapidly that he could only snatch the meaning from a portion of what she said. She was miffed but only as much as she'd be if young boys had tracked mud onto the kitchen floor tiles.

"My dog, he's not here?"

"I believe he has run off, *signore*. He will come back, *si*? He knows his master's voice, not mine. So he did not return to me. You rest, and then you go look for him. He will come back. You will see."

Antonio moved slowly to a sitting position. "Your nephew, Joseph?"

"He was not the one who hit you."

"No, he was not. He ran from me, though. I saw him earlier, at my home. He came to warn me." Antonio did not want to speak badly about this woman's family. He needed information from her.

"The other ones, they cause trouble. Those boys need something to do so they are not loitering around. I tell Father Lucci, but there is only so much he can do. They should get work, like Joey tries to do, just not from the *padrone*."

A cough came from a shadowed corner.

The nun held out her hand. "Luisa, come here, child." She turned to Antonio. "A neighborhood girl, so helpful. She shook out your coat."

The girl slowly emerged. Her large dark eyes showed fear.

"*Grazie*," Antonio said, nodding.

The girl, a teenager he estimated, did not reply. She tiptoed up the stairs and out the door.

Antonio turned to Sister Stefania. "The *Padrone*. Yes, that is why I came." He noticed the woman staring at something near the ceiling. He looked up too. A Victrola sat on top of the icebox, not where one would expect to find a music machine.

"To save it from the rains," she said.

He glanced around for the accordion and spotted it next to the table where he'd been drinking coffee. If someone wanted what his father had—this instrument, as though it was a Stradivarius or something of true value—Joseph could have forced his way into Antonio's apartment. Just now he could have barged in and stolen it from the nuns' kitchen. The men following Nicco could have taken it from him long ago. They wanted money, they'd said. If this instrument held the secret to what they wanted, they obviously didn't know.

"Sister, if you know why someone is after me, if you know anything about my father, I beg you to tell me."

"All I know comes from following my Master's voice."

"Excuse me?"

"I cannot help you, *signor.*"

She cannot help.

Antonio had to find Luigi. As he prepared to leave, he stared at the case, thought about the way the instrument was a moveable box of sorts. He wondered.

29

Sofia was astounded when Minnie escorted Father Lucci into the parlor.

"I was at Ellis Island meeting a new immigrant. When we arrived in Battery Park, her family surprised us. Her parents had not been able to get away from work to claim her at the immigration station, but they managed to get to the Battery so I released her into their capable arms. Since I found myself down here with a bit of leisure time, I decided to call upon you, Sofia, to see how you are getting along."

She wanted to embrace him, a bit of home here in the English woman's boarding house, but that would not be proper. "I am so happy to see you, Father. Please sit down. I will get coffee."

Minnie cleared her throat. "Hold the train! That's my job, Miss Sofia. And I don't want to miss a chance to make coffee instead of tea around here." She chuckled at her own humor as she shuffled down the hall toward the kitchen.

The priest sat on the sofa. Sofia took the chair between the piano and the fireplace. The space seemed somehow foreign with the presence of her neighborhood priest. Father Lucci was a man who embodied the essence of Little Italy—American in speech, but Benevento in appearance. The two of them sitting in Mrs. Hawkins's parlor made her think of two mountain goats climbing the steps of the Waldolf-Astoria—a scene not at all believable. Seeing Father Lucci now reminded her of where she did belong—with Mamma and *la famiglia*.

He glanced around, taking in the room. "You are well here?"

"I am. Thank you for coming."

He lifted a hand. "And at work? It is going well, Sofia?"

"*Sì*. I thank God for my employment. I could not go to work the last few days because of the weather—the factory was closed—but I did visit my mother."

"She is at Ward's Island, then?"

"She is." Sofia drew in a breath to keep the tears away.

"And...how is she?"

"As anyone would expect, Father." Sofia rubbed the heel of her hand at the corner of one eye.

"I am so sorry, Sofia. If only I knew of a way to commission those doctors over on Long Island."

Mrs. Hawkins shuffled into the room, her scurrying footsteps quieting as she reached the flowered rug.

"Mrs. Hawkins, may I present our priest from my neighborhood, Father Lucci."

Father Lucci stood and shook the woman's hand. They were cordial, not adversarial. Most anyone from Mulberry Street would be surprised to see it. Sofia was pleased.

Minnie brought coffee, tea, and round, white biscuits topped with sparkling sugar. She refused Sofia's offers of help. "You just relax and enjoy, honey. You have had it rough, what with your mamma and all."

A few minutes later, Annie Adams and her husband Stephen joined them. Mr. Adams still wore his postal uniform. Sofia was a bit embarrassed for the Father because they had come in to gawk at the Italian priest. But then, how different were Italian families when outsiders came to call? They would have done the same.

The postman addressed Father Lucci. "You say the new medical attitudes toward the infirmities of the mind are quite progressive, Father?"

Father Lucci nodded. "I have been to the hospital myself and witnessed the relative calm, the assurance that the doctors understand the patients as men and women still in possession of their right minds. Underneath it all, of course."

Sofia noticed Annie and Mrs. Hawkins exchanging knowing glances, but for all the lemon trees in Benevento she could not understand what was happening. She twisted her fists in her skirts as she tried to ignore her rushing pulse. Father Lucci, despite being the most friendly and open person in Little Italy you could ever hope to meet, would not talk so freely about his parishioners here despite the questions. It was not done. These Americans did not understand.

"Father?" This time Annie addressed him. "If a charitable group of Christians wanted to assist these doctors, what should they do?"

Father Lucci cocked his head to one side. "I do not understand, Mrs. Adams."

"Well." She straightened in her chair. "I run a library here, to encourage newcomers to read and learn. And to tell stories." She laughed nervously. "I imagine you have libraries in your community."

"We do." His coffee cup rested in his hand. He had not taken a sip.

Annie continued, although Sofia thought she really should have given up. "I am sure you will agree that Jesus himself was the quintessential storyteller."

The Father's expression gave away nothing. "Indeed, you could say so."

"Aye. Well, we try to follow his example, as I know you do as well. We are very charitable here, and there are so many who need assistance these days. What if we wanted to help?"

Father Lucci placed his china cup on the tea table and crossed his long legs. "We have charitable groups, as well, Mrs. Adams. The Catholic church tends to her flock."

Mrs. Hawkins cleared her throat. "Of course, Father. We did not mean to imply otherwise. I am afraid we are not making ourselves clear. What we are proposing is to retain the services of a doctor to tend to Mrs. Falcone."

Sofia gasped. Humiliated by her outburst, she covered her mouth, sucked her lips tight, and then plopped her hands into her lap.

"Very generous, Mrs. Hawkins." The priest tapped his fingertips together as he spoke. "But you may not realize how much in fees it would take to bring one of the doctors out to Manhattan. I am afraid that is the reason it has not been done already. *Signor* Falcone would have sacrificed much to do it if he could have. The church, with her limited resources, would have donated toward the treatment if it were within reach. But alas, it is not." He glanced at Sofia. "I am sorry for the dismay this brings you, Sofia."

She nodded, not taking her hands from her skirt less her trembling hands reveal how very much she was troubled. She wanted help, needed it for Mamma, but the price was too dear. No one could afford it.

"Oh, Father, please have some more tea or uh, coffee, won't you?" Mrs. Hawkins rose to serve him herself. When she saw that his cup was still full she smacked her lips and placed a confection on his saucer. Then she returned to her chair.

Father Lucci smiled. "I can see you are taking quite good care of Sofia. I shall give her father an excellent report."

The older woman blushed. "It is our privilege to help her, Father. In fact, we consider it our mission from the Lord." She waved her fleshy arm around the room. "There are several of us combining resources so that we may help whomever God sends to us. Sofia is not our only girl here, and she won't be the last. There is plenty of money to fund our efforts."

Sofia caught the Father's puzzled look. Hawkins House was nice, but in no way opulent. He obviously was not convinced. She wasn't either. She believed that Father Lucci understood the situation better than Mrs. Hawkins did. After all, he actually knew these doctors and had visited their hospital.

"Despite our humble dwelling, indeed perhaps because of it, I assure you we have deep pockets, Father."

Mr. and Mrs. Adams agreed. Why were they so insistent? They lived well at Hawkins House, but this home could not compare to the mansions uptown that Claudia and others were always fawning over while reading the society pages in the newspapers. Claudia's cousin worked as a lady's maid in one of the colossal homes. She had told Claudia the curtains were sewn with gold thread, and diamonds glittered across her mistress's evening dresses. Hawkins House was nothing like that, but they were acting as if it was. Those rich uptown people, they were the ones who could afford these doctors. She had heard the names of the wealthy: Astor, Du Pont, Forbes, Roosevelt. Definitely not Adams or even Hawkins.

The Hawk made a chopping gesture with her hand. "Now, if you will give us a name of a doctor to contact, we will make arrangements and get poor Mrs. Falcone out of that terrible place at once." She said it as though it were a simple matter.

Father Lucci finally sipped deeply from his cup. "Excellent coffee, madam."

"Thank you, but the doctor?" Mrs. Hawkins could be embarrassingly direct.

Sofia spoke up. "Mrs. Hawkins, I thank you very much for trying to help. And Father, I thank you for coming out here and for your prayers in Mamma's behalf." She stood. "I am sure the Father must be going."

Mrs. Hawkins appeared flustered. "But—"

"It would be an intrusion to keep him past the evening confessional time." Sofia took his coffee cup and he stood as well.

"Minnie? His coat?" Sofia did not wish to direct the housekeeper, but she had to step in to help the Father save face. These were not his people, despite their kind intentions.

Sofia thought the priest looked relieved. "If something can be worked out, I will send word, Mrs. Hawkins." He bowed his head toward her. "Thank you for your kindness." He was being most gracious indeed.

"Uh, thank you for coming, Father. Come back anytime you wish." The woman's face was white and her cheeks puffed. Clearly, Mrs. Hawkins had never encountered the Italian proclivity toward privacy and did not know how to respond. She peered through the front door that Minnie had opened. "Thank the good Lord it seems the rain has slowed considerably."

"Yes, I will need to attend to the mopping out of my church. Good evening, ladies, Mr. Adams." He turned up his coat collar against the autumn wind.

After he had left, Annie Adams sighed heavily. "He did not believe us. No one considers the possibility that an Irish lass like me could have money."

"Now, dear," Stephen said, patting his wife's hand. "It is the nature of your benevolence that has contributed to this. You did not wish people to know of your wealth, remember? Despite the popularity of your father's stories, you chose to follow Mrs. Hawkins's example and keep your generosity a secret for the most part. If your name appeared regularly in the society pages, then people would believe."

Annie grinned and touched a heart brooch she wore near her throat. "Aye, and I don't want that. If people only understood the depth of our Mrs. Hawkins's generosity, they would be as inspired as I have been."

"You two must not go on so," Mrs. Hawkins scorned. "Let us stay focused on what God instructs us to do rather than on ourselves."

"You are most right." Annie stood and flashed her sparkling smile in Sofia's direction.

Sofia leaned against the pocket door. "I do not understand."

"Well," Annie began.

Sofia held up a hand. "Please, it does not matter. If Father Lucci could have helped Mamma, he would have. What I have to do now is get her back home. The rest we will figure out later, my papà and me." She hoped they would understand it was a family matter.

Mrs. Hawkins wrapped an arm around her. "Of course, love. Do not worry so. I will help you get her back to your home and then the matter of her treatment can be sorted out."

Sofia dabbed at her eyes with a handkerchief from her sleeve. "*Grazie*, but please leave Father Lucci be, Mrs. Hawkins. The people from my neighborhood…they are not like you here. Please, understand, and do not bother him. He is so busy."

"I would not dream of it, love."

Sofia thought she caught a glimpse of the woman winking at the couple. They seemed to be in on some secret. They would learn, however, that Italian families take care of their own, one way or another. If not Papà, then someone else from home would help out.

As Sofia prepared for bed she counted the hours until she could return to Ward's Island. Tomorrow, Saturday, was normally a short day for the shoe factory workers who were released at two o'clock. However, Mr. Richmond would expect the workers to make up for time lost due to the storms. The ferry did not run late. Perhaps she could make a telephone call to Ward's Island. She would practice her English and make sure the attendants there knew that Mamma was to be released to her family. Mr. Richmond might be convinced to allow her to use his telephone so long as she did him a favor in return. She didn't know what that might be. Spy on Claudia and the others? That's what he wanted, although there was nothing to tell. That she knew of. She would pay attention, though, just in case.

The sun was beginning to rise as Sofia headed to the trolley. She needed forty minutes to get to work but since she'd left early she might get there in time to talk to Mr. Richmond, before the others arrived. She hoped to appeal to a sense of compassion that she desperately wanted him to possess. *Please, God, open a door for me to get to Mamma.*

There were a few early birds in the building but the relative silence from idle machines gave the factory an eerie feel. She'd had to wear her old shoes because she'd ruined her special pair in the floods. Without the extra height, she felt insignificant.

Her shoes tapped softly on the workroom floor. A light glowed from her boss's open office. The smell of cigar smoke and slightly aged shoe leather stuck in her throat. When she coughed and peeked in he saw her and immediately pushed his chair back from his desk. "Early, aren't you?"

"*Sì.* Yes, sir."

He smiled, exposing tobacco-stained teeth under his mustache. "I am delighted to see you, my dear. Come in."

She edged her way forward and sat in the chair in front of his desk. He closed the door, causing her breath to catch. She swallowed hard and looked away.

He came in front of her to lean on his desk, uncomfortably close. "What can I do for you?"

"I need to use your telephone."

"I see. And in return?"

"I...please, Mr. Richmond. Have mercy. I need to get my mamma back home."

"Yes, so I understand." He ran his hand over the black telephone as though stroking a puppy. "It's a wonderful instrument. So handy. But, it does cost the company money and I am not at liberty to loan its use for employees to waste time talking on it."

"I understand, Mr. Richmond. I am sure I won't be long, and I am here before the shift begins. Please."

"Certainly."

She blew out her breath.

"Go on. You know how to use it?"

Of course she did not. She needed his help. She shook her head.

"Perhaps in return for me helping you make a call..." He put his hand on her knee and she flew back in her chair, sending it against the wall. He came toward her, eyes flaring. "Oh, come now, Miss Falcone, you have been flirting with me since you started working here. Don't act so surprised."

"No. I have not. I only want to use the telephone."

He pinned her against the wall. "And I only want a kiss." He laughed, breath hot on her neck. "That's no more the truth than what you just said." He began kissing her neck. She could shove him painfully, like she had the man in the bawdy boarding house, but he was her boss. What would happen if she did that? When he rubbed his hand down her waist, the debate in her mind ended. She lifted her knee and would have given him cause to crumple to the floor in pain if he had not stepped back just then.

He turned away and moved to the opposite side of his desk, the place he should have been all along. "This is not the time, sadly. That is to say, I would like you to tell me what you have learned from your co-workers."

She glanced up at the huge clock on the wall. Voices and footsteps coming from the work floor told her she had only minutes to decide what to say. If she gave him a crumb, he might leave her alone.

"Uh, Claudia, she is the only one who talks, uh, she says workers should have rights."

"So, she is inciting the workers, then?"

"No. She just talks…ideas. Thoughts she reads in magazines. Only talking." The pounding in her head made it difficult to find the right words.

He narrowed his eyes at her like a wolf after prey. "I see. Claudia. Well, that is good information for now. I shall keep an eye on her. Now, let me help you with that call."

It took several minutes to get connected.

"I am sorry, miss. No patient information can be given out without the permission of the attending doctor."

"May I speak to him, please?"

"He is not here on Saturdays."

Frustrated, Sofia thanked the person on the other end of the line and handed the earpiece back to Mr. Richmond.

"Cheer up, girl. You may call back on Monday. I look forward to our little rendezvous."

She forced a smile and escaped back to the sewing floor. After routinely punching the time clock, she moved to her machine as if in a dream. Nothing happening around her mattered. Not even her boss's advances. She would manage him somehow. Mamma was alone in a strange, cold place and needed her.

It was lunchtime before she realized Claudia was not present.

"She was called to Mr. Richmond's office at the beginning of the shift," Maria told her. "I have not seen her since. Perhaps she's ill."

A man working a row behind Sofia, the fellow who always seemed to be sticking his nose in where it did not belong, leaned his chair backward to speak to them. Sofia didn't like him. He was the one who had first frightened her with his talk about Ward's Island and other mysterious asylums. "I hear she's been dismissed."

Sofia was getting worried so she acknowledged the man's intrusion. "What does that mean? Dismissed from what?"

"Her job. The sewing floor. She's been sacked. Surely an Italian would understand that." He sniffed. "None of you can hold on to a job. I'm surprised you are here and she's the one who was sent away."

Maria marched over and gave the man's chair a shove before returning to her place.

The man laughed.

Sofia had not imagined Mr. Richmond would send Claudia away just because of what she said. She must make amends as soon as she could but first she had to finish her work or Mr. Richmond would make her stay late.

Finally, she stood to leave her sewing machine just as the floor boy arrived. By the time she finished giving him her completed soles, the shift whistle blasted and workers scurried toward the clock. If she hurried, she might reach the train in time to get to Ward's Island. If she waited to speak to Mr. Richmond about Claudia, she might miss her opportunity. With a measure of guilt that sank in her stomach like a brick, she got in line to punch the clock, planning to dash off to the cloakroom and then hurry to catch the train. *La famiglia* was her first obligation, and she was somewhat surprised she had briefly considered anything else. Monday she would explain and tell Mr. Richmond it was a mistake. She would make sure someone came with her to his office. Claudia was his best worker. He would want her back, so convincing him should not be difficult. So long as he asked nothing more of her.

30

ANTONIO LIMPED from the nuns' kitchen toward the train, calling for Lu as he went, though it hurt when he yelled too loudly. He tossed the accordion in a waste can, then backed up and retrieved it. He wasn't sure why.

He gritted his teeth as he searched about, knowing he could not leave Little Italy without his dog. He slipped into a pharmacy and paid a nickel to use the telephone.

Mac did not sound pleased. "That's a shame, losing your dog, Tony. I am sure he'll show up. He might not have the senses of a Border Collie, but he's a smart one. He'll take care of himself."

"I can't leave here yet, Mac. I have to find him. He's all I've got. Listen, I know you can say a good word for me. Explain to the theater."

"You better get over there, Tony. There are…talent managers, shall I say, who are coming to hear that opera. I'll let the manager know you've had a mishap and will be late. With the weather we've had, he'll buy it. But you still need to skedaddle if you care about your future career, lad. Believe me when I tell you getting this job for you was worse than navigating the Firth of Clyde under Viking attack, not that I minded."

Mac always liked to make his point with some Old World reference. But he was right. If Antonio hoped to secure enough work to pay his way to Oberlin, he could not afford to appear irresponsible. He should have never gone to the Italian enclave so close to show time.

"I will be there as soon as I can."

When he left the shop he questioned some children. "Some say he looks like the Victor dog."

They gave him puzzled looks.

He tried the Salvation Army, but Lieutenant Delfino hadn't seen Luigi. He apologized because a planned rally was about to begin and he couldn't help look.

Next Antonio stopped in what appeared to be a library. Several young people milled about inside. He spotted the girl he had seen in the nun's kitchen. "Luisa? That's your name?"

She nodded and moved to the side to pass him.

He stepped in front of her. "Have you seen my dog?"

"No, *signore*. I am sorry your dog is lost." She turned her sad eyes up to look at him. "You should not be in here."

"Why?"

"Go, *signore*. Please. It is not safe."

"Hey, are you the one? Have you been sending me messages?"

Her eyes moistened and she ducked under his arm and got away before he could stop her. He stepped out into the street and yelled Luigi's name. His voice seemed to wallow in a puddle of sounds—people talking, bells on carts jingling, laughter, singing, and then the toll of church bells. Antonio was not an opera singer. His voice would not carry above the throng. Finally, he decided the sister's promise to look for Luigi and the lieutenant's pledge to ask around would have to do and he reluctantly boarded the train.

Later, when he finished at the Twenty-third Street Theater, he would walk over to the Fourteenth. Lu might be waiting for him outside Mac's theater, like he had so many times before.

At 8:20, Antonio met the attendant at the stage door who led him to the piano and thankfully handed him some sheet music. Even if Antonio had brought what Mac had given him it would be soaked through by now. As the performance before his came to a close, Antonio dropped the accordion and took his place at the keys. Not rehearsing with the singer prior to a performance was not unusual at the Fourteenth Street Theater, but the nervous look from the young woman with a painted face standing stiffly in the center of the stage told him this was not typical here. He had imposed on more than just the stage manager by being late. He hoped to apologize later. Accompanying a congregation at St. Anthony's had done nothing to prepare him for this venue. This theater was a professional place, not a church service or nickel show where improvisation was acceptable. Why had they invited him sight unseen?

Antonio drew in a breath and shifted uncomfortably in his wet shoes. Then he raised his fingers over the black and white keys. He was capable. All he had to do was push away thoughts about where he was and how he'd left his dog somewhere in

Little Italy. His father would be proud to see him in this theater. Antonio had God-given talent. God might be silent as far as Antonio was concerned, but he had blessed him with ability and sent him off into the world. He could do this.

Fortunately, the accompaniment was at a slow enough pace that he could follow the singer without mishap, at least without any that he could detect. Then came his solo piece, a fast paced, bouncy rag he had practiced earlier. His fingers flew over the keyboard in a celebration appropriate to the style of the composer. He actually enjoyed it and the resulting applause.

The rest of the opera, lasting nearly an hour, left him both exhilarated and exhausted. His shoulders ached and his throat had run dry but when the manager insisted he come on stage for a bow, to a thunderous audience response, Antonio knew he had done well. Very well. He would probably be called back for more work.

❦

Late that night when he arrived at the Fourteenth, Lu was not posed outside the stage door as Antonio had hoped. The attendant spotted Antonio and motioned him inside. Mac had anticipated his coming by and thumped him soundly on the back as burly Scotsmen are prone to do, nearly knocking the accordion off his shoulder. "How did you do, lad?"

"A standing ovation."

The man's ruddy face glowed in the dark hallway. "Brilliant. Just brilliant, son. Let's head over to the saloon. Whiskey's on me."

Antonio refused. "I have to find Lu."

Mac pushed open the outside door. "Where is he? Wasn't he outside the Twenty-third while you played?"

"No. I lost him before that. Remember I called you?"

Mac rubbed his chin. "Sure, but I thought he'd make his way up there, or at least here. He may not have the smarts of a sheep dog, like I said before, but he is pretty keen, that one. He'll show up. But good for you. You made the best of the opportunity, then." Mac slapped Antonio's back again, causing Antonio to lunge a step forward.

"I guess I did. They asked me to come back."

Mac winked. "They'd be off their heads if they didn't, lad. Say, have you taken up a new instrument?"

"This thing? Nah. It belongs to my uncle. I should throw it in the trash as much trouble as it's been toting it around. I had thought it was worth something, but not likely."

"Do not do that, lad. Instruments are hard to come by. Go home and dry the thing out. See what you have left. That is what I would do."

"Thanks, Mac." He shook the man's hand. "Thank you for all you did for me. I wish I could repay the kindness."

Mac's fair face flushed. "No trouble, not for someone as talented as you, Tony."

Antonio was beginning to tolerate being called that, especially by someone as generous as the manager of the Fourteenth.

Antonio watched the shadows falling over the seats of the trolley in front of him as he rode back to his apartment. Surely Lu would be there waiting for him. Despite the acclamations,

311

tonight did not feel like a real victory when he was no closer to finding out why his father had been killed. And on top of it, he had lost his dog. He tucked the accordion case to his side and thought about how worthless it was. It didn't play right, never did, even though his father said he had planned to fix it, since the buttons did not push down properly. Maybe there was something inside impeding their movement. The bottoms of the broken keys, probably. But what if it was easily fixed? Mac was right when he said something that can make music should be cherished.

When Antonio got home he found a note shoved under his door. Fine linen paper and exquisite handwriting, definitely not another note from Little Italy. He laid it on his piano bench while he removed his overcoat in the dark, quiet room. Without his companion's tail-wagging welcome, the room felt empty. First his father. Now his dog. He shook his head. No, the nun would find him. Lu was probably snuggled on a cushion in the parish kitchen right now, perhaps enjoying a better feast than Antonio could provide. Surely that was true. God would not do this to him, would he?

He flicked on the electric light and paused a moment to listen to its buzzing. A neighbor upstairs shouted something he could not understand. It was loud enough, but in another language. Czech or German, he thought.

He washed his hands in the sink. He was not about to pick that note up and soil the paper. Perhaps it was meant for Miss Josephine in Apartment B and had been misdirected.

Finally, with clean hands, he examined it. It was addressed to him all right, from Ignacy Jan Paderewski, probably delivered by a late night courier. He placed it on the music stand and stared at it for a moment. Paderewski—or at least his name, in his handwriting—right here, looking over Antonio's keyboard. He slipped the note free, leaving the addressed envelope prominently displayed.

Dear Mr. Baggio,

I applaud your performance earlier at the Twenty-third. I hope you will forgive me for not announcing my attendance in advance, and for not greeting you afterward, but by not bringing attention to my presence I hoped to witness your passion for the keyboard without any apprehension my being there might have caused you. I wanted to hear you play in this environment after watching you in vaudeville, which was quite good, by the way, although on an inferior piano. You, my boy, are a natural talent. Now that I have heard you myself, I would like to invite you to become my protégé. I will await your answer, if it is a positive one, at my suite of rooms on or before Monday. I will be traveling soon after. If you decide, as much as I hope you will not, to decline my offer, no response is necessary. But do accept my sincere compliments on your performance.

With all my best wishes,

I.J. Paderewski

The note was signed with a flourishing pen stroke, as a great pianist would be expected to do. Antonio was stunned. This could not be. All his life he had wanted to be someone half as talented as Paderewski, and to have the master compliment a mere ragtime opera performance? It was nearly incomprehensible. But it had happened. He had proof in his hands. This was the reason Mac had pushed him so hard to show up. Why hadn't he told Antonio what he was up to?

Antonio turned to look at the envelope on the piano, the black ink letters bold against the white linen paper. Mac hadn't told him because he knew how in awe Antonio was of the man. He didn't want Antonio to freeze up.

He marveled at the events, how things had unfolded. He'd been struggling to find work when he met the writer in the pub, who had then helped Antonio make the musician's acquaintance. It seemed like happenstance, but things could not have fallen in place without help, without a conductor orchestrating his life. Antonio had not planned this. He could not have even dreamed it. His gaze fell to the Bible on his bedside table. How he had not trusted. How he had pondered whether God heard his prayers. It was Sofia Falcone who had insisted that God hears our prayers always and obviously she had been correct. He must thank her for helping him realize this. She would be the first one he would invite when he finally held a concert in a great hall one day, as an Oberlin graduate.

"Hey, boy, isn't that something!" He glanced at Lu's empty bed. He was so used to having him there, and now he felt foolish. If it hadn't been so late he would have found a telephone and called over to the abbey to see if Lu had shown up. He'd have to wait until tomorrow to share this good news with his most loyal companion.

As he prepared for bed, he noticed again the old accordion. He felt that now was the right time to show gratitude toward his father, and his unwavering support, and to care for his one possession left behind. After lifting it from its case and discovering it had stayed relatively dry, he brought it to the table and dug in a cabinet drawer until he found a screwdriver and pliers. Before he did anything that might render the instrument musically useless, he set it on his knee and examined the keys. The instrument was what they called a button accordion, smaller than most but still weighing as much as a smoked Christmas ham. Running a finger over the lettering, he noted the make, an Italian company called Soprani. Papà had most likely brought it over from the homeland. But he'd never played it, so far as Antonio knew. Antonio had never tried the thing despite his father's proclivity for leaving it in plain view. Antonio's father had collected various instruments to see if his son might be drawn to something—harmonica, a guitar, and this. The piano had been Antonio's choice. He'd never once considered the accordion. Perhaps, he thought with a twinge of shame, he'd deemed it an old world instrument, something for paupers and beggars to use. Had his father been insulted by his choice? If he had, he'd never shown it.

Antonio pressed his fingers to the buttons and tried out the billows. The only thing broken, it seemed, was a few of the keys, one more resistant than the others. When he pushed on it, he heard a clunking sound, as though something was in the way. Why on earth would his father insist Nicco protect this?

He set it down and went to boil water for coffee and to talk sense to himself. There was no possible way this thing contained buried treasure, but perhaps Papà could have put something inside. A note. An explanation of what he was doing at Cooper Union. A clue. If he found something he'd have to apologize to Nicco. If he found nothing, no harm done.

31

SOFIA MOANED when she heard Mrs. Hawkins's wakeup call for church. She had not been able to get to Ward's Island yesterday. When she left work a messenger boy met her at the trolley with a note. She was expected to hurry home to Hawkins House because Annie Adams had invited a literary speaker, someone Mrs. Hawkins wanted Sofia to meet. She had considered refusing by sending the message boy back with her regrets, but when she realized she didn't have enough money for the train and the ferry to the island, she knew there was no use. In addition, she had no plan to convince them to release Mamma. With a heavy heart, and a vow to visit Mamma the next day no matter what, she returned to Hawkins House. However, she had been able to make a call on the Adams's telephone. No treatment had begun for her mother.

The guest turned out to be a dreary college professor who spoke English too rapidly for Sofia to understand. He read poetry, something else Sofia could not comprehend, at least not as completely as the others seemed to.

So, after a dull evening, she had gone to bed with a headache that even Mrs. Hawkins's flowery tea blend could not remedy. Now that the morning alarm had been given, she threw back her bed quilt. She could not miss mass. It took her nearly an hour on Sundays to reach Most Precious Blood, what with the limited transportation going that direction on the Sabbath.

"Why don't you go to St. Anthony's today?" Aileen called from her bed when Sofia returned from the washroom. "Then you won't have to rise so early."

"And not wake you, you mean."

"What if that is what I mean?" The Irish girl pulled a blanket over her head.

Sofia did enjoy the organist at St. Anthony's. Antonio. She could get lost in his deep, serious eyes, but she had no time for romance. She wanted to see Papà and Father Lucci, and mass was her best opportunity. She would press them afterward for a plan to free Mamma and set a time for when they would go up to get her. "I need to see my family today, Aileen." Sofia ran a brush through her hair. Then she twisted it into a bun at her neck and pinned a lace scarf in place.

Aileen sat up. "You know, Professor Malcolm was here last night not just to read from his sad story books."

"What do you mean?"

"He was invited here for you."

"Nonsense. I could barely understand him." Although she had wondered why she had been given such direct orders to come.

Aileen huffed. "Isn't that the truth, now? I could barely understand him myself. His droning on about fate, and gray mountains, and something laughing. A crow, wasn't it?" She snapped her fingers. "Aye, if it wasn't a magpie it was surely a crow, so. A wee bit of feathers bringing more gloom than a banshee. You know, heralding anew of death and despair, that's what. I tell you, that man must abide with nothing but spiders, rats, and goons whispering in his ear."

They both burst out laughing.

"'Tis a good thing, it was, that you did not understand his English, Sofia."

Sofia wiped her eyes. "You have told me all I need to know about his writings. Why do you say he came for me?"

"He is plenty wealthy, I tell you. Inherited money, I hear. I expect Annie and The Hawk wanted to squeeze a bit out of the old bird to pay for your mother's treatment."

Sofia felt her jaw tighten. Her summons now made sense. "They should not do this. We do not need help. I will talk to Papà today."

"They don't mean to be busybodies, Sofia. They only make suggestions. They know who likes to give money away and who doesn't."

"I understand."

Aileen placed her tiny feet on the floor and held out a hand. She was not finished yet. "Don't mind me. I was just having a bit of fun. They do mean well, Sofia. Mrs. Hawkins knows all the rich people in town even though she's not a bit uppity herself."

Sofia finished lacing her boots and stood to leave. "There are some things money cannot fix. For those things we need family. And God." It sounded good, like a loyal, old world Catholic. But inside, Sofia feared God was telling her no. He would not do as she asked and get Mamma out of there. She drew in a breath to shift her focus away from such negative thoughts. "I will see you for supper tonight, Aileen."

꘎

Mass seemed especially long as Sofia sat beside her father and siblings. No one spoke before. There had not been time. Beads of sweat swam under her collar even though the sanctuary was cool. She tapped her fingers on her rosary, unable to concentrate on the prayers being spoken aloud. She stood, knelt, said the Our Father, but out of routine. She continued to think about Mamma. What was she doing today? Had they let her out of her room for mass? What was she eating? Was she cold? Afraid? Sad?

And then the grayest thought came to her. What if Mamma was sitting in her tiny room, blaming Sofia? Perhaps she despised Sofia because Sofia lived and Serena hadn't. As angry as she felt sometimes, especially toward Papà, this fear was worse. On Ward's Island Mamma had hinted at it: Serena died because Sofia lived. She pushed the ugly thoughts from her mind. Getting Mamma better was what mattered most.

As they stood for the recessional, Sofia put her hand on Papà's arm. She would not let go until they had the opportunity to talk.

Papà patted her fingers. "What did you think of the homily this morning, Sofia?"

She didn't think anything. She hadn't heard it.

While she was trying to decide what to say, Gabriella spoke up. "About hearing God speak to us, Papà. The story of Rachel."

He turned to Sofia's sister. "Ah, *bene. Bene.*"

He slipped away from Sofia. Papà and Sofia's brothers approached the Russo men.

Sofia sighed loudly. "Carla Russo is not at mass today. I hope she is all right," Sofia said to her sister.

"I would not worry about that. She misses often. But what is the problem with you?" Gabriella took her arm. "You seem especially distracted this morning."

Sofia's face warmed. She moved away from her sister. "What is the problem, you ask?" She chopped at the air as she spoke. "Everything is falling apart. Mamma is in an awful place, Gabriella. Did you not notice?" The girl's self-absorbed nature irritated Sofia today more than usual. Was there no one in this family to help?

"Of course, Sofia, but she is in a hospital. She will get better."

Sofia closed her eyes a moment. They were in church. She would not scold her sister. Not here. She gritted her teeth. "She will not get better there. I have visited and seen with my own eyes."

"You saw Mamma?" Gabriella's lips parted slightly as she considered this. "I did not know she was somewhere bad."

Sofia whispered. "So, because you did not know, you think it could not be so, Gabriella?"

"No. I mean, no one told me there was anything amiss there. How was I to know?"

You might try to find out.

"How bad, Sofia?"

Drawing a quick breath to calm herself, Sofia realized her sister was ignorant because their parents allowed her to be. They had always done so. Gabriella was obedient. Always doing what they said without question. This was not Gabriella's fault. "I am sorry to be so irritable. She is bad enough that we must convince Papà to get her out. Today."

Gabriella's face turned white. They both looked toward the men who were laughing and slapping each other on the back. "That could be difficult," Gabriella observed.

Later, as Sofia and her sister cleaned up after the Sunday meal and Fredo worked on repairing the heels on Sofia's shoes, even though she had insisted she could do it herself, Sofia suggested a plan. She whispered to her sister. Not even her brothers thought the Falcone women should have any say when it came to their elders. Gabriella might be her only ally. "We will tell Papà we are going together to get Mamma."

"And bring her back here? We cannot do that. You saw how distressed and unmanageable she was when she was at home, Sofia."

"We must manage nonetheless. She is worse off there, I tell you."

Sofia had thought she had convinced Gabriella, but apparently she had not. Why must everyone fear what they don't understand? Why would no one talk about it? Mamma needed her family around her. Maybe not Sofia, not right now, but she would heal with time. Here. At home. With her family near.

Sofia hoped to convince even herself that was true. She prayed for it to be so, but if God would not grant this, she would arrange it herself.

Joey stomped in, latching the door behind him.

"Where have you been?" Papà shouted. He rose to meet his youngest son before he came fully into the apartment.

"Getting work." Joey took off his coat with the patched up elbows and flung it toward the coat tree, missing it. He shoved it to the corner with his foot.

Papà stood so close their noses nearly touched. "And for this you missed mass? You shame me. This kind of work, this bullying work, no Falcone will do this living under my roof."

Joey stood his ground. "What are you talking about, Papà? I have been looking for a job."

Sofia's other brothers sprang from their seats and joined in. There was so much shouting no man could hear the other. Neither did they hear the faint knock. Sofia unlocked the door.

Joey put a hand on it. "Ask who it is."

"Carla Russo," came the answer.

Sofia opened the door to find the woman standing in the hall, shivering. She joined her out there despite being in her stocking feet. She closed the door to the shouting. "*Signora* Russo, what is wrong?"

"*Signor* Russo…he…" She sucked in her breath and began again. "I have to leave my apartment. I come here. I need to come anyway. Sofia, your mother."

Sofia put an arm around her and tried to warm the woman they called the healer but she cried out in pain. "You are hurt. Let me help you."

"No. Please, never mind me. He strikes me because I question him but he will not keep me silent. He and his brother and your papà were talking as they returned from mass. I did not go this morning because…God forgive me, I did not feel well. But I awaited their return so I would know when to bake *pane di saragolla* out back."

The families in the building kept a wood-burning oven in the outside courtyard to bake bread the way they had in Italy. Whether or not Carla Russo felt well, she would be expected to put the bread on the table. "Go on," Sofia encouraged.

"As I was going out the door I heard them coming. I waited in the shadows and listened. I heard things before, so has Luisa, but we did not think we could do anything. Perhaps we cannot, but I will not keep silent."

Sofia guided her to the staircase and when the two of them sat down a rosy bruise showed just above the woman's ankle. Sofia cringed, but did not know if she should mention it. "Where is your daughter?"

"She is helping the nuns this afternoon. They are putting together baskets for the needy. I am glad she was not here."

She paused a moment but Sofia knew she would not explain fully what had happened behind their apartment door.

"I had to come down to see you. Your papà, he did not know. He could not have known. Please, Sofia, do not blame him."

"*Signora* Russo, known what? What about Mamma?"

"The men, the bad ones. *Signor* Parrella's men." She began to weep. "Your papà, he thanked my husband for helping his son get work, but until *Signor* Russo told him today, he did not know." She was nearly hysterical.

324

"Please, *signora*. I do not understand what you mean."

The woman pinched her eyes shut as if what she was about to say was going to cause her pain. "Your brother Joseph. He should have stayed away. Your mamma, if she were here, she would have kept him away."

The woman's words seemed to bounce against each other in the damp hall. She was trying to tell Sofia something, but what? Papà was scolding Joey still. She could hear them through the thin walls. Something about the work he was doing. "Joey is involved in something bad, *Signora* Russo? Please, tell me."

A door slammed above them and the woman jumped. Vanessa, one of the children Gabriella tended to, came bounding past them carrying a hoop. "I am going outside to play," she announced.

"You should. While the sun shines," Sofia said. "Go along now."

Carla Russo relaxed her shoulders but she seemed skittish.

"Why don't you come in for a hot drink, *signora*? Papà won't mind."

As the two of them entered the apartment Sofia felt the woman stiffen beside her when she looked at Joey. But it was Papà who shouted at them. "Her husband. He is the one who got you into trouble, Joseph."

"Papà!" Sofia shouted back. "Whatever happened, it was not our healer's fault."

"No, it was her husband!" Papà lowered his voice. "Carla, Sofia is right. Forgive me. It is not your fault. Sit down. Sofia, get her caffè, *presto*."

Carla was still shaking when Sofia helped her to a chair. She saw Papà looking at the woman's bruise before she quickly pulled her skirts down to cover it. Papà wouldn't ask her about it, either. It was another man's business. Well, Sofia would not follow tradition the next time she saw *Signor* Russo.

"He should not be here!" Carla Russo pointed at Joey. "They will come. Hide him. Run away, Joseph!"

Joey flattened himself against the wall and drew back the window curtain with one finger. "I must go, Papà."

Tears filled Sofia's father's eyes. Sofia looked from him to the healer, but could not comprehend what they were talking about. Her three brothers were about to leave when she blocked the door. "Joey, what is this? We have to help Mamma. There is no time for foolishness." But a glance at the healer made her realize this was no joke.

Joey smiled sadly at her. "Do not worry, my sister. They won't catch me. I was a greenhorn before, but I've learned."

He had grown tall and handsome, but when she looked at him she saw the little boy he used to be, the kid brother he still was in that smile of his. She wanted to believe him. Wanted assurance that Fredo and Frankie would know where to take their younger brother in order to protect him. If she could believe he would be all right, she could turn her focus to helping Mamma. But a gnawing in her stomach and an unexplainable crushing realization told her, it was possible she might never see her youngest brother again. She hugged him and he returned the embrace so tightly she thought he knew it, too.

There was a disturbance on the street below and the brothers rushed out without any more discussion.

Carla stood awkwardly on her injured ankle. "As a healer, I cannot help him. Cannot even help myself." She paused at the door. "But your mamma? There is still time." She sent Papà a pleading look. "The stranger who was asking after his dog yesterday. His name is Antonio Baggio. Your own Joseph was sent to influence him with his fists. To make him tell them what they want to know. But it did not work because this man, this stranger, he knows nothing. I tell you this from *Signor* Russo, even though it could cost me my life, Giuseppe Falcone! These same men murdered *Signor* Baggio's father."

Sofia startled at the mention of Antonio's name. She had hoped, had tried to believe, that Joey had been mistaken. Now it seemed Antonio really was involved. Carla said Antonio was innocent. Sofia prayed it was true.

The healer jabbed a finger in Sofia's father's direction. "I do not know why, but I know God has put the two families together in order to put an end to this. Lose your pride, old man. Joseph is gone. Sofia is banished from the neighborhood. Do something before you lose your entire family! And start by getting your wife out of the hell hole she is in." She slammed the door on the way out.

Papà flung his hands in the air. Sofia looked at her sister. They were both in shock that the healer would speak to their father that way, but now was the time to push him.

"Let's go get Mamma, Papà. Right now."

32

ANTONIO HAD AN UNPRODUCTIVE SUNDAY searching for his dog. He had missed mass, and missed seeing Sofia, but he could only think about Lu. He had returned to his apartment in hopes the dog had found his way back, but there was no sign of him. Antonio glanced at the accordion lying in pieces on his kitchen table. That search had come up empty as well. No note inside. No clues.

Evening shadows fell over his floorboards. A call to the abbey revealed that his dog was not in Little Italy. No one had seen him. Still Antonio looked, to no avail. He may have been run over by a trolley and tossed aside. Things like that happened in a big city.

The note from the musician was still sitting on the piano. The excitement Antonio had felt over it yesterday had waned. He was cold, lonely, and helpless.

Dragging the kitchen chair to the window so he could look out over the street, Antonio thought about what Sister Stefania had said over the telephone line. Because her nephew Joseph, the one who had accosted Antonio, was no longer working for the thugs, his life was in danger. She insisted Antonio could help because he too had been wronged by the *padrone* and his men. Living in a different neighborhood, being more American than Italian, and Northern Italian at that, he had no connection with those people. Sure, Nicco had said he and Ernesto had met some of them in a saloon, but that had been very long ago, a casual meeting of acquaintances. Was this the most the nun could do to help Antonio solve the mystery? He still did not know who wrote those notes. Perhaps Sister Stefania had put that young girl, Luisa, up to it, but for no good use.

He rubbed his stubbly chin and sipped his coffee. Antonio would focus on his music, like his father had wanted, and become the best he could be, someone who could inspire audiences to rise to their feet. He still wished for Sofia to be in that audience, but he did not see how he could help her with her troubles.

Antonio's gaze fell on the empty dog bed. He was alone. So very alone.

A slip of paper flew across the floor from under his door. A boy's voice shouted, "Message!" Then Antonio heard the boy's feet clatter down the stairs.

When he picked it up, he recognized the handwriting. Thick, boxy letters and plenty of ink blots, just the way he signed his checks. Why on earth was Mac sending him a message?

He tore open the envelope.

Tony,

Get on over to the Fourteenth as soon as you get this. Make haste, lad! Paderewski stopped by. He will soon be boarding the Oceanic for England. There's something here ye'll be interested in.

Mac

Well, there was nothing Antonio was interested in over at the theater. He didn't even want work. Not today.

Sofia paced the dark backstage of the theater where Antonio was employed. Performers squeezed past her. Women wearing headbands with large peacock feathers. Musicians carrying black instrument cases. A plump lady practicing squeaky vocal scales. The smell of roasted peanuts and salty popcorn made her think of street vendors. Being indoors, however, the smells mixed in an unappealing way.She received an occasional raised eyebrow look from those who realized she didn't belong there. She would have left when the manager told her Antonio wasn't there, but he was so insistent he would arrive shortly. It was impulsive, coming there, but after they checked Mamma out of the hospital and got her settled in, Sofia hadn't wanted to delay a moment longer.

The manager had said to wait. He had sent a messenger to Antonio's apartment.

She wrung her hands as she walked, wondering how she would explain this to Antonio, and yet she knew she had to. His father's death troubled him. He had searched all over her neighborhood looking for clues. And the entire time her brother Joey had the answers.

"Excuse me." A curly brunette pushed a harp toward the stage.

"Sorry." Sofia stepped back and began her pacing a little farther from the curtain.

She was miffed at her brother for this. And worried about his safety. Surely a job could not have been worth getting involved in such a viperous business. Others in the family had work. He had not needed to resort to working for savage criminals.

A drum sounded from the stage, making her jump. If her nerves were not already electrically charged from the distressing news she'd learned, being backstage in a vaudeville theater would be enough to ensure she was a jumbled mess.

She began a long, slow walk toward the business offices. If it weren't for Sister Stefania they still might not know the whole story. She told the sad tale when Papà summoned her to join them on the trip to Ward's Island. He had thought the presence of Mamma's sister might calm her, and he had been correct. Together those two were more complete. They complemented each other. The two of them even completed each other's sentences.

Sofia rubbed her gooseflesh arms. Life might have been much easier for her if her twin had lived.

"Why don't ye come inside and sit down, lass? You'll wear yourself out with all that marching back and forth. I'll get ye some coffee." The manager had asked her into his office earlier and she had been too uncomfortable to accept. She owed Antonio the explanation he had been searching for so she couldn't leave. And if he could tell her what happened to that money? Well, maybe Joey could come back and the Parrella gang could go to prison, where they belonged.

The ruddy-cheeked manager stuck his head out of his office again. "I will telephone his landlord and tell him it's an emergency."

Sofia nodded and kept walking the hall. A performance had begun and the stage hushed. A few moments later, he brought her coffee. "*Grazie*. I mean thank you," she whispered.

"I know what you meant, lass. There's no need to hide that you're Italian from me. I'm in theater, don't ye know? All sorts of folks here. Even Italians like yourself. A couple of Sicilians are about to go on now. Remarkable guitar players, they are. Have a listen." He pulled a chair toward an opening in the curtain and this time she sat.

They were quite good. She had never been to a theater before. She observed a monkey act next and laughed so hard she cried. This must be why people came here. To get away from their sorrows, even for a little while. She turned when someone called her name.

Antonio's shadowy form came toward her, followed by someone. She pushed back her chair and met him halfway.

"You *are* here. I thought Mac must have been mistaken. Are you all right? I was told there was an emergency of some type." He looked worried. And tired.

The man standing behind Antonio was a policeman. She was not sure whether that was appropriate or not. One never knew about the police. But when they invited her to go ahead of them back to the manager's office, she realized she had seen this officer before. "Are you the man who helped me find my mother on the streets? She was very confused that night."

"Indeed, I believe I was. Sergeant McNulty," he said, dipping his chin.

Ah, yes. The man Aileen had referred to as wonderful. They admired him over at Hawkins House. "You were very kind."

"Doing my job."

"You work up here?" She could not imagine why he had come.

"No. I encountered Antonio outside the theater. I was on my way home after visiting with my mother and her friend. They live a few blocks east. I was getting on the train when he got off."

She must have been staring at his uniform and he guessed her question.

"Oh." He dusted a hand across his brass buttons. "I just completed my shift. I haven't been home yet. But when Antonio told me he had been summoned to the theater because of an emergency, I decided to come along in case I could be of help."

"That is good of you, sergeant."

"What is this about?" Antonio asked the manager when they were seated.

"I will get to that later," the man behind the desk said. "This lady came to talk with ye, Tony."

All eyes turned toward Sofia. She did not realize she would have an audience when she told Antonio that her brother had been involved in his father's killing. She set her empty coffee cup down on the desk, folded her hands in her lap, and cleared her throat to begin. "I have learned something. Something my aunt was trying to tell us before, in her own way."

Antonio's face darkened. "This is about my father?"

"*Sì*, your father. It seems both he and my brother were wrapped up in *Signor* Parrella's ill doings."

"Valentino Parrella? The *padrone*?" the policeman asked.

Sofia turned toward him. "You know him?"

"He's not on our Wall of Shame yet, but he no doubt will be someday. Small time Italian boss that the department's been keeping watch on. When I make detective, these are the kind of riffraff I'm going after."

Sofia stared at him, unable to decide whether this would be a good thing or not. This policeman surely was helpful in keeping the streets clear of pickpockets and finding lost people, like her mother. What could he know of the Italians' business?

Antonio put a hand on the arm of her chair. "Sofia, are you saying your aunt knew something about my father's death? That it wasn't an accident? That the Benevento men were involved in it?" He did not wait for an answer as thoughts seemed to come to him like a runaway trolley car. "My uncle mentioned this. I thought he was just a mixed up old man. But I still don't understand how my father could have been involved. We aren't from your village. We don't live close to Mulberry Street."

She held up a hand. "Please. Let me explain."

He leaned back in his chair, breathless, as though he'd been running after something or someone and had now given up.

"My brother, Joey, he is a good boy. He only wanted to earn money for *la famiglia*. But he was foolish. When he could not find work, he went to the *padrone*. There are plenty of Italian bosses who can help find employment, but he went to this one, a man who is especially brutal, giving all Southern

Italians a bad image in the papers." She didn't know if she was making herself clear. Frustrated, she raised clinched fists in the air. If Joey were there she might have slugged him and made him face what he had done.

"She is right," Sergeant McNulty added. "Not all Italians are extortionists. Not all cheat and lie. They have a bad reputation because of a few. And this Valentino? He is growing into one of the worst."

Sofia squeezed her restless hands together in her lap. "Perhaps, Sergeant, Antonio and I can help you. And my brother Joey. Help you...to...get justice. For the people."

The policeman bobbed his head. "And put this man in jail? I'm at your service."

She glanced to the theater manager who sat with fat hands folded on top of his desk. "You are kind to open your office to us. But we should not keep you from your work, *signore.*"

His brows shot up. "Oh, aye. I should go check on the next set. It's starting in ten minutes." He wove around his desk and between Antonio and the policeman. "Stay as long as you'd like, gentlemen." He turned and saluted her with two fingers to his forehead. "And you, miss. Take yer time."

When the manager closed the door Antonio stared at her.

"I...uh, you see, my family went to Ward's Island today, to get my mother."

Antonio's expression brightened. "Excellent. She is better?"

"No, not better, but she will be now she is home."

"I am sure of it. That is not a pleasant place."

The policeman made no comment. In New York, there was plenty for the police to do and not enough of them to do it. Mrs. Hawkins had told her the night he had brought Sofia home that this man was most trustworthy. She believed Aileen was right, when she told Sofia that Mrs. Hawkins knew a lot of people in Manhattan.

Sofia licked her lips, hoping she did not look as disheveled as she felt. "And my aunt, she came with us. I had not realized it before, but my aunt has the ability to calm my mother. My father is looking for someone to care for Mamma while he works, but for today Sister Stefania will stay with her."

"I hope she gets the treatment she needs, Sofia. I truly do. But what were you saying?"

She inhaled deeply to give herself time to respond, taking in the smells of leather furniture and musty sheets of music. How did one tell someone such terrible things about one's own brother?

"Joey was there when your father was shot. He said he was not part of it and he did not know it would happen, but he did see it happen. He thought the gang would just go and get the money from your father before he met with the lawyer up at Cooper Union."

"Oh. Uncle Nicco."

She did not know what he meant.

The telephone on the desk rang and the manager charged back into the room. Sofia thought he must have been standing right outside to get back so quickly. He talked rapidly into the shiny black receiver. "That so? No kidding? Aye, he's here. I will tell him." He hung up and slammed both of his large hands down on his desk. "Tony, they've found yer dog! He's down at St. Anthony's mission."

33

Antonio and Sofia exchanged glances. She clearly wanted to know what he would do next. After Mac assured him the janitor at the mission said Luigi was fine and the attendant would be there for a few more hours, Antonio relaxed.

Sofia shifted in her chair. "The healer, I mean, *Signora* Russo mentioned you were asking about your dog. I did not understand that he was lost."

"Yes. I asked around in your neighborhood. We got separated in Little Italy a couple of days ago. He is usually so good about staying put. Someone must have distracted him."

"I am sorry, but glad he has been found. What caused you to be on Mulberry Street? Did you come to see my aunt again?"

Owen McNulty stood. "Pardon my interruption. I really must be going but before I do, Miss Falcone, I would like to know if I...if the New York Police can do something to help you."

Antonio thanked him and turned to her. "I would like to know, too. The thugs that assaulted me? They asked about money. Do you know what they want?"

"*Sì*. I know. It is a long story, I am afraid."

Owen McNulty had his hand on the doorknob. He wished to leave and Antonio knew Sofia's limited English prevented her from summing things up quickly.

The sergeant nodded. "Why don't you come around to the main station tomorrow? Ask for Detective Long. He can help you."

"But...I would like to tell it you, Sergeant. I...uh, Mrs. Hawkins said I can trust you."

"Of course you can. I will be there for a meeting tomorrow afternoon. I can meet you before it begins, say two o'clock?"

"I, uh, I have to be at work."

Her eyes welled up, more out of frustration than fear or sadness, Antonio thought.

Owen sat back down. "Now, now. I understand. Where do you work, Miss Falcone?"

She gave him the address of the shoe factory.

"I will come in the morning and ask your supervisor for permission to speak to you. Don't worry. I won't be wearing my uniform. I will tell him it is a personal matter because it truly is, yes?"

"*Grazie*. Thank you."

Owen McNulty left.

Antonio pressed down on his knee to keep from tapping his foot impatiently. "Tell me what you can, Sofia." She turned liquid eyes toward him. This was painful for her. "Mac, give us a moment, would you please?"

"Aye. I have to check on the stage lights, anyway." He slapped Antonio's shoulder on the way out. "There is a note for you on my desk. Do not leave without it, lad. I called ye here for that."

"Thank you."

When they were alone Sofia's tears came freely. He handed her a clean handkerchief.

"Joey did not know, Antonio. I know he made a bad impression on you. But I tell you he is not like what he pretends."

"It's all right. I had a feeling about that. Go on." He reached for her hand and was pleased when she did not pull away. He would have preferred to wrap his arms around her because he could see how distressed she was. He knew the pain of grief, the disappointment when life took turns you weren't prepared for. "Has something happened to your brother?"

She shook her head, dislodging the lace scarf many of the Italian girls wore on Sundays. She released his hand, unpinned it, and placed it on her lap. "I do not know where he is but my twin brothers Fredo and Frankie saw to his safety. He betrayed those bad men. I fear for his life now."

"I spoke to your aunt earlier. I suppose it was before you went to get your mother. She did not tell me this, but she did tell me your brother had seen the error of his ways." He sat quietly a moment and allowed her to regain her composure.

"I am concerned about his safety. I also fear you will hate me." Her voice came out almost inaudible, like the squeal of a mouse.

"Oh, no, Sofia." He knelt on the floor before her chair. "This is not your fault. Were you there when my father was shot? Did you send your brother to that *padrone*?"

She slowly shook her head.

"Well, then. See? You had nothing to do with this."

"But…it is *mia famiglia*. That is the same as if I were there."

"No it isn't." The look on her face told him she didn't believe it. If anyone in her family was guilty, she was too—that was how Italians saw things. All together no matter what. He held her hand, still on his knees. "Sweet Sofia. Listen to me. I felt the same way. I thought I had to do something to bring justice for my father. To honor his memory. I thought I had to rescue my uncle from the power of drink. I thought I had to…" He couldn't say it. He still felt compelled to succeed in the occupation his father believed he was gifted in. Perhaps he had been too driven. But the feeling that he must press on would not go away. "I mean, I took on the problems of my family and now I know…" He let out a nervous chuckle. "You see, I have enough of my own to deal with. We each make our own decisions and mistakes. It's all a part of the journey God has us on in this life. We can't carry our family members' burdens, as much as we'd like to. It's their cross to bear and there is value in bearing it. We should not take that away."

She smiled and the whole room seemed to brighten. "You are so kind, Antonio."

"Would you like to tell me the rest?"

"I do not know much more. Joey was there, working for the *padrone*. They searched your father's pockets and found no money. There was a crowd, something…uh, a political rally going on when it happened, something about anarchists. Your father was pushed into a crowd and shot, but not before they heard him say his son will never be like them. He is a musician at St. Anthony's and one day they all will know his name."

"He said that?" Antonio's voice cracked, surprising him. He hadn't meant to show emotion while she was telling such a difficult tale.

"He loved you, Antonio."

He stood. "And I loved him."

"I am sorry my aunt did not tell you this. We do not speak of family matters. She thought she would betray Joey if she did."

So that was where the messages had come from, Antonio realized. The nun probably thought that by sending him secret clues she would not openly oppose her nephew. That was how the Mulberry women were heard in their culture, by circumventing the Old World order of things. Unnecessary, he thought, but it was their way.

"Since you are telling me this, you do not think like she does."

"No."

Her look softened and so did his heart. He would never hold this against her. "We cannot change what has happened. But what money?"

"I am afraid Joey knows the answer but he is gone. I was hoping you knew something that might free him from exile, something the police can use."

"I am sorry I do not. You tell the story to Sergeant McNulty tomorrow and perhaps the police can take care of the matter. You should get home to your mother now."

She frowned. "Not yet. I upset her and I want her to get better before I come home."

"So back to Hawkins House?"

"*Sì.*"

"I will see you home."

She stood, smoothing her long fingers down her skirts. "You should go see about your dog."

"Uh, yes. Why don't you come with me?"

Before they headed out the door she stopped him. "Do not forget your note."

He glanced at the paper on Mac's desk. He recognized the handwriting as Paderewski's. He stuffed it in his pocket and escorted Sofia outside.

34

"OH HEAVENS, WHAT'S HAPPENED?" Mrs. Hawkins ushered Sofia down the hall while Antonio shut the door.

"Don't leave that dog outside," she said over her shoulder. She waved her arm. "Bring him in too."

When Sofia sat, the dog lay at her feet. She felt spent. It had been a long, emotionally drenching day. Antonio sat next to her on the sofa but kept a respectable distance. She longed to fall into his arms. He was the only one she drew comfort from today. Wouldn't Mamma be surprised at that, since he was of northern Italian descent. Joey had an Irish girlfriend Mamma knew nothing about. It would take patience to convince her, once she was feeling better, that people are worthy no matter where they came from. In this country, the past was the past and easily left behind. Although Mamma hadn't been able to cope with her past, what happened to Sofia's twin, she would have to learn. Soon. She must.

Sofia smiled up at Mrs. Hawkins. How kind and motherly she had been. A substitute when she so desperately needed one.

Leena and Etti wandered in to join them for tea. Two shy girls from a part of Europe Sofia knew nothing about. She enjoyed the stories of their homeland, a place often snowy, they had said, where everyone wore fur and reindeer were as common as dogs. She would have never met these women on Mulberry Street. She thought about Annie's library upstairs where even more worlds were beginning to open to her as she learned to read in English. It was good, if she had to be separated from *la famiglia*, to have come to Hawkins House.

She reached down to pet the dog and noticed how well Antonio filled that formerly cold space next to her. She would certainly go home soon, but these people had become important to her. She ended up needing their companionship more than she had first imagined she would. Could this have been God answering her prayers after all? Perhaps Hawkins House was not the solution to everything, but she had asked for belonging, for understanding, for a place of warmth again. She had wanted that with Mamma, the way it had been. Perhaps God answered the cry of her heart in this place instead.

"You say your dog Luigi was lost?" Mrs. Hawkins asked, accepting tea from Minnie.

Sofia realized she had not been listening to the conversation. Luigi perked up when his name was mentioned.

"I've got a bone in the kitchen," Minnie said. "All right if he comes down with me?"

"Sure." Antonio whistled and made an away gesture with his hand and the faithful dog trotted off with the housekeeper.

Mrs. Hawkins returned to her inquiry. "I wonder why he came to the mission? Wise dog, none-the-less. And very well disciplined." Mrs. Hawkins took a bite of one of the pastries Minnie brought and wiped powdery sugar on her napkin.

Sofia glanced to Antonio, wondering what he would say. Would he share his family matters with someone he hardly knew? True, things were more relaxed here, and these were good people, but he was still a guest.

He dipped his chin, seemingly not bothered by the question. "My uncle, I'm afraid, battles an addiction to strong drink. Has most of my adult life."

Sofia saw recognition light in the sisters' faces. They hadn't spoken of their parents but Sofia guessed the drinking sickness had had some affect on their family as well.

"Oh, love, I am so sorry. The demon drink has control over so many." The sad admission brought Mrs. Hawkins to tears, as many things did. The woman wanted to help people. Always offering whatever she could, and when nothing she had could remedy things, Mrs. Hawkins became wholly overwrought.

"It has consumed so many, even in this country," Leena finally added. "I help many a sick man at the hospital, I am afraid."

"Vaar Maslov was one," Etti whispered. "Our grandfather. Very sad. He died too young."

"Oh, I am sorry, lovies." Mrs. Hawkins wiped her nose and blinked away tears.

"My condolences, as well," Antonio said. "It is very hard, sometimes impossible, for family members to do anything to help."

Sofia smiled at the two girls. "I shall light a candle for him at mass."

They thanked her and then relaxed back into their chairs as if the tea they drank was the most soothing sympathy of all.

Antonio addressed Mrs. Hawkins. "They look after my uncle at the mission. I try to get him to stay with me but I'm not successful very often."

Sofia coughed, not comfortable with the sharing of family matters. Perhaps Antonio felt pressured by The Hawk and that should not be. She whispered. "You do not have to—"

"It's fine, Sofia. I don't mind Mrs. Hawkins and the Maslov sisters knowing. There is no reason to hide it. I am not ashamed of him, although I do pity him."

Mrs. Hawkins patted the air with her free hand. "Well, I am pleased he is getting help, son. There are many charitable Christian men and women acting as the Lord's hands and feet in this city. And God knows they are needed. Did your dog go there because of him?"

Antonio looked toward the hall, obviously wondering how they were getting along in the kitchen. "Nicco wasn't there when I picked Lu up. And truly, my dog never really liked my uncle."

"Oh?" Mrs. Hawkins picked up her teacup, which appeared oddly tiny in her large hand. "I assumed that was the reason your dog appeared at the mission. He had a long walk from Mulberry, where you said you lost him. He is a smart wee thing, now isn't he?"

Antonio pulled at his collar. "I hadn't thought of him seeking out my uncle, Mrs. Hawkins. Perhaps you are correct."

Annie Adams knocked at the edge of the pocket door and then came into the parlor. "Minnie was in the kitchen and let me in back there," she explained. "There is a phone call for Mr. Baggio."

"Me?" He stood. "Why would anyone ask for me at your home?"

She smiled. "The operator knows I take calls for Hawkins House. 'Tis someone at St. Anthony's shelter for men. He explained that you were there earlier and said you were stopping by here." Annie popped into the parlor and helped herself to a powdery cookie.

Antonio excused himself and Annie led him out.

"Oh, dear," Mrs. Hawkins said. "I wonder what the trouble could be. I hope his uncle is all right."

Sofia hoped so too. She didn't know how he could cope with one more difficulty tonight.

Several minutes later he returned, crossed the floral rug to say good-bye, and whistled softly for his dog. "We appreciate your hospitality, Mrs. Hawkins, Miss Falcone." He nodded at the sisters. "Ladies." He put a hand on Mrs. Hawkins's chair. "We will not impose on you any longer. It is getting late."

Mrs. Hawkins wiggled up from her fluffy seat. "Not at all, love. Is everything all right?"

"Oh, right as rain. My uncle returned to the shelter and refused to believe that Luigi was all right until he talked personally with me. So the attendant made the call."

"How very kind of them, love."

Sofia saw him to the door.

"Thank you for sharing about…your uncle. It was none of our business, but I am happy to hear that he has people to help him."

"Thank you for inviting me in, Sofia. Mrs. Hawkins runs a fine establishment. The Sunday dinner here is delightful, but an informal gathering for tea reveals the true character of a place. I am happy to see that you are well taken care of."

"I am. It is…temporary." She pronounced the word like a question, not knowing if she'd chosen the appropriate expression, but he nodded as though he understood. "I will go home as soon as my mother is well."

They stood alone at the front door with Luigi at their feet. Mrs. Hawkins and the others had gone to their respective rooms to retire. He had said everything was fine with his uncle, but she felt an uneasiness between them. She spoke at the floorboards. "Are you sure you are all right? I mean, has this phone call disturbed you?"

He lifted her chin. She stared into his eyes and instead of annoyance she saw gentleness. He nudged her chin a bit more and placed his lips on hers. When they parted, he said, "Now everything will be in order."

He and Luigi slipped out into the inky night. How incredible that one day brought her from bleakness to joy due to the spark of one long, lingering kiss. Knowing that God was indeed seeing to her requests—but in his own way—she went to her bed full of dreams of what might lie ahead.

Before she could clock in at the factory, a floor boy summoned her to Mr. Richmond's office. She had not settled matters with him yet. What would Antonio think of her if he knew how her boss had handled her? She breathed easier when she saw the policeman named Owen. She had momentarily forgotten he was coming. Instead of his uniform, he wore a plain navy suit. He removed a bowler hat from his lap before he stood to greet her."Miss Falcone," Mr. Richmond said in his most authoritarian voice, "this man says you have a personal matter to discuss. Come in and shut the door."

The palms of her hands were wet with worry. Joey was gone. The twins worked sporadically. Gabriella brought in only eggs and a few coins the neighbor gave her for minding her children, and Papà had lost time at work due to meeting with Mamma's doctors at Ward's Island. Sofia could not lose her job. Her family needed her. This planned meeting was a mistake, but it was too late to fix it.

She slowly lowered herself to the cold, wooden chair in front of her boss's desk. His face was gray. His fingers constantly moving as though he was as nervous as she. "Uh, *sì*, Mr. Richmond. I have not clocked in yet. I will only need a few moments."

Mr. Richmond rose and squeezed past them to leave. "Take your time," he said over his shoulder.

"He seems unsettled about you being here," Sofia said when she and Owen McNulty were alone.

"I'm afraid he recognizes me from my old beat. I told him there was no problem with the factory, but he didn't seem to believe me. However…" He pulled out a pad of paper and turned past a used page. "Some of the workers have been more than a little eager to tell me some things about him. Nothing for you to worry about, though." He cleared his throat and positioned his pencil over the pad. "Now, tell me what you know about *Signor* Parrella and your brother Joseph."

Later that day, about an hour before quitting time, Claudia returned to the floor. She had her hair drawn up into a bun and instead of a sewer's apron, she wore a fine shirtwaist and a long wool skirt. Sofia watched her weave among the workers while making notes on a clipboard the way Mr. Richmond normally did. Sofia glanced back to the office. It was dark, seemingly unoccupied. In fact, she hadn't seen her boss since the policeman left that morning.

"Maria," she called to her friend. "Claudia is back and she looks as though she has taken Mr. Richmond's position."

The nosey man behind them spoke up before her friend could answer. "Oh, she has. Richmond has been behaving inappropriately, I hear, and he has been sacked. Carrying on with some of the girls. I do trust you two were not harmed by him."

It was a statement meant to probe for information, not given out of concern, Sofia realized. She had not stopped to think that Mr. Richmond might have been molesting others. She bit her lip. She should have spoken up. She crossed herself and offered thanks for the protection God had provided. She would see Father Lucci in confession as soon as she could.

Maria leaned forward away from the man. "Claudia was a victim of Mr. Richmond's wrath. He knew she cared about the workers and wanted to be promoted. He fired her because he was afraid she would take his job. And now she has been restored. I am happy for her."

Sofia watched Claudia laughing with one of the workers across the room. She would be a much more benevolent supervisor. She had probably been preparing herself all along, not trying to destroy the company as Mr. Richmond had insinuated. Sofia had misjudged the woman, thinking her to be a busybody, when in fact, she had been trying to help the employees.

When she made her way to Sofia's row, Sofia wondered if she would despise her. Sofia spoke first. "I did not mean to give Mr. Richmond reason to dismiss you, Claudia. I hope you…uh, forgive me, *per carità.*"

Claudia paused from counting Sofia's stitched soles. "My girl, you did nothing wrong."

"But…I told him you were asking questions and speaking about workers' rights. He wanted me to spy in payment for using his telephone. I did not know anything so I told him only that. I did not know he would fire you for it. He thought you were going to…uh…" She could not think of the English word to tell her friend that Mr. Richmond thought Claudia was about to lead the workers to strike.

"I know, honey." She put a hand on Sofia's shoulder. "He thought I was a woman intent on taking his job. No matter what he told you, that was what he truly was afraid of." She laughed, throwing back her head. "And he was right, wasn't he? The most amusing thing is, if he had not been such a louse, I would have had to wait for him to retire to get this position. He did it to himself."

"You…you are not angry with me?"

"Whatever for, honey?" She tapped her pencil on her clipboard. "You are one of my best workers. You know that shoe you designed? I am going to recommend it for production and you will get a bonus."

"Hurray!" Maria cried out.

Immediately after work Sofia headed to her parents' tenement building, proud of her work day, but still concerned about Mamma. She would go see Carla Russo, just in case Mamma was not ready to see her yet. She had so many questions. Who should they ask for help? What kind of help did Mamma need? Sofia believed Mamma needed to be coaxed to tell the truth about what happened the day baby Serena died. With that secret out healing would follow. But how was it to be done?

She skipped along, dodging girls with hoops, boys playing stickball, and several newsboys hawking the evening edition of the papers. The smell of meat cooking made her stomach rumble. She had considered splurging at her favorite delicatessen near the factory for supper, but should they need to pay a doctor, one of those doctors of the psyche, she dared not waste a single penny, not even her promised bonus. Perhaps *Signora* Russo would spare some bread, enough to ease Sofia's complaining tummy.

She marched past the door to her home and up the stairs. She was about to knock on the healer's door when Luisa, Carla's daughter, opened it and came out into the hall.

"Papà is angry tonight, Sofia. I am on my way to the Free Library for sewing school. I do not know if Mamma will speak to you." She started to walk away and then retraced her steps. "Sofia, have you spoken to your friend Antonio?"

"About what?"

"The money." She sighed. "I know about Joey and that he was looking for money the night *Signor* Baggio died."

"Who told you that?"

"I overheard. I hear lots of things. Mamma says we cannot change things, but I think Antonio Baggio can. Has he said he will try?"

"Luisa, these are not things you should worry about. Go along to your sewing class."

She scooted on past Sofia, and then whispered low but Sofia heard. "I wish Papà would leave us." The door was slightly ajar.

Signor Russo was shouting something. A whimpering sound came from near the door, low and animal-like. Heartbreaking.

"*Buongiorno*," Sofia called out. "I have come for the healer. With money." She thought that might cause the man to back away from mistreating his wife.

A moment later *Signor* Russo burst through the door. "Another Falcone?" He pinched his fingers and tapped on his forehead. "You are all crazy! I leave this place, shake the dust off my boots, and never come back." He stomped down the stairs.

Sofia cringed for a moment at the word crazy. She went in and found Carla huddled on the floor. Her face was tear-streaked but she did not seem hurt. "He is a monster," Sofia said, helping the woman to her feet.

"He says he is leaving for good," Carla sobbed.

"*Finalmente*! You are better off."

Carla was shaking. "I cannot provide for Luisa alone. What will we do without his earnings?"

Carla had no other family on Mulberry Street and Luisa was her only child.

"I want her to stay in school. Learn things. Become a good American and marry well." She kept squeezing Sofia's arm. "I do not want her to work to support her poor, old Mamma."

Like I do?

After Sofia made coffee, the two women discussed the cost of rent, food, and fuel. "Papà will pay you to sit with Mamma." Sofia urged the sugar bowl toward Carla before realizing it was empty. "He might even take you and Luisa in. There is room in the apartment."

Carla sprung from the kitchen table and began opening cabinet doors. She scooped ingredients from several jars and began mixing with a large wooden spoon. Sofia could smell dried lavender and olive oil. She knew the woman was making a salve for Mamma. "May I help?"

"I earn my way, Sofia. I am the healer."

"Of course you are." Sofia gathered clear jars from a hutch and the two of them filled as many as they could with the mixture.

"I will make all I can before we are put out of here," the woman explained.

If *Signor* Russo really was gone for good—and Sofia hoped the terrible man never came back because he was a disgrace to all Benevento men—Carla and Luisa could not stay here. Immigrant women in this neighborhood were not permitted to live alone. If the landlord did not hear of their predicament, the priest would and shame would come to them. Sofia was beginning to see how women could be business owners and fare well because she'd seen Mrs. Hawkins handle matters. Even

Annie Adams, who was married to a postman, thought of herself as an independent businesswoman, despite bemoaning the fact that some did not respect her as they should. She was making strides, getting somewhere. Like that woman she'd spoken about, Miss Julia Richman. Those women were strong and resourceful. She glanced to the bruises Carla tried to hide. Here on Mulberry it might as well be another country. For some having a husband, even a bad one, was better than being left alone to starve and beg on the streets.

Sofia had to help Carla if she could. "Tell me about Mamma," Sofia asked. "Have you seen her since she has been home?"

"Only for a moment. She is pitiful, Sofia. Always looking out the window with no expression. Her thoughts drift from her when she does try to speak so that her words flitter like sparrows. Here and there. Back and forth. She needs the high cost doctors, Sofia."

Sofia brushed a stray strand of hair from her face as she worked. "Perhaps, if we cannot heal her first. You, here. And me offering advice from a distance. Get her to talk about what happened the day my twin died. It will be painful at first, but then she will heal. You will see."

Carla stopped stirring and gripped Sofia's wrist. "Listen to me, child. Some things are better forgotten. You will stir up terrible things with this talk."

"I do not think—"

Carla held up her hand so Sofia relented. For now. Until she could speak to Papà alone.

35

ANTONIO ROUSED with a growling stomach shortly before nine in the morning—early for him, but then he had not been working the night before. Luigi noticed he was awake and trotted over from his bed near the stove.

"Hey, boy. I wish you could tell me where you went and what you were doing."

Antonio got a sniff of something musty like stale rain gutter water. "Or maybe I don't want to know. You're getting a bath."

As he scrubbed the dog with a bar of Ivory soap, Antonio detected a yeast odor, something fermented. Alcohol? "Were you snoozing on the floor of a saloon, boy? You smell like the inside of a whiskey barrel."

When someone knocked on the door Luigi broke free and went toward the sound, scratching until Antonio got it open. "Uncle! Come in."

Luigi shook his body, sending soap bubbles toward Nicco's trousers. Instead of pushing the dog away, as he usually did, Nicco laughed. He was freshly shaven and wore a crisp, white shirt under his weathered overcoat. "There's the fella." He rubbed Luigi's damp ears.

"Since when did you two become friends?"

Nicco hung his overcoat over the back of the kitchen chair and leaned against Antonio's bed. He gave Luigi a firm pat as the dog sat at his feet. "Since he came looking for me. I was...uh, under the weather."

Antonio huffed. "Indeed."

"Oh, truly, I was. Not drunk. Not very much."

"Well, that is a good thing, Uncle. One day you will give it up entirely."

Nicco smiled. "You know those Benevento men I told you about? The ones I tried to keep away from here? They found me."

"Uncle, are you hurt?" Antonio put a hand on his uncle's shoulder, but he brushed him away. Antonio noticed the redness on one side of Nicco's face that hinted of the black eye to come.

"They shoved me around. I...uh, I am afraid I don't remember much else, but I am not harmed. I woke later in back of the grocer's shop, you know, the one who shares space with the butcher? I woke with this fella licking my face."

"The establishment that doubles as a saloon?" He went to the sink to dampen a cloth for Nicco's eye, wishing he had some ice or even a steak to bring down the swelling.

"*Sì*, that place. Maybe I went there for...pickle from the jar. I do not remember. Probably nabbed me in the alley, but they just pushed me around some. Do not worry." He placed the cold cloth to his cheek.

"I'm glad you are okay, Uncle." Antonio patted his dog on the back. How on earth had Luigi gone from Mulberry all the way back there to help Nicco?

"I know what you're thinking." Nicco pointed a gnarled finger at the dog.

"You do?"

"Sure. My brain's working this morning. How did he do it, that pooch? I wasn't surprised when I saw him, not too much, because I did not know that you had misplaced your Luigi in Little Italy until the attendant at St. Anthony's told me. You said the train drivers let him board, *sì*? That everyone welcomes him because he looks like the Victor dog, and anyway, he is better behaved than President Roosevelt's pets? You say this, *sì*?"

"Uh, yeah, something like that. He knew trouble was brewing. Dogs have a sense about things. Good boy."

"*Sì, sì.* Trouble."

They could have done to Nicco what they did to Antonio's father. They did not. That must mean they thought Ernesto had what they wanted, but Nicco did not. Why rough up the old man? Because they thought Antonio would pay up. This revelation nauseated him.

However, Nicco seemed better despite it all. More coherent.

Nicco rubbed his chin. "Now, where is that accordion case? I just remembered something."

Like one of Mac's actors responding to a cue, Lu jumped up and yelped. He trotted over to the case and sniffed. Antonio picked it up. "Nothing to this, Nicco. I examined it. If you thought there was a clue inside, there isn't. I found nothing—"

"Hold on. There has to be something. Sit down, son. Let me tell you what I remembered, like it was a dream, but it wasn't. Ever hear those soldiers talk about remembering things many months later?"

Antonio sighed. The man's moment of clarity had waned. "Soldiers?"

"The ones coming back from China. The fellas visit the shelter like I do and they talk. *Mamma mia*, do they talk. They tell me they have dreams that reveal lost memories. Flashback, some call it. A spark of something that comes to you and reveals an experience once deeply hidden."

"I know, Nicco. Those men, they witnessed horrible things. They buried memories to protect themselves from dwelling on unspeakable evil. A defense of the mind. I don't see how the accordion—"

Nicco held up a hand. "I don't say I'm the same. I am just telling you that I had a memory brought back to me. That is all."

"All right. What was it?" He rose to prepare coffee, only half-listening to the man's ramblings until he mentioned Antonio's father.

"Your papà, he came to me the morning before he was shot. I was sitting somewhere. *Sì*, the park. Relaxing a bit, you know. And your papà, he found me and he said, 'Brother, if ever you respected me, listen to me now. I am going to do something about those Benevento men. They should not be pressing the poor shopkeepers for protection money like they do. I pretended to help those thugs by collecting some of the money, but I will not hand it over. I will get help. A lawyer. Until I get back, you watch this.' I asked him, why me? Why not your son? And he scolded me harshly. He did not want you involved."

Antonio plunked down on the piano bench with a thud. "My father was a secret informant of some kind?"

"I don't know. All I know is he was trying to help the poor workers who struggle to put food on their tables and coal in their stoves, and he knew it was dangerous. That is why he did not tell you. To protect you."

"They want their money back. Do you have it?"

The man's face drooped. "I tell you the truth, God help me. I try to get better. I try. But...if I had that money all these months I would have spent it at the saloon. You know that. I cannot be trusted because I do not even realize what I'm doing until it's too late."

"Then where is it?"

Nicco glanced toward the case that Luigi sat near. The dog, motionless and rigid, reminded Antonio of the Peter Cooper statue that sat on its stony perch overlooking the violence when his father was killed. "In the case? Impossible. It's so compacted inside, and besides, I already looked."

Nicco shrugged his shoulders.

"Do you remember telling me Papà had told you to give this to me if he didn't come back? Why would he say that if he was trying to keep me out of it?"

"I remembered wrong. He did not say to give it you. He said to keep it away from you. Give it to me. I will hide it in the basement of the shelter."

"Now wait a minute. If it's that important we have to find out why. What if it does hold some kind of clue that could lead to the arrest of Papà's killers?"

The two of them searched inside and out, lifting buttons and feeling along the edges of the billows. Nothing.

"Any pencil writing inside? Nicco asked. "My eyes are not too good."

"It is as clean as a whistle. Nothing. Just this one broken key." He turned the accordion upside down. "Probe with your little finger in that reed opening there. I hear something but it seems like nothing is there."

After a few moments of shaking, a metal key slid through and clinked to the floor. Luigi whined and went over to sniff it.

After Sofia got Carla settled in in her parents' apartment, and carefully avoided Mamma's blank stares while speaking softly so as not to disturb her, she slipped outside to find Luisa. Carla was worried her daughter would come home to a cold apartment and not know where her mother was. Only days earlier Sofia would have expected to encounter Joey on one of the stoops or chatting with the newsboys. It pained her to think she might not see him again. Might not even know if he was alive or dead. As she walked, she drew her shawl tighter around her shoulders. The familiar coldness returned with magnified strength now that she had lost two siblings. Would this ever get easier?

When she reached the church, she found Sister Stefania sweeping the steps next door. She had handed over Mamma's care to Carla earlier that day. "Sister, it is so late. Why are you doing that?"

The diminutive woman looked at her with rounded eyes. "Working while I was waiting for you, dear."

"Oh, well I've come for Luisa Russo. Is she here or at the Free Library?"

"She is here. After visiting that place we have to remind her she is a good Catholic." She winked and nodded toward the yellow light coming from a window a few paces down the sidewalk. "They will be finishing up there any moment and she will come out. Until she does, tell me, Sofia, have you talked to that young man again? The one I said could help lead you to the bad *padrone*?"

"I have. He's a very fine young man, although, Mamma might not approve since he is from Northern Italy. I do not think he can help with Joey's situation, though. It was kind of you to try to help, Sister. Joey is away safely and there is nothing else to be done."

The nun wrinkled her nose as though Sofia had spoken an alien language. "You did not heed my advice?"

"No, we spoke, *Signor* Baggio and me. He does not have what the men want. He knows nothing about it. But I have explained to the police. They are aware of the bad man and I believe they will handle matters. I just wish Joey could come back home, but that is yet to be seen."

"Police?" She tsk-tsked the suggestion. "That young man, Antonio, he is who you need."

Sofia was pleased they could have this conversation but the woman was misdirected. "Why would you think that?"

"Your brother, Joseph, told me. Your brother worked for the bad man." She crossed herself as she said this.

"I know Joey worked for the extortionists. I know he helped threaten people, although I can't imagine he was very good at it. Antonio is not a threat. Parrella's men sent Joey on a bootless errand." She waved dismissively. "Maybe Antonio looks like someone else."

Luisa and a few other girls came toward them, chatting happily now that their charity work was done for the day. When the friends parted, Luisa joined Sofia and her aunt. "Did Mamma send you to walk me home? She worries too much."

"No," insisted Stefania. "She does not worry too much. You two girls should not walk home alone."

"We will be fine," Sofia said.

"One of the boys working on the church might walk you back. The Father retires early. If you wait, someone will be coming down. They have been working on the *predella*." She clapped her hands. "In my lifetime I may yet see the altarpiece installed."

"That is wonderful," Luisa said.

Sofia had no energy to entertain the musings of her distracted aunt. While they stood chatting about the cooler weather and changing colors of the trees in the park, a policeman crossed the street and headed in their direction.

"Miss Falcone," he called out.

"Sergeant McNulty? What brings you out here?"

When he got close enough, Sofia introduced him to Luisa and Sister Stefania.

"I was working," he explained. "I am finished for the day."

Stefania clapped her hands. "Since you already know my niece, perhaps you would walk her and her neighbor home?"

Owen McNulty bowed his head "I would be most happy to, Sister."

Luisa did not budge when Sofia tried to urge her forward. "I have never needed an escort before. We are only a few blocks from home. What is this all about?"

Sofia sucked in her breath.

"Coffee first!" Sister Stefania announced, herding them all toward the convent's kitchen.

Sofia plopped down on a chair. "There isn't time, Sister. We have to get back. Mamma needs us." She glanced up at Luisa. "Your mamma needs you."

"What has happened?" The young girl's expression stiffened. She shook her head at Stefania's offer of a cup.

"Your mamma is fine," Sofia also refused the convent's hospitality. The sergeant, however, supped as though famished.

"There has just been…a change. That is all," Sofia whispered.

"Sofia, tell me." Luisa's eyes watered. "What did Papà do?"

"He left."

Luisa looked at her strangely.

"Do not try to deny it. We know he was a wife beater."

"He was much more than that," Luisa said, plopping her arms on the table. "I must ask. Do you trust this policeman, Sofia?"

When Sofia said she most certainly did, the sergeant took out a pad and pencil and began to take notes as Luisa spoke.

The nun broke in when Luisa paused. "Now, you listen to me. I have something to say." She raised an eyebrow at the policeman and shrugged, apparently deciding she would speak in front of him.

The outburst so stunned them, they fell mute.

The sister drew her hands in front of her as she spoke, clearly and without the fluttering expression that most often accompanied her conversations. "*Signor* Russo behaved badly." She patted Luisa as she said this. "Joseph behaved badly. But the worst is *Signor* Parrella and the way he gets men to follow him, hungry men who are desperate to feed their families. And then someone dies. *Signor* Baggio, the young man's father. Joseph told me. And now Joseph had to leave." She pointed a gnarled finger at the sergeant. "Joseph had nothing to do with the death, you hear?"

He nodded and continued scribbling on the pad.

The nun's eyes filled with tears. "You will go to your father, Sofia. You will tell him enough suffering. It must stop. He will take care of the Russo women. He must tend to my dear Angelina. But you, Sofia, you must go to your young man *now* and get him to tell you about his father, what he did, what he tried to do to help."

"Sister, can you tell me more about that?" Owen readied his pencil over a fresh sheet of paper.

The nun glanced toward the ceiling. "No. Not me. But, Sofia, you ask, and then..."

Music wafted from an open window, a Victrola, perhaps the Sister's borrowed recording. She smiled and turned toward it. Sofia feared the lecture was over and just when she was about to tell them something.

Stefania put a cupped palm to her covered ear. "Hear that? Hear the master's voice?"

Luisa pushed a cracker around on the plate in front of her. "*Sì*, the dog hears his owner's recorded voice. We should go now, Sister."

"*Sì, sì*," Stefania said, eager to finish her thought. "You and Antonio Baggio, Sofia. You follow this and it will lead to answers." She patted Luisa's cheek. "And we will be safe, happy, and fat again. You will see."

After they saw Luisa home, Owen McNulty hired a cab to take Sofia to Hawkins House. On the way he tried to assure her. "Your mother will improve, I'm sure."

Sofia blurted what she was thinking. "The past haunts her. It haunts me also. Papà does not think bringing up the past is right."

"A detective's job is to uncover what is hidden, especially what folks have tried to keep buried, but in your case I shall do it with as much care as possible. I would not want to violate your family's privacy any more than is necessary."

"*Grazie*. You are kind." She sighed. "Mamma always said what begins difficult will end with success so long as we do not give up."

The whole way back to the boarding house Sofia thought about Antonio. She did want to see him again. She wanted to know his uncle was well, that Luigi the dog had endured his adventure away from home without mishap, and that Antonio would find peace with his father's untimely death.

Mamma would get well. This time God would answer that prayer because *la famiglia* had come together in their time of need. Joey? She didn't know what his fate would be, but God would hear Sofia's constant prayers for his safety.

She should be content but she was troubled. Stefania, as daffy as she seemed sometimes, had an uncanny ability to equate two seemingly unrelated things, like the Victor dog listening to his master's voice on the phonograph record labels—the dog that remarkably resembled Antonio's pet—and the search she and Antonio had been on to solve their respective family mysteries. *"You and Antonio Baggio, Sofia. You follow this and it will lead to answers."* She could not get that out of her mind. Follow the same voice? The same clues? What if God was directing the devout woman's words as she was instructing Sofia?

36

NICCO TURNED THE KEY between his fingers. "Too small for a door key. What do you have around here that locks?"

"Nothing. You can see for yourself. No boxes, no closets, no desks. Let me see." The key was simple-looking, no engraving, no numbers. As he studied it a thought came to him. "Uncle, keys turn locks, but sometimes they turn other things, don't they?"

Nicco drew in a breath and stared at the ceiling. "They turn cranks, like for music boxes or to wind clocks."

"That's right." He rush toward the piano, bent down next to the bench and inserted the key into the opening near the right front leg. Perfect fit. As he cranked it a creaking sound came from the seat.

"What the devil is that?" Nicco came closer for a look, Luigi at his heels.

"It's an adjustable bench. You can raise it if you are of short stature. I didn't need it, and besides, Papà said the key was lost." He kept cranking it. Metal scraped metal until the seat elevated slightly. They leaned over, gazing into the compartment underneath. A lumpy piece of burlap had been flattened between the seat and a board on the bottom covering the inner workings. Antonio lifted it out and unwrapped a pile of paper money.

"We're rich!" Nicco slapped him on the back.

"Not so fast. This is money the *padrone's* gang wants. You know Papà. He was no thief."

"No, not your papà."

"So it belongs to someone. And there is a note." Antonio sucked in a breath. This was the reason his father was killed. It had to be. And now he would know why.

Antonio turned up the oil lamp and laid the note on his kitchen table. The high electric bulb would not suffice. Nicco folded his hands against his stomach as he stood looking over Antonio's shoulder. His uncle could not read. Papà had studied hard during his years in America and had taught Antonio to read English, and only English, before he went to primary school.

Antonio stared a moment at the handwriting. It was indeed Papà's. Lacking the flourish and sure hand Paderewski's letters had, Papà's penned words spoke of hard work and determination, if not perfection.

To Whom It May Concern,

I dearly hope this missive does not become necessary. In case it does, I will set forth a list of the men to whom the bills found with this note belong. I was entrusted to defend the businessmen listed here by collecting the "protection money" Parrella exhorted from the blameless Benevento men. I was to withhold it from the gangsters until such a time as these funds could be used to bring matters to the attention of a United States judge. An attorney by the name of J.M. Yates has pledged to aid us. The tyranny happening in Little Italy must end. I became aware of the situation because of a young man I conversed with at an Irish saloon. We met again later on the streetcar. We engaged in conversation and he confided in me, hoping that an Italian man of more prominence than himself would know what to do. I laughed at that. I am a poor immigrant as well, although not nearly as unfortunate as the newest arrivals. God caused a stirring in my heart. I knew I had to try to help.

That was the end save for a list of names and the amounts they had given.

Nicco sniffed after Antonio read his father's note aloud. "That was your papà. *Sì,* he pretended to be gruff with me, but he had a heart as wide as Lady Liberty is tall. A good man. A very good man." He wiped his eyes with a handkerchief. "Too good, wasn't he? It got him killed."

Antonio's throat swelled with emotion. *Why, Papà? Why did you get involved?* "We will return the money to the rightful owners."

"Oh no, you don't." Nicco grabbed the money in his fist and stuffed it in his shirt pocket.

"What are you doing? That does not belong to you."

"You cannot just march over to Mulberry Street like it's the feast of Saint Bartholomew and you are leading the parade. If the thugs hear what you are doing, you will be ambushed, robbed, shot, and left for dead. I won't let what happened to my brother happen to his son."

"I understand. That would be foolish. But we can't keep the money."

"True, we can't do that." He returned the wad to the table. "What to do?"

"I don't know. It's late. Grab a blanket and we will talk about it tomorrow."

Antonio woke to Luigi's whimpering. He blinked his eyes. It was still dark but he had the sense that he had slept a long while. He lifted his pocket watch off the nightstand and struggled to focus on the small hands. When was the last time he'd been awake at 5:45 am? "What's wrong, Lu?"

The dog sat staring at the closed door.

"Is someone out there?"

Lu lifted a paw and gently tapped the door. Then Antonio heard a voice coming from the other side.

"*Signor* Baggio? It is Sofia Falcone. Are you awake? The pastor at St. Anthony's told me you lived here." There was a soft knock and Lu whined louder.

Antonio shrugged into his jacket and allowed Lu to join him out in the hall. "Miss Falcone, what brings you here at this hour?"

"I am so sorry. I am on my way to work at the factory. I did not think I should wait to come speak to you. What my aunt, Sister Stefania, has been saying finally made sense. You and I, we need to work together to stop *Signor* Parrella. I am sorry your father was killed, but I do hope you will want to do something to end this."

Antonio rubbed his chin. "I am not sure what it means, but you showing up here right after my uncle and I found...well, I do hope you can help clear some things up."

Nicco came out of the apartment on his way to the washroom. "Well, what a surprise to have company for breakfast. Tony, put the kettle on. I will return shortly."

"Won't you please?" Antonio opened the door wide, allowing Luigi to lead the way.

"I won't keep you. Your uncle looks well." She accepted the lone kitchen chair and sat while Antonio cracked eggs into a bowl.

"He seems very well. While the episodes of sobriety have been short-lived in the past, I'm hopeful this time he will stay out of the saloons." He noticed her staring at the pile of money they had left on the table. "Uh, that is what I think we need to talk about."

"What is it?"

"Protection money paid by the men from your village to Parrella. Only he did not get it. That is why my father was killed."

She turned her wide, dark eyes to him. "God rest his soul. But I do not understand. What I came to tell you is Sister Stefania believes you and I can help find justice. That our stories overlap by more than just happenstance."

He nodded to the wadded up pile. "And as you can see, they do indeed."

"Where did you get that? Your father..." She pinched her hands in her lap. He would save her from having to say it.

"No, he did not steal it. He apparently, unknown to me or my uncle until we found this with a note, had been working for

Parrella. Well, in fact, he was working for the Benevento men like a spy of sorts. He was trying to help them. They gave him the money under the belief that he would get legal help for them. That they would be able to escape the extortion through the courts. My father heard about the ordeal somehow, through a conversation on a streetcar apparently, and he tried to help. Obviously, that turned out to be a deadly decision."

A tear streaked down her face.

"I do not blame anyone from your village, Miss Falcone, least of all your brother. From the first time I encountered Joey I could tell he was not the type to do these things. Poverty sometimes causes men to sink below their moral standards, but I believe they can rise above it. I would like to see this money returned and the man responsible thrown in jail. He has surely committed more crimes than this. This country is supposed to be the home of the free, the land of opportunity, into which the Statue welcomes the huddled masses, isn't it? This should not happen here."

Nicco returned, stomping into the room while drying the back of his neck with a towel. The public nature of the shelter house had caused him to lose all sense of propriety. Antonio gave Sofia an apologetic grin.

"You are from Benevento?" Nicco asked.

She nodded.

"You know about the protection money the store owners have been paying?"

"I did not until now. I knew Joey was supposed to get money from *Signor* Baggio, but I did not know all this."

He leaned against the bed and Luigi sat at his feet. "Not only store owners, I suppose many laborers paid just to keep their leases on their homes. And the rent kept going up along with payments to the thugs to keep from being thrown out on the streets. And whenever someone wanted a job, he had to pay another fee. God help them."

An odd expression shadowed Sofia's face. She stood. "My papà," she whispered. "He would not tell me, but this is why he would not pay for doctors. He could not." She pointed to the money. "And Joey was mixed up in it. He probably was trying to earn back the fees Papà had to pay." She ran a hand over her face and then flung her hands to her side. Lu trotted over and licked her fingers.

Antonio set the bowl of scrabbled eggs aside. "This." He put a hand on the pile of money. "This was keeping your mother from getting treatment. It must have been tearing your father up inside."

"I knew there was a reason the Sister sent me to you. But...how do we return this while *Signor* Parrella is still out there watching?

"We were just asking ourselves the same thing."

Sofia lifted a finger into the air. "Annie Adams's library."

"Who?"

"You met her the day you were at Hawkins House. She wanted to raise money for my mother. Both she and Mrs. Hawkins offered. It did not seem right to me. *La famiglia* takes care of their own. But, if the *padrone* didn't know any different, we could return this and make a show of *Signora* Adams's benevolence being the source of it, just until Sergeant McNulty shuts down the gang."

Nicco stomped his foot. "What in blazes are you two cooking up?"

"Don't worry, Uncle. Miss Falcone has it all in hand."

Later that day, Antonio made a telephone call to the Adams's house and explained the plan.

"It's a bit unorthodox," Mrs. Adams said.

"I understand, but it would really help us out."

"I would not agree to such a thing unless the police are involved."

"Of course not. Miss Falcone will speak to Sergeant McNulty as soon as her shift at the factory is over."

Antonio hung up the receiver and hurried back to his apartment, wondering what it would be like to own one's own telephone machine. When he got back, Nicco was gone. Luigi whined and dropped to the floor, his paws over his ears. "Well, let's hope for the best, boy."

Antonio went about his chores, whistling the tune he was to play at the theater that evening. Now that he knew the circumstances of how his father came to be at Cooper Union that fateful day, he had a measure of peace. He might never understand the choice his father made, why he had thought he was the one to undertake such a thing. He wished his father had informed him, but he understood that he'd only wanted to protect him.

As he was straightening up, he came across the paper Mac had given him the other night. He'd forgotten about it. It was from Paderewski. He had missed the deadline. He wasn't sorry Sofia had filled his thoughts to the exception of all else, but this could mean his hopes for a career as a concert musician might be over. He sat down on the music bench, the one that had held a secret so close to him, and yet completely beyond his knowing. *Oh, God, you are like that. So close, and yet I don't feel you there. If Oberlin is where I need to be, let me trust that it will happen. If not, help me to accept my circumstances because I have learned the best and most treasured parts of life arrive in the form of people and not by my lofty plans.*

He unfolded the note and read.

Dear Antonio,

If you read this before my ship leaves, there is still time, my boy. But I suppose you will not take me up on my offer. I can only conclude that your plans have taken you elsewhere. Oberlin, perhaps, and I hope you find success there. I will not lie and say that I am not disappointed. Perhaps we can meet again in the future. I look forward to following your career.

He signed his name in the usual manner. Antonio felt a lump in his throat. The ship of opportunity had docked and he had failed to board it. *Help me to accept my circumstances.*

There was something else in the envelope. He shook it out. Another letter and two one hundred dollar notes. With trembling hands he read.

Please accept a contribution to your future education. Use it at Oberlin or somewhere else. It is my pleasure indeed.

"Lu, I can go to Oberlin to audition now. And this will put me on the path to having enough tuition." The dog wandered over and laid his head in Antonio's lap. "What? You aren't happy about this? It's what I was hoping for." As he said the words aloud, they felt heavy and burdensome, not at all what he had expected. "Well, boy, as soon as I help Sofia get what she needs, what my father was trying to do for that community, then this will be the right thing. We are on our way."

37

Thankfully, Claudia was an understanding supervisor. She allowed Sofia to use her office to telephone Sergeant McNulty without asking why.

The large man's voice boomed over the telephone wire. "So, you have a document in which the deceased named the perpetrator and the party he was meeting at Cooper Union?"

"I do not. *Signor* Baggio has it. It was a note from his father that he recently found."

"I will go see him, then. This should be enough to convince the judge to follow through this time. Good work, Miss Falcone. And there will be extra security in the area as well."

"Very well. However, I did not do anything—"

"You put pieces together. Have you ever considered police work?"

"Me?" She laughed.

"We do have police matrons, but I foresee the day when women do detective work."

"Until then, Sergeant, I will leave that to you."

He thanked her for calling and they hung up. Not waiting until she left work turned out to be the best decision. She had called to see when he was available and it turned out he was working a day shift. She hoped this meant Parrella would be off the streets by evening. After work she would confront Papà. It was time they were honest with her, both he and Mamma.

At noon, she was surprised to see Annie Adams on the factory floor. Claudia pointed in Sofia's direction. When they made eye contact the heavily pregnant woman smiled and waved. Sofia left her machine and met her in the aisle. She would never have been able to squeeze between the workers' stations.

Annie was out of breath. "Thank the good Lord you do not work on the fourth floor, Sofia."

"*Signora* Adams, why are you here? Is there something wrong?"

"At Hawkins House? No, not at all."

"You spoke to *Signor* Baggio, then?" She must be coming to tell Sofia that she would not follow the plan. She began to think of other options when the young woman led her toward Claudia's office.

"I did. We have a few things to talk about. Your supervisor, a very nice woman if I may say so, agreed to allow us the use of her office for a few moments. I won't keep you away from your work long."

They entered and Annie shut the door. "I have some very exciting things to tell you."

This sounded better than she imagined. "You do?"

"Indeed. The Benevolents and I not only agreed to deliver the funds Antonio's father collected from the workers on Mulberry Street, but also to employ extra police officers for the beat. Owen McNulty will recruit them himself. They aren't official, but rather off duty police to keep the peace."

"That is wonderful but...if they are not from our part of Italy, they will not be trusted. I am afraid it will create more trouble."

Annie rubbed her immense belly. It seemed to cause her some discomfort. "At least one of them is from the region of Campania. Owen is aware of the situation. He has a unique gift of relating to the people. He is trustworthy and folks can see that." She grunted as though in pain.

"Are you all right, *Signora* Adams? Can I get you something?"

"I, uh, I am not feeling well. I think I will go home now." She forced a smile. "Do not worry, Sofia. The Benevolents also have a plan to speak to your father about your mother's care. They will do so with respect."

"But, why would they do this for me?"

"You are important, darlin'. You are special in God's sight. We understand that doing whatever we can for people only results in more good things. Perhaps you will be the next person to help someone in need. Once you are the recipient, such things spring to your attention as never before. Suddenly you know that any act of kindness you put forth will be multiplied. I have certainly witnessed this myself." She began to rub her stomach with vigor.

"I will help you downstairs."

"Thank you." She stopped in the doorway. "Oh, I almost forgot. Remember when you shared with me about the woman, the nurse in your building?"

"Nurse? Oh, the healer? *Sì*. I should not have, but you are so easy to talk with, Annie."

"Indeed you should have. I would like her to work in the library with me and to bring her daughter."

"Library? But she cannot read. She makes healing ointments and such. She knows nothing about books."

"But she knows about stories, aye? She knows about people. That is how books begin. As stories in the mind. I think we would work well together." She sucked in a breath. "Does she also deliver babies?"

"I will telephone Mrs. Hawkins right now. Oh, she does not have a telephone. Will someone answer at your house?"

"Yes, I believe so. Etti and Leena are cleaning for me today." She gritted her teeth as she spoke.

Grace McNulty paced across the rose carpet in Hawkins House's parlor. "I know that childbirth can be dangerous. I do hope Annie is all right."

Claudia had allowed Sofia to leave work early. She had been too distracted to do much work anyway. A new baby, a new life to celebrate. She had not considered that Annie might not be well.

"Did you see how big she was?" Grace asked, pausing a moment to watch the foot traffic outside the parlor window.

Sofia nodded. "She is carrying a big *bambino*, *sì*."

"She might be swollen up with fluids. That can be very bad. I attended a birth once. 'Tis scary, let me tell you. I've been volunteering at the hospital, too, with Dr. Thorp. The things I've seen."

"Don't go borrowing trouble, dear." Sergeant McNulty had come in from the direction of the kitchen. "The Maslov sisters let me in. They are boiling water. They told me our Annie is about to give birth. Thought I'd pop in before I go track down the new father on his mail route."

"Oh," said Grace. "You better do that. You never know what could happen."

Owen reached for his wife's hand, reminding Sofia that loved ones always warmed troubled spirits. "The sisters said she is doing fine. Mrs. Hawkins is with her?"

"And a midwife." Grace paced the carpet again.

"It is a big baby, I hear," the policeman said before his wife urged him toward the door.

"Oh, Miss Falcone," Sergeant McNulty said. "The judge agreed and an order for that man's arrest has been made. He is being charged with murder. Seems a witness has come forward."

Sofia felt her shoulders relax. "*Grazie*, Sergeant."

Grace kissed her husband's cheek. "And Owen is being promoted to detective, something he's wanted ever since I met him. He does good detective work, but now he is off duty. 'Tis women's work now to take care of Annie. You've done well to help Sofia, but your mission now is to go get Stephen Adams." She sighed as she closed the heavy door and leaned against it. She looked at Sofia. "When God blesses me with children, I am sure I will be a mad woman." She reached for Sofia's hand. "I am happy the trouble in your neighborhood is being cleaned up. That kind of thing is my husband's mission in life."

"He is a good man."

"That he is. When our children arrive I pray they take after him because I will be a raving *eejit* with my worrying on."

"No you will not." Mrs. Hawkins descended the stairs. "It's all those waiting who worry, but the laboring mother knows nothing but joy once she holds the babe, love. In this case the babies."

A squeal came from upstairs. Infant cries.

"Babies? Two?" Grace rushed past her toward the door upstairs that led to Annie and Stephen's house.

"Twins," Mrs. Hawkins said to Sofia. "A boy and a girl. That should keep us all busy for a time."

Twins? Sofia no longer felt envy when she heard the word. She was delighted for them. She imagined them cuddled up together in one cradle. Content and comfortable. Life may deal them challenges as they grow older—as it had for her—but right now they were perfect, the way God intended his children to be. She could not wait to see them.

"Go on up." Mrs. Hawkins inclined her head toward the stairs. "Do not stay long, though. Grace and Annie are quite good friends and I expect Grace will tire her out."

When Sofia entered the passageway between the two buildings, late evening sunbeams streaked through the transom window that overlooked the Adams's tall entryway. The passage was like a catwalk, open on one side above the railing. Sofia had never been past the library before. The sound of infant cries led her toward the correct room. A plump woman was closing the door behind her. The midwife smiled, damp curls tumbling down her forehead. "She is doing well, that one. I suspected twins but the mother wasn't convinced until they came. What a miracle. Go on. Go see for yourself."

Sofia padded toward the door and gently pushed it open. Annie was propped up against the headboard of her bed, a bundle tucked against her breast. Grace was pacing the floor with another, cooing at the squawking child.

"Come in," Annie said. "I guess I should have listened to the folks who said I was exceedingly large for my eighth month. A boy and a girl!"

Sofia leaned over and gazed at the baby Annie held. Pink with a button nose and pinched face. Fresh from the hand of God. "Are you all right, *Signora* Adams?"

"I am indeed."

"Their names?"

"Stephen and I discussed it. When he gets here, he will announce the names, but I will tell you. The girl will be Kathleen Agnes, for my mother and Mrs. Hawkins. And the boy, Martin Stephen, for my father and my husband. I will definitely be needing help in the library, like we were discussing. Can you speak to your neighbor? I do not want to leave the library closed for long and besides, she can help me form a new coalition between the library on Mulberry and ours."

"Listen to her," Grace teased. "A patron of the arts, a supporter of the written word, and a mother. She will be a wonderful mother, so."

Annie winked at her friend. "I am blessed to have Grace to help me. She was a nanny, you know. She understands more about children than I do."

Grace walked over and placed the baby she held into Annie's open arm. Sofia could not stop gazing at them. Two perfect babies. Not two halves of a whole, but two individuals. They would need each other of course, but also their mother, their father, the friends at Hawkins House that were like family. No one was whole alone, only complete in the presence of others, the way God intended.

Etti and Leena marched in next, giggling and jabbering in their native language. One could never be isolated here, and that thought made Sofia long for Mulberry Street.

Sofia went first to Most Precious Blood. She wanted to speak to Father Lucci and then to Sister Stefania. After that, she would check on Mamma and see if any of her siblings had been able to talk to her.

On Tuesdays, especially at the supper hour, the church was quiet. The workmen upstairs had gone home and the nightly confessions had not yet begun. She entered and breathed in the scent of burning candles, oiled wood, and the faint odor of the coal stove pumping too little heat into the room. She prayed, lit three candles, and then turned to look for the Father.

"Sofia!" Father Lucci entered from a side door. "How delightful to see you. Have you heard what has transpired in the last day?"

"The *padrone* will be stopped."

"That is correct. Our prayers for an end to the violence have been answered."

She remembered seeing Luisa at the church so often, her escape. Perhaps an end to the violence in her family had come as well. "*Signora*, I mean Mrs. Annie Adams, would like to employ Luisa and her mother at her library across town. Do you think Luisa will be able to leave her work here? It would be good pay, I believe."

"That sounds wonderful for her. We were her shelter, and always available, but I believe now the Russo women can find their own way, with God's help."

Sofia crossed herself. "May we all, Father."

"Amen," he agreed.

"I wanted to ask if you might help me convince my father to allow others to pay for my mother's treatment."

"Did you not hear? He received a large amount of money recently. An overpayment on his rent, I believe."

"Oh, *sì*. I did hear." The Benevolents had already done their work.

"A fellow man of the cloth came by, said he has met you. Reverend Clarke of First Church."

"He came here with the others?"

"No. Alone. Said he was trying to visit all the churches in Manhattan to see how we might work together to save souls and feed the hungry."

"I am happy you met him."

"All these good things coming so quickly." He shook his head. "Why are we so surprised when God hears our prayers?"

"Maybe because we do not listen for the answers." She remembered the time she had been praying in church with Carla. The presence she'd felt but could not identify. God was with her always.

"I think you are right, Sofia. We must listen. Your papà? He is a proud man."

"*Sì.*"

"But he wants what is best for his wife. Like we all do."

"I know you are right. Excuse me, Father. I must go see Sister Stefania."

"Of course. She is entertaining a guest. Someone you would like to see as well."

Before she got to the kitchen, she was met by the white and brown dog named Luigi. He wagged his tail as he came closer. "Hey, boy. What brings you to the neighborhood?"

Antonio walked up behind him. "I wanted to make sure everything went as planned."

Sofia looked into his soft face, admiring how kind he was, empathizing with the pain he must feel. "I am so sorry about your papà. The Sergeant said there is a witness, so perhaps this will be over soon and you can pursue your dreams of playing in concert halls."

"I believe so, Sofia. And I hope you'll be sitting in the front row."

Luigi trotted away, leaving the two of them alone in the hall leading to the nun's kitchen. Antonio put his hands on her arms, helping to steady her pounding heart. When he leaned over and kissed her, she thought she saw stars under her closed eyelids. The coldness left her body and the kiss was over too soon.

He stepped back far enough for her to admire his smile. "I must be going. I was hoping I would run into you here, though. I wanted to say good-bye."

"Good-bye?"

"Yes. I have run into some good fortune and I will be leaving for Ohio next week. I am going to audition for Oberlin College, the first step in my concert career."

"Oh." Her happiness flew away like an uncaged bird. "It was what your father wanted for you, you said."

"Yes it was." His eyes sparkled with unshed tears.

"It is what you want?"

He swallowed hard. "A great opportunity for me. I will write to you. I promise."

She nodded and he moved away, leaving a wispy breeze in his wake. He called from the front door. "Hurry inside. You will want to see the police witness."

"Here?"

"Of course here."

She saw his shadow first, a long dark figure. When she turned toward the west-facing window she could not believe her eyes. Joey! She embraced him, not wanting to let go. "Are you all right?"

"I am, sister. You will squeeze the life out of me, though, if you don't let go."

She laughed. "I was afraid I would never see you again. Where have you been?"

"In my attic," Sister Stefania said, placing a coffeepot on the stove. "Up there with the phonograph, for safekeeping. The gardener's wife let me keep it."

"Are you safe now, Joey?"

"He will be," the Sister answered. "As soon as the trial is over."

"You are the witness?"

"I am."

"And so brave," their aunt added, placing a tray of cannoli on the table.

They talked a long while and Sofia almost forgot the pain of Antonio leaving so soon after their kiss.

"Go see Mamma for me," Joey said. "And tell Papà not to worry."

"I will." She hurried toward the Falcone apartment, only a few yards away. It seemed life was like a continually turning wheel, throwing off some things and gathering others. She lost Mamma, she gained Hawkins House. She got Joey back, she lost Antonio. Maybe not forever. She hoped not.

Carla met her at the door wearing Mamma's apron. "Are you settled in all right?" Sofia whispered.

"*Sì*. Your papà and your brothers and sister have been very kind to us." Carla reached behind her for her daughter and gave Luisa a big squeeze. "I am proud of her. She tried to fix what her papà did."

"What do you mean?"

"During her visits to the Free Library, Luisa overheard that *Signor* Baggio's father had hidden the money that was supposed to help the men of our village break free of the p*adrone*. She sent Antonio anonymous notes, hoping he would come help."

"Notes?"

"*Sì*, like a message boy," Luisa admitted.

While Sofia wished the girl had confided in her instead, she agreed that it was a brave thing to do. Who knew if her abusive father would have come after her as well as her mother if he'd known? Benevento women always find a way around obstacles.

"And Mamma?"

Carla stared at the floor as she motioned Sofia inside. She kept her voice low. "Your sister spoke to her. At first your mother did very well, almost seemed her old self again. And then Gabriella talked about that day, asked her questions, and Angelina withdrew again. Your sister had to return to the children. Luisa and I have been trying to reach her, but Angelina refuses to talk to us. Your father is not home from work yet. He will be angry with your sister."

Sofia had not realized Gabriella agreed that Mamma needed to talk about it. "He should not be angry. My sister was right. Mamma should remember, tell us what happened."

"There was a cost, Sofia. Your mamma has taken a bad turn.

Sofia whispered a prayer as she walked toward Mamma's room. The space was heavy with anticipation. *Dear God, I need your words to be mine right now. Help us all.*

"Mamma?"

"Sofia?"

"*Sì*, Mamma. I am here." Her mother sat on a stool next to a window encased with a newly installed iron lattice. The window was closed. There were no burning candles and Carla had filled the room with the scent of her tinctures.

"I chose you, Sofia. I chose you." Tears streamed down Mamma's face. "Gabriella asked me, so I told her. And now I tell you. I chose you." She began whimpering, repeating Serena's name over and over.

Sofia clasped her mother's hand. "An accident, Mamma. You remember?"

Her mother nodded and sniffed. "I was home alone with my twins, you and her. Serena headed for the door toward the sound of the goats, like always. But this time someone had left the door open. I was cooking. I left the stove and headed for the door. You stuck out your hand because you knew I was making *orecchiette*. 'Little ears, little ears,' you called because you thought the name of the pasta was so funny. You reached for the pot. Your sister ran for the door. Both in danger. What could I do? I had to choose."

"Oh, Mamma. It is not your fault."

"No, it happened. I chose. And I did not tell you because…I feared you would hate me for not saving your sister, and for not being careful enough with the two of you. I thought we were helping by telling you your memories were nothing but fantasy. I was wrong, I know now. I just did not want you to stop loving me." She wept softly into Sofia's shoulder.

"Oh, Mamma, I would never feel that way. I love you no matter what."

"You forgive me?"

"If I had anything to forgive you for, I would without hesitation. I could never blame you, especially knowing the truth. Thank you for telling me."

By the time Papà came home the rooms were quiet. Sofia's brothers were off at work and Gabriella was in the neighbor's kitchen feeding their children.

"Why are you here so early?" Papà asked her, glancing between Sofia and Angelina.

"The woman who owns the library had a baby. Two babies. Twins. She was visiting me at the factory when she realized the babies were coming. They let me go home to help her."

Papà threw his hands upward, as though this was a ridiculous thing.

Sofia silently reminded herself to explain the offer for work to Carla and Luisa as soon as things calmed down in the Falcone household.

"I saw Joey today."

Mamma's face brightened and Papà raised his brows. Sofia explained how her brother was going to help make the neighborhood safer by testifying in the murder case of Ernesto Baggio. "I cannot tell you where he is. It is safest for you if I do not, for now. But do not worry. He is well."

Mamma breathed deeply. It seemed the weight of a freight train had been removed from her shoulders.

"I have news, too," Papà announced, making them all sit around the room and pay attention. Sofia already knew about the returned money, of course, but she did not say so. Papà was proud that Mamma would be getting the treatment she needed, and just in time for Carla to take on a new position.

"What about your young man?" Mamma said suddenly, surprising everyone.

"My young man?"

"Gabriella told me you have a young man, Sofia. I only hope he is as good as your father."

Mamma would get better. She was talking normally again. The time to tell about Antonio's family's origin in Italy would come later. If there was a future for them at all. "He is going away to college in the west."

Papà nodded and the topic was closed.

38

ONE WEEK AFTER receiving financial endorsement from Paderewski, Antonio sat on a bench in Grand Central Station to wait for a train departing westward. He told himself he wanted to go. He needed to. He should be grateful for the opportunity. Detective McNulty assured him the trial would not happen for months. He had plenty of time to audition and return home. The murder trial should be over by the next term. Nicco was getting better and, with Luigi to keep him in line, he would be fine. Everything was falling into place.

Or so it seemed. His heart told him otherwise.

He gazed up at a round white globe light under which sat a mother, father, and baby. A family. In Ohio, he had no one to greet him. Not even his dog. It was normal to be a little homesick. He glanced up to see someone marching toward him. Sydney, otherwise known as O. Henry. He sat down on the bench next to Antonio.

"I heard you turned down Paderewski."

"You came out here to say that?"

"I might have."

"How did you know I was here?"

"Stopped by your place and your uncle told me."

"I don't know if I'm making the right decision. He told me I could use the money he sent for Oberlin."

"So you are on your way to Ohio?"

Antonio laughed, knowing the man held distain for the place for some reason. "Don't say it with such displeasure. Oberlin is the best music college I could find, one that teaches all academics."

"Fine, fine. And why is that important again?"

"My father—"

"No, what about you, Antonio? Don't pin this decision on your deceased father."

Was he making excuses? Running toward a dream that he didn't even want?

"Nicco, your uncle? He said you are leaving a girl behind."

The woman with the baby lifted her nose at them and the family hurried away.

"My uncle talks too much."

The writer crossed his legs at the knee. "I had a wife once. I ran away, too, but it was necessary, circumstances being what they were. I didn't want to leave her. I'm sure you feel the same."

"Perhaps. I'm not sure."

"Listen, kid. Take it from me. There are always choices. If you don't take the Oberlin route, Paderewski will still be around. For a time, anyway. Going on one European tour with him would teach you as much as the college, I would guess. And if I'm wrong, you still have the girl."

"What happened to your wife, if you don't mind me asking?"

"Fair enough. I brought it up, didn't I?" He set both feet firmly on the floor and rubbed his hands on his knees. "She died. I returned just in time but the years we lost being together, well, I will regret them forever. There were consequences to my returning, but to be with her in the end was well worth it. Have you purchased your ticket yet?"

He hadn't.

Sofia decided to stay at Hawkins House. Mamma was being looked after. Gabriella and Luisa had become good friends. Joey would be home soon and Fredo and Frankie had secured him a job working on the subway construction. Carla had moved into with the Adamses, and Sofia enjoyed seeing her in the evenings at Hawkins House. Life was settling in comfortably. She was even beginning to learn to read some of the books in Annie's great library. She should be happy. But she wasn't.One evening she decided to pay Stefania another visit. She found her listening to her phonograph and tapping her fingers together as she sat in the kitchen waiting for visitors. "Father Lucci gave you the most appropriate job," Sofia told her.

"Oh?"

"There is no one more welcoming, more hospitable than you."

SOFIA'S TUNE

Stefania kissed her cheek. "Have you listened to the Master's voice, dear?"

"What do you mean?"

"I know you can hear him calling, if you will just listen."

"You mean God calling to me?"

"I do mean that." A shout from the door sent the woman away to give bread to a beggar.

Sofia thought about what she'd said. She had petitioned Our Lord. She knew he heard and answered. But was she missing something? She quickly said good-bye and headed home to Hawkins House.

Before she reached the front stoop, she saw the dog. Someone was instructing him. Antonio had left for Ohio. Perhaps this was a different dog. As she came closer, she noticed the animal waiting at attention, just the way Luigi always did. She called out. The dog looked at her. It was Luigi. "Hey, Lu. Come here!"

The dog wagged his tail and whimpered, but he did not come.

The man returned, motioned to the dog, and Luigi immediately scrambled up the steps. The man turned toward her. Antonio!

"I was looking for you." He came toward her, Luigi at his heels. The dog would only listen to his master's voice, not hers, even though he had obviously wanted to come to her. If only Sofia's faith in God was that loyal, that strong. She would work at it.

They embraced.

"I am not going to Ohio. I realized I have opportunities for my career right here. I reminded myself that the concert

400

halls in Europe would always be there, when I'm ready, but right now I want to be in New York, because you are here."

"You changed your tune."

"I what?"

"An old English poem in Annie's library about Robin Hood. It speaks about changing your tune. I asked Annie about it. It means to change your mind, to alter the direction of your life."

"Well, then that's what I am doing. I might even take up the accordion."

"Truly?"

"A story for later."

"Me as well. I am listening to God and changing my tune."

His lips met hers, firm and with passion. Her legs felt feeble. Her head light. Though the day was dreary and damp, she barely noticed. What was inside her heart was far more soothing. She vowed never again to stop listening.

They linked arms and headed to the house where they could already hear babies crying. Her spirit warmed in a way that assured her she would never be cold again.

Author's Note

I CONCLUDED THE ELLIS ISLAND series by featuring Italian immigrants because by this time the Southern Italians were coming over in large numbers. For most Italians, family is central to their lives, so I wanted to explore how my characters might expand their definition of family while still keeping their immediate family ties.

As with my other novels, there are some historical characters and some fictional. Readers have told me they like to know the difference, so here's a summary. Most are figments of my imagination, but O. Henry and Ignacy Jan Paderewski, of course, were real people who were in New York City during this time period. O. Henry did visit Healy's Café, which is now known as Pete's Tavern, and legend says he wrote *The Gift of the Magi* in one of the booths. Paderewski was known for supporting struggling musicians. Their friendship, as far as I know, is fictional.

Also fictional are the priests and ministers in this story. The Italian churches do exist, but the aid society at St. Anthony's and the abbey at The Most Precious Blood are fictional. First Church and Rayburn Street, which are continued from my earlier novels, do not exist in real life. Neither does Hawkins House or The Benevolents, but they are based on the many charitable organizations of the era in New York City.

Mental illness, alcoholism, and emotional trauma treatments were evolving during this time period. Unfortunately, many people were locked up and not given much help. Some received treatments that were hurtful and even destructive. New and more effective approaches were emerging as Father Lucci says in the story.

While some *padroni* were abusive and many Italian workers suffered under their control, the *padroni* in *Sofia's Tune* are fictional. The Free Library and the Salvation Army in Sofia's neighborhood did exist. I always try to stay true to the historical time period, so there are many other elements in the story that either could have happened, or did in fact, such as the colossal rainstorm that saw over 11 inches of rain in a 24-hour period.

When I heard about the Twinless Twins Support Group (http://www.twinlesstwins.org) and spoke to one of their members, I was inspired to share the special challenges and emotional trauma some experience when forced to carry on while missing a twin. As someone who is not a twin, I gained an understanding of how difficult that must be.

I have enjoyed writing about Ellis Island immigrants. If you have ancestors who came through Ellis Island, be sure to visit www.ellisisland.org.

Discussion Questions

- Family was most important to Sofia at the opening of the story. What do you think was the most important to her at the end?

- What do you think was the biggest betrayal, that Sofia's parents hid the fact that she had been born a twin or their insistence that she move out of the home?

- Why do you think Antonio wanted to be a concert musician?

- Have you ever had to deal with a loved one's addiction? Do you agree with the way Antonio handled his uncle?

- What do you think Sister Stefania meant by instructing Antonio and Sofia to "listen to the master's voice?" Why do you think she did not tell them directly about the *padrone*'s extortion scheme?

- Why do you think Luisa resorted to sending Antonio anonymous notes?

- Have you ever felt a loss as severe as Antonio and Sofia? How was your reaction different or the same?

- How do you think Sofia's definition of "family" changed throughout the story?

50628849R00250

Made in the USA
Charleston, SC
03 January 2016